MW01137658

THE

BROTHERHOOD

OF THE

BLADE

A NOVEL BY S.A. COSBY

"When the swords flash let no idea of love or piety or even the face of your father's move you." -Julius Caesar

ISBN-13: **978-1500641757**
ISBN-10: **1500641758**

Cover art model Hunter Jordan

HAPTER ONE

Swords.

Pretlow Creedence loved swords. He loved their strength and beauty. He loved the history that some swords carried. He loved making swords. Molding and shaping the steel in his home made foundry in the back yard. Steel never betrayed you, never lied, never lost its courage or broke its word. Once it was shaped and tempered he brought it here, to the basement of his two-story Cape Cod style home in the suburbs of Glenn Allen Va. The basement was his finishing room where he transformed the swords from billets of metal to weapons and works of art. He put his heart and soul into the swords he created. He took a deep breath. The smell of oil and steel filled his nostrils. He loved those scents. The scents of his labor. Lying on his work bench was his latest creation; a four and a half foot long cutlass. A polished chrome handle with a wide hand guard shimmered under the florescent lights in the ceiling. The sword was a replica. Pretlow had created it specifically for a Ren-fair in Norristown Pennsylvania. The blade was simple Bessemer steel .The handle was encrusted with six black obsidian stones. Pretlow had worked for weeks filing and shaping those stones. Obsidian was one of hardest most durable material on earth. It was no match for the steel that Pretlow used to create swords for the Brotherhood. Pretlow's clients were always amazed at how he shaped incredible minerals with relative ease. He was known far and wide throughout the Ren-fair community for his skill in fashioning mock swords with dull blades and ornate handles. Swords that had filigree etched into the very blade or an elaborate fir-de-lis design sewn into the scabbard. Blades that would serve to coax nubile young women dressed like tavern wenches out of their breeches. Blades that would never spill blood. Pretlow stood and grabbed the sword. He was a tall man with a lean wiry frame, broad of chest and narrow of waist. His pale gray eyes changed to green when he was angry. His curly black hair was cut into a rather severe flat-top. His ears were large and cupped on the edge. Pretlow had tawny golden brown skin that betrayed his mixed ancestry. The sword was perfectly balanced. It was not overly weighted toward the handle or the end of the blade. Pretlow tossed it lightly in the air and caught it in the middle with two fingers. It teetered just the slightest bit.

Pretlow sighed. Not his best work. Lately his mind was wandering from his craft. The mundane concerns of life were intruding. His son was defying even his simplest most benign rules or requests His daughter had entered the terrible twos and was now, six years later, in the midst of the awful eights. Re-enactments and Ren-fair shows were not as plentiful as they had once been ten years ago. Income was harder and harder to come by these days. That would have been enough to distract a normal suburban man. But he was not a normal suburban man. He was a member of the Brotherhood. His domestic doldrums paled in comparison to the responsibility he shared with the other Men of the First Order. His father had once told him." When the world in all its brutal stupidity and ignorant self-involvement presses upon you, push back with the sword. The sword will make the crowded places clear and will lay the crooked paths straight. There are not many problems that can't be solved with a swift decapitation." Astor Creedence would then wink at his young son. Pretlow bowed his head for a moment. His father had been a man of great skill and great humor. An honorable man in dishonorable times. A man who died in a car crash when Pretlow was twelve years old. His death had been so incongruous with his life that at first the other members of the Brotherhood had refused to believe. Such a mundane death for such a dynamic man struck many of them as incomprehensible. Yet Pretlow knew, even then, that death was not just invertible but ignoble. It made you soil your pants or piss yourself or drown in your own vomit or a stomach full of blood. There was no honor in death only release. The honor could only be found in what brought you to death's door. A man's action were what were honorable not his death.

Pretlow tossed the cutlass in the air again and this time he caught it by the handle. He stabbed it forward then slashed the air quickly to the right. He spun around for one full revolution before launching his entire body forward .He slid across the concrete floor with his right hand fully extended. His left leg was raised and extended from his body like a rudder. His momentum carried him at least six feet. Using his powerful quadriceps muscle he jumped backwards off his right leg. Shifting his weight in mid-air he landed on his left leg before planting his right. He slashed the air to the left then the right. He sliced the air vertically until the tip of the cutlass scratched the ceiling of the basement then he brought the blade back down while at the same time dropping to his knees. Sweating a bit he stayed in the kneeling position for a moment before using his iron-like abdominal muscles and strong core to rocket himself back to his feet. He heard a footstep behind his left ear.

Instinctively he tossed the sword to his left hand, spun on the balls of his feet and brought his blade to the neck of his assailant. The metal just kissed the skin below the jaw of the intruder. It lay there cool against her skin with the dull edge barely making an indentation in her skin.

"Next time dinner is ready I'll just holler downstairs," his wife Darnicia said coolly. Pretlow immediately pulled the blade from her throat and placed it back on the workbench. He allowed himself a slight chuckle. He turned and picked up a cloth.

"My love how long have we been married?" he asked as he wiped down the blade with a soft microfiber cloth.

"More years than I care to say," Darnicia said with a smile.

"And after all those unsaid years why would you ever come into my workshop without announcing yourself? What if I had been practicing with a real sword?" he asked with his back to her. He tried to keep his tone conciliatory.

"My love. I worry about you. You seem distant and yes I will say it, moody. More so than usual." She walked up behind Pretlow and wrapped her dark brown arms around his waist and leaned her head into his broad back.

"But I know that you, above all other men I have known would never spill blood unless it was absolutely necessary .I trust your skill and your temperament. I trust you with my very life," Darnicia whispered into his back.

"You are my life. The only commitment that equals my commitment to the Brotherhood," Pretlow said as he grasped her left hand and raised it to his lips. She was always surprised by his strength. This man who was the father of her children was a gentle and tender lover. A man who was as light on his feet as a cloud. The hand that now gripped hers had stroked her cheek, wiped away their children's tears, had
disrobed her with the shyness of a monastic devotee. Yet behind his

soft caresses she could feel the power there. She had seen these hands; the same hands that had massaged her full and ripe breast would wield a sword like Zeus hurling lightning bolts. Twirl heavy katanas around and over his fingers like a drummer spinning his sticks during an extensive encore. His hands were not so different than the steel he shaped at his forge in the backyard.

"If only our son shared your admiration," Pretlow said in a low voice. Darnicia released her grip and tugged at Pretlow's belt loop .He turned around to face her and as always was struck by her simple beautiful face. Her skin, dark and brown like the finest leather. Her almond shaped eyes with irises the color of honey. They had enraptured him since he first saw her at a gathering of members of the Brotherhood twenty years earlier. Her features were bold yet delicate. Full sensual lips that promised the fulfillment of every desire a man conjure. The high cheek bones and sharp forehead that were the hallmark of the men and women from the House of Sand and Fire. Her brother Saed had the same stark African features.

"Pret he is a young man and like many young men he is chafing under the weight of who we want him to be and what he thinks he should be," she said as she stared into his eyes.

"I know this. Don't you think that sometimes I wish he was just like other boys his age? That he could just jump on his motorcycle and ride off into the distance and strike out his own path? That we were... ordinary? But we are not. We carry a bloodstained banner for a war that is not yet won. And I fear the time is drawing very near where his dreams and our reality are about to collide."

Darnicia stroked her chin. "My love you could never be ordinary" she said. Pretlow smiled.

"Have you received the Invitation?" she asked. Her voice was calm. But her eyes, those beautiful languid pools were roiling in turmoil. Pretlow grasped her tiny hand in his and kissed it.

"No, not yet. But I have consulted the Book of Seven Swords. I have read over the journals of my father and my grandfather and his grandfather .I have been in touch with the Grand Hall and the archivist there. Everything I have studied and analyzed tells me the Invitation could arrive any day now. So you see, now Catlow's insolence could have catastrophic consequences. The entire Covenant could hinge on him."

"And he could die. Our son could die. You could die, Pretlow. Do not forget that,". she whispered.

"Don't talk to me as if I don't love our son, Darnicia. I know this. Every man who picks up a sword and swears his oath to Brotherhood knows this. Death is always near. But our lives are insignificant when measured against the lives of every person on the planet. The suffering and misery of every single solitary soul on earth depends on what we do or don't do when it's time to fulfill the Covenant," Pretlow said. His voice rose and he felt ashamed. Darnicia was raised in the arms of their fraternity .She knew what was at stake.

"The lives of my husband and son are not insignificant to me, Pretlow," she said . She touched his chest and turned to walk up the stairs. Pretlow shook his head slightly then turned back to his work bench to pack up the cutlass for the trip to Pennsylvania. He loved his wife. He loved his son. But the Brotherhood was not just a group to which he belonged. It was his religion. And every religion required sacrifice. He and the other men of the First Order carried a weight that no one else could comprehend. Except maybe the men of the First

Chaos.

Catlow Creedence sat on his old beat up pan-head Indian motorcycle watching his friends play football in the park. He straddled the bike with his long legs and watched as his friends from high school ran and jumped and played. They played for the sheer joy of playing. They played for the intrinsic male need to conquer and defeat your rivals. To establish dominance. They played just for fun. Catlow wondered how that felt. To just grab a monkey bar and swing from it without someone yelling in your ear to improve your grip. To jump off a picnic table and not have someone criticize your form as you landed. To just run for the feeling of wind against your face.

A break in the game came when Catlow's friend Ronnie Denton laid out a player for the opposing team with a vicious flying tackle. Ronnie, all 245 pounds of him, slammed into the willowy boy at full speed. The other boy, who Catlow thought was named Jeb, flew backwards a few feet then landed in a crumpled pile of arms and legs. Ronnie jumped up and started doing the Cabbage Patch dance while the willowy boy's friends attended to him. Ronnie looked over and saw Catlow sitting just outside the chain link fence that separated the park from the parking lot. He jogged over to the fence, hopped over it by bracing himself with one hand and landed indelicately on his feet.

"You see me knock that fool out his Jordans? He gonna try and come to my side of the field? Somebody done told him wrong!" Ronnie said as he held his hand up for a hi-five. Catlow slapped his friends hand and laughed to himself. Ronnie was a big broad example of genetic inheritance. 6'1', 245 pounds, and quick enough to run a fifty yard dash in 5.6 seconds. His father was huge. His mother was huge. All his cousins were huge. The Denton family had cornered the market

THE BROTHEROOD OF THE BLADE

on muscles and girth. Ronnie had once told him they had been banned from half the buffet restaurants in Richmond and Catlow half believed him.

"Yes you definitely knocked him out of puberty. His balls probably went back up". Catlow said. Ronnie laughed.

"Hey your boy want to play? Jeb gotta go home. I think he shit his pants," Cory Gray said as he leaned on the fence. Before Catlow could speak Ronnie answered for him.

"Man he don't play football. It's against his religion," he said .That was what he had told Ronnie because that was the easiest way to explain his father's moratorium on sports of any kind. The truth was far more embarrassing.

"Come on man your daddy ain't here. Don't be a bitch," Corey said shaking his head. His dreads fell into his face.

"I am not a bitch," Catlow said calmly. Now another boy holding the football had trotted up to the fence. He was a short stocky boy with overly fat bottom lip. Catlow hoped t that was the result of some incident in the game and not his normal appearance.

"He playing?" Fat lip asked. Corey shook his head.

"Naw his daddy got him shook. Or he scared," Corey said. Fat lip laughed. Catlow did not laugh.

"Throw me the ball." he said. Fat lip hesitated.

"Throw him the ball man!" Ronnie yelled. Fat lip threw the ball at Catlow as hard as he could. It sailed through the air in a nice tight spiral zipping past Ronnie like a bullet. Catlow caught it with one hand before it hit his face. He swung his leg over his bike and stood. At 6'4 he towered over most of his classmates. He was narrow of waist and broad of shoulders like his father. He had a tawny complexion like Pretlow but he had been gifted with his mother's honey brown eyes. His forearms rippled with cords of muscle. As if his antebrachium was wrapped in ropes. His hair was twisted into tight black cornrows that hung to his shoulders.

Catlow looked out over the park. About one hundred yards away was a spotlight. When lit it provided much need illumination for night time transactions in Byrd park. Catlow glanced at Corey and Fat lip. He planted his feet and threw the football. It flew like a missile through the air. Ronnie felt a slight breeze hit his face as it left Catlow's hand. It struck the light and shattered the large tear drop glass shade that hung from it .Corey and Fat Lip stood there with their mouths agape.

Catlow punched Ronnie lightly in the shoulder and climbed on his bike. "I'll holler at you later my friend," he said before starting his bike and tearing out of the park.

Catlow zipped down the jagged streets of Virginia's capitol city with a reckless abandon. He wore no helmet and sneakers instead of boots. Because of his father's relentless emphasis on physical training he had superb balance and strength. He could do things on a bike only daredevils would attempt. He could do things off a bike that normal boys his age could only dream about in Dungeon and Dragons fantasies. Like throwing that ball the length of a football field with the accuracy of a hawk. Catlow sighed. He had let his temper get the best of him, again. Those boys would tell friends and families that Catlow had an NFL arm and a sniper's eyesight. Questions would be asked. His father would catch wind of the incident and once again he would have to sit through a lecture about the fate of the world being on his shoulders.

He thought it was all bullshit.

The stories his father told him about The Brotherhood of the Blade sounded like the ravings of a zealot. Which they were. Pretlow Creedence was fanatical about the Brotherhood and his fanciful belief that they held the fate of the world on the edge of their swords. The myth of the Covenant and the Duel of Generations. That myth had been preached to him ever since he could remember. That every one hundred years Men of the First Order and Men of the First Chaos met on a predetermined field of battle to duel for three days .A duel to the death. That whichever group had the most living members at the end of the three day melee were declared the winners. And this is where, in Catlow's mind, it reeked of unmitigated bullshit. If the Men of the First Order won, well the entire human race enjoyed one hundred years of peace, prosperity and good will. But if the men of the First Chaos won, well then thing went all to hell. War, famine, natural disasters, all this and more would plague humanity for the next hundred years.

Catlow had once believed in this story with his whole being. He had also once believed in Santa Claus and the Tooth Fairy. Now what he believed differed greatly. He believed that his father and his mother and his uncles and their friends were really just mental. Oh there was a Brotherhood but they were not the gatekeepers of humanity's destiny. They were just some misguided men and women who believed they really were the sentries protecting mankind. Much like members of Heavens' Gate believed that they were going to intersect with a space ship if they poisoned themselves. An outsider might say Catlow was exaggerating his father's dedication to his delusion. An outsider might say what harm was it if Pretlow Creedence believed he was responsible for saving the world? Wasn't that what Christians believed? Catlow could tell that outsider that his father and his uncles were deadly serious about their fantasy. That the years and years of practice and drills and mock duels had given his father lethal skills with which to indulge his misbelief. Catlow could tell that outsider about the long summer evenings that were not spent playing hopscotch or a pickup basketball game. Summer evenings filled with pushups, fencing lessons and deep breathing exercises. Days and days of sword fighting while blindfolded on the edge of balance beam. He could tell that outsider of forgotten birthdays and blown off school plays. He could tell that outsider there was no harm done. Not really. Except his father made him sacrifice his childhood to this false crusade. Except that his father loved swords more than he loved his own son. Except his father and uncles lived their entire lives in the grip of a dissociative episode of epic proportions.

No harm. None at all.

Catlow guided the bike into the parking lot of the Highgate Mall. It was Saturday and Harmony Dejesus would be working the morning shift at Panera Bread. Harmony was his....well Catlow didn't know what to call her. He had never stayed in one place more than a year or two so he had never had many friendships, outside of the other children in the Brotherhood. His father's paranoia about the mysterious Men of the First Chaos and their nefarious intentions necessitated their frequent moves. However time and circumstance had forced his father to relax his rigidity. Renaissance fairs and re-enactments were the main source of the Creedence family's income. The recession had put a dent in the frequency of these festivals. Fewer and fewer people were clamoring for a Pretlow Creedence sword. His father had no other marketable skills and his mother was a proud homemaker. The other members of the Brotherhood helped as much as they could while fighting their own battles for financial survival. The Brotherhood of the Blade was a spiritual, not materialistic cult. The men and women of the Brotherhood eschewed any overabundance of monetary accumulation. It took time away from studying their craft or preparing for the coming battle. Combine their natural frugal tendencies with their limited job experience and you got a bunch of poor broke swordsmen who could slice the wings off a butterfly but couldn't afford braces for their children. Catlow knew his Uncle Saed taught fencing in Maryland .This was looked at with disdain by most of the Brotherhood, including Catlow's father.

However, even the eternally proud Pretlow Creedence had to admit times were tough and money was tight. He allowed Saed to use his connections in the fencing world to get Catlow a part-time job at the Richmond Fencing Academy. Pretlow had also not moved his family in the last three years. Catlow had attended Huguenot High School during that time. At first it was hard for him to be a social person. To interact with kids who didn't know the difference between a rapier and a saber. Kids who had not been taught what major organs could be pierced and cause immediate death. Kids who didn't know the difference between the femoral and aortic arteries by the age of twelve.

Gradually he started to learn how to socialize. He had gained Ronnie's friendship in history class when chance had thrown them together as partners on a project. He had a deep and thorough understanding of world history thanks to his father's constant tutelage. Pretlow Creedence believed that most major historical events had been and will be affected by the actions of the Brotherhood. So he taught Catlow all about the Battle of Hastings, The Hundred Years war,

Suleiman the Magnificent and the battle for Jerusalem, the influenza outbreak in 1918 and other world events at a young age. Ronnie had appreciated Catlow's intelligence and his dry sense of humor.

"You saving my ass from my mama and daddy. I gotta keep my grades up to stay on the football team. You my boy Cat.!" Ronnie had exclaimed when they got their grades back for the project. Catlow had to admit it felt good to have a friend that didn't want to talk about the coming battle or practice fighting with a sword in each hand. Someone who just wanted to be a seventeen year old, nothing more, nothing less.

In the same way his extended stay in Glenn Allen had allowed him to embrace his sense of humor it also allowed him to embrace his love of music. Band was where he had met Harmony. She sat next to him playing her violin with a tenderness and passion that shared a spot in her soul. Mr. Langhorne their Muppet-like music teacher had accompanied her on the acoustic guitar for a beautiful rendition of Bach's Cello Suite No.1. They had performed for the entire class .Harmony was first chair violinist for their band. The common consensus was that she was pretty much the best musician in the entire school district. Catlow had watched her play. The joy and concentration on her face reminded him of his father when he practiced dueling against his Uncle Saed. The sheer magnificence of knowing that you are magnificent was clearly evident in their body language as they did what they loved. Catlow was moved by her skill and her beauty. Harmony was a striking young girl on the cusp of womanhood. Her smooth flawless skin had a light ecru coloring that helped highlight her gray eyes. She wore her long dark hair in two pigtails that seemed always run along the wonderful hills of her breast. She was short and voluptuous in a way that belied her years. Catlow loved to watch her play the violin or walk or laugh or do just about anything.

That day after the class had ended Mr. Langhorne had left his guitar on the desk. Catlow had lingered. The guitar was not that different from the akonting that his uncle had taught him to play over the course of a summer spent at his home in Maryland. The akonting was a large guitar like African instrument that Saed Barkarhat played with the skill of a virtuoso. Catlow had picked up the guitar and began to pluck and pull the strings with a haphazard frenetic display of dexterity. Soon the notes of Bach's "Fugue in G minor" began to emanate from the instrument. He played with his eyes closed feeling the music flow from him like water from a faucet. It felt right. Right in a way that holding a sword never had. He stopped himself and put the guitar back on the desk. He heard slow, soft clapping from behind. He whirled on his heel and saw Harmony standing there clapping. There was a large dopey grin on her face.

"Well he doesn't speak but he can play," she said.

"I can speak. I just don't have much to say," he said.

"I wouldn't talk much either if I could talk through my instrument the way you do," Harmony said. Catlow looked back at the guitar.

"You are much better than I could ever be," he said softly. Harmony walked over to him.

"You are incredible. And I'm going to tell Mr. Langhorne," she said.

The bottom fell out of Catlow's stomach.

"Please don't .He is going to want me to try out for band and I can't play and it's just gonna make things weird."

"Well why can't you play? You parents can't afford the instrument? Cause you can get help with that. The school helped me get my violin. Won't no way me and my moms could have afforded that," Harmony said brightly. Huguenot High had a program where each student could take a different elective class every grading period. Catlow had taken chorus (couldn't sing but liked the class) Home Economics (his father wanted him to learn how to sew so he could help make gauntlets and scabbards) and now Band. The band class was free. Actually playing in the school marching or jazz bands required the purchase of an instrument. Catlow could plead poverty to Harmony and hope that satisfied her curiosity. Money was tight these days. The real reason was more embarrassing. Pretlow Creedence viewed any activity that took away from training for the upcoming Duel of Generations as frivolous. He would not allow Catlow to join the school band .Or the football team .Or the Drama club. Catlow was beginning to break some of his father's constraints but on this he knew there was no equivocation.

"Well my dad won't let me beg the school for a guitar. "Catlow said. Seeing Harmony's countenance become dark and clouded made him regret his choice of words.

"I didn't beg them for shit. I just needed help. Maybe you shouldn't speak. It ain't your best skill," she said as she walked out the room. Catlow hung his head and sighed.

A few days later as the students of Huguenot High filed out of school Catlow sat on a huge concrete sphere at the end of the steps leading out of the school. He watched and waited. Finally he saw Harmony coming out with a few of her girlfriends. She had almost passed him when he said her name.

"Harmony". Her name felt right coming out of his mouth. She stopped and looked at him.

"Yeah?" Catlow pulled a medium sized rectangular card out of his back pocket. On the card was a hand drawn picture of a cat wearing a dunce cap with a thought bubble above its head. The thought bubble said:

"I am sorry for being stupid."

Harmony looked at the card then burst out laughing.

"Did you draw this?" she asked.

"No my little sister did .But I told her what I wanted it to look like. I am sorry. You were just trying to be nice," he said sheepishly.

"Yeah you was being stupid. And I am nice. Too nice," she said .Her two girlfriends laughed. Catlow looked away from their laughter. He felt her shove the card back into his hand. She and her girls walked down the sidewalk. Catlow felt a pit of pain open up in his chest. He shook his head. Sucking his teeth he looked at the card one more time before throwing it in the trash. That was when he noticed Harmony had written her cell number on the card. Along with the inscription

"Don't be stupid again." and a smiley face.

Now six months later they spent most of their free time together. When she wasn't practicing violin and he wasn't practicing fencing, gymnastics, sword making or martial arts they would talk on the phone or go to Byrd Park or maybe just sit on the bench in the commons area of school, eating lunch together. Harmony said she wasn't really a fan of movies but Catlow thought she was lying because she knew he couldn't afford it. Harmony did love for Catlow to read to her though;

Shakespearean sonnets or T.S. Elliot poems or an Edgar Allan Poe short stories. They would sit on the porch of her house and lay next to each other on her small love seat as her mother peeped out the window periodically. She needn't worry about Catlow taking advantage of her daughter. He was a virgin in every sense of the word. Not in the new-fangled hipster speak of "new virginity". They had kissed a few times, in the park with the summer sun setting in the western sky or on his bike after she got off work. Harmony had straddled his bike with her back to the handlebars, her little work cap turned backwards, her short brown arms around his thick neck. Her lips would lightly touch his with a soft insistence. Despite his Namaste yoga training and deep breathing exercises his heart had started to pound deep in his chest like a circus drum. Kissing Harmony made his head swim. He wanted to do more but was terrified by the idea at the same time.

Catlow pulled his bike up to parking space nearest to the door of the restaurant and parked. Harmony's heart skipped when she saw Catlow pull up to the door. He was wearing a black t-shirt and jeans. The t-shirt stretched across his broad chest. He climbed off the bike and started to walk in the store. She loved to watch him walk. He moved like a cloud that had fallen to earth. Smooth movements like he was dancing to music only he could hear. Her girls called him lame because he was quiet and in their minds he had no swag. Harmony couldn't explain to them that his lack of swagger was his swag. Catlow didn't have to tell the world he was a great guitar player or a great athlete or a great kisser. He knew it and expected the world to recognize it without his prodding.

The door chime rang as he walked through the door. Harmony was talking to a customer who couldn't make up her mind between the turkey and bacon cheddar croissant and the ham and blue cheese

sandwich. The people behind her were trying to be patient but Harmony could feel the thin social contract of civility holding their collective
tempers in check begin to break.

She held up her hand with all five fingers out to tell Catlow she had five minutes until her break. He nodded and sat down at a table in the far corner.

She couldn't wait to tell him the good news. She had gotten him a surprise.

Outside a black Lexus parked six spaces away from Catlow's bike. A thin, sharp-faced Asian man was behind the wheel. He reached into his suit jacket and pulled out his cell phone. He touched the screen and waited for the person on the other end to answer.

"Yes he is visiting someone at the mall. Yes sir. I will await your instructions." He put the phone back and began to whistle a song. If someone had been sitting in the car with him they may have recognized the song. It was "O Death". He loved American Bluegrass music. The man reached into the glove box of the car and pulled out a shuriken. He rolled the razor sharp weapon over his fingers. Back and forth. Back and forth. Back and forth.

Pretlow packed his bags for his trip to Pennsylvania. He wrapped the cutlass reproduction in velvet fabric and then put it in a handmade wooden box .He had constructed the box as well as the sword. He also packed an overnight bag and his real sword. It was a weapon that could pass itself off as a work of art. It was two edged like a medieval longsword. He had added a detachable basket guard and an eye bolt on the end of the pommel. He could string a lanyard through the eye bolt and make a loop that he could put his arm through. The lanyard loop was connected on each end by thick Velcro strips. He could draw his sword in less than a second with this particular rig. The time of the Invitation was close. Pretlow could feel it in his bones. Everything his father and the other men of the Brotherhood had been training him for, everything he had been training his son for was about to come to fruition. He didn't have to see the Judges appear in front of him to know the time was nigh. He also knew that the Men of the First Chaos had acquired a reputation for winning at all cost. They had won the last Duel of Generations in 1913 by hook and by crook. Once the Invitation had been received by all the Houses several of the Men of the First Order had disappeared. They were gone in the twinkling of an eye. The remaining Men of the First Order had arrived at the Duel outnumbered seven to three. Astor Creedence had always gotten a cold look in his eye when he recounted that day for his son.

"I was twelve years old. I watched as your grandfather Oron and Oscar Esperanza and Lothar Crzivell stood against those seven agents of Discordia .I watched as the Judges allowed the Duel to commence. At first the men of order held their own against the men of chaos. Lothar dispatched two opponents with one thrust. Oscar ended the lives of Ian Crisp and Stefan Du Mor with the edge of his two sabers. For a moment I allowed myself to hope. To hope my father would live to tuck me into bed that night. To hope the men of order would triumph. Then Heinrich Lutenburgh cut off Oscar's arm as Stavaros Apothas cut off his head with their gilded sabers. Lothar ran up the nearest wall, flipped backwards with a rapier in each hand. He was trying to get behind them but they had anticipated his strategy. As he landed Stavaros swung his saber like a whip and cut off his right hand as Aaang Saang pierced his guts with a short tanto. He had been dueling with my father but disengaged from him to join the fray. My father stood before the three of them with a saber in one hand and long sword in the other. Blood covered the floor of the old warehouse where the duel was taking place. The smell of death was heavy in the air like the scent of rain before a storm. I could see the light from the setting sun pouring through a dirty skylight. The Judges stood there off to the side, silent as the Sphinx. Stavaros Apothas stretched his sword out and pointed at my father.

"Shall you ask for quarter Mr. Creedence?" .He sneered when he said it.

"I shall only ask that you don't bleed too heavily upon my shoes Mr. Apothas" my father had responded. Suddenly Aaang Sing let out a cry and ran at my father. My father struck his blades together once. The clear tone of pure steel rang throughout the warehouse like a battle cry. Oron parried his first strike then spun into his opponent .As he completed his revolution he took Aaang's head off with the longsword. The other two attacked simultaneously. My father held them off for what seemed like hours. He turned and slashed like a whirling dervish of death. Parried their strikes, blocked their thrusts. They fought at a speed that was hard to track with the naked eye. The light was a fairy running along the edge of bloodstained metal. Finally Heinrich leaned in with a strike that my father sidestepped as he turned to his right. At the same time he slashed at Heinrich's neck with the saber in his left hand. A fountain of blood erupted from his aorta and covered father's face and chest. As he was sidestepping he tried to turn a complete revolution so he could face Stavaros. But the wily bastard had already positioned himself behind his falling comrade and behind my father. He slid his saber into my father's neck like a surgeon. The end of the blade exited out his throat right below his chin.

That cur cut his larynx. He denied me the final words of my father. I don't remember what happened next. I woke up to the sounds of my mother weeping and the beginning of World War I. My father could not speak to me before he died but I will speak to you my son. Do not take the Men of the First Chaos lightly. The path they walk has afforded them an opulent and decadent lifestyle to which they are beholden like bondsman. They profit off of death and war. Disease and agony. Addiction and depravity. They will fight to maintain this lifestyle at all cost. I will be long in my grave when the next Duel happens and the Covenant is fulfilled. So it falls to you my son. Do not fight to avenge your grandfather. He was a great and honorable man this is true but he is not the reason you fight. Do not fight to honor me. You honor me every-time you pick up a sword and practice for what is to come. You fight to spare the world another war to end all wars. To give them a reprieve against the abasement of men and women. To free them from the yoke of drugs and addiction. To give them a chance to flourish on a planet that is lush and green not barren from chemicals eating the very soil upon which we walk. Pretlow, if the Men of the First Chaos defeat you and your comrades all this will come to pass and more. The world you will leave your children will be worse than the one I leave to you. Beware when the time for the Invitation draws near. They will stop at nothing to assure their victory." Astor Creedence would then take a drink from his near omnipresent glass of scotch and close his eyes for a moment. Pretlow wondered if in those times he was trying to remember his father's face .Much as Pretlow was doing now. Astor Creedence was long dead and in his grave. Yet his lessons lived on in Pretlow's heart.

"I will not fail you father," he whispered to himself as he zipped up his travel bag.

Harmony ran to Catlow as soon as her friend Cashona relieved her for her break. He rose as she ran toward him and wrapped his arms around her .The warmth of her body was pleasant to him .She smelled like lilacs and strawberries. She hugged him back fiercely. They stood there a few moments like that until finally she released her grip.

"So you not working today?" she asked as they sat down at a small metal table. She took off her cap and pulled her down her pigtails. Catlow loved to watch her hair fall over her ample bosom. He may have been a virgin but he knew what he liked. And he liked Harmony.

"Naw, my dad's leaving to go to a big Renaissance Fair in Pennsylvania so we are having family dinner later. I just been riding around on my bike today," he said

"Your dad ain't got you practicing for that big fencing tournament?" Harmony asked. Catlow sighed. He hated lying to Harmony but even with his rudimentary understanding of social conventions he realized they were not close enough for him to tell her the truth about his family's beliefs. They really were his family's beliefs. Every day they were less and less his beliefs.

"Well he thinks I'm practicing at the studio but I just wanted to ride. And come see you. I'll go to the studio tomorrow .Saturdays are our busiest days even with school out," he said plainly. Harmony loved how Catlow didn't attempt to be smooth or cool or fly. He just was who he was. She found that irresistible.

"Cat can I ask you something?" she said holding on to one of his hands. His hands were huge with thick calluses on the palms and thumbs. He cocked his head and peered into her eyes.

24

"Of course."

"You say your family is really poor. They couldn't afford a guitar for you to join Jazz band. But you got a motorcycle. I don't understand how you afford it. You not in the game are you?" she asked .Her voice was filled with weariness. For a second Catlow didn't understand what she was saying. Then he let out a low chuckle.

"No. I am not selling drugs. My uncle Saed gave me the bike. One of his fencing students gave it to him in trade for six months of fencing lessons. But she never came in for the lessons .So he was stuck with the bike and when he looked at it closer he figured out it didn't run. So he was going to send it to the junkyard. He was at our home talking about it when he asked me if I wanted it. His son Shian didn't want to ride it .So he brought it down from Maryland one weekend. He gave me the key and a copy of "Zen and the Art of Motorcycle Maintenance". I went online at school and downloaded manuals on how to fix it up. Now it's mine," Catlow said .He smiled as he remembered the look on his father's face when Saed offered him the bike. Pretlow Creedence did not acquiesce to many people. He was a man of strong will with a stubborn disposition. His mother couldn't change his mind, nor could any of the other men of the Brotherhood, except Uncle Saed. When no one else could get through to Pretlow Saed would step forward and speak. Invariably Pretlow would listen. When Saed offered the bike Pretlow's face had become a smooth mask of barely contained rage.

"We will speak about this Saed," he had said without looking up from his dinner plate. Catlow loved his uncle just a little bit more that night. He wasn't there when Pretlow and Darnicia and Saed did speak about the bike.

"What if he breaks his leg and we get the Invitation?" Pretlow had asked in hushed tones. They had adjourned to the workshop. Saed was leaning against the wall with his muscular arms crossed. He was wearing his usual attire. Pressed, white button-down shirt and black slacks with a crease so sharp you could have sliced cheese on it. His dark shaved head gleamed under the pale white lights of the workshop. His face was a smooth as he his head .He shared his sister's full lips and high forehead.

"Listen to yourself for a moment Pret. You are worried he won't be a part of the Covenant. What about if he breaks his leg and is laid up in the house for months? What if he dies on the bike?"

"You're not helping your cause Saed," Pretlow said in a low voice.

"What I am saying my brother is that you don't seem to be concerned about Catlow .I know you are but it doesn't come across that way .You seem more concerned about whether or not he will be with us if and when we receive the Invitation. He is a young man Pret. Not a piece of metal. You can't hammer him into whatever shape you desire," Saed said. His voice was heavy with his thick South African accent.

"We should be like metal. You know the weight we bear," Pretlow said. He picked up a sword and began to swing it and roll it over the back of his hand. Whenever he was stressed he went back to the steel. It gave him peace.

"I also know if you keep riding him he won't give a dam about the responsibility we have been given. He will pack his bags and never look back," Saed said.

"So the bike is a bribe?" Darnicia asked softly. They both looked at her. Saed took a deep breath.

"Yes. We will need all of able bodied, able-minded warriors on our side when the time comes. Call it a bribe if you will .I call it insurance. You see Pret I also take what we have inherited seriously. But while you are Cotton Mather I am Rob Bell," Saed said to his old friend. Pretlow did not respond. He just went through his motions with his sword. The sound of the blade splitting the air was a whisper of blood not yet spilled.

Harmony leaned forward and kissed Catlow on the cheek.

"That's good. I don't like guys in the game. My brother is doing ten years for that shit. Come on walk me to my car .I got you something." She rose and took his hand. They walked out of the restaurant and over to Harmony's weathered Honda Civic. It had once been blue but had now aged into a faded azure color. She unlocked the door and reached into the backseat. When she turned around she handed Catlow a guitar case. It was black leather case that had seen good days and bad days. It had a few stickers on the bottom. One said Amsterdam, the other said London Calling. Catlow stared at the case with a puzzled look on his face.

"It's for you ding dong. It's kinda worn out but you are good at fixing things," she said .The smile on her face threatened to split her cheeks. Catlow reached out and took the case from her hands. He placed it on the hood of her car and opened the tarnished nickel plated latches on the side. A dark mahogany acoustic guitar was in the case. The A string was missing and frets were chipped. Catlow thought it was the most wonderful thing he had ever seen. No one except his Uncle Saed had ever given him something that was not sword or dueling related. Not his Father, not his Mother. No one.

"I can't take this. How much did this cost you?" he asked.

"Oh no don't start that noble shit with me. You are going to take it and you are going to fix it and we are going to play together at the Winter Music Expo this year. We are going to play your Bach piece. Just say 'Yes Harmony.'," she said with her hands on her hips staring up into his light brown eyes. God she loved his eyes.

Catlow took her face in his hands and kissed her. A deep kiss that sent a lightning bolt through his body. His tongue slid into her mouth and touched hers. Like a circuit was being connected he now felt the electricity flow through his body down to his ten toes. Instinctively she reached up and touched his firm chest. Heat began to rise from the center of Harmony's body spreading to all her extremities. Suddenly she pushed him gently. He released his grip and stroked her cheek with his right index finger.

"Thank you. Thank you so very much. I guess I owe you one now." Catlow said with a grin.

"I gotta go back to work. You can make it up to me later," she said with a wink.

The Asian man sitting in the black Lexus turned on his IPod. It was sitting in the port in his dashboard. "Man of Constant Sorrow" began to pulse through the Bose speakers. The shuriken was still in his hand.

CHAPTER TWO

Carcone Apothas sat at his huge mahogany desk in the study of his chateau in Bavaria sipping 100 year old cognac while his son Carcine entertained an entourage of friends downstairs His longish black hair fell to his shoulders. His pale blue eyes contrasted with his tan skin. He was born in Greece in the city of Patras. He was raised in Greece but spent summers here in the Apothas family chateau .In between attending boarding schools in Switzerland and then entering Oxford before becoming a part of the secondary family business, Majoria Incorporated, A multinational weapons and ammunition supplier and development corporation. He had been educated about the real family business here in this chateau, in this dark and somber room. The books here were tools for his true vocation. The study was lined with oak shelves filled with books that covered a wide array of subjects including politics, philosophy and military history. He had read each and every one of the books on the shelves. Carcone counted Alexander the great among his ancestors. History says Alexander did not have any children. Historical record did not recognize any of his bastards. An enormous stone mantle filled the right wall of the room. The dying embers of a fire gave off an eldritch glow. The chateau was heated by electricity with a gas back-up but Carcone still used the fireplace from time to time.

Carcone leaned back against his leather chair and swirled the cognac. The amber liquid caught the dying embers of the fire and for a moment seemed to ignite. The lamp on his desk was the only other light in the study. Carcone sipped his glass and savored the pleasant burn the liquor sent down his throat. A portrait of his grandfather Stavaros was hung above the mantle. His stern visage stared at Carcone with pitiless eyes. Carcone thought the artist, whoever he or she was, had captured the essence of his grandfather. Pitiless.. A bastard in the other sense of the word. Carcone heard music and laughter coming from the great room downstairs. Carcine was no doubt drinking and dancing with his guest. He was probably doing a little cocaine as well. Just a bump or two...Carcone denied his only son nothing. Whatever Carcine Apothas wanted he received. Women, cars, drugs, anything and everything could be had for the right price and the Apothas fortune afforded him all of it. Carcone allowed his son to take full advantage of this fortune. There could be a day when his son would have to defend that fortune with his very life.

So Carcone allowed him to "party up" as his friends called it. He allowed him to enjoy his freedom and indulge his desires. Their lives were tied to a dark destiny that would soon be fulfilled. He allowed these indulgences with one caveat. Carcine had to become a master swordsman. He practiced six hours a day every day with the best instructors in the world. Gymnastic coaches from the former Soviet Republic. He was taught kung-fu by disgraced Shaolin Monks. He was drilled day in and day out with Parkour specialists and Olympic caliber decathlon athletes.

Carcone himself taught his son swordsmanship. The multiple styles of fencing the Men of the First Chaos employed .A hybrid of German Kunst des Fetchens, French and English fencing combined with Japanese Samurai techniques. Two-handed longsword melee fighting co-mingled with their native Greek single handed short sword attacks. The ring of steel style, also known as the Master's wheel. All these styles and more Carcone taught his son until they congealed into a specific amalgamation of deadly skills, as his father and grandfather had once taught him. Every day. Without pity or sympathy. The regime was repeated over and over again until Carcine sometimes cried or threw up from his exertions. Carcone was the bastard and the son of a bitch and whatever else his son wanted to call him when they locked themselves in the training room. Once they left that desperate place he became a benevolent benefactor. . A subtle mea culpa for the pain he inflicted on him in the House of Blood and Steel. Carcone took another sip from his glass. He rose from his seat and walked over to the fireplace. He had a compact muscular frame .At 44 he still had a flat stomach and broad shoulder. His red button downed shirt was open at the neck allowing a thicket of gray and black chest hairs to burst forth. His four hundred dollars a pair black slacks were from his casual clothes collection.. His Ed Boon leather loafers had been around the same price. His wife Agrippina, Carcine's mother, once asked him if he was being too hard on their son .Their only child. After he slapped her and picked her up off the ground he had grabbed her by her hair and turned her in a slow circle around their palatial estate in Athens.

"Do you see all this? Do you see the clothes you are wearing? The car you are driven in? The twice a week fuck sessions that you call massages? The Louis Vuitton purses and the thousand dollar dinners? All that will turn to dust if I do not prepare him for what is to come. I will not let what my family has built and has stood for over a millennia be destroyed because of the softness of a mother's heart. Our fortunes are built on blood and steel and thus are subject to the whims of the blade. You know this and yet you ask me such foolish questions."

"Carcone, my father told me all the tales. I was raised in this world of covenants and duels to the death. But that's all it is, a tale. You really believe it. I pity you and I pity our son more," she had said once he released her. Carcone could have grabbed her, struck her again and then told her she had the luxury of not believing. He could have told her it didn't matter what he believed. The old men in the ivory tower believed. They believed wholeheartedly. The old men who controlled the purse strings of their world. Call them the Illuminati or the Bilderberg Group or the Freemasons. He called them the Men of the First Chaos and their belief would dictate the fortunes of Carcone and all the houses of chaos. These men had known his father and his grandfather. These men held the Book of Seven Swords in higher esteem than the bible. Their belief, their total submission to the ideas of the Covenant meant that if the Invitation came and Carcone and his brethren lost they would swing their influence away from war and destruction, Away from death and disease. They would turn their backs on decadence. They held fast to an ancient code of honor .At least once the Duel of Generations began. It was ironic that the power and influence they had amassed from thousands of years of chicanery and discord would be used to fulfill the Covenant and bring a hundred years of order to the world. If Carcone and his comrades lost.

Carcone had no intention of losing. The more esoteric details of the Covenant were up for debate. Did he believe in the deification of the Judges? Did he really believe they were all powerful beings who gave man a chance to control his own fate in an unfathomably large and dangerous universe? In the end it didn't matter. The old men believed it all. All Carcone could do was make sure he and his son were ready. He had to give them the best chance to win. By any means necessary.

A scream roused Carcone from his reverie. He dropped the glass and ran toward the door. Were the Men of the First Order here? There was nothing in their recorded interactions with the Men of the First Chaos to suggest they would strike outside the confines of the Covenant but Carcone prided himself on being ready for every eventuality. As he ran toward the door he grabbed a cane from a small basket by the door. Hidden in the cane was a single edged saber. Carcone might have had a few concerns about the quality of the steel but not about his skill. He threw back the study door and ran toward the grand staircase. A lacquered white pine railing ran the length of the upper floor landing and lead down the stair case. Carcone moved with ghostlike grace and cheetah-like speed. He hopped up onto the railing in one jump .Breathing fast he balanced himself there for a moment and looked down into the great room.

Carcine was standing in the middle of the room in front of another enormous fireplace. He had a sword in his hand. Carcone recognized it as one of the swords that adorned the dining room wall. It was a cheap piece tin that was worth barely a hundred dollars. A few of his guests were chopping up small piles of white powder on the glass top coffee table and then bowing their heads in prayer to an alabaster master. Others were sprawled across the white leather furniture like beached dolphins, bodies at odd angles in the midst of their drug induced stupor. One nubile young woman in a devilishly tight pair of ski pants and a form fitting white sweater was holding a piece of fruit. It was one of the large red apples that Carcone had the staff ship in from Wisconsin.

"Go ahead. Throw it at me as hard as you can," Carcine said grinning. As he grew he looked more and more like his mother .Tall and lean with pale skin. His father had contributed his dark hair to the DNA equation but everything else had come from Agrippina. The young lady was laughing and wiping at her nose.

None of the guests had looked up yet and noticed the imposing sight of Carcone Apothas balanced on one leg on the railing 25 feet up in the air above them. Carcone watched as Carcine implored her again. "Throw it Candy! Come on don't be a scared little bitch!" he howled. The girl stopped laughing and wiping her nose. She cocked her head to the side for a moment.

She hurled the fruit at Carcine as hard as she could .It was an underhand throw .Carcone remembered she was an Olympic softball player. Carcine was currently fucking her quite frequently. Something in his choice of words had unlocked her competitive spirit. The apple left her hand as a red blur.

Carcine had been standing with the sword down by his side. He adjusted his feet and brought the sword up faster than Carcone's eyes could register the movement from his perch. He extended his arm and rapidly rotated his wrist as the apple met the point of his blade. In one fluid motion he snapped his wrist straight up toward the ceiling. The apple flew toward Carcone. He reached out and grabbed it deftly. The apple was now hollow. The core was gone.

Carcine looked up toward the ceiling with a puzzled look on his face. Upon seeing his father his eyes fell and he dropped his sword. Carcone held the apple for a moment. He shook his head and tossed it back to his son. Numerous times he had told Carcine that their training was not a circus act. Despite his permissiveness, despite the grandiose lifestyle he provided Carcine often defied his one rule. Being a master swordsman did not entail parlor tricks. Tonight's training would be brutal. Carcone would make sure of that personally.

"Carcine what's wrong?" Candy asked .She was too high and too drunk to really verbalize what she had just seen but somewhere deep within her drug addled brain she realized that Carcine had just caught an apple that she had thrown at him full speed on the point of a sword. If she had been just a little bit more sober she would have been able to register her astonishment in a more articulate way. During the Olympic qualifying game against China she had once thrown an 85 mph pitch at an opposing players head. She had done it purposely because said player had slid into her friend Lily spikes up earlier in the game. Nong Park had seen the pitch coming but had not been able to duck fast enough. The softball had opened up a gash that had required sixteen stitches to close. The apple was lighter than the softball and she had thrown it as hard as she could after Carcine had called her a bitch. In the bedroom he could and did call her worse but she did not appreciate him using that word in front of their friends. So she had planted her feet and curved the apple up and to the right. Straight at his head. There was no way he should have been able to dodge it, let alone pierce it with a sword, catch it and throw it up in the air. It was impossible. If she had not seen it with her own eyes she would not have believed it. Yet she had seen him do it. Somewhere past the haze of cocaine and Scotch she knew she had just witnessed something she probably shouldn't talk about to anyone else. She had the feeling people would lump her in with individuals who reported seeing Bigfoot or experiencing an alien abduction.

"Nothing, lets get ready to go into town. I want to go to the club .I'm in the mood for some Rammstein," Carcine said. He would go into town and drink the bitter warm German beer the tavern sold then fuck Candy in the backseat of his Bentley. He would build a buffer of pleasurable memories to hold onto when he was in the training studio later tonight. A wall of delightful distractions to protect his psyche from the draconian instruction he would endure at his father's hand.

"You sure?" Candy asked. Carcine turned and faced her. She subconsciously took a step backwards. His eyes were ice blue lakes that burned with a hellish fire. The nostrils of his aquiline nose were flaring violently.

"Oh I'm sorry I forgot you are an idiot. I forgot that you are just a dishonored former Olympian who is now a two thousand dollar a day coke whore. It must be hard to comprehend any statement that doesn't have the words 'blow' or 'suck' in it. You know what, stay here. I am going into town by myself. Why don't you fuck Roderick? He has about an ounce in his left front pocket. I'm sure he would give you a line in exchange for a handy." He brushed past her and headed for the door.

Candy stood there for a moment. The other guest Carcine had invited to join them at the chateau only gave her a cursory moment of silence to register her humiliation before they returned to drinking and laughing and snorting. After a few seconds she walked over to the glass bar in the back of the room and poured herself a shot of scotch. She told herself she didn't have to take his shit. She told herself that what he had said wasn't true.

She didn't approach Roderick for 30 minutes. She was proud of herself for holding out that long.

Carcone returned to his study and sat at his desk. He pulled a new glass and the bottle of Cognac out of his desk drawer. It was a vintage of spirits that was no longer produced .His was the last bottle of Du Mor cognac in the entire world. Agrippina's cousin Vivian Du Mor had given it to him two years ago when she visited the chateau. Agrippina had elected to stay in Greece while he and Carcine had gone to the chateau for their annual retreat after the end of the school term. Vivian had visited with two sons Henri and Febre. Their father Louis had died years earlier. Vivian was the prefect of the House of Love and Agony. Carcone was the prefect of the House of Blood and Steel. Vivian was a Du Mor by birth. Louis had actually taken her surname when they married. The Du Mor fortune was built on the foundations of the world's oldest profession. The Du Mor's owned hundreds brothels throughout Europe. These were for the common man. For centuries they had also operated an exclusive and unique escort service for the world's most powerful men and women. They traced their lineage back to concubines in the entourage of Cyrus the Great. Her grandfather had invested some of the family fortune into early stag films. Today the Du Mor's owned or had controlling interest in 95% of the porn studios throughout the world. He and Vivian had carried on an affair for years. Agrippina knew but she did not confront Carcone. She had her own stable of lovers. Theirs was a tacit non- aggression agreement.

Vivian had given him the bottle after he took her bent over the very desk he was sitting at right now. He could see her luxuriant blood red hair whipping back and forth as he slammed his hips into her thighs. He remembered how he had flipped her on her back and she had brought her legs up until her heels were on his chest. He remembered her razor-sharp stiletto heels that were on the end of her black leather knee-high boots. They had dug into his chest until they split his skin. He had slapped her when he came .She had slapped him back, hard. Breathing heavy and walking ungainly she had gone to her purse which lay on the floor in front the mantle. She pulled out the bottle and handed it to him as he pulled up his pants.

"A drink before the war. The Invitation is coming. My sons will fight for our House. I would train them myself but they need a man's skill.

My style will not serve them well," she had said as fastened her bra. Carcone let out a bitter bark of a laugh.

"Your style. Has a woman ever fought in the Duel? Why do you even train?" He knew that Vivian trained with the rapier and the epee every day, a useless endeavor in Carcone's mind. Vivian leaned forward as quickly as a bolt of lightning and slapped him again. She was as fast as a thought. He hadn't been able to move his hand because he was holding the bottle.

"My father informed me of his disappointment at my lack of a penis every day of my life. I took up the sword in the hopes that he would be just a bit less ashamed of my gender. You are the greatest swordsman of our generation. And I just ambushed you with a hundred year old bottle of liquor. I played on your greed and could have taken your life if I so desired. I watched you duel Louis when he found out about us. I saw your skill and your power. I watched as you eviscerated him before my eyes. And I have thanked you ever way possible ever since. But do not take my insatiable desire for your cock as a weakness. I am not my cousin. I will not suffer your tantrums. For all your skill and prowess I see your flaws. If the Judges allowed it I would fight for my house and I would win. If needed to I would defeat you my dear Carcone. Alas nowhere in the Book of Seven Swords does it record a woman fighting for the Covenant. So I turn to you to train my sons. Do not fail me," she said. She turned on her heel and began to walk to the door. Carcone put down the heavy thick glass bottle onto his desk. Moving like a breeze he ran past Vivian to the basket by the door and grabbed his cane and an umbrella out of the basket.

"A quick sparring session Madame Du Mor if you would be so kind," he said with a deep, sarcastic bow.

"Oh my dear Carcone is your ego bruised? Better your ego than your face. I think not," she said as she brushed past him. Carcone sucked in his breath then tossed the umbrella at her back. Vivian threw her torso forward and landed on her hands. She caught the umbrella between her feet. Grunting she kicked her legs into the air thrusting the umbrella toward the ceiling .Like a coiled spring she pushed off her hands and landed back on her feet just in time to catch the umbrella in her outstretched hand.

She replaced it back into the basket.

"Better your ego my dear than your face," she whispered as she left the study.

Carcone sipped the cognac. Agrippina was his wife but Vivian was his woman. He would love to spar with her .Loser serves the winner for a month. He would show her the true meaning of love and agony. A vibration went through his left leg. He reached into his pocket and pulled out a smooth rectangle of plastic. It was his IPhone: a cutting edge prototype that would not be released to the public for several more months. Wealth had it perks. He looked at the screen. There were a few letters on the screen to indicate who was calling him

"MOTHFC" Carcone swallowed his drink in one gulp. He touched the screen. "Yes?"

"Go to your front door." The voice on the other end of the phone was wispy and soft but stern. A hammer wrapped in velvet. It was Barton Crisp, the ancient prefect of the House of the Poison Soil Carcone walked slowly down out the study and down the staircase. His stomach felt bottomless. The sights and sounds of the party faded to the background as he parted the sea of revelers to head to the door. The closer he got to the ornate wooden double door with the wrought iron corbels the more his heart thudded in his chest. By the time he grasped the handle he could hear nothing but his own breathing.

He swung the door open with a slight grunt. The frigid air was so cold it almost felt like he was being burned. At the very bottom of the chateau's six-level front step was a black box. The light from the full moon played across its surface. Carcone walked down those wide brick steps breathing slow and deep. He knew what was in the box. Barton Crisp would not have called him personally for anything less than the fruition of all his training and sacrifice. The entire weight of all he had and all he would ever have was suddenly pressing down on his chest. His destiny, his son's destiny, the destiny of everyone he had ever known rested on the contents of that small black box at the bottom of his front step. By the time Carcone reached the box he was sweating despite the frigid temperature. He squatted down on his powerful haunches and picked the box up off the ground. It was light, nearly weightless. It seemed to be constructed of some sort of rigid black material. It was hard like stone but only 1/8 the weight. The surface had been polished to a mirror finish. His face stared back at him twisted into funhouse shapes. He turned and sprinted back up the steps taking them two at a time. Party goers were knocked aside as he barreled through the living room. Sprinting now he ran up the staircase up to his study.

Carcone slammed the door to his study so hard a few books fell off the shelf. He strode over to his desk and sat down in his chair. He grabbed the bottle of cognac and took a swig straight from the bottle.

"The Invitation. I'll be damned," he whispered to himself. He pulled out his phone again and touched the screen. The person on the other end picked up on the second ring.

"Make them the offer. Yes I just received mine so they will all be getting theirs. If they refuse kill them all," he said to the person on the phone. They hung up and Carcone put the phone on the desk. He had no doubt in his skill. He had virtually no doubt in Carcine's skill. He had spilled blood twice in his life at the end of a sword. He was not a coward. But he was no fool. If there were no Men of the First Order to fight then the Duel would be won by default. His son would not have to even pick up his sword.

"We will train intensely tonight anyway," he thought to himself. The Men of the First Order were nothing if not resilient. He had hired the best assassins money could buy. He had done this on his own without the knowledge of the old men. They would have admonished him about besmirching their honor. All the while conveniently forgetting they had tacitly allowed his grandfather to do the same thing a hundred years ago. While outwardly appalled at what Stavaros Apothas had put into motion in the weeks prior to the last Duel, privately they applauded his foresight and panache.

Still the Men of the First Order had arrived at the last Duel. Outnumbered and out maneuvered they had still managed to kill all but one of The Men of the First Chaos. Carcone would push himself and his son and Vivian's sons until The Men of the First Order either accepted his offer or were dead. By his hired killers or by his own hand it made no difference.

Catlow left Harmony reluctantly and headed home. He drove the old bike hard and fast on his way out of the city and towards the peaceful suburb of Glen Allen. "I love Harmony." he thought. He could finally admit it to himself even if he wasn't yet ready to say it to her. The old guitar case bounced against his back as rode. He would accompany her at the Winter Music expo. Pretlow Creedence wasn't going to like it but Catlow didn't really care. For the first time in his life he could glimpse a life outside of the Brotherhood. One where he crafted songs instead of swords. He found the idea very appealing.

He loved her in a way he didn't know was possible. He loved her brassy laugh and her long pigtails. He loved her eyes and her twisted sense of humor. He loved the way she played Mozart on her violin but also knew all the words to "Single Ladies." She was Brunhilde to his Siegfried. On some level Catlow knew that was a strange way for a seventeen year old to think about his girlfriend but he was a strange seventeen year old.

Darnicia stood before her counter top slicing tomatoes with a wide butcher's knife. As a daughter of the House of Sand and Fire she was well acquainted with bladed instruments. Her father had not forbidden her from training with swords as some of the other fathers of the Brotherhood had done. She looked over her shoulder. Pretlow was upstairs taking a nap before dinner. He didn't sleep well during the night and lately it had gotten worse. Darnicia threw one of the Roma tomatoes into the air. Her hand moved so fast the blade on the butcher knife nearly disappeared. Perfectly round slices of tomato began to rain onto the counter top.

"Do it again Mommy!" a little voice squealed. Calla was standing there in all her dirty jeans and braided hair glory. Darnicia hadn't heard her walk into the kitchen. She silently cursed. Not because she had not wanted Calla to see her skill but because she often just seemed to forget about her youngest child. Shame fell over her like a wave.

"Oh no, not again. Your father would not approve my little dirt diver." Calla looked around.

"I won't tell if you don't,"she said with a conspiratorial wink. Darnicia laughed in spite of herself. Calla was unlike anyone in the Creedence or Barkarhat families. She was wholly her own person. Quick witted and ferociously curious she sometimes exasperated her father and her brother. Even Darnicia could sometimes lose her patience with Calla. The little girl didn't seem to really care though. She was unnervingly self-assured for an eight year old. Whenever anyone chastised her or admonished her she responded by drawing a horribly accurate caricature of them with thought bubbles full of supposedly self-inflicted insults. She had once drawn one of Pretlow with the caption "I am a mean daddy because with my big ears I can always hear people talking about how big my ears are." Pretlow had been enraged when he had found the drawing on his workbench. Out of respect for her husband Darnicia had gone upstairs before she burst out laughing.

"No...we don't keep secrets in this house. Now go upstairs and get washed up for dinner. Your brother should be home soon," Darnicia said.

"Catlow Cat slow Cat go Catlow," Calla began to sing. In addition to being a talented artist Calla had a beautiful singing voice. Catlow hated when she made fun of his name but he loved her voice and his little sister. That was something that she knew would never change. His commitment to the Brotherhood was an entirely different matter. Darnicia had heard of men and women who had walked away from the Brotherhood. Not many but enough that it was recorded in the Book of Seven Swords.

Pretlow would not even entertain the idea of Catlow joining those besmirched ranks. Darnicia didn't want to believe that Catlow would do such a thing. However she could feel his restlessness. She saw how the light went out of his eyes when Pret made him go down to the basement and practice. The threat of him abandoning the Brotherhood was a black raven flying over their lives. She tried to make Pret understand that pushing Catlow too hard would make that raven land in their midst and take their son away from the Brotherhood and from them. Pretlow didn't seem to understand that sometimes.

Darnicia sighed. Squaring her shoulders she went back to shopping vegetables for her beef stew.

She often found herself conflicted. She didn't want Pretlow to be so hard on Catlow but she also wanted him to be ready when and if the Invitation arrived. She didn't want to lose her son to her husband's stubbornness or to the swords of the Men of the First Chaos. She knew Catlow didn't really believe in the Covenant anymore .She was his mother and there was little he could hide from her. She saw as he rolled his eyes before his he and his father recited the oath of Brotherhood prior to their practicing. His copy of the Book of Seven Swords lay on his bookshelf gathering dust.

She could also see he was in love. She didn't know with whom yet but she could tell his heart was enchanted. He talked on the phone for hours at a time. He listened to ballads on the radio until late into the night. His steps were lighter and his spirit seemed buoyed. He didn't scowl as much these days. She didn't know who his beloved was but she owed her debt of thanks for that little blessing.

Darnicia heard the front door open and Calla started yelling at the top of her lungs.

"Cat Slow is home!!" she screamed.

"Don't call me that you stinkbug!" Catlow yelled back. Darnicia could hear as Calla ran toward the kitchen with Catlow in hot pursuit. Calla was giggling manically. She ran into Darnicia and grabbed her legs.

"Mommy don't let Cat Slow get me!" she whined. Darnicia pried her daughter off her legs and picked her up off the floor.

"If you would not make fun of his name he would not be out to get you," she said as she looked into her eyes.

"But it's funny," Calla said plainly. Darnicia shook her head and put her back down on the floor. Catlow stood at the edge of the kitchen leaning against the wall. He had his arms folded across his chest and in that moment she got a glimpse of the man he would become. A man very similar to his father.

"I don't want you stink bug. What would I do with you? Oh I know I could hire you out as a pest repellent. Your stink could clear a house of mice and roaches in matter of hours," he said. Calla launched herself at him and began beating him about the legs and thighs. Catlow reached down and grabbed her, flipping her upside down then holding her with by her ankle with one hand effortlessly. Calla squealed with delight.

"All this noise could raise the dead," Pretlow said. He was standing behind Catlow with his arms crossed. Calla got her stealth from her father. Catlow flipped Calla and placed her on her feet. Catlow then stepped out of the door way to the kitchen. Pretlow walked past him and embraced his wife as she stood by the counter top.

"So I guess dinner is a little ways off," he said. Darnicia punched him softly in his chest. A small spasm scampered across Pretlow's face. It was as close as he came to a smile. Catlow went to the fridge and grabbed a bottle of fruit juice.

"So where did you get the guitar?" Pretlow asked as his son stood at the door of the fridge sipping his juice. Catlow held the bottle to his lips a few moments longer than was necessary. He was physically as tall and as big as his father. Perhaps one day the man wouldn't terrify him. Today was not that day. His father had never ever laid a hand on him in anger or abused him in any way. That did nothing to ease his fear. His respect for his father's belief may have begun to wane but his fear of what his father could do was as strong as ever. He had seen firsthand what Pretlow's years of dedication made him capable of doing. He intrinsically knew his father would never do to him what he had seen him do to those men at the 7-11 all those years ago. He hoped his
father had done what he did to protect them. Somehow that didn't make him feel any better or any less afraid. Catlow took a deep breath.

"Harmony gave it to me. I am going to fix it up…" His father cut him off mid-sentence

"Who is Harmony?" Pretlow asked.

"Ooooh she is the one I drew the cat for!" Calla squealed.

"SHUT UP!" Catlow yelled at her.

"Lower your voice Catlow," Pretlow said evenly. He knew this day was coming. His son was a young man and woman always seemed to gravitate toward the Creedence men. His mother said women could sense their power and their danger. The combination was hard to resist. When he had been young, long before he met Darnicia he had not understood this statement. He had not understood that as a man the worst thing you could do to a woman was awakening love in her heart without the intention of loving her in return. His mind reflected for a moment on a summer spent in Italy apprenticing to Garn Whiteborne, sword maker extraordinaire and a young woman who belonged to a House of Chaos and the pain he had seen on her face. He pushed that memory away.

"Catlow, who is Harmony?" he asked again.

"Pret let's talk about this after dinner. The stew will be done in a little while," Darnicia said.

"No. We will talk about this now. Time is getting short. We can afford no distractions. If I had not given my word to Hollis Prudence that I would deliver his sword personally I would not be going to Pennsylvania tonight. So I will ask for the last time Catlow, who is Harmony?" Pretlow asked with his arms folded across his chest. Catlow took a deep breath.

"She is my…girlfriend. She gave me the guitar so I could play at the Winter Music Expo," Catlow said. He stood against the fridge, the door handle pressing into his back.

Pretlow unfolded his arms. Seconds ticked by. Catlow could hear the low hum of the refrigerator and the subtle tick tock of the Cat in the Hat clock on the wall. Darnicia stood against the counter with one of her hands covering her mouth. Calla looked toward Catlow then back toward Pretlow with her eyes wide and her mouth open exposing her missing front tooth.

"I would have preferred that you were involved with someone from one of the seven Houses," Pretlow said finally. Catlow pushed himself off the fridge and started to protest .A dark scowl moved across his face like a white squall. Pretlow held up his broad callused hand.

"When I come back from Pennsylvania I want to meet her. As long as the guitar doesn't interfere with your training too much I am not opposed to you studying it. God knows there are worse things you could be doing," Pretlow said wryly. Darnicia smiled. Calla laughed. Pretlow held his hand out to Catlow. His son grasped his hand and pumped it once, then twice. Catlow went to release the handshake but Pretlow held him fast.

"Catlow, I am not fighting you on this because I know this girl obviously makes you happy. But know this. When the Invitation comes we are all leaving here. We may never come back. And once the Invitation comes we will all be in danger. This includes anyone that is in our presence if the Men of the First Chaos try to win the duel before it even starts. For her sake, don't lead her on, don't promise to run away with her or love her forever. Just enjoy this for what it is. A distraction, a moment of calm before the coming storm," Pretlow said as he stared into his son's eyes. Catlow pulled his hand out of his father's grasp.

"She is not a distraction. I love her. She makes me happy. Happier than I've ever been! She loves me even when I don't have a sword in my hand. You don't! You don't care about me; you don't care about any of us. You only care about your precious Brotherhood! You tell us we are warriors, that we are meant to save the whole world. That we are honor bound to defend humanity. What honor is there in tossing someone aside like a rag that I've wiped my hands on? What honor was there in letting that old lady get beat up in that 711? And don't say you saved me; you just didn't want to be one player short for your

LARP team. You want me to abandon her. And for what? For an imaginary duel and some fake-ass gods. You have dragged us around the country, friendless and awkward and lonely. You have wasted your life and ours waiting for an invitation that is NEVER GOING TO COME!!" Catlow screamed at his father. He felt so light he thought he might float away. Finally saying out loud what he had been thinking for years made him feel like a millstone had been cut from around his neck. He could breathe and that breath was unhampered by responsibility and sacrifice. It was a clear cool inhalation of freedom.

Pretlow had trained his entire life to maximize his reflexes. He had endeavored to link his thoughts and his movements in a seamless synchronicity. Thought equaled action. So he was as shocked as anyone else in the kitchen when he slapped Catlow. The thought of slapping his only son had not entered his conscious mind. His body, a body dedicated to a single unquestionable purpose reacted to the insult his son had hurled at him with such invective before his mind could process what was happening. His son had just spit upon everything he had ever taught him. Pretlow knew some of what he had said was the wild and immature ramblings of a young man on the cusp of adulthood. A young man pushing the boundaries of his existence in an attempt to find his path out of childhood and into the world of men. A young man who thought like countless young men before him that he had figured out the riddle that was life. The answer was so simple. His father was wrong. About everything that was normal for young men to think. Pretlow could wrap his mind around that idea, no matter how misguided it may have been.

What Pretlow could not comprehend was Catlow disrespecting his family's heritage. It was like someone was trying to explain the color yellow to a blind man. His mind could not even begin to process it effectively. Catlow had been witness to Pretlow's dedication to their destiny since he could walk. Catlow had been at his side through countless hours of sparring and practicing. He had traveled with him over the highways and bi-ways of this land visiting their brethren to train with the masters of every form of bladed combat. Catlow had watched as he poured his blood and sweat into a forge to create swords that helped clothe and feed heathen shaping metal that would someday save their lives. Pretlow had taught him the history of the Brotherhood since he had spoken his first word. He had educated him in the importance of their commitment since he had been a child. Had it all been for a naught? Had he wasted his time on a son that regarded his beliefs as fairy tales? Did Catlow think that every member of the seven houses denied themselves the trappings of a conventional existence on a whim? What did he think, that they were a sharing the same delusion? His son had basically called him a fool. Disparaged the cause to which he had pledged his entire being. His only son. Who he had held in his arms the day he was born and vowed upon everything he held dear to love and protect. A son who used to giggle at the silly faces he would make when he fed him. A son who he had rubbed down with alcohol to break a fever that almost killed him. A son who used to beg to hold a sword and learn to fight like his father and his uncle. Now that son spoke sacrilege in his house. Belittled what his ancestors had died defending.

Pretlow's arm articulated his grief in a way his lips never could have done. Catlow spun around and fell to the floor in a heap. Darnicia let out a short sharp cry like the bark of a small dog. Calla covered her mouth with her hands. Catlow rolled on his back drew his knees to his chest then kicked upward and landed on his feet. Shaking his head he turned and ran through the kitchen and out the backdoor.

Pretlow rubbed his face with his hands. Darnicia turned around and looked out the window over the sink. Catlow was running across the back yard like a gazelle. Tears began to flow down her cheeks.

"Can I get Catlow's share of the beef stew?" Calla asked.

Catlow jumped on his bike and tore out of the driveway. He rode without any idea where he was going. The wind wiped away his tears. The suburban civil-engineered trees were blurry sentries as he zipped down the smooth pothole-free streets. His father had struck him. In the very moment when he had felt most free his father had done what he had most feared. He had laid his hands upon him with violent intent. He turned the throttle and pulled the shifter on the bike and drove even faster. He darted in and out of traffic like a hummingbird gathering nectar from iron flowers. He would go to Harmony. She was still at work .He would sit in Panera until she got off then go to her house until he was sure his father had left for his trip. Right now he couldn't think of any circumstances that could make him want to speak to Pretlow Creedence. Harmony was his only shelter now, the only port for his wayward tortured soul.

Pretlow dabbed at his mouth with a napkin. The beef stew was excellent. Calla was licking her bowl. Normally he would reprimand her for such behavior. Tonight he said nothing. Darnicia finished her stew and sipped from her glass of wine. Pretlow was a teetotaler. He told himself it was because he didn't want to risk his skills being compromised by alcohol. He never considered perhaps he there was one thing his father did that he didn't want to emulate. Where Darnicia had gotten the wine was a mystery he didn't have the heart to investigate tonight. He sipped from a glass of pineapple juice.

"So is Cat coming back?" Calla asked as she finished licking her bowl.

"Yes Pretlow is Catlow coming back?" Darnicia asked .Her tone was unusually sharp. Pretlow decided he would ignore that as well. He finished his juice and rose from the table.

"Your brother will come home. Maybe not tonight but he will come home," he said.

"Well you sound very confident about that," Darnicia said. Pretlow looked at her.

"And what exactly does that mean?" he asked. Darnicia finished her wine.

"It means you slapped our son. It means you pushed him and pushed him and now you broke something inside him and now he is gone .My baby is gone," she said through her clenched teeth.

"You would have him stand there and make a mockery of all that we are for some girl and a beat up guitar? Where is my wife? Has she crawled inside that glass of wine and drowned?" he said his voice dropping an octave.

"I would have you be like a father and remember when you were once a boy. I would have you pick your words more carefully," she said. Pretlow slammed his hand down on the table. "My name is Pretlow Astor Creedence. I will not be a footman in my own house. I will not kowtow to my own son! I will not choose my words based on the criteria of whether or not they will offend him! No one wants to admit but what I said was right. If we get the Invitation and we have to meet the members of the other House at the Grand Hall we may have to leave at a moment's notice. And my dear wife and mother of my children as you said we may die. Either at the Duel or before at the hands of the Men of Chaos and their hired minions. I love my son. But if he truly believes that our lives have been a fool's errand then that is my failure as a father. I accept that. What I won't accept is his disrespect. A small part of me sometimes wishes he was right. That this was all a fantasy. But I know who we are and what we are," Pretlow said. He tossed his napkin on the table. "I am leaving for Pennsylvania. When and if he returns he will live here under my rules. This is not open to discussion," he said as he turned and stomped up the stairs. Calla put her bowl down and sipped her pineapple juice.

"I think-" she started to say but her mother cut her off with just a raised hand.

"Not now Calla. Just ...not now." Pretlow came back down the stairs with his bags. He walked up behind Calla leaned over and kissed her cheek.

"I love you crinkle head," he said into her ear. He walked around the table and put his hand on his wife's shoulder, leaned over and whispered in her ear. "I know you are angry with me. I am angry with myself. But you know the cause we serve is real and so is the danger. Forgive me my transgression but respect my position. I love you Darnicia. As I love Catlow and Calla." He moved her long braids aside and kissed her neck. He strode toward the door. He pulled it open and began to walk out into the night. He stopped and turned to look back at his wife. The straps of his bags crisscrossed his chest like a bandolier. Pretlow held his left hand vertically and parallel to his face. He grasped it with his right hand then kissed his wrist. It was the universal symbol among the Men of the First Order for devotion. It was the hand sign presented when they recited the Oath of Brotherhood. Then he was gone.

"Mommy do you think Daddy loves the Brotherhood thing more than us?" Calla asked .Her big brown eyes had a dark shine.

"No my little one," Darnicia said to her daughter. "But its close," she thought to herself. Catlow pulled his lime green Ford LTD out of the driveway and headed for the Interstate. It was 7 o'clock. He could be in Norristown by 2 am and then he would get up first thing in the morning to deliver the sword to his old friend Hollis. Hopefully Catlow and Darnicia would have calmed down by then. He turned on the radio and "Hurt" by Johnny Cash started pumping through the speakers.

If Pretlow had looked in his rear view mirror he may have noticed a figure clad in black jeans and a black hoodie walking the well maintained streets of his neighborhood. He might have noticed that figure was headed for his house. Pretlow's eyesight was 15/20 so he may have even noticed that hooded figure was carrying a small shiny black box. But Pretlow was not a man who looked back often if at all. When they sparred Saed called him Jaws. He was always pressing forward, never backing up, never giving an inch. So he never saw the figure. Fate is peculiar that way.

HAPTER THREE

Catlow got to the restaurant just as Harmony was getting off work. He pulled up next to her car and leaned his bike on the kickstand. Harmony was walking out the door with her head down and her cell phone pressed against her ear. When she raised her head and saw Catlow a smile broke out over her face. She half-ran half-skipped to Catlow. As she got closer the smile faded.

"Aw baby what's wrong?" she stroked his cheek. Catlow gazed off in the direction of the setting sun.

"Got into it with my dad," he said simply. Harmony hugged him tight. He could feel the solidness of her begin to fill the empty pit that had developed in his stomach ever since his father had slapped him.

"So what you doing now? You going home?" she asked when she released him.

"No. I guess I'll just ride around. Maybe I'll sleep on a bench in Bird Park." Harmony rolled her eyes.

"No you won't. You can come to my house. My mom will let you crash. You just can't come into my room…"

"Your mother is not going to let me spend the night at your house."

"She won't care. She will be upstairs drinking by nine o'clock. By ten she will be drunk. Trust me I know her schedule," she said. Her voice was tinged with sadness at the edges. Like a blanket that had gotten too close to an open flame.

"You sure?" he said. She pressed her body to his and kissed him full on the lips.

"Yes I'm sure," she whispered. Catlow kissed her back and fired up his bike. Harmony climbed in her car and he followed her out of the parking lot and further into the city.

Thousands of miles away in Las Vegas Nevada Davi El-Aki was sitting at a diner eating a piece of apple pie. Besides the pie he was enjoying a strong hearty cup of coffee. He was headed to a warehouse out near in a secluded part of the city. There waiting for him were men with two precious works of art that had been stolen from a private collection weeks earlier. Davi would pay them the agreed upon price for the paintings then he would kill them both and bury their bodies under the white sands out in the Big Empty. He would return the paintings to his father whom they had been stolen from and the honor of the House of Black Rivers would be restored. Davi El-Aki was the adopted son of Abdul El-Aki the prefect of the House of Black Rivers, one the houses of the Men of the First Chaos. Abdul had found Davi living on the streets of Tel Avis when he was just six years old. If pressed Davi could describe his mother. Her dark almond shaped eyes and her wide beautiful smile. If pressed even more he could tell you what the man that killed her looked like. The abusive, belligerent Israeli art dealer that had taken Davi and his mother in during the 80's. After a particularly nasty fight the art dealer shot his mother. No preamble no threats he simply shot her and then tried to shoot Davi. Davi had jumped through the window to the street and had run for his life.

The art dealer had certain connections within the government. He was never arrested or tried for the murder of Davi's mother. He never knew his real father so he found himself on the street. On the day that

Abdul found him he had been foraging through a trashcan outside a loud boisterous bar.

Abdul had called him by his name. He was so used to people Ignoring him that at first he didn't think Abdul was talking to him. Then Abdul called him again. Davi stopped foraging and stared at the man calling his name. He was frightening. He had long black hair flowing almost to his thighs. His nose had a hoop through the septum like a bull. He was tall with dark burnished skin. He was wearing a pair of khaki pants and a white flowing long sleeved shirt. He had crossed the busy street and trotted over to where Davi was standing.

"God you even have her eyes. Listen to me Davi. I was a friend of your mother's. A very good friend. I was saddened to hear what happened to her. Do you think you can take me back to where you used to live?" he had asked Davi .His voice carried the authority of a man who did not take no for an answer so Davi said yes. He took the man through the maze of dusty streets and darkened alleys. It took them quite a while and Davi had to turn around more than once. But finally he led them to the large bungalow that he had lived in with his mother and the art dealer for six months. It was on the outskirts of the city in a fairly secluded area. It was only one story but it sprawled over a huge amount of land like a dying cat. The art dealer was not rich but he was wealthy enough to have a gate at the end of his driveway. The gate stood as the way station between the fenced in property and rest of the masses of the distant city. The gate was a great wrought iron monstrosity with a lock in the center that could only be opened from inside the gate. Or so it seemed.

Abdul had stood in front that gate for a few minutes mumbling to himself. Davi stood there quietly shaking. He did not want to be here.

He did not want to remember what his mother's face had looked like after the first bullet.

"Stand back little one." Abdul had said. Suddenly a sword appeared in his hands like a magic trick. He would learn later it was called a shamshir. It gleamed under the blistering sun. It was beautiful to Davi. It consisted of a bright brass pistol style handle and wickedly curved blade with deep fillets running down its length. Abdul had raised it high above his head and slashed it across the gates from right to left. Davi held his breath for a minute. The gate fell from its hinges like a child's puzzle knocked from a table. Abdul walked through the opening and Davi scampered behind him. As they got closer to the house he could hear the sound of merriment. The art dealer was having a party. As they got closer to the wide picture windows that ran along the front of the bungalow Davi could see the art dealer and two women without shirts. Their pendulous breasts swayed as they danced in front of the art dealer. Standing against the back wall of the room was a huge dark-skinned man that Davi didn't recognize. Abdul walked around the side of the bungalow and up the steps to the side door. He knocked with the curved pommel of his blade. Davi stood on the bottom step. The door opened and Davi could see the dark-skinned man filling the doorway.

"Who are you? Mr. Shavone is busy." Davi didn't know who the dark-skinned man. He had not been there when his mother had been shot but something in the way he spoke made him angry. It made him hate the dark-skinned man just a little bit.

"I am Death. Come to exact a debt long overdue." Abdul had said. He brought the shamshir up from his left side with his right hand in one smooth practiced movement. The blade moved from left to right effortlessly. Unfortunately for the dark-skinned man his torso was in the path of the blade. It sliced through him as easily as it had sliced through the gate. His upper torso slid on along the diagonal slit that Abdul had created. His upper torso tumbled down the steps while his lower torso which held most of his intestines fell back into the house. Davi jumped to the side as the dark-skinned man's huge head and shoulders and part of his broad chest came to rest at the bottom of the step. Abdul stepped over the pile of legs and guts and walked into the house. Blood, thin and watery ran down the white bleached steps like drunken sprinters. Davi ran up the steps and stood in the doorway. The art dealer was standing .He was holding a gun. The Gun. The women had fallen to the floor screaming. The art dealer fired at Abdul.

Abdul leaned to his left and the bullet whizzed past his cheek. The art dealer shot again and Abdul leaned to the right. His motions were so fast and so succinct that Davi could hardly say he had moved at all. He had covered the distance between him and the art dealer very quickly. He sliced the shamshir to the left then the right then the left again .His last blow started as he held the blade aloft...then slashed down he completed one complete revolution of his entire body. His long black hair fanned out behind his head like a flag unfurling as he spun. Blood flew in every direction. The art dealer fell to the floor in pieces. As each part of his dissected body fell it made wet slapping sounds. The blood covered the tan travertine tiles on the art dealer's floor. Blood stained Abdul's shirt and pants. The art dealer had been cut into six neat sections. The women huddled together in the floor in front of the couch. Abdul noticed that their full brown breasts were splashed with blood. He held his hand out to them

"Rise little ones. It's alright. Rise," he said smiling. The two women looked at each other then rose still clinging to each other like new born pups. Abdul smiled at them again.

The shamshir flashed through the air once more. Both women were decapitated at one time. Their heads landed next to the ruined remains of the art dealer.

"Always smile at someone you are about to kill. It puts them at ease," Abdul had told him. It was the first of many things Abdul had taught him, including the family business. The El-Aki's were smugglers of the highest class. They would move stolen goods, people, and weapons, all for a price. They would make sure their clients products moved down the black rivers of the world.

Davi thought back on that day thirty years ago as he sipped his coffee. Abdul had made a phone call and from the art dealer's ornate gold plated cradle phone. He sat down on the couch seemingly oblivious to the carnage he had created. Davi could smell the harsh coppery scent of the blood and the dark bitter smell of human waste. Living in the streets had given him a high tolerance for both odors.

Abdul had motioned for him to come over to the couch. Davi stepped over the remains of the art dealer and the women and sat next to Abdul. He looked at his sneakers. They were stained with gore.

"You are going to come and live with me and my family. I promised your mother if anything ever happened to her I would take care of you," he said in his deep rumbling voice. He was speaking Hebrew. Davi would learn that Abdul was fluent in ten languages as were most of the members of the House of Black Rivers. Davi just sat there looking at him. Fifteen minutes later a black jeep pulled into the art dealer's driveway and a man got out of the vehicle. Davi watched as he walked past the big picture window to the side door. He stepped over the dark-skinned man and entered the living room. He looked very similar to Abdul. He was wearing a white t-shirt and black khaki pants. His arms were covered with tattoos and he had a septum piercing as well. He was carrying a duffel bag. The bag had a change of clothes for Abdul.

"You all done playing Shashti?" the man with the tattoos said. Abdul stood and took off his shirt. His upper torso was covered in strange sigils and designs.

"Shut up. Let's get out of here. Are the ships ready?" Abdul asked the man. Davi would come to know this other man as Uncle Oman.

"Ready and loaded with 2500 pounds of C4 headed to the Congo. We chopped it up into wedges the size of a block of cheese then stuffed them in jars of peanut butter. We should be good," Oman said. Abdul pulled on a t-shirt and glanced at Oman.

"We better be," he said. The two men headed for the door. Davi sat on the couch. Abdul stopped and looked over his shoulder.

"Come. We are leaving" Abdul said. Davi got up and stepped over the corpses. Once he had stepped over the remains of the art dealer he stopped turned around and spat on the remains. Abdul laughed.

"I think you will fit in just fine," Oman just shook his head.

Davi did fit in just fine. He would do anything for Abdul El-Aki. Abdul had indeed made him a part of the family. He had also introduced him to the sword and the Men of the First Chaos. Davi relished the coming Covenant .He wanted nothing more to make the man who had saved his life proud. Davi secretly suspected that Abdul was indeed his father. Davi's mother had once worked for one of the brothels owned by the Du Mor family from the House of Love and Agony. Abdul had been one of her most dedicated clients. Davi had discovered all this from his Uncle Oman. After an especially harrowing encounter smuggling sex slave to Thailand the entire crew had gone to Bangkok and drank copious amounts of rice wine. Oman had divulged the history between Abdul and Onca with the style of a medieval bard. His telling of the tale made Davi yearn for a happy ending even though he had lived through the conclusion. Abdul had never once come close to admitting the truth. Davi would have liked to hear some sort of acknowledgment but that did not lessen his gratitude. Abdul's legitimate son Alton tolerated Davi's presence with barely concealed disgust. Abdul's wife Nazir tried her best to pretend he did not exist. So Davi tried his best to stay out of the way. He spent his time in the studio Abdul had built at the seat of the House of Black Rivers' power in Turkey on the coast of the Black Sea.

He knew his swordsmanship skills were better than Alton's. So did Alton which did nothing to placate his disdain of Davi. Bravado was not a part of his personality, it was simply a fact. It was evidenced by the trust Abdul showed in him when he sent him on missions like this one. Davi would face his enemies with the same words he had heard Abdul speak that day. "I am Death." He was Death; Inevitable, unstoppable and utterly without remorse. He finished his coffee and left a twenty dollar bill on counter. He left the little diner and stepped right back into the sweltering Las Vegas heat. The heat was nothing like the heat in Tel Avis or Libya or Somalia or any of the other places he had gone on behalf of his House and his family. Dressed in a light tan sport jacket and a v-neck black t-shirt with jeans and loafers he appeared to be nothing more than an attractive tourist. A few of the women he encountered thought he looked like a rich Arabian shah or his son, or perhaps a model.

The thieves had been friends of Alton, or more precisely

individuals who had pretended to be friends of Alton to gain his trust. That trust had been cemented with the help of some casual sex with beautiful men young men and women catering to Alton's tastes. After that, the strike was easy. Davi thought it was not a coincidence that the thieves had taken the two pieces Davi had purchased for Abdul for his birthday a few years earlier. Nevertheless here he was about to reclaim his family's property without one cross word in his mouth for his "brother." He would take his rage out on the thieves.

His cell phone vibrated in his pocket. He grabbed it and answered it .There was only one person that ever called him. Abdul El-Aki was on the line.

"Davi, come home. We have preparations to complete." Abdul took a deep breath. "We received our Invitation today," he said finally. Behind his Michael Kors sunglasses Davi's eyes lids fluttered. The Invitation. It was real. Not that he had ever really doubted it but hearing the words sent a shudder through his body. Yet he was conflicted.

"Father what of your property? It won't take me long to reclaim it," he said.

"Davi come home. I need you. What are two paintings of fat Italian women measured against our very way of life? No, come home .We must prepare for the Covenant. There are only two things I believe in, my son. Money and the Covenant. We must fulfill the later to continue receiving the former" Abdul said.

"Of course Father," he said. Davi ended the call and began walking toward his rental car.

Lavell Carson saw the towel head walking down the street in his fly ass clothes and talking on his phat cellly that probably cost a thousand dollars. Motherfucker deserved what he was about to get. Lavell checked to see if his boy Rashad was ready. They were about to roll this bitch for his goodies. Lavell took one last look up and down the street. No po-po to be seen and no good Samaritans either. Lavell inhaled deeply. As he exhaled he began to run toward the Arab dude. He had a sawed off pool stick in his hand. One clap to the head and motherfucker would be out for the count .Rashad would come up from the front and help relieve Al-Qaeda of all the contents of his pockets. By the looks of him they could score enough for ten or fifteen Mollys. One would be popped for celebratory reasons and they would sell the rest. Probably. They might pop two depending on how good they were. Drug purchases varied in quality.

Davi heard the footfalls behind him. He listened as they increased in speed. Ten feet behind him. Then six. Then three. Davi reached inside his sport coat and grabbed his own shamshir. It was a replica of the one Garn Whiteborne had made for his father. He simultaneously ducked and spun to his right. A young black man was in the process of falling into the wall of the diner. He had a short club in his hand. He had swung it at Davi's head with all his might. Davi's flanking maneuver had caused him to miss his target and he had over committed to the strike. His momentum had carried him right into the wall. His shoulder hit the concrete hard. He recovered fairly quickly (for someone not trained in the ways of the Brotherhood) and turned to face Davi with his club held high over his head. When he did, Davi put the tip of his blade against the man's throat and the would-be robber froze in place.

"Yo man. You got me. We good right? Look I ain't got nothing," Lavell said as he dropped the stick.

Davi smiled at him.

"No we are not good. You tried to rob me. I, who do not know you or ever did anything to harm you," Davi said. Lavell could hear the trace of some Middle Eastern dialect in the man's voice. It was subtle like the taste of cumin in his mother's jerk chicken.

"No doubt my bad homes. But look I'm unarmed and shit," Lavell said. His arms were indeed extended from his body in a Christ like manner.

"Yes you are," Davi said. He smiled again. He slowly pulled the tip of the blade from the man's throat. Lavell swallowed hard.

Davi lowered the blade. Flicking his wrist he flipped the sword in his hand so that the cutting edge was facing up toward the azure sky. As quick as a hiccup he sliced upward with the shamshir and amputated Lavell's right arm at the elbow. A slow stream of blood spurted from the wound. In one fluid motion Davi brought the blade up and over Lavell's head and separated his left arm from his body. He re-sheathed the sword in the scabbard under his coat and walked away before each limb hit the ground. Lavell opened his mouth to scream but no sounds emanated from his gaping maw. He fell to his knees as the blood continued to flow. Davi sidestepped another young black man who ran past him and grabbed Lavell around the waist and tried pull him up off the sidewalk.

Davi could tell the man he was wasting his time. In advance of his meeting with the thieves he coated his blade with liquefied ricin. The young man would be dead within 24 hours even if he did receive medical attention to suture his wounds.

"I am death," Davi whispered to himself as he got in his car. He could return home in peace. He found an emotion coursing through his veins that was foreign to him. Fear. The Covenant was real. So were the Judges. And if they were real so were the consequences. He did not fear death .He only feared disappointing his father. He would do everything in his power to ensure the House of Black Rivers continued to live in the lifestyle to which they had become accustomed. He owed that to his father. Adoptive or biological, it didn't matter to Davi. He would repay his debt to Abdul El-Aki with the lives of the Men of the First Order.

Catlow sat on the couch in Harmony's house pensive as a long tailed-cat in a room full of rocking chairs. In all his seventeen years on this planet he had always slept under the same roof as his family. He had never stayed out past his curfew. He had never spoken to his father so defiantly or stormed out of his house. This was a night of multiple firsts. It was frightening, and a little bit exciting. The most frightening part of the evening was happening right now as Harmony spoke with her mother. He couldn't imagine what would have been his parents' response if he brought Harmony, or any other person with ovaries to his house to "crash". By the lack of yelling and screaming coming from the kitchen it was beginning to seem like Harmony's mom had a more laissez-faire approach to child rearing. That did nothing to lessen Catlow's apprehension. So he sat seemingly quiet and self-assured ignoring the knot of fear tightening in his stomach like a noose.

Finally Harmony emerged from the kitchen.

"Okay .You can stay down here on the couch. You just can't come up to my room okay?" she said as sat beside him. Catlow exhaled and fell back against the couch.

"Thank you. I really didn't want to go home tonight," he said. He grasped her hand. Harmony gazed into his eyes.

"I didn't want you to go home," she whispered. Catlow felt his face get hot.

"Well can you stay down here til I fall asleep?" he asked. Harmony leaned forward and kissed his cheek.

"Of course. Do you wanna talk about your Dad?" she asked. Catlow shrugged his shoulders.

"He is just...I mean he is just crazy. My whole family is, except for my little sister." Harmony laughed.

"Everybody's family is crazy," she said. Catlow nodded and bit his lip. He almost told her everything right then and there, the whole insane story of his life and his father's beliefs. At the last second he changed his mind. He just couldn't bring himself to tell her about the Brotherhood. He was afraid that his family's insanity would frighten her and make her distance herself from him. Later he would wonder if the events that transpired could have been avoided if he had told her the entire story. Forewarned was forearmed after all. It was a question that could never be answered. Instead he said:

"My father is just crazy about fencing. He wants me to be in the Olympics one day. I mean he saved our lives once all because of his fencing skill." Catlow was shocked how easy he melded the truth and falsehoods.

"Wow really? I guess if he like saved y'all with his fencing stuff I can understand why he takes it so seriously," Harmony said as she nestled her head against his chest. Catlow stroked her hair.

"You have no idea," he said softly. Catlow thought of that night at the 7-11. The night he first saw his father for what he really was:. a deadly fanatic with the skills to back up his fanaticism. His mind went back to that night five years ago...

Twelve year old Catlow sat on the steps of their old house in Mathews County Virginia playing with some second-hand action figures that his mother had given him. He had affixed toothpicks to the action figures hands to represent swords. He manipulated the figures in mock duels recreating the moves he saw his father and his Uncle Saed perform in their fenced in backyard. Catlow would flip them and twist them to match the things he had seen his father and uncle do with their sabers or scimitars or katanas or rapiers. He loved to watch his dad and uncle practice. It was like living with Batman or Wolverine. It was so hard not to say something to the kids at school when they got into debates about whose dad would win in a fight. Catlow wanted to tell them his dad could beat ALL their dads. At the same time. By himself.

Uncle Saed had just left a few hours ago. His father was in the garage putting the finishing touches on a new sword he was making for somebody. Catlow was fuzzy on the details of who his dad made swords for but he knew it was important work. His dad took it very seriously. He could hear the whir and whine of the grinding wheel as his dad sharpened and shaped the sword. Catlow hoped his dad would be finished soon. It was Saturday and sometimes on Saturday after his father practiced and worked on his swords he would take Catlow to the Tastee-Freeze in town. The Tastee-Freeze was a close second behind Kings Dominion in the race for Catlow's favorite place on earth. The little ramshackle restaurant made the coldest, sweetest most delicious milk shakes in the entire world, or as much of the world as Catlow was privy to at that time. It was a treat that gave Catlow an almost unfathomable joy. The cool sugary goodness of a Tastee-Freeze shake could bring a smile to the most dour of faces. Catlow played on the step all the while harboring a quiet, desperate hope that his father would come around the corner and tell him to jump in their car and head into town.

"I guess somebody wants to go to the courthouse and get a milkshake," Catlow said. He had, as always, eased around the corner of the house noiselessly. Pretlow was shirtless, his bare chest shimmered with sweat. Catlow smiled.

"Not somebody me Daddy!" he responded. It was their traditional way of heading out on a milkshake mission.

"Well I guess somebody better go get in the car while I get a shirt," Pretlow said. His cheek barely twitched. Catlow laughed a bit too hard. His father didn't make jokes often so when he did Catlow savored those moments. His father could sometimes seem distant, almost robotic. However there were times like their milkshake runs where he let the mask of solemnity slip just the tiniest bit. Catlow jumped up and ran to the car. Pretlow watched him as he ran. His wavy black hair trailed behind like streamers on a parade float. His son moved with a grace that belied his years. Pretlow knew some of that agility was natural genetic inheritance.

The majority of his son's physical prowess came from hours and hours of training masquerading as games. The milkshakes were just one of many carrots that Pretlow dangled in front of Catlow to encourage him to train his body to the peak of it's potential. But as he ran to the car at that moment he looked like any other exuberant twelve year old boy. Pretlow silently wished that he was a normal little boy. He also knew that wish was as futile as wishing the sun didn't shine. They were of the Brotherhood. There was nothing normal about them or their destiny.

Pretlow went into the house walking as quietly as he could, which was very, very quiet. Darnicia was asleep…a summer cold had taken her off her feet. Saed had taken Calla to his house for the evening to give his sister a bit of a break while she fought virus. Pretlow went upstairs and grabbed a black t-shirt out of the dresser drawer. Humming, he went to the closet and pulled out his shoulder rig, his scimitar and a short, black, light waist jacket. Actually it was more like an oversized shirt than a jacket. He put on the rig and slid the scimitar into the scabbard. Next he put on the jacket. He paused to look at himself in the mirror. The scimitar was virtually unnoticeable.

Catlow was literally bouncing in his seat when Pretlow reached the car. He climbed into the old green Ford LTD and turned the key. The beast came to life with a roar. Catlow tapped his hands on the dashboard and howled.

"The Green Pepper rides again!" Pretlow almost smiled. They drove in silence. The silence was not uncomfortable however. It was a silence born of a deep and abiding understanding between the two individuals in the car. They understood that sometimes you don't have to ruin things with words. Father and son rode along the rapidly darkening roads of Mathews County content with each other's company.

Finally they reached the intersection of route 198 and route 14, pulled into the Tastee-Freeze and Catlow hopped out before the car had stopped completely. Pretlow watched him run up to the small rusty window with the ancient sliding screen. As he ran he did a full cart wheel landed on his feet and kept running until he was standing in front of the window. Pretlow could see the foundations of a master swordsman in his son. He was a lithe coil of potential energy. He was shaping up to be as tall if not taller than Pretlow. He had the dexterity of a cat. He was truly ambidextrous, as strong in his left hand as his right. Soon Pretlow would do away with the pretense of playing and begin his training in earnest. No more jungle gym races in the rain or walking around the house on their hands. He would start with wooden replicas then with swords with blunt dull edges .Finally he would take up a real blade.

Catlow ordered their shakes and Pretlow paid for them. They sat on a metal bench that was still warm from the heat of the sun earlier in the day. Father and son sipped the cool chocolate goodness that is a Tastee-Freeze shake in comfortable silence. Finally Catlow spoke.

"Dad, when do I get to use a sword?" Pretlow was taken aback for a moment. He was shocked that his son's thoughts were so close to his own. Pretlow sipped the last of his milkshake and wiped his mouth.

"Next year. We will start with the wooden replicas then move on to the short bladed Gladius sword then on to the rapier because it is fairly light. Why did you ask me this Catlow?" he asked.

"Cuz I wanna do the cool stuff you an Uncle Saed do. I wanna slice grapes in half in mid-air and do back-flips with two swords in each hand and..." Pretlow held up his hand and his son closed his mouth with a soft plop.

"Catlow, what we do is not for fun and games or some tricks in a sideshow. You are too young to fully understand but what we are doing is training. Training for something very important. It is not something to show off to your friends at school," Pretlow said quietly.

"Aw Dad I know that," Catlow said. Actually he had no idea what his father was talking about but he tried to pretend he fully understood. He had heard his father talk to Uncle Saed about the Book of Seven Swords and something that was coming soon. All he really knew was that Dad was cooler than Batman or Spider-man or Superman because he was REAL. He had watched as Uncle Saed fired golf balls at his Dad from a modified pitching machine and his Dad had sliced the ball in half. Every time. Over a hundred times. He had counted from his seat on the back-step. He had watched with wide eyes as his father and uncle pretended to fight with swords in each hand. He had been awe-struck the first time he had seen his father run up the wall of their house and do a back-flip off the building and land behind his uncle with a sword at his throat. His Dad didn't understand. What they did was cool!

"Come on let's get home. I've got to stop at the convenience store and get your mother some cold medicine. That woman is the love of my life but she is the biggest baby when she gets sick. Don't tell her I said that Catlow," his father said with a tremor of a smile playing across his lips. Catlow smiled a little too. It was another episode of jocularity from the usually taciturn Pretlow Creedence. Catlow could hardly believe it. His father was not a man prone to hilarity. They climbed back into the car and started on their way home. The drove along the blacktop roads as a rapidly setting sun threw strange shadows in their path. They drove until the darkening sky was illuminated by the yellow glare of a 7-11 sign. The store sat at the border between Gloucester and Mathews counties and was a way station for most people in both counties. It was the last place to get gas or cigarettes or cold medicine for miles. Usually a rag-tag crowd of regulars were milling around in the parking lot or leaning lazily against the counters. Not tonight. Tonight the parking lot was almost empty. Catlow saw a small blue two-door Geo Metro parked around the side of the building and a dilapidated pick-up truck parked in the front. Pretlow parked the car and opened his door.

"Can I come with you Dad?" Catlow asked. Pretlow hesitated for a moment.

"Why not? Come, hurry so we can get back to your mother." Catlow bounded out of the car and ran to the door. Once inside he made a beeline for the candy aisle. He grabbed two candy bars and a lollipop. Pretlow went to the medicine aisle intent on getting his wife something to soothe her aching chest and her quiet her incessant cough. As was his nature he noticed the pale, sallow-faced clerk behind the counter. A woman who looked as if life had kicked her ass so much she had learned to enjoy the beating. In contradiction to his nature, however, he did not notice the two men who came into the store after he and Catlow had entered.

The two men were nondescript white men. They both had on brown hoodies and baseball caps. They milled around the store for a few seconds. Then the heavier of the two nodded as his partner. They both pulled their shirts up in unison and pulled out semi-automatic pistols.

"Give me the fucking money, bitch!" the heavier one screamed at the clerk. For a moment she didn't react so lost in her reverie of sadness that she barely heard the request. The man moved forward and smacked her in the forehead with the butt of his gun.

"Money. Now!" he yelled. His partner pointed his gun at Pretlow. Catlow was behind the second man, frozen in place. His candy had fallen to the floor, forgotten now as fear gripped his very soul. Pretlow raised his hands and gazed at the second man.

"Sir we do not want any trouble but my little boy is behind you and I am sure he is very scared. Could you allow him to come to me?" Pretlow said evenly. The second robber whirled on his heels and grabbed Catlow by the arm.

"Get your fucking ass over there!" he yelled as he pushed Catlow toward his father. Catlow grabbed his father and held him as tight as he could. It was then he felt the weight of his father's scimitar against his right arm. The second man bounced from side to side on the balls of his feet. He was biting his lip and his eyes darted side to side like a caged weasel. His skin was red and scaly and had a greasy film over it that gave him a slightly tan appearance. Catlow heard the clerk crying as the first man hit her again. And again. And again.

"I-i-i- can't open the safe and I only got …twenty in the drawer I swear!" she moaned between sobs.

"You got five seconds to give me the fucking money. I am not motherfucking playing with you, bitch!" the first man screamed. The man hit her again. Catlow could hear the sound of the gun meeting the woman's flesh. It was like someone was chopping up a ham with a hammer. Her cries became more frantic. Catlow could feel his father's abdomen tighten. Catlow loosened his grip on his father. He wanted to scream at the men with the guns that they were in trouble now! His father was a sword swinging, one hundred one-hand push-ups, one hundred percent bad-ass! Pretlow Creedence was the last man that you wanted to mess with and they were in for a quick ride to a city called Ass Whupping where Pretlow was the mayor. He waited and his breath started coming quicker and quicker. He waited for his father to pull his scimitar, kick the robbers' collective asses and save the clerk.

He waited for his father to make these bad guys sorry they were ever born.

It didn't happen.

Pretlow just held his son and looked at the second robber with a cool and impassive visage. The second robber stared back at Pretlow and began scratching his chin.

"What the fuck you looking at? You know what hoss, give me your fucking wallet," the man said with a heavy southern accent. Pretlow didn't move at first. The man stepped forward and struck Pretlow in the forehead with the butt of his gun. Pretlow didn't cry out or stumble. The man struck him again and Pretlow grunted deep in his chest.

"Give me your fucking wallet, nigger!" the second man howled.

"Stop it!" Catlow screamed. The second robber looked at him as if noticing him for the first time. He pointed his gun at Catlow's face. He then raised the gun to strike Catlow.

"Do...not...strike...my...son," Pretlow said. Blood was dripping down his cheek from the wound on his forehead. He said his statement through clenched teeth. The second robber looked at Pretlow and without saying a word, pointed the gun at him and turned sideways just like he had seen in the gangster movies he loved so much. Catlow started to cry.

Pretlow moved his right hand to the left side of his body under his jacket. He moved so fast and so smoothly the second robber did not register that movement with his periphery vision. In one fluid motion he grabbed the handle of his scimitar, pulled it out of its cracked leather scabbard and swept it up and to the right like a tennis player hitting a backhand shot. The blade sliced through the first four inches of the gun like it was made of butter. The bright Damascus steel had been tempered by the sword-smith Garn Whiteborne with an ancient technique known only to the men of the Brotherhood. He had taught Pretlow this technique when he was just a young boy. Common metals of modern design were no match for the blades of the Brotherhood. The barrel hit the floor with a loud clatter. Pretlow let the scimitar go and it spun in midair on an invisible axis for one complete turn. He grabbed the silver and black handle and brought the blade down over the second robber's wrist. The man's hand fell to the floor with soft slap.

The second robber opened his mouth and peered at his hand. The appendage had been amputated so quickly that for a moment he still held his arm extended as if he was still holding the gun. One heartbeat then another, then blood began to spew from his stump. Catlow watched the blood flow like a geyser.

It was so different from the blood he had seen in the movies. It was not thick and viscous. It was watery and thin and it splashed across the white tiles like rain.

Before the second robber could say or do anything else Pretlow brought the scimitar back again in a backhand motion and slid it through the man's neck. The blade was so sharp and the blow so strong the man's head did not immediately tumble off his shoulders. The second robber's body crumpled to the floor in a kneeling position. Then his torso fell forward. His head tumbled backwards. Catlow covered his mouth with the inside of his elbow and started mewling. The first robber stopped beating the cashier just long enough to shoot her in the leg. The sound was like the thunder of Thor inside the store. Catlow's ears popped. The first robber looked up and saw Pretlow advancing upon him.

"What the fuck?" he yelled, then began firing.

Pretlow swept the scimitar in front of him. He turned the blade sideways so the broader part of the blade was in front of him. As the robber fired Pretlow swatted the bullets aside. His arm moved in a blur of motion and concentration. Catlow could see sparks fly up when the bullets hit the blade. Yellow sparks that glowed for a moment as the blade made contact .The first robber was grunting and groaning in an indecipherable language. Perhaps it was the language of fear. His last bullet was not deflected Pretlow flipped the sword and split the bullet down the middle. The two halves pierced two bottles of soda on a shelf behind Pretlow. The sugary contents escaped their containers with a low hiss.

Pretlow sliced through the first robber's wrist as easily as he had his partner's. The first robber let out a bloodcurdling moan. Pretlow's blade silenced him by cutting through his neck and spine, decapitating him. He flew past the falling corpse and stepped over the dismembered head as he headed for the door marked "employees only". He ignored the river of crimson flowing from the vivisected neck of the first robber. Once inside he found the DVD drive for the recording system that was connected to the cameras had had noticed when he entered the store. He slammed the scimitar into the drive and cut it in half. He grabbed the bisected DVD and put the pieces in his pocket. He came out of the room and grabbed a handful of napkins from the hotdog counter and wiped the blood off his blade. He returned it to the scabbard under his jacket and walked toward Catlow. He grabbed his son by the arm and pulled him out of the store. Pretlow opened the driver side door of the LTD and tossed Catlow inside.

Catlow scrambled into the passenger seat. Pretlow jumped in the driver's seat and started the car. The old rolling tank came to life with a roar. Catlow heard the tires squeal as they peeled out of the parking lot.

Silence. Now an oppressive, uneasy cloud filled the car. Catlow looked out the window Pretlow stared straight ahead. The moon chased their car as they traveled home. Pretlow pulled into their driveway and shut off the motor.

"My son, we will be leaving this place soon. We ...we can't stay here now," he said in a soft voice. Catlow didn't look at him; however he spoke in a quavering whisper.

"Why didn't you stop and help that woman? Why did you let them beat her up like that? I've seen what you and Uncle Saed can do! You're like Batman or Hawkeye! She was crying, Dad" Pretlow rubbed his eyes with his gnarled fist.

"Catlow I know this will be hard for you to understand but what Uncle Saed and I do is not a game. It is deadly serious. We are heirs to a duty that you cannot yet fathom. There are questions that police officers will want to ask me that I cannot answer. I did not want to intervene because I have a responsibility that is more significant than one cashier in a gas station or even my own life. Soon I may be called into service to engage in a battle that will literally decide the fate of the entire world.

I am a soldier in a war that has raged since shortly after the time of Jesus. Your Uncle Saed and I are not heroes. We are members of the Brotherhood. The skills that we have acquired are not just for us, they belong to the whole world even if they don't know it. If I were imprisoned for my actions in that store tonight and we receive the

Invitation and could not attend to the Covenant then I will have dishonored my father and his father and all the houses of the Men of the First Order. There are things that I have not told you yet. Things that you are not ready to comprehend. But believe me when I tell you I am no coward. We are yoked to the fate of all mankind. It is not something that we can just abandon or disregard," Pretlow said, his voice never rising.

"Then why did you kill them?" Catlow asked. His head was leaning against the cool car window. Pretlow turned and grabbed his son by the arm and pulled him close until their noses almost touched. His eyes scanned the boy's face.

"Because they were going to hurt my son. I tried to do what fathers are supposed to do without pulling my blade. I took the brunt of their violence so that they would not touch you. The world is a cold and cruel place and you will have to fight your own battles soon enough. But I will do my best to save you from the inequities of the world for as long as I can. We are fated to a higher purpose, Catlow. There may come a day sooner than I would like when we will be asked to give our very lives for billions of people who do not know us or care about us. They do not love us the way I love you my son," Pretlow said, his voice finally cracking. Catlow looked away with tears in his eyes.

"I am tired .I want to go to bed," he said. Pretlow released his grip and boy opened the car door and walked to the house. Pretlow sat in the car for a few moments more. He would call Saed in the morning to help them pack. The robbery would make the local paper and the details would surly catch the attention of the Men of the First Chaos. The rules of the Covenant did not dictate that the Men of the First Order and the Men of the First Chaos had to wait until the Duel to engage each other. The Men of the First Chaos were notorious for exploiting this loophole. He watched his son walk into the house. His shoulders were slumped and he seemed to have lost some of the lightness in his steps.

Not for the first time did Pretlow wonder what good it was to save all of the humanity and lose your own...

"BLOOD!" Catlow sat up screaming. He had drifted off to sleep and found himself transported back to that convenience store so many years ago. Harmony sat straight up and touched his face.

"Baby baby...shh...it's okay," she said in his ear. The house was silent. Catlow felt it was very late. He didn't have a watch. He looked at the clock above the door to the kitchen. It was two in in the morning.. Harmony wrapped her arms around his chest.

"Shh baby, it's okay you are safe. You're with me boo," she said. Catlow hugged her tight then pressed his lips against hers. She murmured something as he kissed her.

"What? I'm sorry. I ...don t know why I did that..." Catlow stammered. Harmony put her finger to his lips.

"I was saying do you have a condom?" she said. She smiled at him and suddenly the horrible dream which was a memory faded away.

"I, uh I don't have one," he said. "But I can go get one or we, uh I don't know what we can do." Catlow felt his face get very hot. Harmony laughed.

"I have one, it's just old but it should be okay. Let's go upstairs," she whispered.

"But I'm not allowed in your room!" Catlow said. Harmony laughed.

"Do you always follow the rules Cat?" She stood up and walked to the staircase. She stopped at the bottom step and pulled her shirt up over her head. Her full brown breasts were held at bay by a tight white lace bra. The tops of her breasts heaved with every deep breath she took. Catlow felt a fire ignite in his belly and spread to his extremities. His loins tingled then he felt himself harden like a diamond. He flew off the couch and placed his hands under Harmony's armpits. He picked her up off her feet and carried her up the stairs two at a time. A hollow feeling, like the first drop on a roller-coaster, filled Harmony's chest. They reached the landing and he put her down. She took his hand and led him to her room. The first door on the right. Once inside she fell backwards onto her small twin bed. She held out her arms and Catlow climbed on top of her and felt those arms embrace him and for the first time in his entire life he wasn't thinking about his father or the Brotherhood or swords or blood or death. All he could think about was touching Harmony and having her touch him in return. Her lips were heaven, her hands were salvation and her body was the temple at which he would lay his troubles down.

# CHAPTER FOUR

Pretlow awoke in his small motel room and sat straight up in the bed. He had been dreaming of his father. He and his father and his mother were walking in a park. Pretlow didn't know where the park was but it was a gorgeous verdant field alive with flora and fauna of all types. He was a little boy in the dream and he was walking hand in hand with his parents. His father had his pale hand entwined in Pretlow's tan one. His mother Eugenia had her dark ebony hand wrapped around his wrist. They were walking and laughing but in the dream young Pretlow knew this was the day before his father died in a car accident. His mother was smiling at his father. His father was telling her a joke and Pretlow the child in the dream was smiling, but Pretlow the adult wanted to scream at them. He wanted to tell them not to let his father drive to the store the next night. He wanted his mother to take his father's keys because he had had too much to drink. He wanted his father to fall asleep on the couch like he usually did on Sunday afternoons. He implored Pretlow the child to say something. It was then he saw through his child eyes his father looking down at him. His father had blood running down his face .His head was spit open from the right eye to the crown of his head. His dirty blond hair was soaked in crimson and his brain was visible through the crack in his skull. It was pink like the inside of a conch. His father spoke to him.

"Death has no honor, Pretlow. Only the manner in which you meet your death can be honorable. I was drunk and I pissed on myself when I hit that tree. Die more honorably than me my son. Die with a blade in your hand."

It was then Pretlow felt himself sit straight up in the bed. The sun was shyly peeking through the cheap curtains. Pretlow swung his feet around and they hit the cool thin carpet with a thud. He stood and stretched his arms wide. He fell forward and caught himself on his palms before he hit the floor with his face. He began to do push-ups. Fast rapid movements. Up and down. At the apex of the exercise he clapped his hands. Then he put his right arm behind his back and used only his left to push himself up off the floor. He switched arms. One hundred push-ups with the right, one hundred with the left. Next he got into a kneeling position and popped up onto his feet. He repeated this move one-hundred times. By the time he started his handstand push-ups he was sweating, his arms burning, with an old familiar sting. Finally he stood and wiped his face with his hands. He walked over to the other side of the room where he had placed his bags and pulled out the shoulder rig that held his sword. His true sword made with the techniques of the Brotherhood and forged by his own hand. He pulled the sword free and held it out in front of him. The edge was as sharp as the edge of a diamond and just as hard. The blade shone, kept shining from obsessive cleaning and sharpening. Pretlow had designed it to be used as a cutting and stabbing sword. It could work as a cutlass or a rapier. In addition to the detachable hand basket the guard cross could be folded into the handle so that it could be used with a katana style of fencing. The Book of Seven Swords warned against falling into the pit of pride in one's sword. You could appreciate the artistry of a weapon but one did not want to hold that weapon in too high of esteem. There was a quote in the Book attributed to one of the old masters Bartholomew Winston in 1794: "A work of art can enliven your soul but it can't save your life."

Pretlow knew what that quote meant. But he couldn't help being a little proud of his work. He even gave the sword a name. It was a name he never spoke aloud but whenever he picked up the sword he thought "Aequitas," the Latin word for justice. Aequitas was not his favorite sword. His training and his nature kept him from having a favorite. A member of the Brotherhood was well served to be well versed in the usage of any bladed weapon. Aequitas was the sword that felt the most natural in his hand though. He put Aequitas on the bed and pulled out his sharpening stone and his oil and his soft cloth rag. He always felt a sense of calm fall over him when he sharpened his swords. A sense of ...order in the repetition that soothed his spirit. It would help to assuage his feelings of guilt concerning Catlow.

He had not misspoken when he had described the girl as a distraction .But he could have used kinder language. In the aftermath of the argument he could see that now even if he couldn't verbalize it. Pretlow sat in the edge of the bed and slid the stone along Aequitas's edge in long even strokes. The sound of the stone against the steel was a gritty background chorus to the thoughts in his head. If Catlow didn't return he knew the fault was his and his alone. Had he been too hard on the boy? In comparison to their responsibility, no. But could he have been a little more flexible, and perhaps a little more lenient. Perhaps. As he slid the stone back and forth he realized he wanted Catlow to come home so he could try and repair their rift not just so that he would be in place if the Invitation arrived. Maybe that was some sort of progress in and of itself. Because if he was honest there was some truth to what Catlow had said. His loyalty to the Brotherhood did, at times, supersede his loyalty to his family. His love his family could not be bested by anyone or anything but he had made decisions that were for the good of the Brotherhood at the expense of his family.

A pang of guilt fluttered through his chest. He pushed it away. Gently. He whispered the Oath as he wiped the blade down with his cloth. It was the Oath that every member of the Brotherhood spoke before they took up the sword. Men of the First Order and the Men of the First Chaos. No matter what their house or their affiliation.

"WE ARE THE MEN OF THE BROTHERHOOD

WE PLEDGE OUR LIVES TO THE DUEL OF GENERATIONS.

WE PLEDGE OUR LIVES TO THE FULFILLMENT OF THE COVENANT UNTIL THE END OF ALL TIME.

WE PLEDGE TO TAKE UP THE SWORD, THE FIRST WEAPON OF ORDER AND THE FIRST INSTRUMENT OF CHAOS.

NOT FOR LOVE

NOT FOR HATE.

NOT FOR VENGEANCE.

NOT FOR PLEASURE.

NOT FOR PAIN.

BUT FOR THE LIVES OF ALL THE PEOPLE OF THIS WORLD..

CRY DISCORDIA, CRY DECRETUM!

LET OUR BLADES STRIKE TRUE!"

Pretlow put the sword down and walked toward the shower. He put his hands against the stained tiles and let the hot water flow over his aching muscles. It was all worth it. All the sacrifice all the pain all the tears. If it changed the course of the next one hundred years it was all worth it.

"It's worth it," he mumbled as the water ran.

Catlow felt the sun tickle his face as his eyes fluttered. He opened them fully and saw a poster of "The Rock" staring at him from the ceiling. Somehow it was disconcerting that he lost his virginity under the watchful eye of Dwayne Johnson but he felt too good to let that get to him. Harmony was spread across his chest like a sleepy cat. Catlow stroked her hair. Her pigtails had come undone during the night and all the shenanigans therein. She yawned and then looked up at him with a smile rushing across her face.

"Hi.' she said.

"Hi," Catlow whispered. Harmony propped herself up on one elbow. She pushed her head forward and kissed him. Catlow kissed her back then cocked his head to the right.

"You sure your mother isn't going to come in here shooting at me," he whispered. Harmony's smile faded then quickly re-emerged.

"I told you she gets good and fucked up. She will sleep in until noon. So baby can I ask you something?"

"You can ask me anything," Catlow said. Harmony traced her finger along his jaw line.

"This was your first time wasn't it?" she asked. Catlow looked away, toward the rising sun coming through the window.

"Yeah. Why? Did I do something wrong?" he asked. There was no inflection in his voice but his guts were tied in Gordian knots.

"Oh no baby! Not at all. I could just tell you was nervous. No baby it was incredible. Was it everything you dreamed it would be?"

"No," Catlow said. Harmony frowned .Before she could ask him what she had done wrong he cupped her face and kissed her.

"My dreams were never this good," he said. Harmony kissed him again. He grabbed a fistful of her hair and pressed his lips to hers. She forced herself to pull away from Catlow.

"No, no, no. We ain't starting that right now .We don't have any more condoms and I am not trying to have any babies right now. I want to try out for the Shenandoah Conservatory this spring and I ain't trying to play Schubert with a basketball under my shirt," she said, laughing. Catlow kissed her again.

"Okay, okay I understand that. It just felt so...good, much better than sword practice." Catlow said

Harmony giggled. "Oh I think you were doing pretty well with your sword. You did make me feel really good though baby..." she said. She ran her finger along his bare chest. Actually no one had ever made her feel so good. She was not a virgin but she was far from experienced. Counting Catlow she had been intimate with three guys. Neither of the other guys had made her feel the way he did last night. He may have been a virgin but he was a natural. He had given her kisses down below and she had felt her body explode and she knew that had been her first orgasm .Or to be precise the first orgasm someone had given her. However she kept this detail to herself. There was a part of her that didn't want to give Catlow that bit of information. She had watched with ever growing disgust and despair as her mother fell heels over head in love with this man and that man because he was in her words "a beast in the bed a real pussy pounder." Her mother only talked this way when she was drunk, which was happening more and more frequently. She loved Catlow she knew that. But she meant what she had said. She had plans. Plans that would take her out of the River

City. Plans that would take her to places she only glimpsed in her dreams. She would love for Catlow to come with her but if he couldn't she would go alone. So she kept her satisfaction to herself. Catlow was sweet and kind but even the nicest guys could ego trip if you told them they made your legs shake and your body explode when they touched you. If you gave them too much of yourself there was nothing left for you.

"Well if we are not going to play anymore I should get up and head to work. I am teaching an advanced class today," Catlow said. Truthfully he wanted to stay in Harmony's bed all day. He was enraptured with every aspect of this girl; her skin, so soft and smooth and without blemish. Her lips, full and sensual that tasted like cherries. Even her scent enthralled him. It was sharp and acrid yet with an underlying floral aroma...the musk from last night's exertions mixing with her body wash. It entranced him. But his uncle had gotten him the job and he would not disappoint Uncle Saed.

He was the only one in his family that seemed to understand him even remotely.

"Hey you wanna go with me? The class is only an hour then we can go to the mall. We can even leave early and I can show you around the Academy," Catlow said. He wanted to show her where he worked He wanted to share more and more of his life with her just like she had shared her body with him. And truth be told he wanted her to see a glimpse of his skill with the blade. Despite his ambivalence toward his father's beliefs there was no denying his expertise with a sword. And through his father's constant draconian training methods Catlow had attained a level of swordsmanship that few could equal. Catlow realized that in some strange way deep down inside he was just a bit proud of his ability no matter how it was acquired. That did not lessen his resentment toward his father for the dysfunctional life they had lived. He was still angry that they had sacrificed so much to his father's fanaticism. But some of the things he could do with a blade were pretty dam cool. In his mind he could see himself showing Harmony the true extent of his abilities one day. That would of course necessitate a conversation about how attained said skills .He hoped by that time she would love him enough not to run screaming into the night. Maybe she would understand his father's delusion. It was a disease like her mother's drinking. Perhaps that's why they had met. They were kindred spirits .Warped souls created from broken molds.

"Yeah I'd like to see where you work since you always stalking me at my job," she said, laughing. Catlow reached down and pulled her onto his body. He made her feel as light as a feather. She straddled him and looked down at his face. Her hair fell in loose curls around her shoulders. He was more than just cute. There was something about him that made you feel safe. Harmony was not accustomed to that feeling. She liked it.

"I am not stalking you. Just making sure no one is bothering you. I'd hate to have to throw somebody over the bagel counter but I would if I had to," he said grinning.

"You would, wouldn't you? You would do that for me," Harmony said. She didn't smile as the gravity of what she was saying and feeling settled upon her. He loved her. He really loved her. Catlow raised himself up onto his elbows. Their faces were only inches apart.

"I will never let anyone hurt you. I promise," he said. Harmony kissed him lightly.

"I know," she said softly.

Carcine stumbled up the steps of the Apothas chateau. The air was frigid. A steady harsh wind was blowing. It felt like the cold air was slapping him in the face. His gorge threatened to rise out of his gullet and cause him to spew the contents of that evening's gastronomic adventures all over the brick steps. He was drunk and a little high. He vaguely remembered taking two hits of ecstasy last night in the club. His body had become one huge erogenous zone. Everything he touched or that touched him aroused him sending his sex drive into the stratosphere. At one point he had looked around for Candy before he realized he had left her at the chateau. Then it was more drinks. Bitter Germanic beer and smooth Bavarian liquor mixed with the X and the two lines of coke he had done earlier that evening to wrap him in a warm cocoon of disassociation.

Now that cocoon was unraveling. He was home. It was incredibly late and his father would still be awake. He knew this from past experiences and transgressions. His father would tell him to go down into the sub-basement through the door in the wine cellar. Down to the House of Blood and Steel. The name of their noble fraternity within the Brotherhood was also the name of their training facility. Carcine would go down into that nether world and would emerge covered in sweat and vomit and quite possibly drops of blood.

He despised the training but he couldn't argue with the results. He was not as others were. He was not one of the sheep that wandered the earth in search of a shepherd. He was an Apothas, a descendant of Alexander the Great, himself a god among men. He was Superman. Not the comic book character of dubious origin and monumental naiveté. He was the Nietzsche ideal come to life. He was what existed on the other end of the rope that good ol' Fredrich spoke of so lovingly. On one side of the abyss stood the animalistic, the weak, the moronic, and the sickly. On the other side were the Men of the First Chaos: the strong, the iron-willed, and the brilliant. The Supermen. His party pals were on the first side of that abyss. Slaves to their passions, bondsman to their desires. Not Carcine. He mastered his vices and enjoyed them accordingly. It was why he could enter that dark place at the bottom of the stairs and emerge stronger than before. He knew his father sometimes looked at him disparagingly but even he did not know what he was creating in that harsh and unforgiving theater of pain. Carcone Apothas was fashioning his replacement. A younger, stronger version of himself to one day defeat the Men of the First Order and fulfill the Covenant. His time was coming. He would lead the House into its greatest period of prosperity in its long and storied history. His mother would tell him every time they talked that it was his destiny to defeat the Men of the First Order and replace his father as Prefect. So he would endure his father's cruel tutelage. For now.

Carcine opened one of the two huge doors to the Chateau de Apothas. All his guests were gone. The building was as quiet as a tomb. His father was sitting on the couch in front of the glass coffee table. There was a black box sitting on the table. Carcone was sipping a drink with his legs crossed at the ankles. He raised his head and stared at Carcine for a moment.

"Come. Sit. We need to talk," he said. Carcine plopped down on the love seat across from Carcone. Carcone took another sip of his drink before he spoke.

"Do you know why they call us the Men of the First Chaos? It is because we represent freedom. We were the first rebels. We tossed aside the empty platitudes of gods and God and took our freedom from their ethereal hands. Because really what is chaos but freedom without the fine clothes? Order is just another word for control. It is control of what you do or don't do, over how you make a way for you and yours. Control of what you can have, and what you can possess. We cannot be controlled. We cannot be cajoled or bound to unrealistic standards of behavior. They fear freedom, Carcine They abhor it. If I want a piece of bread I take it. If you think you are strong enough to stop me you can try. Whoever survives that encounter gets to make the rules from there on out. That is what we are Carcine. Chaos is freedom's less sophisticated twin. It is rough and uncouth, but it is vital to our existence. They would take away all that we have built and deny us our right to gather as much as we want."

"As much of what?" Carcine interjected. His father glared at him.

"Everything! Money, land, women. POWER. Order is a fantasy that men use to pacify us .To sedate our true nature. Chaos allows us to embrace that nature. We are the strong and we have and always will survive. I know I have pushed you Carcine. Harder than I push Vivian's sons. I do this because I know you can take it. You are made of sterner stuff than the smut peddlers. I pushed and prodded and yes sometimes beat you. But now it all will make sense. Now you will see why we have trained and will continue to hone our skills," Carcone finished his drink with a flourish.

"That my son, sitting in front of you, is The Invitation. THE. Invitation," Carcone stressed. Carcine leaned forward and inspected the box. It was beautiful. He could see his reflection in the smooth surface.

"What do we ....I mean what does it say?" Carcine asked.

"I don't know .I was waiting for you to come home before I opened it. This is something we should do together. All the Houses have received their Invitations. Each generation receives a different Invitation with different instructions so I have no idea what it will say. But we will find out in a few moments," Carcone said.

"Then it begins. "Carcine said.

"It already has," Carcone said.

Pretlow walked across the fresh cut green grass in the Norris-town square with the cutlass in a long wooden box that he had fashioned especially to hold the sword. His long tan jacket fluttered around him as he walked into the breeze heading for the information desk of the Time after Time Renaissance Fair. Hollis Prudence would be there directing traffic, coordinating demonstrations, arranging entertainment, soothing egos and putting out fires. The Renaissance recreation community attracted open-minded intelligent people who were dedicated to preserving a way of life and a culture that much of the world had forgotten. Their skills were very specialized and unique and because of that there were a finite number of competent performers and artists. Theirs was a close-knit group with a multitude of interpersonal friendships, relationships, rivalries and grudges that often overlapped. Hollis had a certain talent for keeping all those delicate balls in the air and ensuring that the show did indeed go on with a minimal amount of breakdowns and temper tantrums.

The day was glorious. The sun rained down a gentle blanket of daylight that bathed every tent and booth in a golden hue. The temperature had not yet reached a hellish degree. Later in the day it would be nearly unbearable but right now it was comfortable. The gentle morning breeze helped. People filled the square with the sounds of raucous laughter and the rumble of disembodied chatter.

Interspersed among the townspeople were performers and artists taking breaks and gossiping. Sipping from water bottles and networking. They wore chain mail and heavy woolen shirts or dresses in spite of the coming July heat It took a combination of a certain type of dedication and madness to be a Renaissance fair performer. Performers often made their own period clothing from flax and wool spun on homemade spinning wheels. Chain mail painstakingly created ringlet by ringlet in garages and sheds. Helmets created from salvaged metal and of course swords of all description, made with varying degrees of craftsmanship.

Pretlow noticed them all. Swords that were constructed with an incredible attention to detail and a fine artistic flair he admired from afar. Other swords that appeared to have been created by a blind person who suffered from epilepsy garnered his derision. Saed had once called him a sword snob. He disagreed with that description. He just knew good work when he saw it. There was some good work at this Ren-Fair, but nothing as good as the swords he owned.

The Information Tent was positioned at the base of the courthouse steps. Pretlow could see Hollis flitting back and forth in the tent his hands flying in every direction all the while maintaining a huge toothy grin. Hollis was thin bean pole of a man with a huge shock of white hair that fell to his shoulder blades. His skin was a ruddy road map of creases and wrinkles obtained from long days in the sun at countless fairs just like this one. He had started first as a performer and reenacter, but now was an organizer and promoter. Despite his leathery skin he looked considerably younger than his 74 years. Pretlow had met him fifteen years ago in Gloucester Virginia at a small fair in that sleepy little hamlet. Hollis had seen his work at a previous fair and had contacted him about giving a metal working demonstration at the Gloucester fair. Once they had met and discussed the compensation and the itinerary they found that they shared a love for the blade. They had discussed metallurgy and blacksmithing. They had talked for hours about the history of the sword. From the first simple spears and pikes to the finest epee swords of the early 17th century. Hours later they finally parted with promises to keep in touch. At the next fair Pretlow was asked to attend, Hollis invited him to dinner with his wife and other performers after that day's events had ended. The adventures that ensued helped cement their friendship. It was the first time in his life that Pretlow had felt like an ordinary man. The nights spent talking with Hollis and his band of merry anachronists eased the weight of his destiny if only for a few hours. That first night of camaraderie had ended with Pretlow carrying a drunken Hollis up two flights of stairs to a loft he and his wife were squatting in that week thanks to the hospitality of a local Renaissance fair enthusiast. He had laid the older man across the bed while his wife began to take off his shoes. Pretlow had turned to go when Hollis had sat up and pointed at him.

"You're a king my good fellow. A king in a world full of pretenders to the throne." he had slurred. Then he turned his head and unceremoniously vomited in the floor. Pretlow had smiled. It was one of the few times since his father had died that he could remember smiling. Even the birth of his children could not elicit a smile from his face. Destiny and duty kept him from being able to completely let go and fully embrace their lives. He lived under a very real Sword of Damascus. His oath to the Brotherhood meant that his children could very well end up fatherless. Something in that realization prevented him from being able to truly enjoy their childhoods. Or his marriage. Or his life. There was a tragedy in that kind of devotion but he would never be able to articulate it to anyone.

Hollis saw Pretlow and ceased his flitting and hand waving and strode over to his old friend.

"Pretlow, you made it!! How was traffic? I've got some medieval swordsman apparently stuck on the turnpike," Hollis said. His voice sounded raspier than Pretlow remembered.

"I drove up last night. So the only people on the road were me and some truckers. I didn't ask them if they were medieval weapon experts though," Pretlow said. Hollis rolled his eyes.

"Humor is not your strong suit my good-fellow. Well let's see the latest Creedence creation!" Hollis said as he clapped his hands together. He was wearing a distinctly non-medieval t-shirt and a pair of plaid blue and green shorts. Pretlow sat the box on the plastic fold-out table that acted as a makeshift desk. He flipped the brass latch and opened it without fanfare. Hollis stood next to him and whistled when the lid was raised.

"It is exquisite my friend. Beautiful work as always. Are those obsidian chips in the handle?" he asked.

"Yes. I shape them with a diamond edge grinding wheel and polish them with wet/dry sand paper then a fine cloth," Pretlow said. He did not tell Hollis he also shaped them with steel from a Brotherhood sword. He hoped his voice did not carry a trace of arrogance. Hollis clapped him on his broad back and laughed.

"Your like is becoming more and more rare my good fellow. No one wants to learn the true skills. If we have a zombie apocalypse we will be so screwed. We have a generation of technophiles who couldn't sharpen a knife if their lives depended on it. And the way the world is going it very well may," Hollis said. He laughed again but this time the laugh turned into a deep hacking cough. The older man double over and coughed up an ugly wad of greenish phlegm. Pretlow grabbed Hollis by the arm.

"Are you alright? he asked. Hollis waved his hand with a dismissive aplomb.

"Just dying my friend," Hollis said after his coughing had ceased. Pretlow pulled his friend's arm roughly until Hollis was facing him.

"What?"

"Yes my friend. The big C is waging war on my liver. But buck up dear fellow. In truth are we not all dying? Every day we die by inches. Honestly the way the world is going I hope I won't be around to see humans evolve over-sized thumbs for the express purpose of faster texting." Hollis said smiling.

Pretlow felt like his head was spinning. Hollis dying? It seemed incomprehensible. Hollis always seemed like an ageless imp full of energy and vigor. He couldn't believe what he was hearing.

"Have you gone to the doctors? What do they say?" Pretlow asked.

"They give me a year...two at the most. Don't let it trouble you my good fellow. I plan on fighting this as much as I can and when I can't fight anymore I plan on drinking a few bottles of absinthe and then taking some OxyContin and going to sleep for the rest of eternity. Did you know the Archangel Michael is always depicted carrying a sword? Perhaps if I am judged worthy I will get to meet the fellow and inspect his blade myself." Hollis said .His smile faltered a bit but Pretlow could see him force it back to its full strength. "But you are not a member of the faith of the zombie carpenter are you?" he asked.

"I practice an alternative religion. But my father told me stories of angels. He had a special affinity for Michael. He called him 'God's Sword'. He would tease me that we were agents of Michael. My mother would tell me my father drank too much," Pretlow said. He had shocked himself. That was the most he had spoken about his father in years. To anyone, even Darnicia. In the years after his father's death his mother had grown more dedicated to the Brotherhood. She had not been born into one the Houses but she had accepted what she called his father's strange devotion. Once he had passed she immersed herself in the Brotherhood She sent Pretlow to the Grand Hall to study the history of the Brotherhood. The Archivist in turn sent him to study with the master sword-smith Garn Whiteborne in Italy. His mother never spoke of his father in the past tense. She refused to discuss his death. She did not pretend he was still alive but she would not accept that he was dead. She didn't want to hear of Pretlow's grief. She did not want to know of Pretlow's heartache. It made her heartache real.

"We will not grieve Astor. We will honor him. We will honor his life. You will be the greatest swordsman the Brotherhood has ever seen. You will make your father proud, Pretlow," she told him when she sent him to live with the Archivist in the Grand Hall. He had been sixteen. She had kissed him on his forehead. He remembered she had to stand on her tiptoes to do it. He had smiled. Two days later she hung herself in the basement of their house that had served as his father's workshop.

Pretlow put his hands on his friend's shoulders and locked his eyes with a steely gaze.

"Don't give up on this world just yet .There are many of us who

THE BROTHEROOD OF THE BLADE

have not forgotten the old ways. And don't give up the fight just yet. Please." Hollis patted his arms and laughed.

"Enough of this morbid, melancholy talk. Come on let me show you around the compound. I've got a few serving wenches you just gotta see over by the tavern tent! That's where we hold the raffle for you gorgeous work of art here," Hollis said. Pretlow's cheek twitched and he followed as Hollis started for the far end of the fair grounds.

Three men stood ten feet away from Pretlow and Hollis. They were men of Asian descent but they did not garner much attention. People of all races and cultures were welcome at a Ren-fair. The three men watched as Pretlow walked behind Hollis heading for the recreation of a medieval tavern. The man in the middle of the three gentlemen pulled a cell phone out of his pocket.

"Yes he is here. Yes I understand," he said in Japanese. His associate took a shuriken out of his pocket but the man in the middle held up one finger.

"Yes we will call back once it is done." the man in the middle said into the phone.

"He does not look so tough," the man with the shuriken said. The man in the middle put the phone back in his pocket.

"Those are the ones that are the most dangerous. A wolf does not have to tell you he is a killer. You can see it in his eyes. But by the time you do it is too late. We will wait until the crowd thins out a little. Then we will approach. His family is still in Virginia. We will move on all of them at the same time if he refuses the client's offer," the man in the middle said.

"It's good to have proper information about a target for once," the man with the shuriken said.

"We have a good source," the man in the middle said.

Catlow rode his bike over to the Richmond Fencing Academy. Harmony followed in her car. It would be an overstatement to say he felt good, but he felt...alright. He knew that eventually he would have to return home but he had a safe haven at Harmony's house. He was just beginning to conceive of a life with her and without the Brotherhood. Not marriage or children, nothing as mature as that. But perhaps attending the same college or even moving in together after they graduated. Those ideas were just snapshots in his mind. Pieces of a waking dream that he wanted to make reality. He drove up the hill to Broad Street and pulled up to the curb of the main thoroughfare of the city of Richmond. The "Academy" was really just a small office space that the director, owner and chief instructor Frank Corbin rented from his cousin for half the market value. They had a total of fifty students. About half of them were really dedicated to learning the art of fencing. Half of those students were actually talented. Frank Corbin was a fifty-year-old former Marine who had taken up fencing as a way of rehabilitating a fractured knee cap. Even at fifty he was whipcord trim with a short gray and black crew cut. He had interviewed Catlow for a few minutes then stood.

"Alright let's see what ya got." And with that they engaged in an impromptu sparring session in the middle of the studio. Uncle Saed had warned him about Frank Corbin.

"He's a little brusque and rough around the edges. But he is a good man. A proud man. Do not embarrass him. He will ask you to spar. Please do not hurt him. You must, and I stress this, YOU MUST hold back without appearing to be weak. I am trying to help you nephew .Do not make me regret my decision. This man is a friend of mine," Uncle Saed had said before giving Catlow the address of the Academy.

"I promise I won't hurt him or embarrass him Uncle Saed," Catlow had said, but once they began sparring Catlow found it hard to keep his promise. Compared to his father, Frank Corbin was incredibly slow. His defense was as porous as a sieve. He telegraphed his moves so much Catlow thought he was trying to send Morse Code. When he was going to strike high he tapped his foot three times. When he was going to strike low he switched his stance so that he led with his right foot. Catlow had deciphered his entire style in about thirty seconds. Afterward Frank had been impressed with his footwork and his skill but criticized his technique.

"You try to use your power too much. You're strong but fencing is not a game of just strength. It is a game of finesse and skill and technique. You strike like you're trying to break my sword. The object of the game is too score points not kill your opponent. I'll let you teach the novice class. Don't teach them any bad habits that I will have to break," Frank had said after their practice session. Catlow bit his tongue .He had not been taught to fence for "points" or style. He had been taught to kill, as quickly and efficiently as possible. He held his piece and took the job.

Harmony parked across the street then ran through traffic to hug Catlow before he went into the studio.

"You sure they won't mind me watching?" she asked as they laced their fingers together and walked into the studio hand in hand.

"I'm telling you they won't mind. It will be nice to have an audience," Catlow said. The novice class, or what was left of it, was already there. They were all stretching and warming up on the floor near the fencing strip. Frank was sitting at his desk near the back of the studio looking over some papers. He looked up and waved Catlow over.

"You're late." he accused as he looked over what appeared to Catlow to be some kind of bill.

"Yes sir I know. I am sorry. I'll go change immediately," Catlow said sheepishly.

"And who is this young lady? A new student?" Frank asked.

"Uh no sir. She is my girlfriend. I told her she could watch today's class," Catlow explained. Frank sat back in his chair.

"Alright. Maybe she will watch the class and want to become a student. God knows we could use some more students," Frank said wistfully. "Go get changed." He went back to looking at the papers on his desk. Catlow started for the back of the studio toward the locker room, but stopped.

"Dang, I forgot my headband," he said under his breath. Harmony was wearing a blue bandanna. She took it off and held it out to Catlow.

"Here wear mine .It's not a girlie color." Catlow took the bandanna and leaned down to kiss her. He heard Frank clear his throat.

"Let me go put on my uniform. Promise you won't laugh at my knickers," he whispered. Harmony giggled.

"Too late," she whispered back.

A black Lexus was parked across the street from the studio. The thin sharp-faced Asian man sat in the car. His IPod was playing "Foggy Mountain Breakdown". He pulled his cell phone out and pushed a button.

"Yes he is in a fencing studio. Yes. I understand. I await your instructions." He ended the call and sat back in his seat. He reached back behind his seat and grabbed a black polished wooden scabbard. He placed the scabbard in the passenger seat leaning against the dashboard.

The Windsor Hotel was twelve blocks from the Richmond Fencing Academy. The thin Asian man had placed a call to his superior. His superior was in a suite in the Windsor Hotel. When the call came through the superior, who was named Kenton Kashigi, he was sitting on the floor in the lotus position with a Japanese katana across his lap. He was shirtless. If anyone else had been in the room with him they would have seen a kaleidoscope of colors etched into his back. Bright red and black dragons surrounded by electric blue and florescent green lotus flowers. In nature lotus blossoms did not come in such bright colors but nonetheless these were the colors of the Clan Junoksiwi Shi. Clan of the Swift Death.

Kento sat with his eyes closed. He had just received reports from all his sons. Traditionally the head of a clan of was called Father and all those that were of that clan were his sons or his daughters. He loved them and tutored them and disciplined them as any father would his own children. One was not born into a clan. The very nature of the clan made having blood relatives prohibitive. Certain assignments could be suicide missions. One did not want to send their real son or daughter to face almost certain death. The Clan was comprised of the "unwanted". Orphans, homeless children, runaways, these were the individuals that filled the ranks of the clan. Kento was the youngest clan leader in recorded history. At 32 he had assumed control of the clan from his predecessor in an honor duel at the base of Mt. Fuji. Now at the age of 45 he was the undisputed master of his clan and the only living Clan master in the world. His clan numbered 300 members. They were the last and only clan left in the world. They were the last Ninja.

These hired assassins were agents of sabotage. Masters of the deadly arts, they were proficient with all manners of silent weaponry. Daggers, shuriken, katana, wakizashi, harigata shuriken, kusarigama, all could be fatal in the hands of a properly trained ninja. Kento prided himself on properly training his children so that they did nothing to bring dishonor to the Clan. He and his council of instructors pushed the strong and eliminated the weak. There was no room in the clan for those who could not meet the exacting standards that were set hundreds of years ago. Those who could not were cremated, their ashes were then scattered to the four winds, far from the clan's home. It was as if they had never existed. Their failure was a dishonor the clan could not bear. Kento breathed in, then out deeply.

Suddenly he pushed himself up in the air with his quadriceps. The katana flew up with him, reached its nadir and began to fall back to the floor. Kento landed on his feet and caught the sword before it hit the ground. In one smooth fluid motion he unsheathed the sword with his left hand and raised it above his head while still holding on to the scabbard with his right. He began to slash through the air with the katana. Harsh, rapid motions that made the air sing. Kento kept his breathing slow and steady even as his skin began to glisten with sweat. Normally the Clan Master did not personally oversee an assignment. He would send his children with a full dossier on their target to various locations around the world. They would return, confirm the completion of the assignment and retreat back to the clan's village. This was a unique assignment that presented Kento with a rare opportunity.

This assignment involved the Brotherhood of the Blade.

Every individual on earth has pride. Some have more than others. Kento was a proud man. Pride in his leadership of his clan, pride in his children. Most of all he was proud of his prowess as a warrior. As a child he had heard whispers about the Brotherhood. The former master of the clan and his council of instructors spoke of the men of the Brotherhood in hushed tones and quiet reverence. They told tales of men so devoted to their swordsmanship they could slice shurikens in half in mid-air. Men who could take a ninjas' own sword out of his hand and use it against him. Men who were so fast that if they slit your throat you would not know it until you nodded your head. Kento listened to these half-mumbled tales with a mix of awe and curiosity. When he first went to live with the clan he was terrified of the instructors, of the other members. His training did nothing to allay his fears. Seeing his fellow clan members in all black garb, the deadly tools of their trade hidden within their robes, it was a frightening sight. The clan members wore a black mask with a small opening above the nose to allow them to see. As a child Kento hating looking into that slit and seeing the eyes of his brothers and sisters. A cold darkness lived behind those eyes. A darkness Kento finally learned to embrace after many years. The idea that these fearsome creatures might actually be afraid of someone fascinated him. As he grew and rose among his brothers and sisters he made himself a promise. If he ever got the chance, if the day ever came that an assignment involved the Brotherhood he would personally fulfill the contract. He would be the Ninja that bested the men of the Brotherhood. Kento would go down in history as the greatest clan leader the world had ever seen. His chief instructor and second in command

Hiro Makai had advised against personally carrying out the assignment.

"My Master. These men are not as normal men. They move like the wind and strike like lightening. There are tales about these men defeating whole clans in the ancient days. Send a competent team and observe the results from afar. If they are dispatched easily then the mission is completed to everyone's satisfaction. However if for whatever reason they are not dispatched so easily then we may study the situation and devise a more effective course of action." he had said in Kento private study in the clans main house in the middle of their compound.

"Hiro, are there not tales of ninjas who can fly, ninjas who can turn invisible? Did we not spread those tales ourselves to inspire horror in our enemies and targets? These men are accomplished swordsmen and duelists. But they are still men. I am sure they have some skill but nothing to compare with us. We have existed since the fifteenth century. We have killed samurai and lords, kings and queens, presidents and prime ministers, captains of industry and drug kingpins. And we will kill these men of the Brotherhood. Because to do otherwise calls into question everything you and I and our clan has ever done or sacrificed. I will personally take their heads and bring them back to the house of Jinkosi shi to show my children we are the danger that lurks in the dark. That we are the reapers of men and the demons that mothers warn their children about," he had said. Hiro left the room walking backwards and bowing profusely.

Kento twirled the katana above his head then slid it back into its scabbard. He held the sword out in front of him and nodded curtly. He would vanquish the men of the Brotherhood. It was his destiny.

He sat on the king-size bed and checked his cell phone. There was no further report from his sons in Pennsylvania. As soon as they notified him whether or not Pretlow Astor Creedence took the deal offered to him by Carcone Apothas he would alert his other children to begin eliminating their targets. It was possible that Pretlow would take the deal. But Kento did not believe that he would accept Carcone's offer. He had studied Pretlow as any good hunter studies his prey, learning his habits, his personality.

Like Kento, Pretlow was a proud man. A man of honor.

Kento wished he was the one killing him.

HAPTER FIVE

Calla Creedence sat up and rubbed her eyes. Her hair stood off from her head in unruly twists and corkscrews. She yawned and hopped out of bed. The house was quiet, very different than last night. Last night Daddy had hit Catlow. Her Mommy had cried and Catlow had run out the house. It was all strange to her because her Daddy had never struck her or Catlow before last night. Oh he had punished her for drawing a picture of him or putting mayonnaise in Catlow's shoes but he never ever hit them. She heard other kids at school talk about their parents hitting them and she thought that sounded awful.

To be fair Catlow had said terrible things about the Brotherhood. She didn't really understand everything that Catlow had said but she got the idea that he had called Daddy and Uncle Saed and Mr. Darn stupid. Catlow didn't believe in the Brotherhood. Even though Daddy had let him play with the swords and taught him to do stuff that was so cool she could hardly stand it. She had once asked Daddy when she would be able to learn to do handstands on the point of a sword and her Daddy had just ruffled her hair.

"Little bit, don't you worry about that. I am training Catlow so that you will never have to pick up a sword," he had said. She put her hands on her hips.

"What girls aren't allowed to pick up swords?" she asked. Daddy had chuckled.

"No not at all Little Bit. I just don't want you to have to pick up a sword. Do you understand?" he had asked.

"Yeah but I don't like it," she had said.

Calla walked downstairs and into the kitchen. There was an empty bottle of wine on the table. She pulled a chair from under the kitchen table and pushed it up to the cabinet. Humming she climbed onto the chair and got her cereal out of the cabinet. Froot Loops were her favorite. She was climbing down out of the chair when she happened to look out the window over the kitchen sink. There was a man standing in their backyard. which bordered against the front yard of Billy Kenton and his family's house. The man was wearing a black t-shirt and black pants. He had his hands behind his back. He was just staring at her house. She blinked her eyes and looked again.

The man was gone.

Calla thought that was strange. The man kind of looked like Jet Li with longer hair. Jet Li was once been one of her favorite kung fu actors. Then she saw her Daddy practice down in the basement with Uncle Saed. After that, Jet Li seemed kind of boring. Calla moved the chair and got a bowl out of the other cabinet. Then she pushed the chair with the box of cereal and bowl in it over to the table. She went to the fridge and got the milk. She poured her milk into the bowl first then the cereal. Then she sat in the chair. The first spoonful of cereal was always the best.

Calla didn't know why Catlow didn't believe in the Brotherhood anymore. Everything Daddy told them was true. The Judges had told her so in her dreams. The first time they talked to her she had been scared. They were scary to look at. In her dreams they were as tall as her house .Dressed in dark red robes from head to toe. The robes had hoods so you couldn't see their faces. But two blue spots where their eyes would have been glowed deep within the hoods. As they appeared again and again to her she gradually came recognize they were three different beings. The first one she thought of as the Nice One. He would speak to her about the upcoming duel thing Daddy was always talking about. He told her that it would get real dangerous when it got closer to the duel and she would have to be careful.

The second one she thought of as the Mean One. He would tell her that they would all probably die and that she had to prepare herself to accept that. Calla did not like the Mean One. The last one she called the Quiet One. He never spoke to her but only stared at her with those glowing blue eyes. While the Nice One and Mean One lost their scariness the Quiet One still frightened her when he showed up in her dreams.

Like last night. She had been dreaming she could fly. She flew across the top of her school and to the mall. She could feel the wind against her face and the sun on her back. Birds tried to keep pace with her and she would just fly faster. She flew down to the Maple Leaf Mall and flew straight through the doors like she was a ghost. In the dream she landed in front of the Kay Bee toy store. She was going to get the big giant easel and oil paints that she wanted for her birthday. Mommy had told her she wasn't old enough for oil paint yet but this was a dream and in dreams it didn't matter how old you were. As she was about to walk into the toy store she heard a crack of thunder. Calla turned around and saw the Judges standing there. They towered above her like great red oaks. Their hands were hidden in the sleeves of their robes. The Nice One spoke to her. It seemed as if she could hear his voice in her head and not with her ears.

"The time is drawing near. Be ready little girl."

The mean one spoke next.

"Death is coming Calla. All the things that you love are coming to an end."

The Nice One spoke again.

"Beware of men in black."

The Quiet One didn't say anything .He just held his arm up and pointed to the fountain in the middle of the mall concourse. It was spewing blood.

Calla had sat up in bed wide awake. The dream hadn't really scared her. It just woke her up. But then she saw the man in the backyard .In all black. She decided she would tell Mommy about the dream when she came downstairs. It just seemed like the right thing to do. She wished Catlow was home. She would tell him first and see what he thought about her dreams. She like to pick on him and make him mad because he was funny when he got mad , but he would never be mean to her in return. He looked out for her. He always gave her his dessert at dinner. He took her trick or treating last year when Daddy had gone to some knife show. Yeah, she really wished Catlow was there.

Catlow was putting his students through their paces. He paired up each novice and had them practice foot work on the fencing strip, a six by forty foot long mat. The Academy had three strips and Catlow had all his novices moving back and forth on one of them. Catlow insisted they use their swords slowly at first until they got a feel for the weight and length of the weapon. He taught them a distinctly French style of fencing with emphasis on the foil and epee. The saber was for the more advanced class. Harmony couldn't stop looking at Catlow in fencing attire. His calf muscles bulged in the tight white socks he wore. His knickerbockers hugged his firm thighs. Even though the buttons on his jacket reminded her of Dark-wing Duck it looked sexy on him. It was skin tight and showed off his impressive arms and chest. He looked so professional and commanding in his uniform.

She had no idea what he was teaching the class but he looked dam good doing it.

Catlow would glance at Harmony occasionally. He liked that she was watching him. Once the class started doing full-speed drills he might show her a little of his skill. Maybe. If Frank wasn't looking his way.

The man in the Lexus was listening to "Carolina Moonshine Man." He looked at his phone. He was not impatient just vigilant.

Pretlow enjoyed talking to Hollis. The sun had risen in the sky and now released its full power on the crowd gathered in the town square. A thin sheen of sweat covered Pretlow's brow but he hardly noticed. The performers and the vendors, the patrons and the attendees all swirled around him like a tornado made of laughter and smiles. Hollis was telling him a ribald joke while at the same time directing an assistant to make sure there was an adequate supply of bottled water for the fair goers. The man was an expert at multi-tasking. Pretlow leaned against a tree watching his friend. He couldn't see the shadow of death hovering over Hollis. The idea of him not walking the earth was incomprehensible to Pretlow. He was a living being whose energy could be measured in joules. Pretlow shook his head and tried to think better thoughts.

The three men of Asian descent watched Pretlow from behind a booth selling handmade leather goods. The one with the phone was named Saito. His two brothers were named Liu and Aiko respectively. They had dressed in traditional medieval garb. All three were wearing wool breeches and leather boots with a tight from fitting tunic and mulch-patterned jerkin. All three had on bright steel close helms. An observant Renaissance aficionado would have noticed the swords the men wore on their hips were not traditional medieval swords. They did not have a cross guard or a basket. The scabbards were ebony, not leather or iron. The handles of the swords were wrapped in crisscrossing red and black fabric. The men stood waiting for Pretlow to walk back toward his dark green vehicle.

It was incredibly hot inside the helms. None the men seemed to notice. Each of them had survived harsher conditions during their training. They waited patiently, their hands on the handles of their swords.

"Here, my dear fellow, have a glass of mead with me!" Hollis exclaimed as he handed Pretlow a mug of mead. Pretlow held up his hand.

"Hollis you know I don't drink." Hollis put the cup in Pretlow's hand and folded his fingers around it.

"Pretlow ...my dear Pretlow. I don't expect you to join me a celebration of inebriation. I just want to share a drink, a sip of this golden elixir with a friend. I don't know how many more days I have upon this poor stage but I would surely regret never imbibing at least once with a man I have grown to love like a son. Please grant an old man this one request." Hollis said staring into Pretlow's face with sad eyes. Pretlow took his cup and clanked it against the other one that Hollis was holding. Raising the mug to his lips he let the sweet and cloying liquid flow over his tongue and down his throat.

"To you my friend," Pretlow said. Hollis smiled

"To us all my good man," he said then threw the cup to his head.

Darnicia walked down stairs dreading every step. The creaking reverberated inside her skull like canon fire. She was not a woman taken to solving all her problems with a bottle of wine but last night it seemed like a reasonable solution. Tannins coated the inside of her mouth leaving behind a bitter acidic taste. Darnicia walked into the kitchen and saw Calla sitting at the table finishing her bowl of cereal.

"How many bowls have you had Calla?" she asked with her hand on her head.

"Counting this one?" Calla asked.

"Yes Calla, counting this one."

"Oh well four," Calla said calmly. Darnicia picked up the box off the table. It was empty.

"Calla you can't eat that much cereal. You ate the whole box by yourself! "Darnicia said.

"Well you drank that whole bottle wine by yourself," Calla said under her breath.

"Excuse me?" Darnicia said sharply.

"Nothing mommy," Calla said. She hopped out of the chair and walked to the fridge.

"Can I have some juice then? Oh and there was a man standing in the backyard this morning." She was running her finger across the surface of the fridge and shaking her curly hair.

Darnicia's skin turned cold "What did you say, Calla?"

"I want some juice."

"No! You saw a man in the backyard?" Darnicia shouted. Calla turned around and looked at her mother.

"Yeah he was a standing over by Billy's house. He was just looking at our house. What's wrong Mommy?" Calla asked.

"Nothing. Go to your room. Stay there. Don't back talk now, just go," Darnicia said. Something in her mother's voice stifled Calla's sarcastic tendencies. She ran up the stairs singing a song of nonsensical words. Darnicia walked to the phone on the wall of the kitchen and dialed Pretlow's cell phone.

Darnicia was born to the House of Sand and Fire. Her father had been a chief of their House.   He had never tried to hide anything about the Brotherhood from Darnicia or Saed. Theirs was a destiny inexorably tied to death. The Duel of the Generations was to the death. The Men of the First Chaos lived to kill them. Death could come for them or their loved ones at any time.   But until that very moment she had always been able to put the idea of harm coming to her or her family in a locked room in her mind .Exiled from all her pleasant thoughts and memories. In that locked room the idea of cradling her dead children or her husband lived like a mad aunt that lived in the attic. Calla's statement had blown the lock off that room. Now the idea filled her mind, made her chest tight and left a hollow feeling in her stomach.

Pretlow's phone rang and rang.

Darnicia wished that they had gotten Catlow a cell phone. She wished Saed didn't live in Baltimore. She wished that Pretlow was there with her .For twenty years whenever she felt sad or lost or angry he would put his arms around her and make her feel like she was invulnerable The night they had met they had both been attending a

116

gathering of the Houses in New York. The Men of Order met at a hotel under the guise of a Rotary Club convention at a small hotel in Manhattan. Back then the Men of Order met frequently. They discussed matters ranging from the status of the records in the Grand Hall discussing sword making techniques, fight styles, and information about the Men of the First Chaos

They analyzed the various portents and signs in the Book of the Seven Swords. The Brotherhood's entire history was inscribed in that book. Every one hundred years it was updated by the Archivist. Throughout the centuries, men and women were culled from both the House of Order and the House Of Chaos. They were tasked with giving an unbiased account of the history of their blood-soaked fraternity. The Brotherhood also used these meetings as a thinly veiled attempt to pair off their progeny. The complexity of the Brotherhood's mission made dating rather difficult. Unless one left the Brotherhood entirely it could be awkward trying to build a life with a significant other. There was more than altruism at work. To fulfill the Covenant the Brotherhood had to replenish their supply of viable warriors. Adoption was an option but the elders, the Council of Prefects, felt that the bloodlines should remain intact as much as that was humanly possible.

So at their bi-annual meeting young men and women of the various Houses were allowed and encouraged to mingle .The Men of the First Order did not go as far as the Men of the First Chaos in their attempts at manipulated procreation. They did not actually arrange marriages. Darnicia always thought how oxymoronic the Men of the First Chaos could be. An order devoted to the chaos and randomness and anarchy of life regularly made their children marry people they did not love.

She had first seen Pretlow at the meeting of the Men of the First Order. He was 21, two years older than her. He had been standing in the lobby of the hotel by himself with a weathered back-pack over his shoulder and a tattered denim jacket and jeans. His hair was cut in that severe flat -top that she would learn he favored. He would tell her it got in the way when he was training In truth, he didn't like to grow his hair out because then it resembled the long and flowing hair of his father. Darnicia had been sitting by herself on a circular bench in the lobby waiting for her father and Saed to come down the elevator so that they could all go to dinner. Her family had immigrated to America in 1980 when she was 5 years old. Her father Ket Barkarhat, prefect of the House of Sand and Fire, had fled the Apartheid regime of South Africa for the welcoming shores of the United States. Ket was a bit more financially secure that most members of the Brotherhood. While in Johannesburg he had learned the art of cutting and shaping diamonds from a kindly old Jewish man who had fled Israel under circumstances so dire he never explained them to her father. Ket took his skills as a gemologist and carved out a fairly decent living for his family .All the while he maintained his family's devotion and commit to the Covenant.

Darnicia remembered sitting there alone because she was the first one in her family dressed for dinner. As Pretlow's phone rang she recollected that she had been wearing a tight pair of Guess jeans and a floral print blouse open to the waist with a black tank top under it. She would not have called her younger self vain. But she was very aware that she had a body that made men stare. The attention stirred something....primal in her. She liked it. She liked more than she should have. So when the drunken white men came in the door of the lobby and looked her up and down she smiled. They had stumbled over to where she was sitting and leaned around her. She could see then that they were not just drunk but totally inebriated. The scent of bourbon poured from them like the ghost of hangovers yet to come.

"Hey you look like you could use some company over here." the first man said. He pronounced here like "heyeah" in a thick Brooklyn accent. He rubbed his hand across her cheek. It stank of tobacco and liquor. The second man sat beside her and put his hand on her leg.

"You wanna party, sweetness? You can come party with me and my boys. We going upstairs to a party. Come on it'll be fun. We got some drinks and some other party favors." he said. Darnicia remembered he had tried to charm her with his smile but it looked more like a lascivious leer. The third man burped then laughed.

"Come on guys she ain't bout it." The first man didn't look at him but held his hand up to his face.

He was stocky and muscular with a pock-marked face and thick greasy black hair that was slicked back away from his forehead. He wore a tight white t-shirt and even tighter jeans. He had prominent bulges in both articles of clothing. His companions were dressed much the same way. The third man had a long scar across his neck .It looked like someone had attempted to garrote him. Darnicia had started to stand up and walk away from these three hard looking men.

"Um my parents are probably looking for me," she said as she tried to rise. Black-greasy hair put his hand on her shoulder and held her in place.

"What, you think you're too good to party with us? Huh? Is that it? What we not gangsta enough for you?" he asked. Spittle flew from his lips and landed on Darnicia's face. The second man touched him on the shoulder

"Hey Sid come on let's go." But Sid pushed his hand aside.

"Is that what you think you fucking bitch?" he asked quietly. The third man shook his head. Darnicia tried to look calm and worldly. She turned her head from Sid and looked longingly at the elevator. Sid grabbed her chin and forced her to look at him.

"You goddam nigger bitch, I asked you a question. You sitting round here showing off ya fucking tits and ass and now you wanna get quiet? You fucking sluts are all the same," he said. His hand was gripping her chin tightly.

"Get off of her." she heard a deep voice say. Sid let her go and turned around .They all did.

Pretlow was standing there. He was holding a weathered black scabbard. The hilt fit perfectly against the scabbard. It appeared to be made of ebony wood. It was a weapon even without the blade exposed. Darnicia did not know his name at that time. She had never seen him before but at that moment she had never been so happy to see anyone in her life.

"Hey fuck off moolie," Sid said. He laughed. His friends started laughing as well. Pretlow did not laugh. In her time in America Darnicia had become accustomed to the rhythm of a street fight. They lived in Baltimore, Maryland and saw such confrontations frequently. Most fights she had witnessed lasted about ten minutes. Eight minutes of posturing and preening and two minutes of actual fighting.

As she would learn later in their life together, Pretlow Creedence did not posture. He did not preen. He acted. He moved. Her brother would nickname him Jaws after one particularly intense sparring session. He was always moving forward. He never gave an inch. He was an engine of action.

Pretlow stepped forward. Sid raised his fist.

"Oh boy I'm going to fuck you up!" he yelled. Pretlow swung the scabbard, blunt end first, into Sid's throat. Hard. He moved with such speed that the scabbard blurred as it moved through the air. It connected with Sid's larynx with such ferocity that the man immediately dropped to his knees. The second man ran at Pretlow, his fist flailing. Pretlow dropped to one knee while swinging the scabbard at the man's right shin. The sound of the unyielding wood sheath hitting bone made Darnicia's ears hurt. The second man tumbled to the floor writhing in pain. The third man stood still as a statue. His hands were balled into fist but he didn't advance on Pretlow. As soon as the second man fell to the ground and rolled on his back grasping his shin and howling in pain, Pretlow jumped onto his chest with both feet and performed a front-flip punch out like a gymnast doing a floor exercise. As he completed his revolution he held the scabbard above his head so that at the end of his flip it absorbed all his centrifugal force. He brought it down on the head of the third man as he landed on his feet. A crack reverberated through the lobby as the third man dropped to the floor unconscious. The entire altercation had taken about one minute.

Pretlow surveyed the scene and then slid the scabbard back into his large green backpack. He then came over to Darnicia.

"Are you okay?" he asked her. Darnicia remembered how melodious his voice had sounded that day. Like a cross between James Earl Jones and Patrick Stewart. He asked her how she was like he really cared. He seemed oblivious to the carnage around him or the startled looks from the other hotel guest in the lobby. Darnicia could see the concierge dialing the phone. One particularly harried woman was running to the phone-booth.

"Uh yeah I'm okay I just..."

"Darnicia!" Her father's voice cut off her response. Ket Barkarhat was striding toward her. He was not as tall as Pretlow but his shoulders were just as wide. Skin as dark as obsidian. A gleaming bald head that was held high as he walked toward his daughter and the stranger standing among the litter of unconscious bodies on the floor. A black double breasted suit was stretched tight across his wiry frame.

"Who is this? What has happened here?" her father had said in fast clipped tones.

"He saved me. He is a member of the Brotherhood," Darnicia said. She had shocked herself with her assertion. But there was no mistaking the skill and power the man had displayed. Even without showing her the hand sign or saying the Oath she knew he was of the Brotherhood. Ket stopped and angled his head. He gazed at the man.

"Is this true?" he said softly. The man then displayed the hand sign.

"I am Pretlow Creedence. Prefect of the House of Green Hills. The only member of the House of Green Hills," he said. His eyes seemed on the verge of misting then they retained their steely glare.

"Where are the other members of your House?" Ket asked. Pretlow dropped his head a bit.

"My father was Astor Creedence. He had no brothers or sisters. His father died in the last Duel. Along with his uncle who disappeared before the Duel commenced. He had no children. My father had me late in life. He died in a car accident when I was twelve. My mother died when I was sixteen. There are no other members of the House of Green Hills," he said in a flat monotone. Darnicia felt a warm sensation fill her heart for this man. He was utterly alone in the world. She could tell by the way he told his tale that he had recited it many times before. Ket sighed.

"Well come on up to our suite. We are going to have to hide you. These people are not used to violence like this that is so personal and tangible. They have acclimated themselves to the way of the gun. A coward's way. But that is not the way of the Brotherhood, is it, Master Creedence? Come now before we have to gather bail money for you. I am in debt to you for defending my daughter." Ket shot Darnicia a glance that intimated they would discuss why exactly she had needed defending. He motioned toward the elevator. Pretlow seemed not understand for a moment then he hurried toward the carriage. Darnicia did not know at that time that they would become lovers or husband and wife or parents. She just knew that he was unlike any other man she had ever encountered and she wanted to learn everything about him. He was a king among peasants. Nothing in the intervening years had changed that opinion. Not even the argument last night.

Pretlow's phone went to his voice mail. Darnicia hung up and sat down at the kitchen table. It was then she let the fear touch her. Tears slowly slipped down her cheeks. It was beginning. After all these years it was beginning. And Pretlow was in Pennsylvania and Catlow was somewhere out in the world and she and Calla were alone at the house. It was a perfect storm of chaos.

She wiped her tears and shook her head. She had the key to Pret's workshop and the sword cabinet. She would defend her house if it came to that .She would defend both her Houses. She was a daughter of the House of Sand and Fire and a lady of the House of Green Hills.

She would defend her House.

Pretlow and Hollis sat on a wooden bench under a large oak tree. His friend Richard Darn, prefect of the House of The Olde Grove, thought that trees and nature itself were a conduit through which the Judges spoke to them. That the very ecosystem they lived within was a sort of God. Of course Richard Darn and his House were descendants of former pagans who had been drawn into the Duel the same way Pretlow's ancestors had. Richard was a well-respected member of the Brotherhood but he held fast to some of his ancestors' beliefs and tenets. He ran a furniture store in Birmingham England. He hand crafted each chair or table with the idea that he was honoring the spirits of the trees from which they came.

Pretlow did not share his friend's attachment to any other religious system. His father had told him once upon a time the House of the Green Hills had been the largest house in the entire Brotherhood. These were hard and earnest men who farmed the earth for their sustenance. Men who had been plucked from the comfortable monotony of a life on the farm to be champions for the entire human race. There was no room in their hearts for any other philosophy. They submitted to the Covenant wholly and completely.

Christianity, Islam, Hinduism, Judaism, and any other of the great theological movements had no place in their world once the Judges had pulled back the curtain of reality. If someone had asked Pretlow just who the Judges were, he would have recited for them the description of the Judges from the first chapter of the Book of Seven Swords

"They are and always were. They Judge. They stand as wardens amidst the pillars of creation. When the Universe had lost faith in us they intervened and forged a Covenant with us that will last for all of time. Through our honor and sacrifice we strive to be worthy of their interdiction. The Covenant they have entered into is not for the weak or the fearful. It is a covenant of blood and death. But that this blood shall be a balm to heal the troubles of this world for a little while and from this death shall life spring anew is their promise. Their power is infinite as is their patience. For the latter we must be grateful, for the former we must watchful." --The Book of the Seven Swords as written by Aron the Wounded Eye, champion of the first Duel of Generations. Pretlow had memorized that passage when he was thirteen years old. It was all the explanation he needed. Everything he had seen in his life left no doubt to the complete and total veracity of those words written over a thousand years ago. As he sat on the bench with his old friend he reflected that for Catlow those words were now meaningless.

"So I have sent half the money for your beautiful sword to your PayPal account my friend. The other half will come from the sale of the raffle tickets. I wish I could just pay you straight out Pret. It is a masterwork. Just masterful," Hollis said as he finished his fourth cup of mead. Pretlow looked at his watch. It was approaching one 'o clock. The crowd at the fair had begun to thin out a bit and he needed to get on the road. He would call Saed on his way home. Perhaps Catlow's uncle could talk some sense into him. Saed was a smooth tongued devil when he wanted to be. Pretlow stood and held his hand out to Hollis.

"I am going to head off my friend. Promise me you will take it easy today. The heat is hard on you old men," Pretlow said. Hollis laughed.

He grabbed Pretlow's hand with a grip that still had quite a bit of strength behind it.

"Sure you won't hang around for the after party? We are going into town in full garb to freak out the locals. Should be a roaring good time," Hollis said with a twinkle in his eye. Pretlow gave the idea the briefest of considerations. He could just call Darnicia and tell her he was staying. But he wouldn't be staying for Hollis's company. He would be staying to avoid the situation with Catlow. And avoidance was not a part of his code of honor.

"No my friend I should be off. Just make sure you get the rest of the money to me as soon as possible. I have a gift I want to make for my son," he said softly. Hollis pumped his hand vigorously.

"Safe journey my friend. If the Gods find it in their divine providence I hope they will see fit for our paths to cross once more." he said. His eyes lost a little bit of their twinkle.

"We will see each other again Hollis. Life isn't done with either of us yet," Pretlow said and took his hand out of Hollis's with little effort. He gave him the Brotherhood's sign for devotion and nodded his head sharply before turning to on his heel. Hollis watched him walk away.

"I think not my dear friend. But I hope I'm wrong," he thought to himself.

Pretlow walked through the fairgrounds heading for his car. He cut across a lush green field bordered on three sides by a waist high old crumbling brick wall. A silver and black sign mounted on a pole just outside the wall stated this was the site of the original courthouse of Norristown .All that remained was this brittle foundation. If Pretlow hopped across the foundations remains instead of going around it he would be at his car in ten steps. As he walked into the field he heard footsteps behind him. He turned slowly. He saw three men dressed in period garb sporting full helms standing in front of him. The man in the middle stepped forward.

"You are Pretlow Creedence yes?" the man asked. He had a thick accent. It sounded like his first language was Japanese.

"Yes I am Pretlow." Pretlow felt his muscles begin to twitch and tighten. A cloak of concentration was beginning to envelope him. He noticed the swords the men were carrying were katanas not broadswords. He also noticed they were standing two feet apart. It was a common formation for sword fighters. It gave each man enough room to pull his weapon. Pretlow didn't think the men even realized they had arranged themselves in such a fashion. That spoke to rigorous training.

"I have a message from Carcone Apothas for you. Ignore the Invitation. Remove you and your House from the Duel and he will give you 25 million American dollars. I have been instructed to get your signature on a contract. Once that contract is signed the money will be deposited in the financial institution of your choosing. He says that no one will know of your decision. You will not lose face among your comrades. What say you Mr. Pretlow Creedence.?"

Pretlow felt his pulse rate quicken but just enough to register an increase in his adrenaline. Of all the emotions he expected to experience when he realized the time of the Covenant was at hand excitement was not one of them. Carcone Apothas was the prefect of the House of Blood and Steel. He was the grandson of Stavaros Apothas, the man who had killed his grandfather and won the last Duel for the Men of the First Chaos. He was also married to Agrippina Du

Mor. Pretlow kept in contact with the Archivists. They kept detailed genealogical records in the Grand Hall He had inquired years ago about Agrippina's marital status. He was just curious. He didn't know Mr. Apothas personally but if he was married to Agrippina he had to be a man of great will and strength. He didn't think she had changed much since that summer in Italy He pitied and envied Carcone a little bit in that moment. It was a bold move offering that kind of money. If Pretlow had known the man personally he would have told him not to waste his time. There was no price on his honor.

"Shall we begin?" Pretlow said as his hand moved toward his sword.

HAPTER SIX

Taang Sang sat on the patio of his house eating a bowl full of pineapples slices and papayas. The morning sun was finally coming through the clouds and the breeze eased up a bit. The rain storm that had saturated the island for the past three days had finally dissipated. The island had no name it was simply the Island. It had belonged to Sang family for over two thousand years. It was on no map that had ever existed. In the past the Sang family used intimidation and murder to keep their island a secret. Nowadays they just greased the right palm to keep their ancestral home secret. Cartographers compensated to ignore the 15 mile wide land mass in the South China Sea. Satellite researchers and government officials were paid to forget the location of the small tropical oasis eighty miles off the coast of mainland China. It would never show up on any GPS or Google Maps search. Taang bit into the sweet papayas and savored their sugary taste. The patio was covered by a rattan pagoda that cast slits of shadow on the cobblestone floor. Taang was wearing a loose fitting white linen pull over shirt .It had a small v neck that showed the top of a greenish black shark tattoo on his chest. Long black shorts and a pair of sandals completed his ensemble. He was a large man, wide through the middle with bowling ball shoulders and thick meaty hands that could crack open a coconut with the right amount of leverage. His hair was parted down the middle and was flecked with spots of gray. His beard likewise sported gray strands interspersed among the jet black hairs. Humming he licked his fingers and finished his bowl of fruit. The climate on the island was mostly temperate, never too hot or too cold.

The pineapples did not grow here naturally nor did the papayas. Taang had them shipped in especially for his own enjoyment. He interlaced his fingers and stretched his arms out cracking his knuckles. He rose from his breakfast table and walked down the rough cobblestone steps that led away from the main house and toward the beach. The Island had four main ports that could accommodate any size ship, from a tramp steamer to a cargo freighter.

There were two hundred men and women on the Island. With the help of the large mobile crane he had built and paid for through a dummy corporation they could strip a cargo freighter bare in three hours. A smaller ship took even less time. Taang and his family would then sell the products taken from the various ships to various manufactures for half the retail value. The companies made a much higher profit that if they paid even the most meager of wages to small children in third world countries. The Sang family didn't hijack every ship that they encountered nor did they attack ships randomly. They received valuable intelligence from various sources, evaluated the risk versus the reward and responded accordingly. The Sang family had first mastered then plundered the high seas for over two millennia.

The Sang family members were the masters of The House of the Lost Sea.

They were pirates through and through.

Taang had no qualms about calling himself a pirate. Or a crime boss. He was not ashamed of the empire that his forefathers had built. They were what they were destined to be. How could anyone be ashamed of that? Oh the rest of the members of the Men of the First Chaos tried to reform their images with fancy titles and obtuse double talk. They like to call themselves arms dealers and pleasure merchants. Pharmaceutical corporations and mineral traders. Years ago Taang had seen Barton Crisp at a meeting of the great Houses in Antwerp. He had been wearing a deep brown and gray seersucker suit and carried a cane made of polished oak with a gold handle in the shape of a lion's head. His iron gray hair had been clipped and coiffed within an inch of its life. The prefect of the House of Poison Soil looked the part of a captain of industry. One would never know he made his family had built their fortune in the salt mines of ancient Europe and used that as a foundation for their modern chemical empire which now included plants that manufactured petroleum, industrial acids, and had lately branched out into fracking and natural gas extraction. In the course of these business endeavors countless lives had been lost. Slavish working conditions or environmental contamination of the soil, either could have been responsible for the name of their House. Barton Crisp wanted to think of himself as a proud businessman but Taang knew he was just a crime boss like him. Barton tried to dress it up and hide it, as did all the rest of the Men of the First Chaos. Taang embraced it. He wondered who slept better at night.

Taang walked down to the docks whistling to himself. He came upon his son Tenchu and his twin brother Tanchu overseeing the unloading a large container ship. The cargo was mostly clothing that was made with slave labor in China to be sold at exorbitant prices in the USA and Canada. The Sangs would sell these items to the competitors of the stores that had originally paid for them. Those stores would make a hefty profit and the Sangs would get a hefty payment.

Old school piracy was only one of the tent poles that held up the House of the Lost Sea. Taang had been instrumental in the diversification of their operation. Now they worked with the Russian

Mafia as a data bank storehouse for stolen information. In the main house there was now a room with over one hundred stations where workers monitored cloud transactions and wireless purchases. They absconded with tons of personal information which was in turn sold to the Russians for their lucrative identity theft rings. Getting information from a group on a secret island that wasn't on any map was much safer than stealing credit card numbers out of gas stations card readers. Taang firmly believed that those who stagnated died a slow pitiful death. The man with his hands tied behind his back on his knees on the dock would not have to worry about suffering that indignity.

Taang nodded at Tenchu and his son pulled the man up roughly by his arm. Taang stood at the end the dock where the port met the sand with his arms crossed. Tenchu pulled the man along roughly until they were only five feet apart.

"Alu Kiamana. You are captain of the cargo ship 'Catalina'. You tried to renege on our agreement. You notified the U.S Navy you were being boarded. You tried to back out at the last minute even though we had already paid you handsomely. I am very disappointed in you. I do not understand why you did not want to honor our deal. Did you think we would not be monitoring your radio transmissions? Did you really believe we wouldn't know?" Taang asked sadly. The man did not speak. He was a heavy-set man with prominent jowls that fluttered every time he breathed. He was breathing extremely hard.

"I bet you thought you could keep the money and the cargo. Hoping that the Navy SEALs would board your ship, kill my men and you would appear as the hero. Don't you know there are no heroes in this world? Just various degrees of villainy. A spider is a villain to the fly because he eats the fly. The fly is a villain to the spider because it seeks to deny him his food. Now I must play the role of villain because you could not hold up your end of a bargain," Taang said. He nodded to his son. Tenchu grabbed Alu and turned him around to face his ship. His crew was on the bow. All fifteen men were standing with their hands tied behind their backs. Tanchu stood ten feet from his brother and his father. When he saw that Alu was watching he took off running toward the end of the dock. He was tall and wide like a linebacker but he moved with the grace of a gazelle. When he reached the end of the dock he jumped toward his right off the dock and toward the ship. A thick length of rope hung from the bow of the ship. Tanchu flew through air for at least fifteen feet before his wide hands caught the rope. Immediately he began scampering up the length of the rope until he reached the very top of the ship. Tanchu covered a total distance of about seventy five feet in a little over minute. He jumped up and over the railing and now stood on the bow of the ship. Taang men had several AR-15's trained on the crew. One of Taang's men walked over to Tanchu and handed him a sword. It was a Chinese broadsword. Three and a half feet of Brotherhood steel that ended in slight upturned tip. The blade itself was smooth as glass. It had no fillets or lines on its surface. The handle was brass with leather wrapping that wound around it as tight as a snake skin. Taang's grandfather Aaang Sang had commissioned the blade back in 1899. Taang believed it was some of Garn's finest work. Aaang had planned on using the blade in the Duel of 1913 but at the last minute opted for the two smaller tanto blades. Taang often wondered if he had used the broadsword would he have survived. Taang would use the sword if the Duel happened in his lifetime. His father Tong Sang brought him up with an unshakeable belief in the Covenant and his lifestyle, and had offered irrefutable proof of the veracity of said Covenant. Taang had not spoken with the Archivist at the Grand Hall in years but something in the air told him the time of the Invitation was coming. He could smell it like a storm rolling in from the sea. He could feel it bearing down on him and his House like a white squall. It would appear suddenly and without warning. Taang was ready. And so were his sons. They would represent the House of the Lost Sea. They would avenge his grandfather and fulfill the Covenant. Taang looked around the Island .He looked toward the gigantic main house that stretched across 5,000 square feet of terrain. He glanced at the other four ports that took up the majority of the north side of the Island. He looked west and saw the rocky temple built by his forefathers where he and his sons trained and where their mother's remains rested with the rest of the Sangs. He watched as his kinsmen and kinswoman went about the daily business of running a vast empire. The bond that they shared was unbreakable. True there disputes from time to time but they were handled quickly and decisively. Sometimes greed reared its ugly head. Sometimes some kinsmen failed to recognize that they had more than enough wealth to share. Their opulence was not a thing to be ashamed of but to be embraced. This is why he and his sons would fight and this was why they would win.

Taang pointed at Tanchu.

"See what treachery brings you Alu." Tanchu raised the broadsword. "If you had just held up your end of the deal you and your men would have been released into a life boat. But you tried to outsmart us. We who have sailed all the seas of the world since before the time of Genghis Khan. Watch and learn the price of betrayal," Taang said. Tanchu was standing near the port side of the ship. He held the blade chest high. It was lined up perfectly with the necks of the fifteen crew members. Taang nodded.

Tanchu ran toward the starboard side of the boat. As he approached the line of men he spun, once then twice .On the final revolution his blade connected with the neck of the first crewman. Tanchu's blade slid through his neck like a great white sliding through the ocean depths. The blade moved toward the starboard side of the ship as Tanchu ran. It left a fountain of blood in its wake much like a shark. Tanchu reached the starboard rail where he had boarded the ship. Behind him fifteen bodies lay in a haphazard pile like pieces of firewood. The heads of the men littered the bow of the ship. They had fallen like overripe apples from a tree. Blood flowed across the steel plates and seeped in the worn cracks where the welds were weak. Tanchu had decapitated all fifteen men with one strike in less than five seconds.

Alu tried to drop to his knees but Tenchu held him fast. Without warning he vomited onto the dusky black deck. Taang whistled .It was a high sharp sound. Tanchu pulled the broadsword over his head and with his right hand hurled it toward his father. It tumbled through the air end over end. It flew like some great steel bird of prey. Taang plucked the sword out of the air. He held it aloft for a moment.

"Now captain, join your men in eternity. Perhaps you can lead them better across the River Styx than you lead them today." Taang said. He swung the blade from right to left across his body. The steel sliced through Alu's neck with little resistance. His body and head tumbled to the ground near Tenchu's feet.

"Get all this cleaned up. Take the ship back out away from the Island and away from the mainland. Scuttle it and then..." but before Taang could finish his instructions he saw one of his kinsman running toward the dock. He was carrying something. As he got closer Taang could see it was a gleaming black box.

"Master Taang. This was found on the front steps of the main house. It was not there this morning. I didn't see it during my rounds," the thin little man said breathlessly. Taang felt the hairs on the back of his neck stand up. He walked toward the little man and took the box from his trembling fingers. It felt as light as a feather.

"What is it, father?" Tenchu asked him as he stepped over Alu's remains.

"It's the Invitation. It is the means by which we avenge my grandfather. It is the key to keeping our way of life. It's the reason I couldn't let your mother take you and your brother away from me," he thought to himself.

"Leave this task to the team on the ship. Get Tanchu and join me in the main house in my office," he yelled over his shoulder. Taang walked back to the house trailed by his sons. The sound of the surf lapping against the shore filled his ears. His mind was awash with a multitude of feelings and emotions. Excitement, fear, vindication, completeness. He walked up the cobblestone steps and across the massive patio. A huge wooden French door separated the patio from the rest of the estate. Taang pulled the door open without much effort. He held the box away from his body like it was full of venomous snakes. Which it could very well be for all Taang knew. He was woefully behind on his Brotherhood lore. Barton and the other prefects would subtly chastise him on the rare occasions they would meet .They reminded him he was a part of a larger world .A world in which he bore a duty handed down from generation to generation. Taang would laugh to himself. They all forgot about him here on his Island until one of the Archivists made some esoteric observation and the talk of Covenants and Duels was kicked up again like a dust devil. The only House he had regular contact with was the House of Black Rivers and that was mainly professional courtesy. They did their best not to step on each other's toes so to speak. Taang and El-Aki had an understanding. Taang wouldn't' attack his shipments given enough notice. From time to time there were unfortunate confrontations but once their membership in the Brotherhood was established most ended without bloodshed. Truth be told Taang thought the other Houses and their leaders, prefects and masters were a bit overly dramatic. The Duel at its core was a blood sacrifice. People were going to die. Taang felt no need to dress that up with superfluous rituals and traditions. Taang always thought that when and if the Invitation came he would pack his bags go to the address on the invite kill some Men of the First Order and go home.

Yet now with the slick black lacquered box was in his hand he felt the presence of countless ancestors reaching out to him from across oceans of time. The voices of his forefathers spoke to him in unison.

He walked down the wide main hall of his home. It was a hall that was wide enough to drive a dump truck across its stone floors with room to spare. Paintings lined the walls and every ten feet there was a potted palm tree. Near the cathedral ceiling every twenty feet there were huge casement windows that open letting the sea breeze flow through the house. Taang turned left at the end of the hall and opened the door to his office. The ivory handle felt cool in his hand. His office had a large bay window that showed a view of the four ports. There was a 72 inch screen TV in the office. The walls were lined with DVD cases. Action movies, westerns, kung-fu flicks and historical epics filled the shelves. Taang loved movies. This was his personal office. There was a 75-seat theater in the west wing of the estate.

Taang sat down at his desk. It had been hand made by a furniture maker from England. Taang had purchased the desk through a third party. He kept layers and layers between him the rest of the world. Only a few mainlanders had ever seen his face. Other than the occasional meeting with the other Houses, Taang never left the island anymore. So he had no way of knowing the desk had been constructed for him with such fine craftsmanship by Richard Darn, Prefect of the House of the Olde Grove and a member of the Men of the First Order. If made aware of this fact Taang would have been nonplussed. He didn't hate the Men of the First Order as individuals but as an entity .They were a homogenous group that had killed his grandfather and threatened his way of life. If told that Richard Darn had built the beautiful desk he now sat at Taang would have shrugged his shoulders. The desk was a work of art. The four legs were the narrow trunks of palm trees dipped in shellac and wrapped at the bottom and the top with rattan cord. The top of the desk was a piece of driftwood found on the west side of the Island by Tenchu when he was six. It had been sanded and polished to such a degree that Taang could see his reflection in its opaque surface. He loved the desk. His disdain for the Men of the First Order would not have changed that at all.

Tenchu and Tanchu sat in dark brown wicker chairs across from their father. The twins were mirror images of each other .Tenchu was right handed, Tanchu was left handed. They were both 6'2 and weighed 215 pounds. They kept their coal black hair short and close to their skulls. They had their mother's dark eyes. Taang didn't like looking in their eyes sometimes. Lilian Malan and Taang had not been married in any traditional ceremony. Taang had met her on a foray into the Bahamas twenty three years ago when he was still leading the raids and his father had still been alive. Lilian had been a vision of beauty sculpted out of pure chocolate. After raiding a freighter in the south Atlantic, Taang and his men found that the manifest had been switched. Instead of big screen televisions they had found a container ship full of grain. Taang contacted his father who instructed him to sink the ship and kill the crew. Tong Sang then told his son to go to the Bahamas and find their contact in the shipping company and silence him as well. Taang did as he was told and then once he had completed his mission he decided to partake of the pleasures that the Bahamas had to offer a young man with light silver eyes and a massive physique. Lilian had been working as a bartender at a club in Nassau. Taang had noticed her as soon as he and his crew entered the club. A blind man would have noticed her. She had cinnamon skin and long, curly, sandy-colored hair. Apparently her work uniform was a clam shell bikini top that was barely able to contain her full light brown breasts. Taang sauntered up to the bar and plopped on the stool.

"Sex on the beach please. And I'd like a rum and coke as well," he had said with a smile.

"Wow that's the first time I've heard that...today," Lilian had said with a smile. It was a smile that said "Tell me your corny jokes, leer at my big ripe titties. Take mental photos of my firm ass but make sure you tip well."

"But have you ever heard it from such a handsome man who was also humble?" Taang had said. Lilian had laughed .Genuinely laughed at that joke. Taang got her number and her email address. He told her a part of the truth. He was a sailor and that he would be returning to the Bahamas very soon. Weeks passed and the emails increased in frequency and intensity. By the time he came back to Nassau they both knew she would be leaving with him. He told her his family ran a maritime salvage operation on their very own island. Lilian was an orphan .She had grown up quick on the streets of Haiti. Bartending in the Bahamas was light years away from turning tricks for fat old tourists in Port Au Prince. The idea of a gorgeous man coming into her life and taking her to a private island hadn't been a hard sell.

At first they had been happy. Deliriously so. The kind of happiness that can't last. Like a shooting star it burned bright and in that burning consumed itself. The truth of the House of the Lost Sea was shown to Lilian in a sudden and brutal fashion.

Some kinsmen had tried to make off with goods from a raid. Since they were kinsman they were not immediately executed. A trial of sorts was held. The leader of the thieves, Liu Ki Sang, Taang's first cousin and Tong Sang's nephew stated his case in the very office Taang and his boys were sitting in right now.

"We eat at your table uncle but we eat scraps. You keep us scuttling around like hungry mongrel dogs. We just wanted a little extra. A little bit to go to the mainland with, to enjoy the spoils of our labor. We risk our lives for you!" he had said. He had been on his knees hands bound behind his back.

Tong Sang sat at his desk. His weathered brown face was as inscrutable as the Sphinx. When he spoke it was in short clipped tones. He spoke in Maori, the native tongue of the House of the Lost Sea His heavy eyelids never fluttered and his voice never rose above a whisper.

"You are my late brother's son. I gave you anything you required. My brother would have been pleased with how I treated you. Yet you forget yourself. My brother was not Master of this House. I am. You don't like your share of the spoils of our labors you come to me and speak to me as kinsman to kinsman .You don't steal from me, from your kin. Everything we take we give to the family, to the House. Your greed is the issue here not my fairness," Tong said. "So now I must..." but before he could finish Liu interjected.

"I claim the right of trial by combat. I challenge you uncle. I challenge you to trial by the sword," Liu said softly. Taang had stood up and walked toward Liu but his father held up his hand.

"Liu, my nephew, I am sorry you have chosen this way to meet your fate. I am sorry you are not a kinsman of honor. Take him to the Temple." Liu was led away. Taang had walked up to his father.

"Poppa let me fight instead of you. Liu is a very good fighter. We practice; I mean we used to practice together. He is not to be taken lightly," Taang had said. Tong had just stood and put his hands on his son's broad shoulders.

"My son. What are we?" he asked. His gravelly voice scratched Taang's ears.

"We are pirates. Buccaneers. Corsairs," Taang said smiling. Tong did not smile.

"No. We are killers. We live by the sword .We will die by the sword. I would have it no other way. Liu has challenged me. Not you. I cannot lose face in front of the rest of the House or we will have everyone stealing Levi's and trying to sail to Beijing with a boat full of button fly jeans. I practice too. I have held a sword since I was six years old. Fifty years later I think I know my way around a blade. Liu sees the lines in my face and the gray in my hair and he thinks I am weak. That I am easy pickings. He will learn that is far from true. It will be his last lesson," Tong said. He walked past Taang and headed toward the Temple. Taang had looked out the window, the same window he looked out of now. Lilian had been down on the beach with their twins. Tenchu and Tanchu were only one year old that day. The wind had taken Lilian's hair and thrown it into disarray. He had watched her futile attempts to keep it straight. Taang wanted to go to the window and tell her he liked it a little messy. But instead he followed his father to the Temple.

The Temple was a rock outcrop that had been shaped over the centuries by wind and workers into an open air cathedral of stone. The entrance to the training ground for the men of the House of the Lost Sea was a huge man-made arch that was carved with images of sea creatures both real and imagined. The Temple overlooked the sea like a ruined crow's nest. On the four corners of the temple jagged rock spires reached toward the sky. The floor of the Temple was forty feet long by thirty feet wide. Generations of Sang men had trained and fought and died on this harsh unforgiving proving ground. On each side of the temple were rough seats that looked more like steps. Members of the House, all men, filled the seats as Taang accompanied his father through the arch. Liu stood at the far end of the Temple. Unbound now, he held a Chines dao sword in his hand. Three and half feet long with a curved quillon hand guard and leather bound hand with an open hoop on the pommel, it gleamed in the orange setting sun. Tong Sang was carrying the Chinese broad sword. Wider than the dao and heavier it was an imposing weapon in its own right.

Tong removed his plain white pullover shirt. His broad brown chest and back bore dark scars from other battles, other wars. Taang was his father's son. They were both tall and wide with huge deltoids muscles. Tong held the sword in his right hand. He waved it back and forth in front a few times. Liu held his dao in his right hand extended out in front of him. No one spoke. Taang stood near the arch listening to the sea crash against the island. Sea gulls cawed to each other above the temple's spires. The wind ceased.

Liu screamed. It was a guttural sound more like an animal than a man. He ran toward Tong forty feet away. Thirty feet. Twenty feet Ten feet. Five feet .The dao held above his head swing toward Tong's neck.

Tong blocked his strike with the broad sword while at the same time moving toward his left .He spun away from Liu and kept spinning until he was behind him. He stabbed forward with the broad sword but Liu brought the dao up behind his back, blocked the thrust, and spun away from Tong. Tong pressed forward thrusting the broad sword at Liu's mid-section. Liu blocked each thrust. His dao moving so fast it cracked the air like a whip. Tong feinted a thrust and Liu readied a block. Instead Tong swung the blade one handed like a back hand slap at Liu's neck. Liu leaned away from the strike until the back of his head was mere inches from the floor. Tong brought the blade back and Liu pushed off the balls of his feet and back flipped .He landed in a split and stabbed forward at Tong's ankle. The wickedly sharp edge of the dao split the skin around Tong's ankle wide open. A stream of scarlet started flowing from the wound. Tong leaped into the air and front flipped. Midair he rotated his body so that when he landed he was facing Liu. Liu spun his legs up and around like a helicopter and landed on his feet. He pressed what he thought was his advantage. He slashed the dao at Tong's head. The larger man brought the broadsword up and stood his ground. He swatted Liu's thrust away as a man would wave away a fly at a picnic. Liu was grunting and panting as Tong blocked every one of his attacks. Liu slashed at Tong's legs. The older man jumped above the blade like it was a child's rope. In mid -air he kicked with his left leg and his foot connected with Liu's chest. The younger man was driven backwards. Tong moved forward. He slashed at Liu's head with the broadsword. He raised it over his head and brought it down toward Liu. Liu raised his dao to block the strike. At the last minute Tong let go of the blade and flipped it at Liu. The pommel cracked into his forehead, splitting the skin there. A wide wound opened on Liu's head. The handle struck him so hard that it bounced back toward Tong.

Tong caught the sword. As the blood filled Liu's eyes, Tong slashed at Liu's midsection from left to right like a maestro conducting an orchestra. Liu jumped back but not quite fast enough. A crimson line appeared across his bare stomach. Liu quickly backpedaled toward the far wall near the entrance. He ran backwards faster and faster. Taang had watched as his speed and momentum allowed him to basically walk up the wall up to eight feet in the air. He then launched himself off the wall and over Tong's head. He tucked his head down and rolled head over feet until he landed on his feet. Tong ran at him. Liu held the dao in front of him and had his right hand behind him taking a defensive stance Tong ran at his nephew. He didn't scream .He didn't yell. When he was three feet away he suddenly leaped into the air and to the right. His right foot touched the craggy wall of the Temple for a brief moment. He pushed off the wall with a barely a grunt. His enormous bulk flying through the air was a sight to behold. As he came down, heading toward Liu he turned his body. He switched the broadsword from his left hand to his right hand in mid-air.

Maybe it had been the blood in his eyes, or maybe it was the pain from the gash on his stomach but Liu didn't move the dao fast enough. Tong came down behind him .As he landed he slammed the edge of the broadsword into Liu's left shoulder and collarbone. The broadsword sliced through muscle and bone effortlessly. Liu's left arm fell to the floor of the temple. The dao clattered on the floor as the hand which held it flopped upon the ground. Gallons of red water blood spewed from the gaping maw that had been Liu's arm pit. Liu stepped forward a few steps then fell face first onto the floor. Taang felt a pang of something pull at his insides. Not grief exactly but a wistfulness. He had liked Liu.

"Taang what is going on!!"

Taang turned and saw Lilian standing just outside the archway. Tanchu was holding her right hand. Tenchu was holding her left. Her eyes were bulging from their sockets. Taang grabbed her roughly and pulled her down the embankment away from the Temple. He held her tight.

"Taang what the fuck is going on?" Taang didn't speak. He just pulled her down the beach away from the Temple. Tenchu and Tanchu followed their parents. They kept up quite well for one year olds.

Once they were out of listening range for anyone at the Temple Taang took Lilian's face in his wide hands.

"My love. What do you think you saw? It was just a sparring exercise. Fencing is a hobby for many of us here." he said as soothingly and calmly as he could.

"No uh uh don't talk to me like you trying to get me to do anal Taang. I just saw your father, my children's grandfather, cut Liu's arm off!! Liu was in Manila with us last year when I found out I was

pregnant. He is your cousin. Taang what the hell is going on?" she
screamed.

"Please stop yelling Lil. Please."

"I just saw a man get cut in half. You're lucky I'm not running into
the ocean screaming. Taang I'm not stupid. I know you and your family
are not just a salvage crew. Give me some credit. But....damn Liu has
changed these boys' diapers!" Lilian said as she pulled Taang's hands
away from her face.

Taang stared at her. He could see something in her eyes,
something fearful and sad. He took a deep breath. He didn't like seeing
that look in her eyes. He stroked her cheek and moved her long, curly
hair away from her cheek.

"My family and I are not a salvage crew. We take what we want.
Some people would call us...pirates. Rarely there are disagreements
about how the results of our endeavors are divided. What you saw
today was how we settle disagreements here. I have hidden this from
you for the last two years and I am sorry. But the way you are reacting
has confirmed I did the right thing," Taang said. Lilian pushed his hand
away and turned her back to him.

"Taang. I am no saint. I have done things that I wish I could erase
from my mind. But this....I don't know...I just don't know Taang," she
said. Her shoulders had slumped and her head was hanging low.

"There is more," Taang said. Lilian turned and to face him.

"More?" she said. Taang ran his hands through his hair.

"We are a part of a brotherhood. We meet every one hundred
years to defend our way of life from those who would take everything
from us. It is a commitment that overrides all others. Our family has

belonged to this brotherhood for over a thousand years. There may come a time very soon when I am called upon to defend our way of life with my life. Lilian everything we have, our home, this island, is tied to this brotherhood. I know this is confusing but it is real and it is very, very important," Taang said in one long breath. Lilian balled up her fists and shook them in at the sky.

"You know how crazy that sounds right? I mean you know that just sounds insane right? I just don't know. I don't know if I want our sons around this," she said.

"You fell in love with me and I was around this. You came here to live with me and you have lived around this. Lilian this is who I am."

"I don't care Taang! I have to protect our boys. No one ever protected me and look what happened. I don't want my boys to go through what I went through," she said.

"What are you saying Lilian? You want to leave? I can't let you do that."

"What do you mean you can't let me? Am I a prisoner now Taang? Is that what you are saying to me?" she said. She put her hands to her face. Tears began to run down her cheeks. Taang stepped forward and took her small hands in his large ones.

"You think this is about you and me? Lilian my family robs freighters and cargo ships. People on those ships don't always cooperate. Millions and millions of dollars of merchandise flow through this island. We break at least sixteen international laws every minute. My father would not allow anyone to leave the House of the Lost Sea. Not even the mother of my children. Do you understand my meaning?"

"You would let him hurt me? The same way you let him kill Liu?

What about our kids? Oh my God what the fuck am I doing here? I was better off on the street." She began to walk away from Taang and her children. She walked toward the main house.

"Lilian!" Taang yelled. He yelled her name again but she just kept walking. Lilian had gone into the main house and opened a bottle of wine and started drinking. Five years later she stopped. Unfortunately it was because she was dead. She had either fallen or leaped from the Temple into the roiling sea. Her body had washed ashore a week later after being trapped in a grotto near the island. His kinsmen placed her on a funeral pyre and Taang spread her ashes in the Temple. A few years later his father died in his sleep. A peaceful death for a violent man. Taang couldn't help but think that somewhere his father was still disappointed. He had assumed leadership of the House and tried his best to raise his boys the way he had been raised.

Sitting in his office looking at the smooth black box on his desk he couldn't help but believe that what he had done had been the right choice. They were what they were meant to be. Men of the First Chaos, members of the House of the Lost Sea. They were killers, living by the way of the sword. Taang looked at his sons. He glanced around his office. He peered out his huge window .He watched his men unload the ship, watched as the soft white caps broke against the shore of the Island. This was his world. He was the unquestioned master here. His sons were heirs to his throne. He would be damned if anyone was going to take that away from him. He looked at his sons.

"Well let's see where the Men of the First Order will die." Taang said as he opened the box.

HAPTER SEVEN

Vivian Du Mor watched the rays of the morning sun break through her bedroom window like a thief wearing slippers. Her long red hair was spread out on her black silk pillow like a bloodstain. To her left was Seville and to her right was Marcel. At her feet was Noel. Seville and Marcel had been her personal slaves for a little over two years. Both were finely muscled men like living representations of Michelangelo's David. She ran her left hand over Seville's golden brown chest. His pectoral muscles rippled under his skin. Marcel stirred and turned so that he was facing her. He was a gorgeous man with strong Gallic features; a fine mouth and wide expressive blue eyes. His shock of hair that was so black it was almost blue trailed down his muscular back. Seville's hair was cut close in a Caesar style. It appeared to crinkle like fine suede in the sunlight. Noel turned and propped herself up on one arm and looked at Vivian.

"Mistress would you like me to go downstairs and tell the staff to prepare breakfast?" she asked as quietly as possible. Noel had been with her for ten years. She was a beautiful sprite of a woman. Her small fairy-like features were deliciously innocent with the promise of decadence hiding just behind her eyes.

"Not yet. I appreciate these quiet moments. I think they will be few and far between very soon," she said. Vivian had gotten a call from Carcone earlier. That was why she was awake. He had told her to go to her door; that the Invitation was there. God she had three of nature's most beautiful creatures laying in her double king sized bed and still his voice aroused her more than the warm bodies lying against her. Just the first vibration of his vocal cords made her golden palace moist with desire. He was without a doubt the coldest, most arrogant beautiful bastard she had ever met and a part of her loved him. Another part of her hated herself for feeling that way. He was married to her cousin. Her uncle Etienne had moved quickly to have Agrippina betrothed to Carcone as soon as she came of age. Her father Lucien had been too concerned about running the House of Love and Agony to worry about the daughter he viewed as a disappointment and her feelings. Vivian's mother had been little more than window dressing to her father. Arlene Lafuer Du Mor was just a convenient way for Lucien to hide his ferociously amorous homosexual lifestyle. He rolled the dice once with Arlene hoping for a boy to carry on his family name. When Vivian came out of her mother's womb sans penis Lucien lost all interest in his wife and never found a reason to be interested in his daughter. After Agrippina's summer in Italy and her engagement to Carcone Vivian resigned herself to being an old maid. She committed herself to studying the way of the sword. Somewhere deep inside she thought maybe this would be the thing that brought them together. Yet even this, the fundamental foundation of their immense wealth and influence could not bridge the gap between her and Lucien. He never forgave her for not having a truncheon between her legs. His love of the penis extended to even his progeny. So Vivian practiced alone in the basement of the Du Mor mansion near Versailles. She studied the Book of Seven Swords with a religious fervor. She took lovers. Men at first, then women, then men and women. The mindless sex and the relentless practicing seemed to take her mind off of Carcone. He of the pitiless eyes and cocksure swagger. She had been enamored of him since she was seven years old. He and his father had attended the Bilderberg Conference as had Lucien and Arlene and Vivian. The

Bilderberg Conference was a very subtle cover for the Men of the First Chaos to meet and exchange pleasantries and sign treaties and make deals that affected the lives of nearly every person on earth. It was during these times her father came the closest to actually acknowledging her. He genuinely seemed to enjoy discussing the power the Men of the First Chaos wielded. At seven she had seen the young boy, a few years older than her playing in the courtyard of the Bilderberg Hotel with the dark hair and the tanned skin. Even then you could see the strength he would one day possess in his arms and shoulders. He was walking on his hands even though the air was frigid. She had been standing by the door when he fell and landed hard on his butt. She had let out a light giggle. He had immediately jumped up and stared at her.

"Oh you think you can do better?" he asked. Vivian stuck her tongue out at him and immediately began to walk on her hands. She was oblivious to the fact her dress had fallen down to her face as she walked and her daisy covered panties were out for the world to see.

"She loves me she loves me not!" Carcone had said laughing. At first Vivian had not understood what he was laughing at. Then she remembered she was wearing her favorite pair of undies with the daisies on them. She flipped forward landed on her feet and started walking out of the courtyard. She got to the door and turned and licked her tongue at Carcone again. He laughed.

"You were really good. Not better than me but good," he had said with a twinkle in his eye. Time had passed and Carcone had grown and so had Vivian. They only saw each other at the Bilderberg meetings and had never exchanged address or phone numbers. Seeing him at the meetings had been her Christmas, her birthday, and

Mardi Gras all rolled up into one. When Etienne and Carcone's father Carlos announced his engagement to Agrippina at the gathering in 1991 Vivian wanted to throw up in her dinner plate.

Two years after their nuptials The Apothases visited the Du Mor estate for a holiday celebration Etienne was there looking as dapper and stylish as a character in a Noel Coward play. Lucien was there as well but he didn't look nearly as good. His skin was sallow and slack and he had been fighting a case of pneumonia for months. Carcone and Agrippina swept into the Du Mor mansion like a storm of wedded bliss. Their affection was nauseating to Vivian. Finally she could take it no more and excused herself from dinner and walked down to the stables. Herod, her fine Lipizzaner stallion, was eating oats as she entered the stable and turned on the light. She entered his stall and started to brush his coat with a stiff bristled brush. The strokes reminded her of strikes she made with her epee when she trained, long fluid movements that capitalized on her gymnastic strength and dancer's flexibility.

"He is a beautiful animal. Strong and wild like his mistress," a deep rumbling voice said outside the stall. Vivian whirled around and saw Carcone standing there. He was wearing his tuxedo but the bow-tie was undone. The white shirt was stretched tight over his flat belly and broad chest. His hair fell to his shoulders. His pale blue eyes seemed to bore through her.

"I am not wild," she said softly. Carcone came up to the stall and leaned on the gate.

"Oh you are wild. I remember a girl who did a handstand and didn't care that anybody saw her rose-covered panties," he said grinning. Vivian turned her head.

"Daisies," she said.

"What?" His forehead wrinkled.

"The panties I had on that day had daisies on them. Perhaps if you were more observant you would have remembered correctly." Her sarcasm was intentional. She wanted to strike out at him even though she knew he probably had little choice in marrying Agrippina. Carcone frowned even more.

"You have a smart fucking mouth."

"I have a smart mouth. It only fucks when I want it to," she said. Carcone looked confused. Did he not understand he was talking to a scion of the House of Love and Agony? Her forefathers had provided concubines for Cyrus the Great .Her fore mothers had brought kings and queens to their knees trembling with pleasure. Sex was an art and the members of the House of Love and Agony were grandmasters of every style. They could use the human body as a canvas. They could paint sweeping orgasmic vistas or dark and disturbing still lifes of pain and degradation. Here in this stable he was a fly and Vivian was a spider and she would suck him dry...if she chose to do so.

"Do you want to?" Carcone asked. His breath was coming quickly. Vivian didn't respond. She was wearing a mauve evening gown with spaghetti straps. Despite the heated stall her nipples were still hard. Her luxuriant hair was piled on top of her head in an up do. She turned to face him.

Hooking both her thumbs in her straps she pulled them down over her shoulders and freed her pale full breasts. Her pink nipples were hard enough to cut glass. Carcone grabbed the stall and prepared to hop over it but Vivian held up her hand. Dismissively she waved him back from the stall door. She kicked off her high heels and took off running toward the gate. She took one hop then pushed off the floor with her powerful thighs. She sailed over the gate with her arms outstretched in a swan dive into Carcone's waiting arms. He caught her effortlessly. She wrapped her strong legs around his waist and forced her tongue into his mouth. She felt him pull at the pins in her hair as she felt him stiffen against her crotch. He spun around and slammed her against a wall covered with tack materials. A few bits and riding crops fell off the wall to the floor. Vivian pulled at Carcone's shirt trying to rip the buttons. He grabbed her hands and pinned them to the wall. She was still wrapped around his waist like an anaconda.

"No, Agrippina will notice torn buttons," he said breathlessly. Vivian smiled at him.

Suddenly she leaned in and shot her head forward like a cobra, seizing his bottom lip in her teeth. She bit down. Hard. Hot coppery blood squirted in her mouth. Carcone pushed her legs down and backed away from her.

"You crazy bitch you bit me!" he yelled. Vivian laughed.

"Oh poor Carcone are you so used to Agrippina just lying there and taking that Greek sausage without a whimper or a moan?. I like to bite Carcone. If you are afraid of fangs best not try to fuck a lioness," she said laughing. She pulled her strap up and over her shoulders. A dark cloud moved across Carcone's face. He stepped toward her with his right hand raised. He swung at her face intending to slap that smile off her churlish face. Vivian leaned back at the last minute and Carcone missed her completely.

"Oh now my dear Carcone you have to be quicker than that. Perhaps I've misjudged you," she said giggling. She turned and started to walk to the door of the stable. She heard Carcone running at her. His footsteps reverberated in the old wooden building. She was ready for him. She would give him a nice spin kick to the rib when he grabbed her arm. This was fun! She felt like cat playing with a mouse. Suddenly his footsteps stopped. / Vivian heard the stall creak like a strong wind was battering it. She looked up .Carcone had jumped into the air and grabbed one of the rafters that ran across the roof. In a feat of acrobatics she had not expected him to be capable of; he flipped over her head end over end until he landed in front of her, blocking the door. He grabbed her by her arms and kissed her again. Hard. She bit his lip again. This time he did not pull away.

"I am a lion. It's fitting I take a lioness," he growled.

"Then take me you bastard." Vivian said thickly.

Later he talked about his marriage to Agrippina.

"She is smart and beautiful. But she is just so.....empty. Something happened to her when she was in Italy. Something that damaged her. We barely touch each other," he said sadly. They were sitting among the jostled tack materials. They were both breathing hard. Their first coupling had been hard and fast yet mutually satisfying.

"You don't have to lie to me Carcone. I enjoy fucking you. I will continue to fuck you. My cousin notwithstanding," she had said with a laugh. Carcone turned his head and looked down the long line of stables.

"No I am serious. There is something missing with her. She knows what drink to have at a cocktail party with our board of directors. She can organize a gala dinner with the Prime Minister so that we can secure tax breaks. But when I look into her eyes, when I try to touch her, there is nothing but emptiness there. Lifeless eyes like the gaze from a pig." His voice had dropped an octave. Vivian rubbed his thigh.

"Well the next time you can take out all your pent up aggression on me," she said as she rose. She straightened her dress and piled her hair back on top of her head. Carcone looked up at her.

"Oh so you want there to be a next time?" he asked. A grin ran across his broad face.

"There will be a next time as long as I desire there to be one," she said as she stalked out of the stables.

That was how it was between them for the next five years. Then Louis entered her life.

Lucien wanted her to marry. He suggested Louis Crisp like one would suggest a Mercedes Benz as a mode of transportation. As he lay on his death bed he finally talked to his daughter about their responsibility to the Brotherhood.

"No woman has ever fought in the Duel of Generations. I cannot impress upon you how important it is that we not only fight in the Duel but we win. Our life, our legacy is inexorably tied to the Covenant. I know you practice my dear. I've seen you in the wine cellar. I've watched you run the along the horse trails. But there has never been a record of any woman fighting for a House. We need male heirs. You need sons. Train them as you have trained yourself. The Men of the First Order would take all that we have and throw it on a bonfire of their vanities. They and their puritanical devotion to the 'common good', bah I spit on the common good. What good is it to be common? Better to be extraordinary. They look down upon us you know. Call us whoremongers, pimps, hedonists. I say yes we are that and more and I have never felt an ounce of shame for what we are. The same Men of Order who deride our way of life spend their meager earnings in our brothels. They come to us like all that come to us. With sin in their hearts and their cocks in their hands," Lucien had said before a fit of coughing descended on him. His face turned bright red. Vivian had sat next to his bed with her legs crossed. Her face was impassive as he coughed. She did not offer him the glass of water sitting just outside his reach. She did not jump up and pat him on his frail back. She sat there in her black leather stiletto boots and black mini-skirt and a gray sarong type shirt that wrapped around her lithe frame like a second skin. She watched as he finally regained control of his breathing.

"If that you were born a man. But we must deal with the situation we have been handed. Louis would be a good husband for you. Not the exciting, dashing fantasy you think you deserve but a good solid man in your life. He will give you sons; those Crisp boys are nothing if not fertile. And full of stamina," her father said with a wicked smile.

"I have asked Barton to arrange for you two to meet. It is my dying wish that you marry this man. You may keep your lovers, yes my dear I know all about them, but you must marry Louis and bring to the House of Love and Agony men to defend her." Lucien said. He lay back and closed his eyes. The advancement of his condition left him very weak. Speaking for such an extended period time was hard for him. He wouldn't tell anyone in the family or the Brotherhood what was killing him but Vivian had her suspicions. She believed his random carousing and indiscriminate sexual proclivities had finally caught up with him. Contrary to what her father thought she was fully aware of the importance of male heirs and how they helped her standing with the other Houses. Louis Crisp was a reasonably attractive man with a spine the consistency of a marshmallow pie. Marrying him was an idea that had crossed her mind two years ago when she saw him staring at her and nearly salivating at the last meeting of the Houses at the Bilderberg. Legitimize herself in the eyes of the other House prefects and also solidify her standing with the board members of Aeon Holdings, the parent company of their pornography studios. The brothels were owned wholly by members of the Du Mor family. She had been running them for three years now, ever since her father took a turn for the worse. Uncle Etienne was at the helm of Aeon Holdings, but having a husband would make her appear more mature to the board. Yes it was an idea that had crossed her mind. She leaned forward.

"I will marry Louis and I will have babies with him. And I will be the first woman to be the prefect of a House. While you ran the streets of Paris sticking your dick in any pretty young stud who glanced your way I have been honing my craft. I have studied the Book of Seven Swords. I have consolidated my support at Aeon and within the structure of our dens of inequity. And I will continue to have my lovers. I will do all this and more. If you had ever stopped to look, to really look at me you would see that I am more than capable of leading this House even without a penis," she whispered. She stood .Her father gazed at her with wonderment in his eyes. She turned and walked out of his room.

"Everything alright, Ms. Du Mor?" a nurse asked as she glided out the room.

"Perfect my dear. By the way you did receive the release my father signed correct?"

"Yes ma'am .He does not want any extraordinary efforts taken to save his life. We have his DNR on file," the nurse responded with a bright smile.

"Good." Vivian said.

Her marriage to Louis was the social event of the year in Paris. Captains of industry, celebrities, politicians, anyone who was anyone or wanted to BE someone came from far and wide. The fact that many of these people could not explain in public how they knew the Du Mors did not keep them away from the festivities.

As she sat on the dais at her reception she saw Carcone in the audience. Carcone raised his champagne glass toward her. He did not do anything as unseemly as wink or blow a kiss. But he did dip his index finger in the champagne and then put it to his lips. He licked the champagne off his finger. Vivian nodded her head. They had met in the coat room an hour later. He had taken her against the wall .Her hands holding on to the closet pole .Her mouth buried in his neck as she screamed her orgasm into his firm trapezius muscle. He came inside her like cannon. She felt her body fill with his hot seed. He spit in her face when he came. She spit back. Then she bit his lip. Hard.

Nine months later her first son Henri was born.

Febre followed soon after.

The day Louis found out about their affair had started much like all the other days of her life since her father passed. She arose at eight. Louis was in the downstairs bedroom. She had told him she had a migraine and absolutely needed peace and quiet. She went to the kitchen in their mansion and had the cook prepare a boiled egg and her special blend of Kopi Luwak coffee. She would go to the actual House of Love and Agony in downtown Paris. A nondescript two story building that served as the epicenter for her vast erotic empire. The offices for Aeon Holdings were in Lyon. A world away but Vivian kept her finger on the pulse the goings on there as well. Louis wandered in and the cook made him his usual. Steamed cod fish and Brussels sprouts. He had a glass of white wine and prepared to go into his law office. He was a patent and contract lawyer and had moved his office from England to France when they had married. He had also changed his name to Du Mor to the chagrin of his great Uncle. Vivian had cajoled and seduced him into doing it when they first decided to get married. She could be very persuasive. And Louis was eager to please. He was a short man with a full meaty face. Not fat exactly but not fit. He had a rather large mouth but a wonderfully expressive smile and a hearty laugh. His sandy brown hair sat on top of his head in a heap. She kissed him on the forehead as she prepared to dress for the day. Once she was done with that she called for her driver to meet her at the front door.

Her driver took her to the House. She went in to her office and Noel was waiting for her there. She sat in the high back leather chair and put her legs up on the desk. Noel was dressed in a smart, modest black skirt and matching blazer. She entered Vivian's office and closed the door behind her. She dropped to the floor on all fours and crawled toward Vivian.

"Slower." Vivian said without looking towards Noel. Noel slowed her pace. Finally she crawled under the desk and between Vivian's legs. She stayed there for thirty minutes. Once her slave had given her a proper tribute Vivian had gone about the business of running her business. She reviewed financial reports from all the brothels from London to Berlin and everywhere in between. She studied the budget reports from Aeon Holdings. She signed off on donations and contributions to various politicians to ensure that the House of Love and Agony could operate without the meddlesome interference of the legal authorities. She had discussed with Noel that week's interviews for new escorts. Once upon a time the House had gathered their escorts from the white slavers of Albania but Vivian had ended that practice. Not out of any moral compunction but just because it made good business sense. She didn't need vengeful relatives bursting into her establishments looking for a long lost drug addict daughter. The House now acquired women from their porn studios or from the disillusioned expatriates that seemed to populate Europe in the late nineties like a plague of lost puppies. They also employed men for the enjoyment of their more progressive customers. Self-assured women who didn't have the time to find a viable man and dress him up shave his back and take him to an elegant business dinner. Women who were not inclined to try and teach a man both the art of small talk and how to please her body. Vivian provided men who were educated in proper dining etiquette and tantric sex.

After attending to the pressing business matters that day she had made two phone calls. One was to Carcone. He was in town to negotiate the building of a new ammunition factory in the French countryside. He was ensconced at the Humanne Hotel in downtown Paris. He and his assistants had commandeered the entire fifth floor, including all of the suites, the gym and the meeting rooms. During the call he assured her that he would be the only person on the fifth floor. He had given his staff the afternoon off to prepare for that evening's meetings. She had a made a second phone call to Louis.

Her driver had driven her over to the Humanne. A light rain had begun to float down from the clouds. A street performer was out in front of the Hotel. He was an ugly young man strumming a guitar. His voice was as gorgeous as his face was hideous. He was singing Je Ne Regrette Rien by Edith Pilaf. Vivian walked through the lobby went straight for the elevator. She had hummed the little tune she had just heard as the elevator creaked and whirred. It reached the fifth floor and the doors wheezed open asthmatically.

She walked down a dimly lit hall over a plush brown carpet. She passed door after black lacquered door to rooms that she knew were empty. Finally she reached the end of the hall and faced the board room. She had told Carcone she wanted to meet there. She wanted him to take her there on the huge oak table. She opened the black door and saw Carcone standing there. He was in a black turtle neck and tan pants. He squinted at her and smiled.

"Madam Du Mor you look like you need a good deep fucking," he said with a chuckle.

"Mr. Apothas perhaps you are the man to give it to me," she said as he pulled the pin holding her hair up out and threw it on the table.

They fell upon each other like animals.

Thirty minutes later Louis walked into the boardroom.

Vivian had been bent over the table with her skirt pushed up around her thighs. She heard the door creaked and watched as Louis entered the room. He was wearing his cream colored suit and carrying his briefcase. She had called his office and had spoken to his secretary. She didn't identify herself as his wife and the secretary didn't recognize her voice. She rarely called Louis during the day. She had told the secretary that she was an assistant for Carcone Apothas and that they needed his services as a contract lawyer and to meet Mr. Apothas in the boardroom.

Louis stood there watching her get fucked .She locked eyes with him for a few seconds before she started screaming.

"Oh God, Louis!" she wailed. Carcone stopped thrusting and pulled out of her and stumbled backwards. He quickly pulled up his pants. Vivian stood up and smoothed down her skirt. None of them had spoken for a few seconds.

"Vivian, what are you doing?" Louis had said. His voice was even and soft but his face was turning a mottled red.

"Louis what are you doing here?" Carcone asked. He voice was deep and resonant. Vivian stood there with her juices running down her leg. Louis stood still as a statue. He was gripping his briefcase so tightly she could see the veins popping up on the back of his hand.

"I could ask you the same-thing Carcone. What are you doing? Here. With my wife?" Louis asked.

"Louis this isn't what it looks like," Vivian said.

"Really? Because it looks like my wife was getting fucked by her cousin's husband," Louis said. He shook his head side to side then slowly backed out of the room and closed the door. Carcone had grabbed her then.

"What the hell is going on Vivian? Why was he here?" he said. He pulled her toward him until their faces were just inches apart.

"I don't know Carcone. He must have had me followed. In the last few months he has become very belligerent and distrustful of me," she said quietly.

"Why, Vivian? You and I have been very careful."

"A few months ago Febre had an accident. He cut himself on an old piece of metal in the stables. We took him to the doctor. They ran some tests on him, completely as a formality and they discovered he carries the gene responsible for sickle cell anemia," she said. Carcone released her.

"So?" he said .His voice was barely a whisper.

"So the only two groups who can carry the sickle cell gene are African Americans and people of Greek Mediterranean descent. Ever since then he has been behaving abhorrently. He has questioned whether either of our sons is his. He has threatened to take me to court for paternity tests. He has threatened to divorce me and take my fortune and take have the Men of the First Chaos take my sons and have them put up for adoption." A small tear slipped down her cheek.

"That is foolishness. First of all he is those boys' father and if by some trick of fate he wasn't what business is it of the old men?" Carcone said. Vivian wiped away the tear.

"You forget his great uncle is Barton Crisp. Prefect of the House of Poison Soil. Nominal head of the Fraternity to the Men of the First Chaos. He wields a great deal of influence. He knows judges and politicians"

"So do you, Vivian." Carcone had said. Vivian shrugged her shoulders.

"Yes but I'd have to threaten them. Barton can just pay them. And our house is in disarray. Lucien is dead, Carcone. We have no male heirs of age and my Uncle Etienne is not the man that can uphold our honor or our responsibility to the Brotherhood in the midst of me fighting a divorce and custody battle. Now having seen us he has his proof. He is probably on his way to talk to his uncle now. Unless..."

"Unless what Vivian?" Carcone said. His voice had betrayed his wariness.

"You could challenge him to an honor duel. Now. Today. You could go to the old men and plead your grievance. He would be honor bound to accept .You both would then be bound by tradition from speaking about your dispute until the day of the duel. You would win and then both our problems are solved," she said. She had caught his gaze and held it. Carcone shook his head.

"No. I don't have a problem. You do. Your cousin is not going to ever divorce me. She has become accustomed to a certain lifestyle and our pre-nuptial agreement is ironclad. I am going to assume yours is not." He kept her gaze.

"I will not kill your husband for you," he said as he ran a hand through his thick hair. Vivian touched his arm.

"So you would see your children sent to live with strangers?"she asked as she touched his arm. He grabbed her hand and twisted her wrist backwards.

"Stop saying that! They are not my children! I will not do your dirty work Vivian. Not because I am afraid to spill blood but because I will not be drawn into your machinations. Now I think you should go. You should find a good lawyer," Carcone had said as he released her. Vivian pursed her lips and closed her eyes. She had been prepared for this.

She had left and gone home to confront Louis.

He had been sitting in their den in front of the fireplace. There was no fire burning there .Just the mute blackened bricks and the weathered old log grate. He was sitting in a Queen Anne chair with his back to the door. He had sat up straight when he heard her stilettos tapping across the wooden floor.

"I remember when we first met that night at the Bilderberg. My great uncle had arranged for us to be seated next to each other. I had passed you a plate with those delicious blueberry rolls on it. I had watched as you applied butter to the roll. Then you licked the blade. I thought you were the most beautiful and exciting woman I had ever met. When my uncle suggested we go horseback riding together I knew that he and Lucien had come to some sort of understanding but I didn't care. I thought given enough time you would grow to care for me the way I cared for you. And I did love you Vivian. I loved the way you walked into a room like a panther. I loved your laugh. I loved that you didn't need me or my money. I didn't care how your family made their fortune. I see now how naive I was. I thought that what you did didn't define you. I thought the fact that you control a fortune literally built on the backs of broken and damaged young women and men didn't mean you yourself were broken and damaged. But I was so wrong. You are like a painting. Beautiful yet devoid of real human emotion. A work of art with no soul," he had said. Vivian had stood by the door and crossed her arms.

"You are so pathetic. You speak in saccharine homilies and metaphors when a real man would do something, anything, to show me his anger. But you are not a real man are you Louis? You are just this thing that scurries around the house like some small unknown rodent. You let your great uncle and my father force us together. You haven't slept in my bed for three years yet you still think you are Febres' father. You disgust me and have disgusted me for as long as I have known you. You are supposed to be a member of the House of the Poison Soil? A part of the Brotherhood of the Blade? You shame your House and yourself. Do you wonder why I let Carcone take me? Because you never tried, Louis. You never tried." She saw his shoulders tremble. He had started crying. She walked up to the chair and bent down over the back and whispered in his left ear.

"Henri isn't yours either."

Then she had left the room.

The next day Louis had sent word to all the Prefects of the Houses of Chaos that he had challenged Carcone Apothas to an honor duel. As was custom he did not disclose the reason for the challenge .Carcone had accepted. As Vivian had known he would. The duel was held in the wine cellar of the Du Mor mansion. Henri and Febres had been taken away to spend the weekend with their cousin Carcine. All the prefects were there as well.

Barton Crisp, Taang Sang from the House of Lost Sea, Abdul El Aki from the House of the Black Rivers. Silas Boon from the House of The Eternal Apothecary, Karl Lutenburg from the House of the Golden Tears, and of course Carcone and Etienne. Vivian was not yet the Prefect.

Vivian could not divorce Louis. They did indeed have a pre-nuptial agreement and it granted Louis a huge chunk of her fortune. A divorce would also have left her weak in the eyes of the Men of the First Chaos. Her father was dead. She had her heirs. She had no use for Louis anymore. Once he was out of the way she would deal with Etienne.

Vivian had watched as Louis entered the wine cellar. He was wearing a loose fitting black shirt and tight breeches. He did not look at her. Carcone entered next. He was wearing a tight black t-shirt and loose fitting brown pants. He glanced at Vivian. His face was grim.

As was tradition Louis had made the challenge so Carcone was given the right to choose the swords. He chose the rapier. A real rapier, not one used in competitive fencing. A wickedly sharp thin bladed weapon. In the right hands it could bring death as quickly as a gunshot. Carcone was wearing a leather glove with a wrist gauntlet. Louis had gloves on both hands. Barton Crisp stood in the middle of the wine cellar. Louis was on his right and Carcone was on his left. The wine bottles had been temporarily removed and the shelves had been pushed back toward the wall in haphazard pile. Barton Crisp leaned on a black ebony cane with an eagle's head on the handle. He was wearing a black double breasted wool suit with a double Windsor knotted silk white tie over a black shirt. His snow white hair was clipped and combed straight back toward his neck. His light brown gunslinger eyes were not watery or yellow despite his advanced age. He took a deep breath.

"We are the Men of the First Chaos. We are men of the Brotherhood of the Blade. We are the first men to embrace the freedom of our own free will. We do not look to others for their approval or their interference. As is our custom when we have been slighted we rectify it among ourselves. Louis Crisp seeks satisfaction. Carcone Apothas has deigned to give it to him. This shall be a duel of honor. To the death. Cry Discordia!" Barton had said. His whispery voice carried in the confines of the wine cellar. All the prefects moved to left side of the room. Two young men that Vivian had not seen before came out of the shadows .They both carried a rapier. One carried it to Louis and handed it to him. The other gave his to Carcone. There was nothing between him and Louis .Carcone raised his rapier and put his left hand behind his back. Louis whipped the rapier from side to side then moved toward Carcone. Carcone did not move. He did not even look at Louis. He was staring at the prefects. At Vivian. Louis advanced on him and stabbed the rapier toward his chest. Carcone blocked the blow. The sound of steel against steel sent a shiver through Vivian's body. Louis slashed at Carcone's stomach. The larger man swung his blade down then to the right, blocking and parrying the blow. Louis began to swing the epee wildly toward Carcone's head, and toward his chest his legs. Carcone blocked every blow. All the while he never took his eyes off of Vivian. Louis backed up and spit on the floor.

"Fight goddam you! Fight you bastard!" he said. He was breathing hard. Carcone did not respond. Louis ran at him with the epee extended out in front of him. Carcone spun toward his right and out of Louis's path. As Louis rushed past him like a bull, Carcone tossed the epee in the air, did one complete revolution and caught it with his left hand. He then carved a gash in the back of Louis's left hamstring with the point of the rapier. His strike was so fast and so precise at first it appeared he had missed. Louis turned and took one step and collapsed on to his right knee. He put his hand to his left thigh and it came away bloody. He tried to stand but his left hamstring had been severed. He tried again and this time he did rise.

"Is that what you wanted Louis?" Carcone asked. His voice was calm almost soothing. Louis screamed.

"Go to Hell!" He charged at Carcone. He swung his rapier at Carcone's head. Carcone blocked the blow and then, using his own blade, forced Louis's blade down and around in a circular motion. Quickly he pierced Louis's hand with the point of his rapier. The rapier dropped out of Louis's hand .As it fell Carcone used his rapier to catch it and flip it toward himself. Carcone caught the sword in mid-air with his left hand.

Louis stood there in front of him .Red-faced and panting.

"I think the time has come to end this farce," Carcone said. He stabbed both blades into Louis' gut. He rammed the blades all the way into to Louis, down to the hilt. Louis let out a gasp, like the air being released from a balloon.

Carcone grasped each sword firmly. Then he pulled his hands apart. A wet ripping sound filled the wine cellar. The swords tore through Louis' midsection like it was made of paper. Carcone tossed them to the floor. They were streaked with blood and gore. Louis grabbed at his stomach with hands that suddenly seemed dumb and awkward. He tried in vain to keep his intestines from un-spooling onto the floor next to the epees. His eyes rolled back in his head and he fell backwards onto the floor with blood streaming down his legs.

The two young men that had brought out the swords came forward holding a blue tarp. They spread it on the floor and picked up Louis's body and placed him on top of it. They rolled him up and fastened the tarp with large zip ties. The assembled prefects began to disperse. There was a large bloody smear on the floor of the wine cellar. The stench of voided bowels was heavy in the air.

Carcone walked up to Vivian.

"I cleaned up one mess for you. I leave the other to your capable faculties," he whispered in her ear.

Vivian smiled. He was angry. Not because he had killed Louis but because he had been forced to do it. Carcone did not like being anyone's minion. Barton Crisp stood against the far wall. He tapped his cane on the floor.

"He will be found in an alley in Paris. You will tell his sons he died in a robbery. We will then take his body back to England. He will be buried at Westminster Abbey. As are all the Crisps," he said. He walked past Vivian and toward the steps. He stopped. He did not turn around.

"Lucien was so concerned about marrying you off he agreed to all our demands and terms. Now not only do you escape the pre-nuptial agreement, you get Louis' shares in our family business. It seems I underestimated you." He turned to look at her. His eyes narrowed to pin pricks. "It seems we all did." Then he ascended the stairs.

Vivian had waited until all the prefects had left the estate then she walked upstairs and went to her den. She found Etienne there, drinking a from a bottle of Du Mor cognac. One of her grandfather's attempts to diversify their holdings. It was a rare vintage. At that time there had been only five bottles in the entire world. Vivian walked to the chair where her uncle was sitting and picked up the bottle. She took a swig and put it back down on the side table. Her uncle was staring straight ahead. He never even looked at her.

"Well you are free now my dear," he said as he sipped from his glass.

"Not quite. Today you will go to the board at Aeon and tell them that you have sold all your holdings to me. Then you will inform the other prefects in that I am now Mistress of the House of Love and Agony. You will then leave and move to our chateau on the Rivera. I will give you a monthly stipend of 25,000 for the rest of your life. Then uncle I will be free." Etienne laughed.

"Just because you whipped that tight little pussy on Carcone and had him do your bidding don't forget that you are a woman. No woman has ever been prefect of any House of the Order of Chaos! I will be going nowhere. What I will do is begin to have your sons trained for the coming Duel. A real duel with real consequences, not this sham you orchestrated today." he said.

"Uncle, you haven't held a sword in twenty years. It is you who has forgotten. Forgotten who we are and what we are. I have read the Book of Seven Swords. I have consulted with the Archivists. The Duel is indeed coming and I have no intention of losing. I will make sure my sons are trained .I will ensure we win .I will ensure The Men of the First Chaos continue to live in the way we are destined to live. And you would do well to take my offer."

"Or what?" Etienne sneered. He heard a sound then, a sound like the air being divided. He was not so far removed from his swordsmanship that he didn't recognize that sound. He stood and turned to face Vivian. She was holding one of the bloody rapiers in her hand. She had sliced it through the air and a few droplets of blood had landed on the right wall next to an original Degas painting.

"I am Vivian Lafleur Du Mor. I am Mistress of the House of Love and Agony. Say it." she demanded. Etienne laughed again.

"I will do no such thing. You're right; I haven't picked up a sword in a while. But I think I can best my little niece," he said.

Vivian gripped the rapier then moved forward. Her motion was so quick Etienne didn't have time to even attempt to move. She slashed at his arms, then his legs. She then slashed at the heavy crystal wine glass he had been holding.

She stepped back.

The sleeves of her uncle's fine silk suit had slid down to his wrist. The legs of his silk trousers had fallen to his ankles. The stem of the wine glass he had been holding fell to the floor and shattered.

Etienne had moved to the south of France the next day.

Now as she lay in her huge bed, surrounded by her slaves she ruminated on all that she had and all that she had done to acquire all that she had. She thought about Carcone. She had trusted him with training her sons. Their sons. The story she had told him about Febre's accident had been a lie but she had no doubt that Carcone was the father of her children. Now as the Invitation sat on her front step she wondered had that been wise. He did not believe they were his sons. Did that color his view of them? Did that in some way hinder his training of Henri and Febres? She didn't know. That troubled her greatly.

There was a knock on the bedroom door.

"Come in," she said. It was her assistant Gavin. He was a large man with a small man's voice.

"Excuse this intrusion Madame but I just received a call from the London house. There is a disturbance there. A man has entered the house and killed the bodyguards. He is holding one of the girls hostage in the ballroom. Madame the madam there told me he is rambling about Men of Chaos. He was asking for the Prefect of the House of Love and Agony." Gavin said. His eyes were rolling around in his skull.

"Tell them I am on my way. Do not call the police. We will take my private plane. I will be there in about thirty minutes. Gavin please pack a bag. And Gavin, please take care to pack my sword." she said.

Noel kissed Vivian feet. "Mistress, what is going on?"

"The quiet times are over," she said. The only people in England who would use the term Men of Chaos were either the members of the House of the Poison Soil or the members of the House of the Olde Grove who were Men of the First Order. She couldn't think of any reason why someone from the House of Poison Soil would be in her brothel killing her guards. So it had to be a member of the House of the Olde Grove. It had to be connected to the Invitations arriving. She did not believe in coincidence. She thought of Carcone again. She remembered a conversation they had had once. He had remarked that not every member of the Men of the First Chaos took their duty as seriously as he and Vivian did. He had also remarked that if the Men of the First Order did not appear at the Duel of Generations that might be the best thing for everyone concerned. He did not trust his fellow Men of Chaos. He did not trust their training .Perhaps he did not trust them to win?

"Oh my Carcone what have you done?" she thought to herself

CHAPTER EIGHT

Saito Kiku had been a member of the Clan of the Swift Death since age 13. His fellow ninja called him Joe, short for G.I. Joe because his father had been an American serviceman stationed in Okinawa in the 70's. His mother had been a young student who had committed suicide immediately following his birth. His grandparents had been doubly shamed. Shamed by his birth and shamed by his mother's suicide. So they had put him up for adoption. Master Kanto had come and plucked him out of the den of inequity that was the orphanage. He had given him a life and a purpose. He had given him a sense of honor and pride in his and his brother's abilities. He had even taught him English so he was the man who made the offer to Pretlow Creedence.

For all that his Master, his father had taught him, none of these things entered his mind in the last moments of his life. His only thought was this:

"The men of the Brotherhood are very, very fast."

Saito had watched as Pretlow's hand had moved toward the inside of his light jacket. Actually Saito had *tried* to watch Pretlow's hand. His hand moved so fast it was just a blur in the afternoon sunlight. Instantly a sword appeared in the tall man's hand like a magic trick. Saito could see it was a beautiful sword. It was a masterwork of bright silvery steel and smooth black leather on the handle. It had an ornate basket guard and two delicate cross guards just above the basket. Saito had not yet drawn his own katana. Pretlow stabbed him through his costume and pierced his heart. Saito felt the steel enter his rib cage like a shot of physical electricity. A pain filled his chest like an anvil was sitting on his sternum and then the world went black.

Pretlow barely had time to register the man in the middle falling to the ground. His compatriots had their katanas out of their scabbards and were on the attack. The two remaining men were dressed in different colored tunics. The one on the right was wearing a bright yellow and green checked tunic. The one advancing from the left was wearing a solid burgundy tunic. Burgundy had a two-handed grip on his sword and aimed a wicked strike at Pretlow's head full of morbid intentions. Pretlow blocked the blow and then slid sideways where he encountered Checked Tunic. Pretlow ducked under the strike from Checked Tunic and kicked at the inside of his right knee. The Checked Tunic went down to one knee. Burgundy tried to slide his katana between Pretlow's shoulder blades but Pretlow heard his boots on the dry grass and was able to swing Aequitas behind his back to parry the blade. While Checked Tunic was still on one knee Pretlow jumped onto his bent right knee. Checked Tunic almost appeared to be proposing marriage to an invisible bride. Pretlow climbed up the man's body like he was a rope ladder on a jungle gym. He stepped onto his shoulder and jumped into the air. In mid-air Pretlow spun his body so that he would land facing his adversaries. Burgundy leap-frogged over his brother with one hand on his heavy helm. He advanced on Pretlow swinging his katana in short wicked arcs. Pretlow matched him strike for strike. Burgundy feinted a slicing blow to the head and instead shoved the point of his blade toward Pretlow's chest. Pretlow blocked the attack with the basket guard of his sword.

"Gotcha," Burgundy thought to himself. He gripped his katana tight and using his wrist pulled up on the blade. At the same time he did that

Pretlow flicked a small button on the handle of Aequitas. Burgundy expected Pretlow's sword to go flying out of his hand. But only the basket guard flew into the air. Burgundy glance up toward the sky for an instant. He had barely registered that only the basket guard was flying into the sun when he felt a sharp violent pain in his chest.

Pretlow drove his blade through the man's chest and out his back. Checked Tunic was advancing again. Pretlow used his left foot to push Burgundy off his blade and drive his body into his compatriot. Checked Tunic jumped to the left side and executed a front flip. He avoided his fallen brother. He also reached inside his tunic as he flipped. He grabbed a handful of shurikens. As he completed the flip he squatted and hurled the shurikens at the tall man. He could see him clearly through his helm.

Pretlow watched as Checked Tunic dodged his fallen comrade with a beautiful front flip. Time seemed to be slowing down to a snail's crawl. Pretlow saw the man hurl something toward him. Flying pieces of metal...they were shurikens. The sun glinted off their five razor sharp points. The man had thrown six deadly throwing stars at him. Pretlow breathed deeply. He focused on the six flying metal blades. He raised Aequitas to block the onslaught. As the blades rushed at him, He moved his wrist six times in rapid succession. Each movement brought his blade in contact with the shurikens. Each contact caused the shurikens to ricochet away from Pretlow. Checked tunic ran behind his flying blades at Pretlow. He couldn't believe the tall man had blocked every shuriken like a man playing tennis with a toddler. He had to put that out of his mind. He had to complete his mission. He had to kill the tall man with the piercing eyes.

Checked Tunic stabbed his blade at Pretlow's upper chest, then stomach, then back to his chest. Pretlow moved his upper body back then to the left then back again. Checked Tunic, also known as Iko, had a moment to think to himself, "The bastard isn't even blocking my strikes anymore." That realization filled him with rage. And terror.

Pretlow dodged the man's blows by contorting his body the way he had been taught, the way he had practiced for over 25 years. As he leaned back the last time he struck at the man's hand with the tip of his sword. Aequitas cut through his leather gloves like a keel slicing through the water. The man seemed not to notice and kept moving forward. Pretlow brought his own sword under and around his opponent's blade. Using the strength in his forearm from countless push-ups and pull-ups and hand stands and one-arm curls and other arcane exercises, he pushed the man's sword hard to the left. His opponent followed his sword and began to spin. As he was completing his revolution Pretlow kicked at his fallen comrade's sword with his left toe. He kicked the katana up into the air. He grabbed it with his right hand while still holding Aequitas with his left.

Iko completed his spin and swung the katana as hard as he could like a baseball bat. His hope was to break the other man's sword. With his lacerated fingers he knew this was his last, best hope. His katana clanged against his opponent's sword. The man held Ayto's katana in one hand. This was what Iko's blade had struck. Iko felt a shock wave run from his the tips of his fingers up to this collar bone. The man's arm did not move one inch. The blade did not break. Iko saw his left hand move forward. Or he thought he *might* have seen it. He was so damn fast. He felt a shock of cold steel enter his lower abdomen and slide through his body like an icicle. The man pulled the blade out without a grunt or a groan.

Iko fell to his knees. He dropped his sword and put both hands over the wound in his stomach. Blood was pouring through his ruined fingers like water through a sieve. A hollow feeling filled his chest like when he jumped from the cliffs near Mt. Fuji to the rivers below. The helm no longer felt unbearably hot. Suddenly the pain his side and his hands and his arms were gone. He fell forward and lay still.

Pretlow surveyed the scene before him. Three dead assassins. He himself was unharmed.

Pretlow heard clapping.

He turned around and saw a large crowd on the other side of the brick wall. They were clapping uproariously. Some were hooting and hollering. There were young men and boys in the crowd, women of all ages, even small children. A sick feeling swept through his body. They thought what they had just witnessed was a part of the fair. From where they were standing they could not see the blood on his blade, or on the dry grass that seemed to be drinking it up like a man dying of thirst. The death of three assassins was just entertainment to this assembled audience. Three assassins.

"Oh no," Pretlow said softly. There were sure to be more than three assassins. His family was a six hour drive away. Pretlow ran for the far brick wall and cleared it without even putting his sword back in its sheath.

"Best reenactment ever!" a portly man in the audience said to his friend.

Catlow was shaking the hands of his students. The class was over and it had been a good one. He could see definite improvement in all his students. Even Edward Tessier who had two left feet and a sense of balance like a drunken donkey. Frank was in the back of the studio doing the same thing with his students.

"I really do like teaching..." Catlow thought to himself. There was an undeniable gratification in seeing his students make progress .Watching as they moved from their first tentative lunges to more complex angulations and fleches. It was rewarding in ways that his own training had never been. Harmony came over after all the students had filed out of the converted office space and put her arms around his waist. She stood on her tip toes to kiss him.

"Look at my man, all sweaty and stuff. Looking good there Zorro," she said with a smile.

"You wanna go down the street to The Lair?" Harmony raised her eyebrows. Catlow laughed.

"It's a vampire themed bar and grille. Creepy atmosphere but good food. I have about an hour before the next class starts." Harmony ran her hands up and down his muscular back.

"Hmm a whole hour? We should take my car," she said with a devilish twinkle in her eye. Catlow felt his face get hot.

"I don't think we will have time for that." he said with a shy smile. Harmony laughed.

"Cat, you never heard of road head?" Catlow smiled. He had never heard of road head but it sounded pretty dam good.

"Well let me go in the back and change clothes. I won't take a shower until this afternoon's class is over," he said.

Harmony kissed him again. "It's okay I like you sweaty." Catlow felt his face get even hotter.

The door chime rang. Three Asian men walked into the Academy. They were all dressed alike, long blazers over plain white button-up shirts and tan, loose fitting slacks. The blazers were all different colors. The man in the middle had on a black blazer. The man to his right was wearing a light navy blue blazer. The man on his left wore a garish red suede blazer. The blazers looked too big for the men. They were not tiny just compact. They appeared solid and wiry like gymnasts. The man in the middle was older than the other too. He had shoulder length salt and pepper gray hair. His face was pock-marked. The three men stood two feet apart. Something in the way they stood made Catlow uneasy. It was the militaristic way they stood. It spoke to training.

"Can I help you?" Catlow asked.

"Yes you can, Catlow Creedence son of Pretlow Creedence and Darnicia Barkarhat. Son of the Green Hills and Sand and Fire. You can help me. You can join your father in the afterlife," Kento said. He knew it sounded dramatic but this was a dramatic moment. He felt nervous. Excited. It was so rare in his travels as a member of the Clan of the Swift Death that he felt any sense of danger or tension. Most of his targets were dead before their bodies hit the floor. So little challenge to killing heads of conglomerates or Yakuza crime bosses. He hoped that in the men of the Brotherhood he had finally found an adversary worthy of his talents.

In truth he had not spoken to any of his sons since he had given the order to begin. He was not overly concerned about that fact. Missions were not neat little bows that could be tied up in a matter of minutes. He had the utmost confidence in his skills and the skills of his sons. He fully expected to receive a full report later from his sons.

When he and Hiro had met with the client he had asked why he had sought out the Clan. Surely there were trained mercenaries who could eliminate these men.

The client had laughed.

"These men would filet any mercs that got within ten feet of them. Snipers might get one or two but that would alert the others to our plans. No it needs to be a coordinated attack. If a merc tried to shoot one of these men they would slice his arm off before he got the gun out of the holster," the client had said.

"How can you be so sure?" Hiro had asked. The client had glared at him.

"Because that's what I would do." he had said finally.

Now standing before one of the targets Kento remembered those words.

Catlow heard what the man said but his mind did not want to comprehend it. He had spoken the names of the Houses that his mother and father had come from. He was a Man of the First Chaos. Or an agent for them. In the end it didn't make that much of a difference. He seemed to suffer under the same delusion as Pretlow. Catlow could see now why the men wore such baggy coats. They had on shoulder scabbards. He could just glimpse the handle of a katana just inside their jackets. It was a rig similar to the one Pretlow wore.

Catlow had one arm around Harmony .In his other hand he held a fencing saber. A dull blunted tool that was nearly useless in a real encounter. Catlow bent his head down toward Harmony and whispered "If anything happens run to the back of the studio. Go through the locker room toward the emergency exit." Harmony's heart was pounding in her chest. But she nodded her head. Catlow took his arm from around her and pushed her behind him. For some reason he didn't even give the statement the man had made about his father a second thought. Pretlow Creedence was delusional but in the midst of that delusion he had become an incredible swordsman. Catlow could not envision anyone beating him in a fair fight.

"I think you have me mistaken with someone else Sir." Catlow said. Kento stepped forward.

"No I have not. You are the son of Pretlow Creedence. You are a member of the Brotherhood of the Blade. And I have been looking forward to this for a very, very long time," he said. The studio was silent save for the sound of Frank showering in the back and the breathing of Catlow, Harmony, and the three Asian men.

Kento stared into Catlow's eyes.

Catlow gripped his saber. It felt silly in his hands now. His heart began to beat triple time. Was it possible? That everything he had been taught since he was born was true? Catlow pushed that thought away. It was inconsequential whether it was real. These men in front of him believed. He could see it in their faces.

Silence...

"You gentleman here to sign up for classes?" Frank asked from behind Pretlow. He had walked out of the locker room wearing a white t-shirt and jeans. It was his habit to walk across the street to Schlotzskys Deli for lunch before the next class came in. Even at fifty his firm physique could be seen under the tight embrace of the shirt.

The man in the suede blazer pulled a handful of shurikens out of his breast pocket and hurled them at Frank.

Catlow watched them fly through the air like metallic dragon flies, buzzing and whizzing as they went by his head. He turned and watched as they hit Frank. They sliced into him like scalpels. Five of them flew in a tight orderly grouping on his chest, in a straight line that went from his neck to his navel. His white shirt immediately began to turn red.

"Fuck." Frank said as he fell backwards.

Catlow reached behind him and pushed Harmony toward the back of the studio. She started to run then slipped on the polished wood floor. Blue blazer, Kento and Suede blazer all converged on Catlow.

A switch seemed to click in his head. Suddenly he was transported back to his back yard in Yorktown, Virginia when he was thirteen. He and his father and Uncle Saed and a man his father called Richard.

"Now when you are being attacked by multiple opponents what is the most important thing?" Pretlow had asked. Catlow gripped his longsword and answered.

"To engage the opponent on your terms. Dictate the fight. Use my speed and my strength to disrupt their rhythm .Don't try and get fancy. Just kill them all."

"Yes. Kill them all." Pretlow had said.

Suede Coat swung his katana at Catlow's legs .At the same time Blue Blazer swung at his head. Kento stabbed straight ahead at his chest. They were trying to get him what was commonly called a pincer movement. Catlow jumped up and above Suede Coat's attack while turning his body so that Kento's blade slid inside his fencing jacket. He could feel the face of the blade slide across his abs as it went through his jacket. The point exited right below his armpit. In the same moment Catlow blocked Blue Blazer's attack with the dull saber. As he came down he turned away from Kento. The katana cut through his jacket and exposed his belly. He was now behind Suede Coat. Catlow struck at his wrist as hard as he could. The blade didn't even break the skin. But a laceration was not his intention. His blow drove the man's wrist down toward the floor. The point of his katana became stuck in the smooth wooden floor. Catlow kicked hard at his wrist. He felt something snap. Blue blazer jumped up and over Kento and Suede Coat. He had his katana gripped with both hands. Catlow tossed the saber at him. He swatted it away with the katana. Catlow reached forward and grabbed Suede Coat by both wrists. He pulled him toward him as if in an embrace. He then spun him toward Blue Blazer like he was exchanging a dance partner. Suede Coat fell into Blue Blazer. He executed a hands free cartwheel to the left to get out of his brother's way. Catlow kicked at the hand guard of the katana. It popped free of the wooden floor. He caught it blind and then swung it with his left hand up and behind his back to block the strike he knew was coming from Kento. He leaned forward and dropped to the floor in a near completed split. Kento had not expected the split and had thrust his blade forward following Catlow's block.

His blade pierced Blue Blazer's throat. Kento's momentum and subconscious training carried him over Catlow's outstretched right leg. His face was splashed by Blue Blazers arterial blood. He extricated his sword from Blue Blazer's throat and spun around to face Catlow. Catlow was now standing. Kento could not believe how fast he was. He stabbed toward the younger man's leg. Catlow parried the blow and then pushed forward with a thrust of his own. Kento leaned backwards as far as he could until his hair brushed the blood-soaked floor. He raised his sword quickly and tried catch Catlow's extended arm. But the younger man had already pulled arm back and was now slicing the blade down toward Kento's crotch. Kento fell to his butt and spread his legs as far apart as he could. Catlow's blade slammed into the floor. He pulled the blade back up and advanced on Kento. Kento rolled backwards, soaking his jacket in his son's blood until he could pop up onto his feet. He lunged forward with his sword held shoulder high. He brought the blade downward. Catlow met his strike with a strike of his own. Kento felt the blades connect and sharp metallic sound filled the studio like a tuning fork pinging. Almost at the same time his blade connected with Kento's. Catlow spun to his right and allowed Kento to slip past him. In the middle of the spin he threw the katana from his left hand to his right hand. At the nadir of his revolution he brought the blade down and stabbed it backwards. Kento had turned and was aiming a strike at Catlow's back when he felt his son's blade enter his stomach. He felt it go through his large intestines. He felt it go through his stomach out exit out his back slicing through his right kidney. For a moment there was no pain. Then Catlow pulled the blade out and pain filled his mind. He stumbled and slipped on his and his son's blood. He landed on his side and rolled onto his back.

Catlow heard the jingle of what sounded like loose metal. He looked up in time to see Suede Coat swing the chain attachment from a weapon at his head. It was a kusarigama. Catlow held up his sword. It was a purely instinctual move. The long weighted chain wrapped around his sword like a python. Suede Coat tried pulling the sword out of Catlow's hand. For a moment a tug of war of life and death ensued. The other end of the kusarigama had a wicked hooked blade. Suede Coat pulled the chain taut. Catlow held fast to the sword. The chain seemed to hum like a piano wire. The pain was excruciating for Suede

Coat, whose real name was Li. He planned to pull the sword out of Catlow's hand but with his shattered wrist that was proving impossible. Better to release the tension on the chain and swing the chain around his head and slice his enemy with the blade on the end. He was just about to do just that when Catlow let go of the katana. The tension on the chain was so great the blade went flying toward Li.

He did not anticipate his enemy letting go. They were taught from an early age within the Clan to never let go of your weapon. He ducked as the blade came flying at his face. But he didn't duck quite fast enough. The katana sliced across his scalp before sticking in the wall behind him like a gigantic dart. He felt warm sticky blood trickle down his neck.

As he ducked down he advanced forward toward his foe. He had his head down so he did not see Catlow execute a one handed cartwheel. As he tumbled he used his free hand to pick up Blue Blazer's katana. As Li raised his head he swung the bladed end of his weapon at Catlow. It was coming around in a whistling arc. As Catlow completed his tumble he gripped the katana with both hands. He landed on his feet and his sword met the flesh between Li's shoulder and neck. He swung the sword as hard as he could. The blade sliced through Li on a diagonal line. It went through his spine, his sternum, his ribcage. His head, left arm and a quarter of his chest was separated from the rest of his torso. His head and left arm fell to the left. The rest of his body fell to the right. A waterfall of blood and viscera splashed across the dark oak floor. Almost absentmindedly Catlow caught the kusarigama blade with his right hand as his opponent fell to pieces.

Harmony had not made a sound. She couldn't. She could not

believe what she had just witnessed. Catlow had killed three men in less than five minutes. Not just killed them but fought them like some character in a Zorro movie. He had killed them and protected her. The fear in her heart began to give way to another feeling. Love. Love for this man. Her man. She rose from the floor and ran toward Catlow.

Kento was dying. The fact of his demise did not fill him with fear or dread. He had come to terms with the fact that he would not pass away in a comfortable bed years ago. The emotion that filled his mind in his last moments on earth was shame, not fear. He was ashamed of himself as a leader. He was ashamed of himself as a father. He had underestimated these men, this Brotherhood and his sons had paid the price for his arrogance. Li was dead. Cut in half by his own brother's katana. The boy had manipulated him into killing his own son. Kyoto's blood was in his mouth, and all because he had been overcome by a fatal hubris. Death was close now. The spirits of his ancestors were whispering in his ear. They were beckoning him to come across the great divide between this world and the next. He could feel the acidic burn of his own bowels poisoning his body. He had failed. This was an incontrovertible fact. He lay on his back holding his hand over the gaping wound in his gut. Slowly his hand slid from the wound to his pants pocket. Something hard and metallic was in his pocket. Shurikens.

Catlow dropped the katana and held his arms out to Harmony. Her face was beatific. Her pigtails were trailing behind her as she ran toward his waiting embrace.

Kento reached inside his pocket. Three shurikens. They were not his favorite weapon; he preferred the wakizashi or even the tanto. He turned his head and saw the young woman running toward Catlow. His failure could not be erased. His dead sons would haunt him in the next world. Perhaps someone else should join them. He gritted his teeth and propped himself up on his right elbow. He moved slowly. He had no choice. The pain was excruciating. Kento pulled the shurikens out of his pocket. Gripping them tight he mumbled to himself.

"Share my pain swordsman." He let the shurikens fly.

Catlow heard the whisper of something flying through the air. He hesitated for just a moment. Just a brief moment before he moved. He couldn't understand what that noise could be. All the attackers were dead. He turned to look at the man lying on his back near the entrance of the studio. He was propped up on one elbow. He had his hand extended. Catlow could see something spinning through the air. His cloak of concentration fell upon him and he could see they were shurikens. By the time he registered what they were they had reached their mark.

The three flying blades slammed into Harmony's throat. All three in a parallel line. Catlow heard a soft *pop pop pop* sound as they pierced her neck right below her left ear. Her eyes became as wide as saucers. Her forward momentum propelled her into his arms. A wet gurgling sound was emanating from her mouth. He caught her just as her legs went weak. They slid to the floor. Her life's essence was flowing out of her like a river of tears. Catlow cradled her in his arms. His mouth was open but no sound came forth. His face was trapped in a rictus of pain. Her hands flapped at his chest and face like lost butterflies trying to escape a glass jar. Catlow held her because he didn't know what else to do. Suddenly her hands fell to her sides. Her eyes stopped rolling around in their sockets. Catlow touched the metal stars with a trembling hand. He did not want to pull them out but he could not stand seeing them sticking out of her neck like some mutated quills made of steel. Catlow touched Harmony's face. It was still warm. But her eyes were dull and glassy like a doll's eyes. He laid her onto the studio floor. Tears, hot and salty, began to run down his cheeks. His mind felt fractured. It felt broken into a million little pieces. What had just happened? Attacked by katana wielding assassins and now Harmony was staring at the ceiling but not seeing the ceiling. He looked into her eyes once more. She was gone.

Catlow screamed then. Screamed from the bottom of his soul. Screamed and screamed and screamed. He was still screaming when he stood and laid her head gently on the floor. He was still screaming when he picked up the katana and walked over to Kento. Kento returned to a supine position. He was still alive. Catlow could see the subtle rise and fall of his chest. He stood over Kento. Kento's eyes fluttered open and he looked up at Catlow. He tried to speak, to say something pithy. He had the notion he would leave the young man with some acerbic parting quip before he transitioned.

Catlow raised the katana and then drove the point into Kento's mouth out the back of his throat into the floor. He heard a loud *crack* as the blade split the wood. Catlow looked around the studio. He felt as if he mind was a drum that had been beaten until the taut skin split. The large picture windows that faced the street in front of the studio were tinted a dark charcoal gray. No one on the street could have witnessed what took place in the Academy.

The phone on Franks' desk started to ring. It startled Catlow. He pulled the blade out of the floor and Kento's mouth and whirled around. On the second ring he realized it was just the phone. He walked over to the desk. Each step felt as if he was walking through cement. He grabbed the handset and put it to his ear.

"Hello," he said. His voice sounded hollow to him, as if he was speaking through a wind tunnel.

"Oh Catlow it's you mother. Son I know you are angry but you must come home. It's very, very important that we all be together until your father gets home," Darnicia said.

"She's dead,." Catlow said flatly.

"What? Catlow, who's dead? Son, who is dead?"

"Harmony. I thought I had killed them all but one was still alive. He.....he cut her throat with a throwing star. Oh God mama she is dead! They killed her!" Catlow chocked out. Darnicia heard his voice disintegrate into sobs.

"Oh Catlow. Oh my son. I am so sorry. Please come home. Please, until you father gets home. Listen to me my son. We are in a very precarious and dangerous situation. Your sister and I are here alone. Please come home," Darnicia pleaded into the phone.

"No mother. They are the ones in danger. When I find the rest of them, those responsible for Harmony, I am going to cut off their heads so that I know they are DEAD!" Catlow screamed into the phone.

"Catlow who are you talking about?"

"You know who I am talking about. The Men of the First Chaos. I am going to kill them all," Catlow said softly. "I'm coming home Mother." he said. He hung up the phone. He walked back over to Harmony's body. He knelt down beside her and closed her eyes. He saw all his dreams for a normal life die with her as the light had drained out of her eyes. He stood and went to the locker room and quickly changed into his street clothes. He had to go. He told himself that Harmony wasn't in the studio anymore. That it was just her body, just a vessel. The real Harmony was gone. He had to leave before the next class arrived and someone called the police. He had to stay out of jail. At least until he found the Men of the First Chaos and watched as the light went out of their eyes. Catlow came out of the locker room and knelt down beside Harmony's body. He kissed her forehead. It was still warm.

"I'm going to get them Harmony. I'm going to get them all. I'm so sorry. I love you. I will always love you. I'm going to kill them for you. I 'm going to kill them all. I promise you." he whispered in her ear. He stood. He felt dirty leaving her here. But his mother and sister were at home alone. He couldn't fail anyone else that he loved.

Catlow walked to the door. He stopped and looked back at the carnage he had wrought. Weeks later the Richmond Times Dispatch would call it "Massacre on Broad Street". Catlow felt fresh tears begin to trickle down his face.

"We could have had it good Harmony. I know that," he whispered.He opened the door and walked to his bike.

Pretlow was driving a hundred miles an hour down Interstate 95. The old green LTD was roaring like a dragon as he flew down the highway. Once in the car he had checked his cell phone and saw three missed calls from Darnicia. When he called her back the phone just rang and rang. He prayed to all the Gods of all the people of the world that she was just on the other line. He prayed that she and Calla and Catlow were still walking and talking and breathing. The time had finally come. All of his life he had trained and studied and waited for this moment. Yet for the first time in years his thoughts were not consumed by the Brotherhood of the Blade but by the welfare of his family. He thought of Calla and her head full of braids. Of Darnicia and the taste of her lips. And of Catlow, with his strong, determined eyes and his infectious laughter.

He had prepared for the Duel his whole life. It was the reason he got up in the morning .It was the reason he slaved away at the foundry. It was everything to him for so long he had forgotten what it felt like to feel anything else. Driving down the highway with the setting sun at his back he now felt something different. He felt fear. He dialed the number to his house again.

Darnicia answered. "Oh Pretlow I have been trying to get you all day!" she said.

"I know my love. Listen to me. I was attacked at the festival. The Men of the First Chaos must have received their Invitations. They sent assassins to attack me. I am fine. But we have to warn the other Houses that it has begun," he said into the handset as he dipped in and out of traffic.

"I know Pret. Calla saw a man in our backyard and..."

"What? When? Are you and Calla okay? What did the man look like?" he said into the phone. His voice was even and controlled but his heart was thudding in his chest.

"I believe he was Asian. Pretlow, they went after Catlow. Pretlow swerved the car over to the side of the road and slammed on the brakes. He slid along the shoulder for a few feet until he finally came to rest near the ditch.

"Darnicia is he ...is he alright?" he asked. The phone was silent for a moment.

"Yes. I called the Academy looking for him. He answered the phone. Pretlow he killed them all but I think they killed his friend Harmony. Pretlow he sounded ...broken. He was talking about revenge and killing all the Men of the First Chaos. Oh Pret how far away are you now?" Darnicia wailed. Her voice had cracked and even though she tried to hide it Pretlow could hear her sob.

"Three hours away my love. Where is Catlow now?" he asked.

"He said he was on his way home. That was about ten minutes ago. Pretlow. I 'm scared. I called Saed and I didn't get any answer at his building," she said more calmly.

"Saed can take care of himself and Shian. When Catlow gets there you all go down into the basement. Lock the door and stay there until I get there. We are going to head to the Grand Hall. It's neutral ground and even the Men of the First Chaos wont' break that oath. We will be safe there until the Duel begins," he said as pulled back on the interstate.

"And then what happens, Pret?" Darnicia asked.

"Then we defend the fates of men. With our lives."

Saed Barkarhat sat behind his desk looking over the invoices from the past month. His fencing academy had recently added a martial arts curriculum to their repertoire. The classes had taken off and the academy was making money hand over fist. Saed could pay all the bills and still have a tidy sum left over to enjoy all that the Baltimore social scene had to offer. Saed enjoyed going out and dressing nice. He enjoyed meeting people and talking and listening to their stories. Especially women. Saed loved women. And women loved him.

He knew he was considered attractive. Tall and lean with a clean-shaven head and a firm athletic body Saed had little trouble meeting beautiful vivacious women. He was an equal opportunity lover. Black, white, brown, he didn't care as long as they were beautiful and could hold a conversation. To him a beautiful woman who couldn't commiserate was like a Christmas present with beautiful wrapping that was empty when you opened the box. Pretlow chided him for his rakish ways but Saed would not be chastised.

"Your dalliances with be the death of you my friend. Either by the hand of a jealous husband or by the Men of the First Chaos. I for the life of me don't know when you have the time to practice. Visiting us once a year and sparring is not going to save your life during the Duel," Pretlow had told him once.

"Pret, who am I to deny these women the pleasure of my company? Life is to be lived not just endured. What are we fighting for if not for that? Don't worry, I practice. My father would turn over in his grave if he thought I was derelict in my duties to the Brotherhood,." he had responded.

His adventures in bed frame splitting had yielded many pleasant memories and many, many, female friends. But the most important thing his adventures had given him was his son Shian.

Shian's mother had been a lover that Saed had met at the Baltimore Crab Fest eighteen years ago. He and Ansa Veracruz had shared more than a few drinks at Mulligan's Pub on Chesapeake Street.

Ansa was a striking woman with coal black hair that she highlighted with blond streaks. Her skin was a creamy light brown that seemed to shimmer under the street lamps. Firm cupcake breasts above a flat stomach and deliciously wicked hips. After five shots of tequila they had wandered out of the Pub and back to his building. He had purchased the five-story former warehouse about a year before he met Ansa .With help from his father he had converted it into a fencing school and theatrical rehearsal venue. He also rented out the space for dance and burlesque reviews. Saed's father did not embrace the philosophy of poverty in regards to being a member of the Brotherhood He taught his children that membership in the Brotherhood did not exclude them from living a life of prosperity.

Pretlow did not agree with this idea and he and his father-in-law had argued many times. Saed thought that both men had valid points but he tended to side with his father. Why did being a master swordsman and making a decent living have to be mutually exclusive ideals? So he had purchased the building and turned the top floor into his personal quarters.

He had led Ansa into the rickety elevator with the accordion style door. She had put her arms around his neck and he had picked her up by her waist and pressed her against the back of the elevator.

"Mr. Barkarhat will you respect me in the morning?" she asked, laughing. Saed had pressed his lips against her neck and nibbled gently. A soft musical moan escaped her lips like the final notes of a violin at the end of a symphony.

"I will respect you in the morning and the afternoon. And tomorrow night. I will respect the hell out of you as soon as we get to my room. I am going to respect you deep and hard," he said with a laugh. She kissed him back.

"God I love your accent," she murmured

"What about the rest of me?" he whispered.

"Well let's see if it's worthy of adoration as well," she said as she dropped to her knees.

Later, after they had finally gotten to his bed and given each other a very respectful round of lovemaking she told him about her job.

"I'm a systems analyst for the CIA. I actually have to be at Langley by two pm tomorrow. I hope you won't be too upset if I don't spend the night," she had said as she lay across his chest. Saed had breathed a little sigh of relief. He had a full plate the next day and he didn't know how he was going to work Ansa into that particular dish. She ran her hand over his stomach.

"Are you in a gang?" she asked. Saed sat up and looked at her with a sidelong glance.

"Why would you ask me that?" he asked. She propped herself up on her elbow and pulled a stray lock of hair out of her face.

"I'm sorry I was just curious. You have a lot of healed scar tissue on your stomach and chest. And you have very arabesque tattoos on your arms and chest. Almost ritualistic." She stared into his eyes and did not drop her gaze. Saed laughed. It was long loud laugh that resonated through his studio apartment.

"No, not in a gang. Just some old fencing injuries. And the tats are just some images from my childhood in Johannesburg. That's all. Are you sure you are just a systems analyst?" he asked as he ran his hand through her hair.

"Well let's just say I analyze a broad variety of systems. Now why don't you analyze that rapier between your legs and see if you can rise to the occasion one more time," she said as she rolled onto her back.

"My dear, unlike the South I shall rise again."

In the morning she was gone.

Two years later Ansa had showed up at the studio with a small, honey-complected boy holding her hand. Saed had been teaching a class in Olympic style rapier fighting when he heard someone walk through the door. The chime had sounded and he had turned to see Ansa and the little boy. Ansa looked very different than when they had first met. Her hair was cut in a short mannish style. She was wearing a pair of tight black cargo pants and functional but nondescript black boots. A brown leather vest and black turtle neck completed her ensemble. Saed had given his students a five minute break and then he and Ansa and the little boy went into his downstairs office.

"I don't have a great deal of time Saed so you need to just listen .This is our son. I realized I was pregnant three months after we met. Up until this point I have been able to manage just fine on my own. But I have received an assignment that will take me out of the country for at least a year. I don't have any relatives. Not any I trust with our son. You will have to take him Saed, she had said with a tight clipped cadence. Saed had let out a low sigh.

"Please do not take this the wrong way. Well that's a stupid statement. There is only one way you can take this. Are you sure the boy is my son?" Saed asked. He was drumming his fingers on his desk in a languid rhythmic pattern. Ansa had reached inside her vest and pulled out a white envelope and handed it to Saed.

He had opened the envelope and looked at the contents. In the left hand corner was a letterhead that said John Hopkins Hospital. There was a list of names on the paper. Saed saw his was the third one listed. Directly across from each name on the list was a name he didn't recognize...Shian Veracruz. All the men on the list, eight in total, had an X by their names save one. Saed had a check mark by his name.

"I had the docs at John Hopkins run a DNA scan. He is your son Saed," she had said.

"How did you get my DNA? I haven't seen you in two years," Saed had said. His tone wasn't indignant or angry, just quizzical.

"Saed, I am in the CIA." she had said as if that explained everything.

"Ansa I..." but she cut him off.

"You remember my name?" she asked incredulously. Saed sat back in his chair.

"I have an eidetic memory. Ansa, I am not equipped to care for a baby. I have certain responsibilities of my own that I cannot shirk."

"Would you rather I put him in foster care? Saed I know this is all a bit much..."

"A bit?" he had asked. She ignored the comment.

"But you have no choice. He is your son. I am his mother .My country is asking me to go overseas and take a mission that I may not complete. A dangerous mission Saed," she said. She had stared into his eyes .She was speaking to him through her gaze.

"I might not make it back Saed." her eyes had said. Saed had stared back at her then at the little boy. He was holding Ansa's hand and sucking his thumb. He had a high forehead and soft full lips. His hair was light brown and curly. He stared back at Saed and never dropped his gaze.

"Is your name Shian?" he had asked the little boy. The little boy had slowly nodded his head. Saed turned back to Ansa.

"When you come back you come get him. We will work out some type of visitation agreement yes?" he had asked. Ansa nodded her head. She had taken Shian's hand out of her own and dropped down to one knee to be eye to eye with her son.

"Shian this is your Daddy. He will take care of you till I get back okay? Be a good boy and behave for Mommy. I will be back before you know it," she told him. She had kissed him on his cheek and stood.

"One year. Then I will come back. If I can. Saed had gotten up and walked around to the front of the desk.

"You will be back," he had said. She had touched his cheek and kissed him on the lips.

"You are a good man Saed. He is a quiet boy. And shy. He needs your fire," she had whispered to him. Then she was gone like smoke blown away by the wind. That had been eighteen years ago. Ansa never came back to Saed and Shian. Three years after she had dropped Shian off and with no contact from Ansa or anyone who had known Ansa Saed had written a letter asking about her whereabouts to the CIA general information office. In all honesty he had not expected much of a response, if any. What he had gotten was visit from two very stern gentlemen in plain blue suits and ties. They had appeared on the doorstep of his building a month after he had sent the letter. They had asked if he was Saed Barkarhat. When he had assured them he was one of the men had handed him a small jewelry box.

Inside the small gray box was a silver locket. Inside the locket was a picture of Ansa and Shian. They were both smiling in the picture. It had been taken outdoors. The setting sun was redolent behind them in the picture.

"She wanted him to have it," one of the stern men had said. And with that they had faded back into the throng of people walking down the street in front of Saed's building. He had looked at the locket for a long time on that cold wintry morning.

Saed had raised Shian as best he could. He had brought him up in the Brotherhood. He had taught him about the Covenant and the Duel of Generations. And he had trained him. Day in and day out until he was his equal. Even with all her governmental spook skills Ansa had never found out about the Brotherhood. Saed had a feeling if she had she would have never brought Shian to his doorstep. The Brotherhood was many things but "safe" was not one of them. Saed would sometimes look at his son when he was young and actually entertain the thought of leaving the Brotherhood. Of pulling up stakes and just going out west, leaving swords and fate and death behind them. But then he would look at his son again and realize if they ran then others might run. And if others ran then there would be no one to stand against the forces of Chaos. And then what? The world would be plunged into another century of death and despair worse than the century before. No, they would not run. They would stay and they would fight.

Saed did not want to even consider the possibility of Shian dying. He trained him hard but fairly. He didn't demand that Shian forsake the joys of being a young man like Pretlow did with Catlow. He had told Pretlow on more than one occasion that he was going to push that boy until he cracked like a cold glass dropped in hot water.

Shian was out and about right now. He and some friends had gone down to the rec center to play basketball. He would come home later and they would train in the studio downstairs. There were only two fencing classes scheduled for today. Saed had a date with a lovely young attorney from Bethesda.

His cell phone rang. He looked at the screen. An image of two scimitars crossed at the handles was on his phone. It was the caller ID for Pretlow. Saed answered the phone.

"Pretlow Creedence, the greatest sword maker I know!" Saed said with a laugh. Something in Pretlow's silence caused him to cut his laughter short.

"Pret what is it?"

"It has begun, Saed. I was attacked at a ren fair a few hours ago," Pretlow said grimly.

"Oh my God man, are you okay?" Saed asked.

"Saed, you are not listening to me. I was attacked by men wielding katanas. It has begun .The Invitations have arrived. The Men of the First Chaos are trying to eliminate us. Catlow was attacked as well. Where is Shian?" Pretlow asked.

"He is out with friends. Pretlow are you sure..." Pretlow cut him off before he could finish.

"Saed! It is happening!" Pretlow shouted. "Arm yourself. Find your son. As soon as I get home we are turning around and heading for the Grand Hall in New York. I suggest you head there now, while you still can. I don't know how long it will be before they get to you," Pretlow said.

"Who gets to me?" Saed asked.

"Ninjas, Saed. They sent ninjas to kill us," Pretlow intoned.

The sun was setting in Baltimore. Shadows were beginning to creep across the streets. A street lamp outside Saed's window flickered and sputtered to life. As soon as it reached its full illumination it shattered. Shards of glass rained down onto the sidewalk. The street was once again bathed in shadows.

"Pretlow I have to go. I think I am about to have some unwanted guests," Saed said. He ended the call to Pretlow without another word and put the phone in his pocket. He was wearing black dress pants and a white long sleeve t-shirt. Saed reached under his desk and pushed a small brass button. A hidden drawer dropped down from the underside of the desk. The desk was a gift from his friend and fellow member of the Brotherhood,. Richard Darn. In the drawer were two beautiful scimitars. Birthday gifts from Pretlow a few years ago. The handles were made of ivory with gold and pearl accents. Saed took both swords and rose from his desk. His office slash living quarters were on the fifth floor. The fourth floor was a storage area. The third floor had a small meeting room he sometimes rented out and more storage. The second floor had fencing equipment and Shian's living quarters. The first floor was the studio and the moveable stage he had purchased last year. There was an elevator and a stairwell. Unless he was with a guest Saed always took the stairs. He went to the door of his office and opened it cautiously. He had not turned on the lights yet but there was still enough light from the setting sun to see his living room and his sectional couch. His widescreen TV was in the corner of the room as were some random pieces of modern art he had been given from a female friend. There was a window behind the television but Saed always kept the curtains closed. It had a view of the alley behind his building. Saed listened.

There was no sound except the usual mysterious grunts and groans of an old building. Saed's office was large at sixteen by thirty feet. Pictures lined the walls of his office:. he and Pret on the day he married Saed's sister and Saed and Shian on Shian's graduation day from high school. There were pictures of Saed and his father and Darnicia and their mother. The walls of his office were just sheet rock and pieces of one by one's. He and Pretlow had built it years ago once the fencing school had taken off and Saed started to diversify his business interest. If you knocked on the walls you could hear the hollow echo reverberate through the walls.

Saed looked out his office door toward the elevator and the stairwell.

Nothing... yet he could feel *something*. That indescribable sense that someone was in the house.

Silence. Saed closed the door. He took a deep breath. He placed his scimitars on the top of the desk and pulled his phone out to call Shian so they could leave for New York.

Saed heard a sound. It was like someone was cutting paper with a pair of scissors. He turned and for a moment he glimpsed a surreal sight. There were blades sticking through the wall on the right side of his office. Three to be exact. Then as suddenly as they appeared they disappeared. Saed grabbed his scimitars.

The ninjas burst through the office wall. They were three men clothed from head to toe in black loose fitting pants and shirts. Their faces were hidden by a black mask that covered their entire faces save for a narrow slit across their eyes. They charged at Saed. One ran up the left wall and the other up what remained of the right. The third one came straight ahead. Saed knew they were trying to use shock and awe to unnerve him. But they had not been trained by Ket Barkarhat. Shock and awe had not been a part of his lexicon. Words like preparation and dedication and concentration were the major parts of his vocabulary.

Saed twirled his scimitars and occluded the sword of the ninja to his right and then the one to his left .The ninja in the middle stabbed forward with his katana but Saed was able to lean just far enough out of the way the blade. He was surrounded now by all three ninjas.

Saed began a deadly dance with his attackers. He dipped and spun and blocked with the grace of a swan. Every strike, every slash, every stab was checked by Saed's gleaming scimitars. Saed jumped on top of his desk and then back flipped off and slid along the floor on top of the fine film of sheet rock dust. The three assassins advanced upon him like black clad wolves. Saed held his scimitars by the handle in such a way the blades were almost resting against his forearms. As the ninjas moved forward Saed ran at them. At the last second he dropped to his knees and slid along the floor. The ninjas all jumped in unison over his head. As they were in mid-air Saed raised his arms and struck at the two on the right and the left. His scimitars found their ankles. Brotherhood steel, sharper and stronger than the steel of the katanas sliced through their talocrural joints with ease. The ninja in the middle flew over Saed without losing his feet. The ninjas on the left and the right were not so lucky. They landed on bloody stumps as their feet flopped to the floor of Saed's office. The two men did not howl in pain but crumpled to the floor like marionettes whose strings had been snipped. They silently grasped what was left of their legs. The last

remaining ninja slid a few feet and spun around to face Saed. As he
did he pulled a handful of shurikens out of a pocket just inside his shirt
and tossed them at Saed.

Propellers. The last remaining ninja thought the man in front of
him looked like he was holding the propellers of a helicopter. That was
how fast Saed was twirling his swords. He deflected each shuriken
with a slash from his scimitars. The last ninja, whose name was Yi,
held his sword in two hands and ran at Saed as he blocked the last
throwing star.

Saed blocked the last star with the sword in his right hand while
blocking the strike from the ninja with the sword in his left. He then
ducked and spun to his right until the scimitar was almost behind his
back. The blade found the lower right abdomen of the ninja. Saed
buried the scimitar in to the gut of the assassin up to the hilt. He let go
of the sword for just a second as he completed his spin move. Then he
grabbed it again and pulled back and up at the same time. The blade
slid through the ninja opening a huge gash in the man's torso as he
freed his sword. His movements were so quick the other man never
had time to even lower his sword for a counterstrike. Blood gushed
from the man's wound as he fell face first to the floor. Saed went over
to the two ninjas writhing on the floor. He stood between them and
dropped to one knee. Unfortunately for them he had a scimitar in each
hand and he buried the blades into their hearts.

Saed stood and pulled his blades free. He heard footfalls on the
stairwell. He looked through the hole in his ruined wall. The door to his
stairwell burst open. More ninjas. At least ten or fifteen were pouring
through the door.

Saed looked out his window. Across the street was an identical five story building. Saed gripped his swords tightly. They were weapons and gifts made for him by his best friend and brother in law. A man he trusted with his life.

"Fuck it." he whispered.

Saed turned and ran for the window. He accelerated all of his 235 pounds and put his head down as he launched himself at the window. The glass cracked and shattered. Saed felt shards scrape across his head and neck as he passed through the window. His legs, strengthened by years of endless training, pushed him further and faster than a normal man. Sailing through the air he raised his head and saw the building across the street rapidly approaching.

Saed raised his blades.

As he slammed into the building the blades bit into the brick surface and grabbed a hold like the talons of some great eagle. Saed kicked his feet at the wall as he slid down to the sidewalk. A sharp screeching sound filled the night as the blades scratched along the surface of the building. Saed slammed both feet on the sidewalk. . He turned around and saw his pursuers standing in the window. Saed saluted them even as they began to hurl shurikens at him. A few cars were cruising down the street and the shurikens struck unsuspecting motorists. Saed took off running down the street toward his parked car. He hopped in his vehicle, started it and peeled off down the street.

Saed had left his cell phone in the office. So he headed straight for the YMCA. He had to get to Shian before the assassins did. He didn't know how they had found them so easily.

"It really has begun. May all blades strike true," Saed thought to himself as he raced down the street.

CHAPTER NINE

Victor Crizwell sat in his leather recliner and sipped a scotch on the rocks. He took long sips and savored the feeling of the cool liquid pouring down his gullet. He was watching "The Deadliest Catch" on television while his sons Edgar and James helped their mother Eileen prepare dinner. Victor and his sons were home after a long day at the scrap metal yard they ran in Camden New Jersey. His boys, both still in their teens were out of school for the summer and helped out at the yard. His wife did the books. It was a true family affair.

Where was he supposed to find the time to work on his swordsmanship?

Victor was the last scion of the House of the Winter Sun. His ancestors had immigrated from Russian to the United States in the late nineteenth century. They had brought their membership in the Brotherhood of the Blade with them. Victor's father had educated him in all aspects of their duty. He had trained his son to use all manner of swords but emphasized the Cossack kindjal, a sword very similar to the scimitar.

Leopold Crizwell had been a passionate teacher and member of the Brotherhood. Victor had shared that passion for years. He had attended the meetings of the Men of the First Order over the bridge in New York. He had practiced in the back of the scrap yard as a young man. He had taken up blacksmithing and sword making at his father's request.

Leopold's death put an end to much of his dedication. An

accident in the yard took his father from him when he was 21. A magnetic crane malfunctioned and dropped four tons of crushed metal on top of Leopold. Victor had been looking out the window of the trailer that served as their office when it happened. One moment his father was standing there with his hands on his hips. The next he was buried under a twisted pile of iron and steel.

That happened around the same time the Men of the First Order stopped having their bi-annual meetings in New York near the Grand Hall. Victor gave up on swordsmanship for a while. Providing for his mother and his young wife became his mission. Edgar and his younger brother James arrived a few years later, short and squat like their father with a swatch of blondish hair inherited from their mother.

"Father, father what would you think of your son now?" Victor thought to himself. He had built the scrap yard from a mom and pop organization into the largest salvage yard in New Jersey. Of course he hadn't done it alone.

He had certain partners. Partners with names like Vinnie the Brick and Pretty Tony. They had shown him creative ways to raise operating capital. Then they had introduced him to the ponies. And the cards. And the dice. And anything else you could place a wager on. They loaned him more and more money and took larger and larger portions of Crizwell Salvage until he was basically working for the DeNucci crime family. After paying the vig and betting more on the ponies or the Super Bowl or the NBA finals and losing Victor barely had enough to keep the lights on in his own house. And the Brotherhood? Where had the Brotherhood been when he was counting pennies after his father died trying to keep the yard afloat? They told him that all of them were struggling. Which Victor knew was a lie. Ket Barkarhat was doing just fine. Raoul Esperanza, the prefect of the House Sun and Stone was living in a fucking villa in Spain. His olive oil business was flourishing just fine. But they told him they were not able to help. Pretlow Creedence had offered to give his family food. Food? What good was food if you didn't have a house to eat it in? Or a table to eat it off of? Fuck food!

Of course he hadn't said this to Pretlow's face. Pretlow frightened him. He, more than any other member of the Brotherhood that Victor had met, believed in the Covenant. His faith made him impervious to doubt. A man who does not feel doubt is a man not to be trifled with under any circumstances. The most dangerous people in the world are the righteous .And Pretlow was as righteous a man as Victor had ever met.

Victor put the glass to his lips. A tremor ran through his arm. The glass slipped from his grasp. It fell to the floor spilling scotch onto the carpet. Victor looked at his hand and flexed his fingers. The tremor persisted. His fingers quivered uncontrollably.

Victor thought it was ironic that after he finally got the salvage yard making money the tremors had begun. At first he had tried to ignore it and begin training again. One day he was practicing alone in the back of the yard with his kindjal. Victor had attempted a simple pass with the blade, sweeping it up then down in front of his body.

He dropped it and the point found his foot. He had cried out in pain. The visit to the doctor came soon after that experience. Many tests later he received the diagnosis. Parkinson's disease. The doctor had patted him on the shoulder and assured him that he could live a long full life with treatment and therapy.

But he would never be able to use a sword again. He could not fulfill the commitment of his House to the Covenant. The House of Winter Night had no other members. He and his boys were the last scions of that ancient House. His boys. He had tried to train them with words alone but after a few months he saw that was a pointless endeavor. Oh they would be decent fencers but they would never be members of the Brotherhood. There was no substitute for having a true master of the blade to teach you how to handle a sword. A mentor that would do a thousand push-ups with you. A sensei that would stand on a balance beam and show you the proper footwork if you happened to find yourself fighting on a power line. A father that could show you how to listen to footsteps and find a home for your blade in your enemy's chest even if you were in the dark.

So he gave up. He didn't try to teach them, or find someone to teach them. Oh he continued to tell them about the Covenant and the Book of Seven Swords. In reality he was a lapsed member of the Brotherhood. As the years passed he had begun to forget the teachings of his father and his grandfather. The Covenant became a blurry image in the rear-view mirror of his mind.

James' nightmares changed all that.

Victor had been sitting in his easy chair unable to sleep. The meds gave him horrible insomnia. A scream erupted from the second floor; a bloodcurdling scream that raised the hairs on the back of his neck. Victor had half-run, half-skipped up the stairs to his youngest son's room. He had pushed the door back with his considerable bulk and fallen into the room. Edgar came running from his bedroom and joined Victor. Eileen brought up the rear. James was sitting straight up in bed. His eyes were open but the eyeballs had rolled back in his head. Victor had pulled himself up and went to his boy. He had wrapped his arms around him and tried to shake him out of his seizure or spasm or nightmare or whatever the hell he was going through. James began to speak in a deep guttural growl. It was very different from his natural speaking voice.

"The Covenant is only as strong as your commitment. The Covenant is only as strong as your commitment…"

James kept repeating that phrase over and over. The sound of his voice hurt Victor's ears. It wasn't his voice. Not the voice of his serious studious son. The voice made his skin crawl. Finally Victor couldn't stand it anymore. He slapped James hard. The boy fell out of the bed to the floor. James started to cry.

Victor slid into the floor and pulled the boy into his arms.

"James, are you okay? What were you saying?" Victor asked even though everyone had heard James as clear as a bell. James rubbed his eyes.

"Huh? I don't know, what's going on? I must have been dreaming. It was the weirdest dream Da. I was standing on an island in the middle of a lake. I had a sword in my hand and I was fighting some dude. And he stabbed the sword into my heart. And there were these three monsters there watching everything."

"The Judges." Edgar said. Victor shot him an evil look.

"I guess but they were like, crazy looking. They were tall as the house and they had on these red robes that hid their face. But you could see their eyes .They glowed like a purple color. You couldn't see anything on them except their eyes. And they were watching this dude cut me up," James said. Victor patted his head.

"You scared the shit out of me, boy. You were hollering and

yelling. Woke the whole damn house up. Jeez." Victor ruffled his hair again.

"Alright everybody back to sleep. Crisis over," Victor said as he struggled to his feet.

"You coming to bed?" Eileen asked curtly.

"I will in a few," Victor said.

"Yeah," Eileen said under breath. She headed for their bedroom. Edgar went over to his brother and cuffed him playfully on the back of the head.

"Next time dream about Jennifer Lopez, poophead," he said. James swatted his hand away and climbed into bed.

"Lemme alone," he mumbled as he settled under his blankets. Victor nodded to himself and walked out of James' bedroom. Edgar was right behind .He closed James' bedroom door and spoke to his father.

"It's coming isn't Dad? The Covenant," he said plainly. Edgar was 19, three years older than James. He could remember when his father still had had some skill with a blade.

"What? "Victor had said as if he hadn't really heard the question.

"Dad, you heard him same as me. He was yelling about the Covenant. He was dreaming about the Judges. It's COMING. And we ain't ready are we?" Edgar asked. Victor had stopped at the top of the stairs.

"Go to bed Edgar,." he had said.

Now sitting in his chair looking at the spilled ruin of his drink, contemplating the ruin of his life he tried to come to grips with the choices he had made. Victor put his face into his hand and began to weep. He wept for his sons, that they had been cursed with such a weak and infirm father. He wept for his father and the shame he must be feeling as he looked down on his only son from whatever world the dead inhabit. He wept for the Brotherhood for depending on him .Some men were like metal. They were plunged into the forge of calamity and came out tempered and stronger than before. And some men melted, liquefying amidst the heat. Victor knew what kind of man he was, he still had enough honor to admit that.

There was a knock at his door. Victor wiped his eyes and rubbed his face. He pulled himself up and out of his chair and limped over to the front door of his house. The meds were supposed to help with his equilibrium but all they really did make him feel like he was walking through wet mud.

He grabbed the door knob and opened the door. There sitting on his front step was a sleek black box. It glimmered in the summer moonlight. Victor bent down and picked it up. It felt as light as a feather. He closed the door and walked back to his seat.

"The Invitation is the key to open the door to your destiny," he murmured. His father used to say that all the time when he was trying to train him in the yard. But what was his destiny now?

Victor felt the hackles on his neck rise. Someone was standing behind his chair. He swiveled his head and saw a man standing there dressed from head to toe in black. The man was wearing a katana in its black ebony scabbard. His face was obscured by a black mask.

"Well I'd like to say I was expecting you but I had convinced myself it would never happen," he said to the man. The man did not

THE BROTHEROOD OF THE BLADE

respond. He reached inside his shirt and pulled out an envelope and handed it to Victor. Victor felt the weight of the envelope and put it on the small side table next to his chair. Victor rose out of the chair and faced the man in black.

"Do what you must," he said to the man. The man pulled the katana from its sheath.

CHAPTER TEN

Arato Hamato surveyed the crowd gathered in his restaurant and felt a warm feeling settle in his stomach. Tonight was going to be busy night. A busy night meant a profitable night. Arato was behind the grill at one of the six tables in the Nakura Sushi Bar and Grill in downtown Philadelphia. The six tables could hold up to twenty guests each and had room for two chefs if needed. Arato was sharpening his knives, and cleaning his spatula and forks. Four couples had been seated in front of him for an evening of good food and showmanship. The Nakura was one of the more famous hibachi restaurants in Philly. Arato thought it was ironic the training and skills he had earned as a member of the House of Moon and Sky were the same skills that made his eatery a success. He had been born and raised into the Brotherhood. His father and his grandfather had put a katana in his hand at the age of five and taught him about the duty he shared with the other Men of the First Order. They shared with him the history of their House. They were descended from a shamed sect of samurai turned ronin for their refusal to kill innocent children at the behest of their shogun. He had been a young boy sitting on the ground next to his grandfather after a particularly hard day of training.

"Arato, have some water. You look like a wilted flower," his grandfather had said. Arato had taken the small porcelain cup from his grandfather's firm calloused hand. Ken Hamato had been 91 that day in the back room of their small Japanese restaurant Arato's father Lin and Ken had built the room to be a hidden place for their training. It was a secret place to practice the art of swordsmanship; a sacred place to learn the Way of the Blade.

"Arato, have you ever heard the story of why our House is called the House of Moon and Sky?" his grandfather had asked him that day.

"No grandfather," Arato had said quietly. His grandfather was larger than life to Arato. He had long white hair and a long white goatee that unfurled down to his chest. His arms and hands were gnarled not from age but with tight hard muscle. One of the first lessons he had taught Arato was that your grip on your sword was one of the most important skills you could possess, almost as important as the act of wielding the sword. He and his father and his grandfather practiced strengthening their grip by plunging their hands into buckets full of sand. Buried in the sand were a scattering of walnuts. They would feel around in the bucket until they felt the walnuts. Then they would squeeze them until they cracked. At first Arato had not even been able to move his hand in the sand. In time he could grasp the hidden walnut and after struggling for some time he could feel it break. The pressure from the sand and their movement against it as they squeezed made their grip incredibly strong. His grandfather could find all six walnuts and crush them with one hand. He did this over and over for an hour.

"Long, long ago when our ancestors were pledged to the service of Shogun Han Kinaku they were charged with the task of slaughtering a neighboring shogunate and all of the people of that shogunate including the children. Our ancestors led by Kan Inoki rebelled against their mad master and became ronin. They wandered the land and eventually settled in a valley near the base of Mount Fuji. There they raised chickens and ducks and tried to live in peace. But they never gave up on their training .They never forgot that they had once been samurai. They married and had families but they continued to practice and refine their skills. When the Judges came to them in their search for men of honor to stand for the world and defend our race and defend our right to exist Kan Inoki and his legion of ronin said:

'We welcome to the chance to die with honor.'

The Judges had told him they would have to leave Japan to fight for the world. Kan had responded.

'We will fight anywhere. If we must fight in the sky we will fight in the sky and bury our dead on the moon.'

Ken had locked eyes with a young Arato and pointed a crooked finger at his face.

"We are the men of the House of Moon and Sky. We do not run from our duty. We are not afraid to die because to die in the commission of fulfilling our commitment to the Covenant is the highest honor we can achieve. Remember, Arato. Do not be afraid to fight anywhere at any time.

Arato looked at his hands. They were gnarled just like his grandfather's had been. He had not forgotten his lessons learned in that hot dark room so many years ago. He looked to his left. His daughter Miko was taking some more guests to another table. He wondered how his grandfather would have felt about him teaching Miko the Way of the Blade .He and his wife Lauren had tried for years to have a baby. When she had gotten pregnant Arato had not prayed to any of the gods for a boy. He had only wished for a healthy child. Miko was their only child and there would be no more. Her birth had taken its toll on Lauren's body. The doctors had suggested she not try to carry a second baby to term. She and Arato had taken the doctor's advice. Arato had read and re-read the Book of the Seven Swords. It did not explicitly say a woman could not fight in the duel. There just hadn't ever been a recorded instance of a woman fighting. Arato hoped that Miko would not have to participate. He was the prefect of the House of Moon and Sky. His father had a nephew named Neko who still lived in Japan but his swordsmanship was questionable at best. Arato and his father would represent his House if the Invitation came in their lifetimes. The Duel of Generations was supposed to happen every 100 years but if one researched the Book of Seven Swords one would note that sometimes there was a 110 year gap between Duels, sometimes it was 99. Arato had his own theories and why that was the case. Perhaps the Judges were beings for whom time had little meaning. Perhaps a hundred years for us was a day to them. They were just his own personal theories; he never shared them with anyone, not even Lauren.

In the meantime he taught Miko. Maybe he was just a proud father but he felt confident that her swordsmanship could stand up to anyone in the Brotherhood. He and his father had instructed her the same way his grandfather and father had instructed him. He hoped she would never have to fight but just in case she did he wanted her to be ready. He did not want it to be recorded in the Book that the House of Moon and Sky had not been able to fulfill their obligation to the Covenant. He trained her hard because he loved her not just because he wanted to protect the honor of his House. All his lessons were not with the blade however.

Arato made her work for her paycheck at the restaurant. Nothing was given to her. Miko earned everything she received. Arato felt that was his duty as a father. His duty as prefect was to ensure that she could take a life while protecting her own.

Arato checked his supplies under the table in a cabinet that was separated from the grill by a firewall. He had his oil and his butter and his lighter. One of his busboys was bringing around a tray of steak and fresh rice and chicken. His apron held an assortment of knives and forks and his grill scraper and some other odds and ends. Some of his other chefs had already begun to cook their various meals. The scent of sumptuous cuts of beef and cups of rice cooking on the grill began to fill the restaurant. Soy sauce and cilantro and cinnamon and a multitude of other smells wafted up Arato's nose. Cooking was his second love behind swordsmanship. There was an art to creating a meal just there was an art to wielding a sword. His father had instructed him in the creation of a meal with his usual aplomb.

"The meal is your reputation. People will tell one person about a good meal. They will tell ten people about a bad meal. They will tell everyone they know about a great meal." Lin had told him years ago when they had first expanded the restaurant from just a take-out establishment. Arato looked around the restaurant and smiled. He was proud.

Every chef was dressed alike, with a tall red chef's hat, white button-downed dress shirt, and red apron and black pants. All the hostesses, including Miko were dressed in traditional silken geisha robes. The whole building rumbled with the clinking of glasses, the clang of knives and forks and an amorphous cloud of pleasant conversation. Arato pulled out his knives, looked at his order sheet and then turned to his audience.

"Ladies and gentlemen prepare yourselves for something you will never forget!" he said with a wide smile.

Two black rental cars parked across the street from the Nakura.

There were four men in each car. They got out and strode across the busy street amid honking horns and copious amounts of middle fingers. One the men, a tall Asian man with a crew cut, absentmindedly pulled a shuriken out of his inside coat pocket and hurled it at the tire of one of the cars. Air seeped out of the tire with a high reedy whine. The driver lost control of the vehicle and ran the car up on the curb. The man with the crew cut was Hasaka. He was a senior member of the Clan of the Swift Death. He was 38 years old .He had grown up with Kento and Hiro in the Clan. Now Kento and at least eight of his brothers were dead. Hiro had been monitoring the news from their base in Okinawa. Kento's body had been found in a fencing studio in Richmond Virginia. Saito and his team had been slaughtered in Pennsylvania. Hasaka had been contacted by Hiro with one order.

"Kill them, Hasaka. We must complete the mission. Avenge Kento. Avenge our brothers. No more offers, no more negotiations. Just kill them all." Hasaka promised Hiro he would do just that. Hiro was now the de facto leader of the Clan. They would address that issue once the mission was done. But for now he accepted his edict and focused his energy on one thing. He wanted to see the blood of the men of the Brotherhood on his hands. He wanted to taste it. Wash his face in it. He wanted to lay his head down on his pillow this night and smell the copper scent of blood in his nostrils.

"So we any couples here tonight?" Arato asked the group assembled in front of him. A shy young white man raised his hand and the young lady next to him raised her hand.

"Aw don't you go breaking her heart."Arato said. He shaped the frying rice into a large heart then sliced his spatula through the middle.

The couple laughed. He grabbed an egg from his food tray and threw it into the air. He looked at the guests and caught the egg on the edge of his spatula. He flicked his wrist and the egg sailed into the air. Smiling he caught it again, this time with his chef hat. Everyone at the table clapped. A few people even oohed and awed. He nodded his head and the egg rolled out of the folds of his hat .He caught it this time with his cooking knife. .Whistling h to himself he let it roll down the edge of the knife and onto the griddle in front of him. Using his thumb he spun the egg on its end.

"So now we see is the spatula mightier than the knife," he said laughing. He sliced the egg open with his spatula and spread the egg yolk on the griddle. Using a surprising amount of grace he picked up the egg shell with his fork and tossed it over his shoulder into the trash. There was another round of applause from his guests.

Arato glanced at the door and saw a large group of men enter the restaurant. They were all dressed in jeans and sport jackets that seemed too big for them. They moved efficiently and quickly. He watched as the group parted to allow one man to come to the front of the group. He was taller than many of the other men who had walked in with him. His hair was cut close in a severe crew cut. His face was sharp and angular like a slab of quartz.

The man with the crew cut looked left then right. Arato had seen hundreds of people do the exact same thing over the years. Scanning the room for their party was a common occurrence. So why was his stomach suddenly twisting into knots? Arato continued with his presentation.

Hasaka scanned the room looking for his target. Finally he saw him. Arato Hamato was standing at the very first table in the restaurant in front of a large group preparing a meal. He was a tall man with a wide light tan face. He was wearing a chef's hat and smiling like an idiot. Hasaka reminded himself not to underestimate this man. Members of his fraternity had already killed more of his brothers in one day than any other enemy had in one hundred years. However, standing here in the man's restaurant watching him debase himself for the grinning faces of these fat Americans made that fact seem ludicrous.

"On my mark we attack. Show no mercy. Let no one get in your way. No matter what happens to us this man must die," Hasaka said softly in Japanese.

Arato looked at the group of men standing just inside the door. The man with the crew cut locked eyes with him. One of the hostesses came up to the group with a stack of menus. The men paid no attention to her.

The man with the crew cut did not drop his gaze.

Arato did not drop his. The sounds of the restaurant rang in his ears .The murmurs of conversation, the clang of forks and spatulas and glasses. This was his home. This was his House. He would protect his House. He gripped his cooking knife tightly.

"Kare o korosu!" Hasaka screamed. Most of the patrons did not know that it was Japanese for "kill him". Hasaka and his men took off running toward Arato .They all reached in their jackets and pulled out shurikens. They hurled the shurikens at Arato in unison. Each man threw five shurikens. Forty shurikens in total flew toward Arato like a murder of metal crows.

Arato dropped to the floor as the shurikens buried themselves in the metal oven hood behind him. The patrons sitting at the table jumped and screamed when the shurikens slammed into the hood.

"Maybe it's a part of the show?" The young man who had raised his hand said.

"Yeah like Medieval Times!" his date said excitedly. The rest of their party nodded their heads enthusiastically. Hasaka and his men were almost to the table. Arato popped up with a two handfuls of razor sharp cooking knives. He began to launch them at his attackers.

Two of Hasaka's men to his left didn't realize the knives were flying toward their heads until the blades crashed into their faces. The two men dropped to the floor with the knives still vibrating in their eye sockets. Hasaka pulled a short wakizashi sword from under his sport jacket and ducked under the storm of knives headed his way. Two more of his men on his right side were not as quick as their leader. They caught a pair of knives with their throats. They tumbled to the floor just as the arterial spray began to erupt from their wounds. Two more of Hasaka's men had escaped the hurricane of blades and were almost to the table.

There was a certain part of Arato's performance that every one of his patrons looked forward to seeing when they came to the Nakura, if they knew or had heard about it... the flaming onion volcano. He would slice an onion into smaller and smaller ringlets and pile them on top of each other largest to smallest to create a little vegetable volcano He would then pour an oil and vodka onto the volcano and light it with his long handled lighter.   People of all ages and backgrounds loved the flaming onion volcano. Arato didn't think that after tonight ninjas would like this particular piece of showmanship. Arato grabbed his oil and his vodka and took a large swallow of both liquids .As Hasaka and his three remaining men reached Arato's table he spit the contents of his mouth at his attackers while holding his long handled lighter in front of his face.

A huge fireball exploded in front of Hasaka and his men. Flaming oil landed on their faces and chest and instantly attached to their skin .Burning oil seared their bodies. The ninjas did not scream in pain but instead patted at the flames in silence. Arato saw a figure approaching him from his right. It was Miko. She was holding a sword in each hand. Beautiful red- and-black-handled katanas. She jumped up onto Arato's table and nimbly ran among the plates and glasses of his audience without spilling or overturning one dish. She flipped over Hasaka and his men and landed behind them.

Burned and in pain and shocked at seeing four of their comrades fall so quickly Hasaka and his men nonetheless prepared to fight. They pulled their swords and turned to face Miko. She was still in her green and black flowered print geisha robes. Arato grabbed his last remaining knife from under the table and prepared to join the fray.

Hasaka attacked Miko with a two-handed overhead strike. She dropped to a deep squatting position and blocked his strike with her left hand and while stabbing his brother who had tried to attack her from the right. Her sword pierced his throat with a soft wet rip. Miko then turned to her left, turning into Hasaka and sliding the edge of the sword in her right hand across his mid-section. She kept turning and positioned herself behind him. She thrust the blade in her left hand straight back without looking and sliced through his spine and into his heart. Moving forward like a tornado of blades she engaged the remaining two assassins. The one to her left swung his sword at her head. The one to her right swung his sword low toward her torso. Miko ducked under the attack from the left and blocked then parried the attack from her right using her blade and to push the assassin's blade across his body at a parallel angle, exposing his neck on the right side. In one fluid beautiful moment Miko brought the sword in her left hand up and then sliced it through the assassin's neck, severing his head from his shoulders.

She used the momentum from her strike to spin around to face her last attacker. He tried to stab his sword between her breasts but she parried that strike with the sword in her right hand while slashing at his head with the sword in her left hand. The man was able to retain control of his weapon and block the strike from her left hand, just barely. As that strike was being blocked she attacked with her right hand. Her opponent was just able to deflect that blow, but not as cleanly as the previous strike.

"Chainsaw. It's like fighting a chainsaw," the man thought to himself. As soon as he blocked her right-handed attack she flipped the sword in her left hand so that the blade was running parallel to her forearm with the sharpened edge facing her opponent. She used her nimble feet to get inside her opponents personal space. With his sword down and toward the left his neck was dangerously exposed. Miko swept her left hand toward his neck. The sharp unyielding steel of a true sword of the Brotherhood made quick work of the man's musculature and spinal cord. His head fell to the left as his body fell to the right.

Arato let his hand fall to his side. His daughter had just bested four highly trained assassins. His heart swelled with pride.

"Um…can we get our steak and rice to go? I love your show and all but it's like going to a GWAR concert, man!" the young man who had raised his hand earlier said. Arato looked at the man and nodded curtly. He scraped the meal on the grill into a bag and tossed it to the young man. Arato then removed his chef's hat and walked out from behind the grill. He stepped over the remains of his attackers and grabbed Miko's hand. She twitched hard. She was breathing deeply and her face was flushed.

"Come now Miko. We must leave for the Grand Hall. But first we will stop by the house and pick up your grandfather and mother. I believe there is an Invitation awaiting us there," Arato said. Miko slid her swords inside her sleeves and followed her father out the door of the Nakura. Neither one of them knew if they would ever return.

CHAPTER ELEVEN

Papu Akinyele walked among his macadamia trees with a three foot long machete in his hand. The warm winds coming off the Pacific Ocean blew through his long curly gray-black hair. Papu walked up to one of the trees and chopped off a small thin branch. He picked up the branch and sniffed it. He looked at the center of the little twig and noted that it was nice and moist. The tree was getting proper hydration. It was about ten feet tall with lush green leaves about five to six inches long and eight inches wide. Long slender flowers wound their way around the branches with light white petals tinged with lavender. The nuts themselves were encased in an extremely hard outer shell. Papu had a small farm comparatively speaking. Only about 200 hundred trees on a small patch of land directly behind his house.

Papu and his wife Kia and his son Logan farmed the nuts with help from his brother Apau and his son Troy and his wife Lisa. The Brothers Akinyele Macadamia Nuts was not the number one selling nuts in the world, but they did pretty well in their native Hawaii. Papu stopped and leaned against one of his trees and let the breeze blow against his face. He was not overly tall nor was he overly short. His forearms were swollen to Popeye proportions by years of swinging a machete and carrying burlap sacks of nuts up to the small processing facility near his house where his wife and his sister-in-law cracked open the nuts and washed them and canned them. He and Logan would also help once they were done in the groves.

Papu tossed the machete in the air. He caught it blind and swung it to his right then to his left as fast and as hard as he could. He let it roll across the back of his hand, driven by centrifugal force. caught it again and sliced it up to the sky then back down to the ground.

Papu sighed. He was fifty-two years old. Old enough to remember the glory days of the Brotherhood. He remembered trips to Grand Hall in New York, reading the original Book of the Seven Swords and meeting all the prefects of all the Houses. Seeing his father Aku spar against the leader of the House of the Olde Grove, Simon Darn, was something he would never forget. The nobleness of it all had showered over him like a summer rain.

The idea of nobility seemed comical now. His father was dead. His uncle Safu was in a nursing home, his mind riddled by Alzheimer's. Safu's son Colon had gotten hooked on meth and disappeared years ago. Only he and Logan, Akau and Troy held to the old ways. They were all that was left of the House of the Sacred Palm.

Papu and Akau educated their sons about the Brotherhood. They taught them about what was at stake when they were called upon to enter the Duel. Yes they ran a farm and yes they had marriages and yes they went over to the Big Island to drink and laugh and enjoy the fruits of their labors. But beneath that veil of simple rustic charm was a hard-bitten intrinsic knowledge...that they were more than what they seemed to be. Knowledge that there would come a time when they would be called upon to sacrifice all that they were for all of the people of this world. Despite the hardships he had endured, despite the dark and desperate cloud that had sometime hovered over his House Papu still believed in the Covenant. He still believed in the Brotherhood of the Blade and what it stood for. Some give all so that all won't perish. This was the idea behind the Covenant distilled to its purest form.

Papu walked a little bit further into the grove. What would happen to the Covenant if all the Houses faded away? Who would uphold the banner for mankind? He wasn't getting any younger and Logan didn't have any brothers or sisters. Akau was even older. There had been a time when such thoughts would have seemed foolish but now they seemed pragmatic. Papu sighed.

A twig snapped in the distance. It was a sound Papu had heard thousands of time before as he wandered the macadamia groves. It was a familiar sound, a comforting sound. So why did the hair on his arms suddenly stand up? Papu turned and around and stared down the row of trees he had just passed. The tops of the trees were swaying gently in the breeze. That should have been comforting as Well, except the breeze had stopped blowing three minutes ago.

Papu held up his machete. Almost too late he saw the shurikens flying toward him, their razor sharp edges glittering in the dying sunlight. He swatted at the flying metal shards with a speed and accuracy inconsistent with his size and girth. The sound of the machete meeting the throwing stars sounded the sharp ping of hail on a tin roof. Papu moved backwards to get into the clearing between rows of macadamia trees to give himself room to fight. He didn't have to think about this tactical move. It was second nature to him, ingrained by years of training.

One of the shurikens found his shoulder and buried itself up to the center hub. Papu grunted and pulled it out and threw it on the ground. He spun around in a circle searching the trees for his attackers.

A man-sized clutch of leaves fell out of the tree and landed about twenty feet from Papu. Papu watched as the leaves pulled out a short washcloth sword. Papu let out a short sigh. His attacker was wearing a very advanced camouflage suit. It was like a gilly suit made of short leaves and twigs. It covered his attacker's entire body and face. Another walking pile of leaves jumped out of a tree and landed in front of him .Then another. Then another. Four attackers faced him in the clearing. Papu was breathing hard.

"So I suppose the Invitations have been sent. Huh...the Men of the First Chaos must not trust that their swords will strike true," he said. His attackers did not respond.

"Well, let's dance, you bastards. I bet you have never had a partner like me," Papu said. The ninjas ran toward him. Papu screamed "KEKOA!" It was Hawaiian for warrior.

Papu slashed at the first attacker. The ninja blocked his strike with his sword but Papu had anticipated that maneuver. As the camouflaged man blocked his blow Papu dropped to one knee and brought his machete down with him. He sliced through the ninja's right leg and immediately popped up and snatched his sword out of his hand as the man fell to the ground. The other three attackers advanced on Papu.

Papu held the machete in one hand and the short katana in the other. As the ninjas attacked Papu spun like a pinwheel. He blocked and parried and ducked their strikes. His machete was not made of Brotherhood steel. It was a simple metal blade from a local hardware store. It was built and tempered for the express purpose of cutting branches and stalks of tall pampa grass. It was not designed to defend a man's neck from a ninja sword made of billets of steel folded 1000 times. As Papu raised it to block one of the strikes from one of his attackers it broke.

Three fourths of the machete fell to the ground and landed among the soil and leaves. Papu jammed the jagged stump of the machete forward and into his attacker's throat. The ninja had lost his focus for one moment. His eyes had strayed from the battle at hand to watch the blade fall to the ground. Papu pushed the blade into the man's throat up to the hard plastic handle. As the ninja fell backwards his companions attacked from both sides. Papu slashed left to right in rapid succession as he moved backwards from his attackers. They pressed forward.

Papu was tired. His arms felt like they were filled with cement. Each breath was a struggle. It was the macadamia nuts' fault. Trying to make the farm a success had taken its toll on his body. His knees ached so he didn't run anymore. His back was always in agony so he didn't do his handstands. Oh he still practiced his swordsmanship. But swordsmanship without stamina was like being a cook who had pots and pans but no ingredients.

"Come...on...you vultures," he gasped. Death was very near. He could feel its cold touch caress his cheek like a lover. His shoulder was bleeding profusely .He suspected the shurikens were coated with some type of anti-coagulate that kept his blood from clotting. He was fighting two well-trained assassins with one short blade. And he was exhausted. Yet he raised his sword once more.

The two ninjas launched a dual attack. One leaped into the air to strike high. The other dropped to his knees and slid along the cool earth to strike low. Papu jumped into the air and stepped on the left shoulder of the ninja sliding along the ground. All 285 pounds of him. He heard a satisfying wet cracking sound. The man's shoulder had snapped and popped out of its socket. Papu pushed off his enemy's trapezes muscle and met his other enemy in the air. Their swords clanged together as they met in mid-air. They passed each other and landed on the opposite sides of the prone form on the ground. Papu felt a pain shoot up his left leg like someone had injected molten lava into his veins. His attacker landed and immediately started to run toward Papu again. Something shimmered on the ground. Papu noticed it was one of the shurikens he had swatted away earlier. As his attacker leaped over his prone comrade and launched himself at Papu, Papu dived toward the ground and grabbed the shuriken. The ninja sailed over him and landed near one of the macadamia trees. Almost immediately after he landed he ran back toward Papu.

Papu turned his hand sideways and flicked the shuriken at his attacker. The man leaped into the air once more with his sword raised above his head. The shuriken skimmed across the inside of his thigh. As he landed Papu raised his sword to meet his assailants. Once more he blocked the strike.

The ninja recovered from the block, brought his sword down and tried to stab it into Papu's gut. The older man brought his elbow down hard. Papu drove his elbow into the ninja's wrist. The ninja's sword popped out of his hand like a jack in the box. Papu flipped the wakizashi and was preparing to bring it back across his opponent's throat when he felt a brilliant pain in his chest. He looked down and saw a metal blade stained with crimson sticking out of the left side of his torso. The ninja with the broken shoulder had pulled himself up off the ground and had rejoined the fight.

Papu dropped his weapon. Suddenly he felt very light, like a hot air balloon untethered from its moorings. His legs went numb and Papu fell to his knees. The ninja put his foot on the big man's back and pulled his sword out with a light grunt.

Papu gazed up at the man standing in front of him.

"See ya soon," he said. The world began to fall away from his vision and he felt like he was being sucked down into a whirlpool. Sound and feeling began to fade as well.

"I hope I trained you better than I trained myself Logan," he thought to himself. Papu fell forward face first into the dirt.

"What did he mean see you soon?" the man who had killed Papu asked his comrade in Japanese. The other man did not respond. He grabbed at his inner thigh and stumbled to the ground in a sitting position. His leg was bleeding profusely.

"Femoral....." was all he said before he fell backwards. His brother Jinko walked over to his body and dropped his sword. His Father had told him that these men were not as deadly or fearsome as the old stories would have you believe. Jinko agreed with that assessment. They were more deadly and more fearsome than the stories had said. Three of his brothers were dead and he himself was in incredible pain. He would have to hike all the way back to the extraction point in agony. If he went to the extraction point. His Father had been terribly wrong about these Men of the First Order. No one had heard from Kento since he initiated the attack. Perhaps Jinko could just blend into the population here. Find a place to stay. Make contact with certain people who could use his specific complement of skills. As he pondered these ideas he did not notice a tall broad-shouldered figure moving through the trees. Perhaps the pain from his shoulder had clouded his senses. Perhaps he too was tired. Caught up in his existential miasma he never saw the young man emerge from the trees.

Logan Akinyele was taller than his father but wide and muscular like most of the Akinyele men. He had soft luxuriant black curly hair that he wore in loose shag on top of his head with the sides shaved close to the skull. His forearms were like his fathers', Popyeesque in their size. They were covered with Polynesian tribal tattoos.

Logan had returned from town after taking a load of nuts to the market in Kameha. He had dropped off his load and then stopped and had some lunch. The whole trip had taken an hour.

Logan had pulled up to the main house and parked the truck in front of the shed they used as processing station for the nuts. He had hopped out and immediately been struck by how quiet it was. It was never quiet around his house. His mom was always doing something. Either she was cooking in the kitchen or she was helping his Dad in the shed or she was on the phone yakking with one of her girlfriends. Kia Akinkeyle was a large, broad-faced woman with an infectious laugh and a mischievous twinkle in her eye.

Logan had walked up the steps into his house. He hardly noticed the sleek black box sitting off to the right side of the porch. The front door was ajar. Logan pushed it the rest of the way open and walked inside. The house reeked of burning meat. Logan turned right and headed for the kitchen.

There was a frying pan on the stove. Two shriveled bits of bacon sat in the pan. The pan itself was burning and smoking. Logan walked around in front of the stove and turned off the burner. A breeze blew into the kitchen through a hole in the glass of the kitchen window over the sink. Logan walked over to examine the hole when his foot brushed against something on the floor; something heavy and solid. He slowly lowered his eyes.

His mother was sprawled face down on the kitchen floor. Her back was covered with metal spikes which stuck out of her at odd angles like a pin cushion. Blood was slowly dribbling from every wound. Her light blue house dress was now a muddy red. Logan dropped to his knees and crawled over to his mother. He grabbed her by her shoulder and rolled her into his arms. The spikes pushed into his chest.

Her mischievous eyes were open and devoid of any life. Kia's mouth was slack and a line of blood was dribbling down her chin. Logan didn't scream. He didn't cry out. He just held his mother and rocked her as tears slipped from his eyes.

The sound of someone yelling came through the broken window. Logan thought it sounded like his father. Blinking his eyes he lay his mother down gently on the floor and rose. His white t-shirt had uneven blood stains on it like Asian calligraphy. Logan walked around his mother's body and ran out the back door. He galloped over to the shed and pulled up the metal roll door. The harsh scent of macadamia shells slapped him in the face. Logan ran to the back of the shed toward a tall free-standing wooden cabinet. There was an ancient padlock on the door of the cabinet. Logan pulled his keys out of his pocket and flipped through them until he found one that looked like a prop in a Dungeons and Dragons game. He pushed that key in the padlock and swung the door wide.

Five double bladed lances lay in notched grooves that ran along the back of the cabinet. Logan grabbed one and ran toward the groves. The lances were made from the whittled trunks of palm trees dipped in paraffin and then treated with resin. On each end of the lance was a three foot long obsidian blade, edged on each side. The wooden part of the lance was painted with red ocher and charcoal before another coat of clear resin had been applied. The intricate red and black designs were traditional Hawaiian symbols that had been used by King Kamehameha to symbolize his power. In the center of the wooden lances was a rod made of Brotherhood-treated steel. The blades were covered in a clear resin created by Garn Whiteborne that strengthened the already hard obsidian and tempered some of its brittleness. The total length of the lance was six feet.

Logan ran toward the groves as fast as his feet would carry him. He ducked under low hanging branches and jumped over piles of fallen leaves. His heart was pounding in his chest but not because he was running.

He came upon the clearing just as he saw his father fall face first into the dirt. Logan saw the man standing above his father list to one side. He appeared to be covered in some kind of camouflaged suit.

Logan threw his lance. It sliced through the air silently. Logan followed it just as quietly. The man in the leaf suit turned around just in time to catch the lance. With his face. The heavy obsidian blade entered his eye and exited out the back of his skull. The man fell forward but did not hit the ground. The other end of the lance stuck into the dirt and propped him up like a human tent. Logan ran past him and grabbed his father. Papu coughed and a blood bubble formed on his lips. Logan was sitting on the ground with Papu's head in his lap. His father looked up at him and tried to raise his arm.

"Dad, Dad just lay still I'm going to call an ambulance," Logan said .He reached into his back pocket for his cell phone. Papu shook his head.

"No...time...listen..." he said. His voice was barely a whisper.

"Shh, Dad. I'm going to call the ambulance now," Logan said. His father shook his head more urgently.

"No.....find.....the Grand Hall. New York. Safe there until.....the Duel....." Papu said.

"Fuck the Duel, Dad we got to get you to the hospital!" Logan screamed. His father grabbed his shirt and stared into his eyes even as blood ran out of his mouth in copious amounts.

"The Duel is our duty Cry decretum...let our blades strike true..." Papu's eyes rolled back in his head.

"Dad! Dad! Talk to me Dad!" Logan yelled. Papu's hand fell away from his shirt. Logan Akinkeyle sat among the macadamia groves with his father for a very, very long time. He thought of days of laughter and love and thought that he may never know days like that again. But he would dedicate the rest of his life to ensuring that the Men of the First Chaos never knew days like that again either.

HAPTER TWELVE

Barton Fitzwell Crisp knew by all rights he should be dead. Every morning he rose out of his king sized goose feathered bed he felt the cold hand of the Grim Reaper grasping at his soul but finding no purchase. Sycophants always told him he did not look his age. He was well aware of that fact and found the "compliment" tiresome. Anyone who had a modicum of sight could see he did not look 113 years old. He didn't need to be reminded of it constantly. To be honest his longevity unnerved him. He was the undisputed Master of the House of the Poison Soil. He was the majority stockholder in Fordham Gleason, Incorporated, the conglomerate that managed all of the Crisps' various interests and holdings. He was the unspoken leader of the Men of the First Chaos. Yet his longevity disturbed him. It was a constant reminder of what was at stake in the upcoming Duel. It was proof of the terrible powers at play in this deadly Covenant called the Brotherhood of the Blade. Barton knew better than most the true meaning of this Covenant and the awesome forces that called themselves the Judges.

Barton was the only living witness to the last Duel. He had watched his father Ian die in that dirty abandoned warehouse one hundred years ago. He had been thirteen years old. He had also seen Stavaros Apothas kill the last man of order on that lurid field of battle. Barton had felt the touch of the Judges, seen them remove their masks and show their real faces. If he closed his eyes right now he could see their incredible visages right now, remember the feeling of immense energy that passed through his body when they touched him and sent him and the remaining Men of the First Chaos home victorious.

In the last one hundred years Barton Crisp had never had a cold. Or the flu or any other virus-borne sickness. None of his senses had dulled as he entered his twilight years. His hearing was as sharp as a wolf, his vision had precise as a hawk. The taste of a glass of chardonnay was as refreshing now as it had been in his twenties. His vigor had not lessened in the last one hundred years. He could, if he was so inclined, still satisfy two women a night for an entire week. His wife Eleanor had died fifty years ago during a particularly vigorous bout of lovemaking. Since then, when he wanted the pleasure of a woman or two he would contact Vivian Du Mor and have her send over two of her more athletic whores. He would then tell them stories of riding in a Model T. He was a living anachronism and that knowledge was a constant black cloud that followed him.

None of that mattered now. The Invitation had arrived.

Barton sat in his study. A soft, sinister rain was falling against the glazed windows. He was in the Crisp ancestral home of Brighton Hill. A huge sprawling estate on the moors, Brighton Hill had been built by his grandfather as a retreat for the Crisps from the daily grind of running a multinational empire. Over the years many modern conveniences had been added to the estate. Clear LED lighting ran throughout the mansion. A huge air handler hidden under a small wooden shed near the back of the mansion provided sufficient warmth for the entire structure. Barton had replaced the fireplace with a large aquarium. A gorgeous lionfish swam in lazy elliptical circles.

Despite the heat bellowing through the floor vents Barton felt a chill down to his bones. That chill had more to do with the polished black box on his coffee table than the weather. He had seen a box exactly like this one show up on the steps of Brighton Hill one hundred years ago. When Bernbridge, their butler, had brought the box to the study his father had dropped his glass of Scotch.

Bernbridge was long dead, as was Barton's father. He had not dropped his Scotch when Stephen, his butler had brought the box into the study. He had been expecting it for at least six months. The Archivists in the Grand Hall had concurred with his own calculations and they both agreed the Judges were near. That could only mean one thing. The Duel was coming. Barton pulled a small glass vial out of his vest pocket and unscrewed the little black cap. He poured a little bit of white powder into his hand and snorted it quickly. He felt a rush of numbness spread over his nose and face. A few moments later he felt a rush of adrenaline fill his veins. His heart began to pound like a jungle cat trying to break the bars of his cage. Because of the touch of the Judges he had no fear of the deadly side effects of cocaine. He could feel his mind focus like a laser. So here was the Invitation to the Duel. It was the first tangible step toward fulfilling the Covenant. Barton breathed deeply.

This was The Duel that determined whether the world that he and the other Men of the First Chaos had built in the last one hundred years would continue. A world where the strong took what they wanted from the weak. Where Darwinism gave way to Self-Actualism. Men and women who had the will would assume their rightful place as the leaders of the world, with no room for the misguided sentiments and useless platitudes of men like Pretlow Creedence or Richard Darn or any of the Men of the First Order. Their order was dilution of the elixir of human development. Their order was a pathetic leveling of the playing field. Barton was disgusted by this idea to his core. Life was a violent storm of the unknown, a vicious raging river of happenstance. Only men and women who embraced this idea could or deserved to not only survive but thrive. Order was a futile attempt to rope the wind, to ride the lightening. This was an impossible proposition. The Men of the First Order could not understand or accept this undeniable fact. So they went about their little insignificant lives trying to defy the Universe, trying to give form and structure to the formless. They spent their lives trying to stop the fire instead of learning to dance among the flames.

They deserved to die if only to put them out of their misery .The Men of the First Order were the Sisyphus of society, forever condemned to roll a boulder of hope up a mountain of reality and watch it roll right back down.

Barton sipped his Scotch and stared at the box. His longevity was both a blessing and a curse. He was old enough to remember what was in that menacingly mute black box. He was also old enough to have outlived both his sons and his brother and his wife. His great nephew was also dead but not of natural causes. He had foolishly challenged Carcone Apothas to an honor duel on behalf of his wife Vivian.

"That cunning wench wouldn't know the meaning of honor if you tattooed it to her face," Barton thought to himself. His nephew Saul, Louis's father, was an invalid felled by a stroke right after his son was killed. It was up to Barton's discretion whether or not the Invitation was accepted but it would be his grandsons fighting for the House of the Poison Soil. Despite his unflagging vitality Barton was not foolish enough to think he would stand a chance against men sixty years his junior. It would be his biological grandson Thaddeus Crisp and his adopted ward Danny Todd facing the blades of the Men of the First

Order. Barton liked their chances. Thad was an Adonis. Tall and broad shouldered, lean like a jaguar with deep piercing blue eyes and long black hair, Thad had been taught the way of the blade by Barton himself. He spent two months every year training with Shaolin Monks in China. He routinely ran super marathons. Right now he was running across the moors, completing a ten mile route that would bring him back to Brighton Hill.

Danny was …just different.

Twenty years ago Barton had gone on a safari with a potential business partner. The trip was a part of the prospective partner's long campaign of seduction to get Barton to invest in his company. Barton had ultimately refused to invest but had his chemist and researchers replicate the prospective partner's technique for developing better industrial diamonds. Barton then used his influence to stop the prospective partner from gaining financial backing from anyone. Eventually the prospective partner was forced to sell Barton his patent just to survive. Barton knew some who would say that what he did was unethical, he just considered it shrewd. He had found Danny on the safari. They had tracked an old male lion down into low lying grassland. Barton and the prospective partner and their guides had stalked the old king for miles. Finally when they felt they had him near exhaustion they had climbed out of their jeep to deliver the coup de grace.

Barton thought back to that day...

"Do you want to take the shot Barton?" Samuel Ganesh had whispered. They were crouched down on one knee staring at a huge old male lion through their high-powered scopes. Barton was hunting with a Bushmaster .30 caliber long range hunting rifle Samuel had a

Smith and Wesson .50 caliber carbine rifle. Barton smiled .Ganesh was really pouring on the supplication. Of course he would take the shot. Only a king should kill a king.

"Yes," Barton had said as he raised the rifle. His breathing slowed as he put the stock to his shoulder and gripped the trigger guard and the understock near the barrel. He looked through the scope and saw the lion in his cross hairs. The old emperor was cleaning his paws about fifty yards away. A hot arid wind blew and made the savannah undulate like a rolling sea. Barton blinked his eyes and looked through the scope again. The lion was gone.

Barton stood up and scanned the grassy terrain. The lion could blend in perfectly with his surroundings and with the strong breeze making the grass dance it would be impossible to track his movements. Barton was about to turn his head and tell Samuel they should get back in the jeep when the lion leaped out of the brittle weeds.

It flew through the air with a grace and power like a shark that lived on land. Barton had a second to register the muscles rippling beneath a tawny pelt before the creature slammed into him. It felt like being hit with a suitcase full of bricks. Lion and man crumpled to the ground. Barton tried to raise his arms to protect his face and neck but the lion was immovable. Its strength was implacable. His rifle lay ten yards away useless as udders on a bull. Samuel and the two guides had run. Run for their lives to be sure but run all the same. Barton could feel the lion's razor sharp claws ripping through the skin on his forearms, exposing tendons and bone. The smell of blood seemed to enrage the beast and it pawed at his extremities with even more fervor. Barton tried to kick or knee the lion in the mid-section but to no avail.

The world began to go dark .Sound faded away to nothingness. Barton had imagined many times how he would finally die. Being eaten by a lion had never crossed his mind.

"AHHHHHKKKIIIIIEEE!" someone screamed. Suddenly the crushing weight of the lion was no longer on his chest. It took all of his resolve but Barton slowly raised his head. The sight that greeted him was surreal.

A large boy was on the lion's back. The youth had dug his fingers into the lion's eyes and was holding on for dear life. The great cat bucked and spun like a Brahma bull but the boy held on tight. Barton reached for his rifle. Inch by painful inch he pulled himself across the dusty ground toward his weapon. His lacerations burned as dirt filled his numerous wounds. He ground his teeth so hard he felt a crown give way. Finally he reached his weapon. Wheezing, he lay flat on his stomach. He put the stock against his shoulder and sighted the lion through his scope. Barton was bleeding and in agony but he positioned the scope so that the lion's head was between the small black lines that ran horizontal and vertical through the center of the scope. He didn't know what the boy's end plan had been but he sincerely hoped the lad would let go in the next twenty seconds. The boy popped his head up like he had heard Barton's request. Catching Barton's gaze the boy released his grip. He had been thrown twenty feet. The lion shook his head and started after the still flying boy.

"Smile you yellow-toothed bastard," Barton thought to himself as he pulled the trigger. The sound of a loud crack reverberated through the valley. The lion, an old male who was the veteran of many battles and failed attempts to end his reign fell to the ground like a sack of potatoes, a mere two feet from the boy. Barton saw the boy get up and kick the lion in the muzzle. The filthy boy appeared to be about twelve years old. He was naked and covered in dirt and dust with a rat's nest of unkempt brown hair. Barton saw him drop to all fours and scamper away into the grasslands leaping high like a gazelle.

Two days later Barton was back out on the grasslands. He had a new guide and a pair of expensive binoculars and a well-regarded tracker with him. The other guests at the hunting lodge were flabbergasted by his remarkably quick recovery. The lion had bitten huge chunks out of his arms and shoulders and ripped his face and chest to shreds. Two days later he was nearly completely healed.

Being touched by the Judges had its benefits.

Barton found the boy among a herd of gazelles near a watering hole. The boy was ensconced within a pile of the fetid animals with his legs and arms curled up to his chest. Barton realized the boy had not interceded for his benefit but because the old lion had probably been snacking on members of his adopted family. Barton had a tranquilizer gun with him and took aim from the back of the jeep. One of the gazelles must have heard him. It leaped into the air and the whole herd took off like a sentient wave .Barton never lost track of the boy. The dart found its mark right between his shoulder blades. A few hundred yards later he fell to the ground.

Barton had not searched the boy out for purely altruistic reasons. While he was grateful to the horrid little feral boy for saving his life he prided himself on recognizing an opportunity when it presented itself. Both his sons were dead. He had one grandson and one grandnephew. Time would tell if either of them were worthy of defending the House of the Poison Soil in the coming battle.

This boy had something that was rare these days. He had will.

Barton had found you could teach a man to fight. You could teach him to master all manner of swords and sword fighting styles. You could teach him to train his body to the peak of physical and mental fitness. But you could not teach him to have will. You couldn't insert will into a man's spirit. It was something genetic and instinctual. In the wild boy Barton saw a blade that could be sharpened to a wicked edge. A weapon that would only be wielded by him. He could mold the boy to eschew all the extraneous human foibles that weighed down most warriors. Pity, fear, arrogance, all these things could be excised from this boy like a cancer.

Barton had named him Danny after his deceased son. He did not give him the surname Crisp. He would not disrespect his ancestors that way. He gave him the last name of Todd. Tod was German for death.

Barton took another sip of his scotch. Danny no longer looked like a poor man's Tarzan .He had grown into a tall muscular man with dark black eyes and long brown hair that fell to the middle of his back. Barton had his investigators try to track down any information about Danny but they could never find any reports of a young white boy lost in the African plains that fit Danny's description. Danny himself was of no help. He never spoke. Barton had gotten the best linguist and behavioral scientist money could buy but he never spoke one word. They assured him that Danny understood the English language and could communicate through sign language and pantomime. He just seemed to choose to not speak. Danny did not like to wear shoes. The pads of his feet were unbelievably tough. They clicked as he walked across the bare wooden floors throughout Brighton Hill. There was a fierce intelligence behind his eyes despite his lack of speech. He was a natural athlete who took to the various fighting styles that Barton taught him in the barn near the western part of the estate. Eventually he seemed to develop his own style that melded the traditional fencing of Europe with strange acrobatic Capoeira-like attacks. Barton had never seen anything quite like it. Watching Thad and Danny spar was like watching a pianist who was classically trained try to match a keyboardist trained through audiation. Both were skilled and both were deadly but Danny seemed to be able to adapt to different situations faster than Thad. Danny had become what Barton had envisioned, a living weapon.

Barton sipped his scotch once more.

Sighing, he pulled out his cell phone and called Thad. After his run Thad was going to go to London for a meeting with representatives from the nation of China about permits for a copper mine. Palm greasing of this magnitude required a personal touch from a Crisp, not one of their lackeys. He got his voice mail.

"Thad as soon as you get this message come home. The Invitation has arrived," he said in his wispy voice. He had called Carcone earlier. As soon as the butler had brought the smooth black box to him Barton knew what it was and what it meant. He had called Carcone first because he was the Man of Chaos that Bart felt was most prepared for the coming storm of swords. Barton had a grudging respect for the swarthy Greek. He didn't hold the killing of his grandnephew Louis against Carcone. Carcone had just put Louis down like the sick dog he was. There was no room in the Brotherhood that he served for the weak.

Barton felt a pair of eyes on his back. He stood and turned around. Danny was sitting on the window sill, his long brown hair spilling over his shoulders down to his chest. He was wearing a loose fitting long sleeved green shirt and blue jeans. As usual his feet were bare. His hair was wet and stuck to his face in places. Barton was on the second floor of Brighton Hill. Danny had climbed up the ivy covered lattice on the mansion walls and entered through the window. He was perched on the sill like a hawk resting on a cliff. Danny had remarkable hearing.

"I assume you heard what I said to Thad's voicemail. The time has come my boy. Are you ready?" Barton said softly. Danny jumped off the window sill and walked over to Barton. He was taller and heavier than the older man. He took his left hand and extended his thumb. Then he drew his thumb across his throat in a slashing motion. Barton smiled. As time passed he found that he enjoyed Danny's silence. It gave him certain honesty. Honesty was a rare commodity in Barton's world. Everyone around him lied and tried their best to placate him with false praise in the hopes he would give them just a little of his influence. Even the Windsors sought his favor from time to time. That nasty bit of business with Diana came to mind. Danny never lied to him. Danny never tried to cajole him. Danny simply did what he was told.

Barton found that strangely endearing.

"Yes my boy I think you are ready," Barton said as he patted Danny on the arm. The wheels of fate were locking together like the gears of Big Ben. Destiny was drawing in all of them, Men of Chaos and Men of Order, like the whirlpool of the Charybdis to their final reckoning. Only the strong could survive. Barton finished his Scotch.

"Only the strong," he thought to himself.

CHAPTER THIRTEEN

Silas Boon perused the menu of the Bellisamo with a critical eye. He was a connoisseur of fine food and drink. A vinophile and a lover of fine cuisine he was hard to impress. He was also not shy about expressing his displeasure when a meal did not live up to his high expectations. Despite his exacting standards restauranteurs loved to see Silas and his entourage walk through their doors. He was as effusive and generous with his praise as he was cutting with his criticisms. A meal that satisfied his discriminating pallet could result in a ten thousand dollar tip. Among the premier chefs and eateries of the world Silas Boon was known as the Black Knight. He could either put your establishment in the black or deliver a death knell. Such was the power one possessed when one was the CEO of the largest pharmaceutical conglomerate in the entire world .And being the prefect of the House of the Eternal Apothecary made him even more powerful behind the curtain upon the stage of life. Silas finally settled upon a seared slice of Bluefin tuna with a hollandaise dressing on watercress and a bottle of Chardonnay from the Montrachet vinyard in the Cote d'Or region of France. His son Hieronymus would say that Silas didn't have high standards, he had the highest standards. These standards permeated his life. They extended into his business, his personal life and the training he gave his sons for the coming Duel. Silas was proud that both his sons Hieronymus and Danelo understood and accepted his dedication and embraced their duty. He could not say the same for his dinner guest.

The House of the Eternal Apothecary traced their origins back to medicinal and alchemistic practitioners from Eastern Europe. From those humble beginning his ancestors built, with help from the Judges and the Covenant, a huge sprawling pharmaceutical entity that controlled most of the legal and illegal drugs in the world. From their current base of operations in Melbourne Australia Silas and his family kept a firm hand on the legal narcotics industry. Using the influence of his deep pockets he kept any research or advancement in the treatment of cancer, AIDS, heart disease, and other deadly illnesses to a minimum. Silas was a firm believer in the idea that there was no money in a cure, only in a treatment.

Through various intermediaries and associates, most of whom never knew they were in his employ, he kept his other hand on the illegal drug trade. The Cartels of Colombia, the drug lords of Asia, the Russian Mafia, they all used his chemicals to cut their product, his influence kept their lines of commerce open ,with help from Abdul El-Aki and the House of the Black Rivers. His chemists and his private security forces made sure that potent and possibly deadly strains of heroin and meth periodically reared their collective heads to keep addicts enthralled to a pitiless Belle sans Merci. He supported regimes with financial gifts that had a certain flexibility as far as drug traffic was concerned. He destroyed those who tried to take a stand. Silas was nothing if not consistent. Death for those stricken with physical illness and death for those with addiction. He viewed it as protecting his bottom line and separating the wheat from the chaff. Addicts and the ill were both weak. Infirmity of the mind or the body it was all the same to Silas. He had no pity for either.

Silas and his family literally had the best medical care that money could buy. They had a personal physician who lived on the grounds of Caterwhal, their family home just outside of Melbourne. In addition he, his wife Jeannie and both his sons awoke every morning at six in the morning no matter where they were in the world. They would then begin an intensive exercise program created for them by the inventor of a popular workout routine that dominated the current infomercial market. Once that was complete Silas and his boys would begin practicing their swordsmanship. Silas was an only child. His parents had died together when their jet crashed into the Pacific Ocean on New Year's Eve 1994. Silas had taken it upon himself to learn the Way of the Sword. At eighteen, after assuming control of the Boon fortune, he traveled to England to study with Barton Crisp. He traveled to Greece and took lessons from Nicodemus Apothas and sparred with Carcone. He created a style of his own utilizing all the techniques he had been taught. He pushed himself even more He entered Iron Man competitions and ran marathons through the Outback. He even tried to get the mysterious sword maker Garn Whiteborne to take him as an apprentice. Garn had declined none too politely.

"I don't like you Silas. You look hungry like a Wendigo," Garn had said. Silas had sent men to Garn's workshop in Florence to the dreadlocked sword smith to rough him up a bit. They never returned but a box with their hands showed up at his office a few weeks later. Silas did not send any more ruffians. A pragmatist, Silas knew that his obsessive dedication to physical fitness was not only influenced by his membership in the Brotherhood but also a pathological need to stave off the cold embrace of death. He acknowledged the irony that a man of chaos that yearned for control. He accepted this personal quirk and then quickly moved past it in his mind. Pragmatism was his philosophy.

That was evidenced by his dinner with Karl Lutenburg, prefect of the House of Golden Tears. The Lutenburgs controlled a majority of all the gold mining, refining and sales in the open market. Yet here was

Karl showering Silas with compliments in an effort to get something. Silas didn't know exactly what Karl wanted but he knew it was something that was very important to the stout little German. He was buying dinner. So he agreed to meet with the towheaded little merchant.

Silas gave the waiter his order and then leaned back in his chair and crossed his hands in his lap. Karl placed his order then placed his hands on the table. Karl had the countenance of a cherub down on his luck. He had huge red cheeks under a thick mop of blond hair. His tiny piggish eyes twinkled with just a tinge of mania. Karl laughed even though nothing had been said.

Karl looked at Silas like a child looked at Santa Claus even though the man was the physical   antithesis of the jolly old elf. Silas was as thin as a rail but with a tight vascular muscularity. His face was so sharp you could have sliced cheese on his profile. Karl took a deep breath.

"Well Silas good to see you again," he said with a broad smile.

"No it is not. You want something Karl. You have asked to meet me here in Melbourne's most exclusive restaurant instead of my offices. You and I are not friends. We have never golfed or god forbid gone skin diving together. I have seen you maybe five times in my entire life and all those occasions were business or Brotherhood related. So tell me Karl what is it that you want so desperately that you have taken the ten hour flight from Berlin to meet with me?" Silas asked. Karl chewed at the inside of his bottom lip and rubbed his hands together in a slow languid motion.

"Well it's interesting that you bring up business Silas. That is why I am here. I want to talk with you about something that will affect all of us and our various businesses. I chose to speak with you first because in the few times that we have met you seemed to be the most practical of the men in our little fraternity. Not a zealot like Barton Crisp and not a psychopath like Carcone." Karl took a sip of his water.

"My father believed in the Brotherhood. So much so that with his dying breath he implored me to take up the sword and train for this mythical Duel that he was sure was coming. Now Silas I don't know what your personal belief system is composed of. I don't know if you are Christian or Muslim or Jewish or Hare Krishna. But whatever it is I bet that you can separate your spiritual devotion from your financial and fiduciary responsibilities. What I mean is we all go to the meetings at the Bilderberg, we read the Book of the Seven Swords, we swear the oath but not all of us are as naive or overzealous as Barton or Vivian. Some of us live in the real world. A world where we don't spit on the beliefs of our ancestors, but we also don't let that belief determine how we will live our lives, run our businesses or raise our families. The idea that this Duel determines the outcome of human history for a century is no more believable or ludicrous than the idea a simple carpenter from Galilee who hung out with dirty fisherman and a prostitute was the son of God. Millions of people pay lip service to the church he founded but they don't let that devotion take food off their tables. Silas, we are members of a patriarchal hereditary, a fraternity that believes that 20 foot tall angels control our fate and the fate of our children and grandchildren. Our fellow members are serious about this. Deadly serious. Silas, do you remember that business at the Du Mor estate? My father was ill but I dared not disobey him and his fanatical adherence to the traditions of his Brotherhood. Silas, we watched a man be eviscerated in a duel for the honor of a woman whose family built their fortune on the backs of broken and abused harlots. Now I have received letters and emails from the "Archivist" imploring me to be ready for the time is close at hand. Now Silas let's say we go through with this insane dance of death .Let's say for the sake of the argument that we lose. Those lunatics like Barton or Carcone or Abdul will actually make us all go through with this "covenant". They will cease and desist with their legal and illegal activities. They will pull their support from any and all endeavors they deem "chaotic" .And we will have no choice but to follow suit. We are all inexorably tied together in some sort of an ancient six degrees of separation algorithm. We use Barton's mining companies to dig for gold in places that legally we shouldn't be digging. You use Abdul ships to move some of your more esoteric products around the world. Taang will no longer rob and terrorize our rivals on the high seas. Carcone will stop inciting unrest in certain countries thus severely curtailing the demand for his weapons. Stable nations charge higher prices for mining rights. Silas, do you see what I am getting at here? So I bring to you a proposal. We join together and we withdraw from the Duel, the Covenant, the whole ridiculous affair. I believe I can get Taang on board with this idea. Once Taang is with us we can join forces to convince Vivian. The only ones I don't believe will acquiesce are Carcone and Barton. Those two have definitely drunk the Kool-Aid so to speak. Silas, my wife Hilda and I have two beautiful wonderful sons, Gunther and Grice. I will not see our family's legacy which is their birthright taken from them by the turn of a blade.

"What do you say Silas? Are you the man I think you are or are you sipping the sweet sugary concoction as well?" Karl said. He sat back in his chair and peered at Silas with his tiny brown eyes.

The waiter arrived just as Karl sat back with the wine. The waiter presented the bottle to both Karl and Silas then he made a great show of uncorking it with lots of panache and flair. Once he had that out of the way he poured a small drop of wine in the glass and presented it to Silas for his inspection. Silas put the rim of the glass to his nose and inhaled deeply. Sharp scents wafted up his nostrils to his olfactory senses. Images of expansive vineyards stretching across rolling hills exploded in his mind. He could almost smell the moist rich soil that gave birth to the exquisite libation. Silas nodded at the waiter and the young man filled his glass. Silas took a sip and let it wash over his teeth and tongue. He swallowed it and felt the pleasant and refreshing shock to his esophagus that always followed a sip of great wine. Silas put his glass down on the table and looked at Karl.

"Once when I was a young boy my father showed me the passage in the Book of Seven Swords that detailed how our ancestor Cyril The Younger came to be chosen by the Judges to fight in the first Duel. It said that one day Cyril was in the woods gathering herbs, flowers, and mushrooms for his various potions and medicines. This was in 185 A.D. He was under the rule of the Romans and so as to not incite their wrath he dressed very plainly but kept a short sword in his belt. He sold medicines to anyone who had the right amount of coin to afford his potions. Roman, Carthaginian, Huns, if the price was right the right elixir could be obtained. He sold poisons and opium and fermented wormwood as well. He had no constraints on his commerce. So when those Judges appeared before him and entreated upon him to enter the first Duel or face living in a world where men of order bound his hands and took away his right to leave a legacy for his family he gladly accepted on one condition. If the Men of Chaos won the duel they would receive compensation in the form of one thousand pounds of gold. Now Cyril the Younger did not survive that first battle but his grandson fought in the next Duel and won. It was Cyril, not your ancestor Heinrich who first proposed to the Judges this rider in the Covenant. I take a bit of pride in that, Karl.

"The family fortune grew and grew until here we are today sitting in a restaurant with a three thousand dollar bottle of wine eating the rarest and most expensive fish in the world. To receive great rewards you must take great risks. Our ancestors understood that and accepted it. You say you don't believe. I say you are being very foolish," Silas finished as he took another sip of his wine. Karl began to laugh.

"Silas, you are a man of science, a business man, and a rational man. I cannot accept that you too have put your faith in this fairy tale. I guess I missed judges you," Karl said.

"You don't accept it Karl? Have you just for your own edification, taken a look at your family's finances for say, the year 1913? Perhaps you would be interested to know that your great-grandmother along with my great-grandmother deposited one thousand pounds of gold bullion into a Swiss bank account. Have you ever wondered where that amount of gold actually came from? Karl I have a suggestion for you. Stop trying to form some cabal to usurp the authority of the Brotherhood and pick up a sword," Silas said after swallowing his wine. Karl shook his head and picked up his own wine glass.

"Well I will tell you now that neither I nor my sons will participate in this insanity. If we receive some mysterious invitation we will politely mark it return to sender. You should really reconsider my plan Silas," Karl said softly.

"Karl perhaps it is you who should reconsider. If you refuse the Invitation and we are victorious you could find yourself in a very untenable position," Silas said as he drummed the fingers of his right hand on the table.

"Is that some sort of threat Silas? Excuse me if I'm not stricken with terror," Karl said.

"You know, Karl when I was in boarding school me and some of my lads decided to play a joke on the headmaster. There were five us in my dorm but only four wanted to play the joke. The fifth boy did not want to participate but he also did nothing to prevent the prank. Yet after the joke was played I took a sock full of washers and nuts and cornered him in the gymnasium and beat him until my arm got tired. Not because I thought he would betray our secret but because he did not join in our rite of passage .He didn't want to be a part of the fraternity so to speak. I could not abide such egotism. He thought he was better than us sitting on his moral pedestal. Just because he didn't participate he thought that somehow exonerated him. He was just as culpable as the rest of us. He just thought his inaction was somehow noble. People who put themselves on those types of pedestals need to be knocked off routinely. All our hands are covered in blood Karl. Now you want to try and wash it off. Too late for that my friend. Make no mistake Karl. If you ignore the Invitation and we survive you will be ostracized and excommunicated from the Brotherhood. No one will buy your gold or patronize your jewelry stores. We will devote the rest of our lives to making sure you end up so destitute and miserable that you may come to the Bilderberg begging for one of us to run you through. You called me rational. I am very rational and pragmatic. There is a Duel, there are Judges and they expect us to fulfill the Covenant with our lives. What I find irrational is your stubborn insistence that this is all a story we were told to tuck us in at night. I for one never found the Book of Seven Sword comforting light reading," Silas said. He threw back another swallow of wine.

Karl stood up from the table. "I see this was a mistake Silas. I pray you will reconsider. I hope you will keep this conversation between the two of us. I will have them bill my account. Enjoy your meal," Karl said. He turned to go before Silas could respond.

"This was a terrible idea," he thought to himself. As he started to walk toward the door a figure in a black suit wearing a black fedora walked into the restaurant. The figure was also wearing black sunglasses and despite the warm Australian weather a black and white checked scarf around his mouth and neck. He had a package in his hands. The package was wrapped in brown paper and tied with a simple piece of white string. The figure weaved in out of the immaculately decorated tables and in and out of superfluous conversations, heading straight for Karl.

Karl watched the man approach him with a bit of bemusement. What was this? Had Silas anticipated why he had asked him to lunch and paid someone to dress up in a spooky outfit carrying an "Invitation?" As a boy before he had realized it was a lie, like the Bible or the Koran, Karl had read how the Judges sent their emissaries to deliver the Invitations to the Heads of the Great Houses. It didn't matter where the prefects lived the emissary would find them and either leave the Invitation or present it directly to the Master of the House. The Book suggested the emissaries were constructs; non-human entities that the Judges attached to each House. Sort of like a familiar.

The figure in black stopped in front of Karl and held the package out to him. Karl laughed.

"Is this supposed to be the Invite? Oh Silas you really are devoted aren't you? Well my dear fellow I'm sorry he put you through all this.

The suit, the scarf, the slow dramatic entrance, the awkward glances of all these well-to-do bon vivants. But I don't want the Invitation. You can take that back to whatever post office or stationary store you got it from," Karl said. His eyes were twinkling.

"Karl Lutenburg, son of Peter Lutenburg, Prefect of the House of Golden Tears, you refuse the Invitation?" the figure intoned. His voice was as deep as the Grand Canyon. It rumbled out of his mouth like a black avalanche of malice. It hurt Karl's ears to hear the man speak. Something in his voice was...painful. Karl suddenly felt very angry. Who was this man to speak to him? He was Karl Gustav Lutenburg. He was worth more than some small countries. He was a captain of industry, a learned man of letters. Who in the hell was this bastard and why did he think he could just talk to him about some goddam mythical duel?!

"Yes I refuse the damn Invitation and I refuse to accept this goddamn box!" he yelled. The other patrons of the restaurant turned back to their plates and immediately began ignoring the scene. Karl watched them turn away and resume their conversations. He felt embarrassed. He looked at the package. He looked at Silas. The thin man was as still as a statue. Karl could feel the condescension coming off him like heat from a campfire.

"Out of my way you miscreant!" Karl howled. He pushed past the figure with a violent shove. The figure moved to his left. As Karl walked away the figure in black touched the knot on top of the package with his left index finger. The string unraveled itself like a stop motion film running in reverse.

The brown paper fell away like falling leaves. The box beneath the paper was smooth and black .It's surface glistened like it was wet.

"Karl Lutenburg, Prefect of the House of Golden Tears you have violated the Covenant," the figure said. His voice seemed to bellow from the bottom of some Stygian pit. The sound filled Karl's ears. A trickle of blood began to drip out of each of them. Karl turned and stared at the figure. The man in black slid his hand back and forth across the top of the box, first to the right then to the left with a black gloved hand.

The lid slowly rose.

"Your ancestors have honored this agreement for 1,828 years. They took lives and gave their lives to honor this Oath. Perhaps you should tell them why you have broken your word," the man in black said.

Karl looked at what was rising up out of the box and he began to scream. Images rose up out of the box like ephemeral holograms. Faces covered in blood and etched with pain. Centuries of death and sacrifice billowed out of the simple black box. Visions swirled around him like a cloud of sentient smoke. Voices howled at him from across great valleys of time. He waved his hands in a feeble effort to dispel these phantoms of history. These were the true founders of the Lutenburg legacy. They screamed at Karl in languages long dead. He could not understand the words but he comprehended the meaning. Karl had broken his word. He had broken the Covenant that they had fought and died to fulfill. His mind felt close to breaking. His head pulsated with the demonic cacophony of his ancestors' admonishments. He felt tightness in his chest that became a crushing pain. Then without warning a seizure tore through his body. Something inside of Karl Lutenburg broke. It just gave way like a rusted water pipe in an old tenement building. Blood filled his stomach and barreled up his esophagus and poured out of his mouth. The front of his fine gray silk suit darkened to a scarlet hue. Karl staggered backwards a few steps then pitched forward. His face hit the ceramic tiles on the floor with a loud crack.

Silas Boon did not see what Karl Lutenburg saw in his final moments. Silas did not hear the man in black speak to Karl. Karl's responses seemed to be the manic ravings of a lunatic. Silas saw the box open but he did not witness any spirits issuing forth from its maw. When Karl vomited blood onto his Spiegelhaus suit Silas was shocked. He watched Karl fall forward like a small shrub felled by an invisible ax.

The figure in black waved his hand over the open lid of the black box. It closed without a sound. The figure placed a gloved hand on the closed lid for a few seconds. The box seemed to glow with a negative light. It was as if the blackness of the box became more intense, darker before it relented. The figure then held the box out to Silas.

Silas stood and took the box in his hands. It felt cool to the touch and incredibly light. Silas nodded slowly and tucked the box under his arm and walked out of the restaurant.

The patrons of Bellisamo's did not seem to notice him leaving. Later none of them would recall really noticing the stout blond man or his companion or what exactly had transpired before the waiter tripped over his prone form on the smooth ceramic floor.

Silas Boon hurried to his waiting limo. Rogers, his driver, hopped out and opened his door without saying a word. Silas climbed in and settled back against the plush leather seats of the limo and placed the box next to him close to the driver's side of the vehicle. He leaned forward and pushed a button on a small console.

"Rogers I'm not going back to the office. Take me directly home," Silas said into a small unobtrusive speaker. He sat back and pulled out a sleek flat cell phone out of pocket. He dialed his oldest son Hieronymus.

"H, meet me at home. The time is finally here. Call your brother for me. We have an Invitation to read," Silas said. He tapped the screen and the call was disconnected. Silas sat back and let out a deep breath. In his heart he never doubted that the Duel was real. He never really doubted the power of the Judges .But seeing it in person, seeing the emissary drive Karl insane in a matter of minutes shut the door to any doubts that may have tried to sneak into his heart. It was all real. The risk was real. But so were the rewards. All he had to do was kill the Men of the First Order. By any and all means necessary. It was simple really. It was ...

Pragmatic...

CHAPTER FOURTEEN

Richard Darn sat in the living room of his two-story Tudor style house in Biggin Hill .Just eighteen miles outside of London it was small, quiet hamlet that offered a respite from the city. Richard Darn rented a warehouse and office in London proper near the Piccadilly Square. Darn and Sons Inc. was a small but lucrative firm specializing exclusive handmade furniture. Chairs, tables, cabinets, beds, Darn and Sons could do it all. Their expertise and attention to detail were legendary among those who enjoyed the finer things in life. Despite their renown, Richard and his wife Sonna, and their two sons Seth and Robert along with their wives lived simple lives in quaint little houses at the end of a peaceful cul-de-sac in the Poppthistle neighborhood. The Darn family had a deep and enormous basement that connected all three houses. You could, if you were so inclined, enter Seth's house and walk down into the basement walk about thirty yards and come up out of the basement in Richard's house. The basement was where they trained. In the middle of the basement was the trunk of a huge oak tree. In the center of the trunk was an inscription written in ancient Gaelic "Ritheann ar rutai go domhain". It was Gaelic for "Our roots run deep." It was the motto of the House of the Olde Grove.

Richard was sipping a cup of Earl Grey tea and eating a scone. At 46 years old he still sported the build of a tougher than average rugby player and a face that looked like it was carved out of the Blarney Stone itself. He had left the office an hour ago but he still had on his red tie, white dress shirt, black vest and black slacks. His black oxfords were creased with aged and immeasurably comfortable. Sonna was down in Blackpool vising her friend Margret and the boys were at their homes with their respective families. Seth and his wife Corrine and their four boys, Ricky, Longfellow, Neil, and Kenneth, aged 16, 12, 10 and 9 respectively, were all watching an episode Doctor Who. It was a family tradition after Seth came home from work for them to have a meal and enter the realm of Daleks and Cybermen and the like. Robert and twelve year old Langdon were playing chess while Robert's wife Becca was making bangers and mash or Brunswick stew or some other delicious concoction.

Richard sipped his tea again and caught a glimpse of himself in the placid surface of the hot liquid. Customers always asked him if he was an actor. They always seemed to confuse him with the bloke from the Lock Stock and Two Smoking Barrel movies, that ex-footballer with the severe scowl. Richard didn't see the resemblance but Sonna liked to tease him that it was why she married him.

"I loves being married to a celebrity," she would say, sliding her ample rump by him in their small kitchen on a tranquil Sunday morning as he made them breakfast. Sonna was a daughter of the House of Sun and Stone, first cousin to Raul Esperanza, the prefect of that House from the Spanish Hills. Richard didn't know how anyone in the Brotherhood made a marriage work with a *slaepan*. Slaepan was Brotherhood slang for all those who walked the earth unaware of the Covenant. The Book of Seven Swords said they ***"were as in a dream, a walking sleep that comforted their souls and embraced their hearts and protected them from the true world. They slept in peace like children unaware that their house was on fire, and surrounded by rough men. Some who were trying to quell the flames and some who fanned the blaze."***

Marriage was hard enough. Richard couldn't imagine trying to explain to a woman that he practiced every day to fight in an ancient Duel that determined the fate of the world. That was a little more to come to terms with than just leaving the top off the peanut butter. Richard sipped his tea and took another bite of his scone. In the living room on the wall above the fireplace were two swords. Colichemardes. They were light weight extremely sharp swords with a half-hasp hand guard and edged on both sides. The handle was decorated with arboreal motifs and designs. Tree branches and pine cones were etched in fine detail in the hilt. The blades themselves had an ivy filigree carved into the entire length of the sword. Pretlow Creedence had made those two swords and given them to Richard as a gift five years ago. The last great gathering of the Men of the First Order had coincided with his birthday. Richard and Pretlow had met when they were young men apprenticing to Garn Whiteborne in his studio in Florence. There had been a nasty bit of business with a young girl from one of the Houses of Chaos, a stolen sword and some rather murderous gangsters. Richard had stood with Pretlow against these men who had grossly underestimated them. They had not been ordinary young men. They had been young men of the Brotherhood. Even at such a young age they were well versed in the Way of the Sword and the awesome responsibility the Way entailed. Once you picked up a sword you became a merchant of destiny and the currency you dealt in was death.

During that last great meeting Pretlow had presented Richard with those very swords. He had invited Richard and his sons to visit his home in the suburbs of Virginia. Richard had gladly accepted the offer. His sons had gotten along famously with Pretlow's boy Catlow. Pretlow was a man who valued loyalty above all else. He told Richard so when he handed him the swords.

"You could have run that night in the down by the docks. You could have gone back to Garn's and left me to face the men holding Agrippina by myself. But you didn't. You stood and were true, Richard. I will never, ever forget that my friend," Pretlow had said to him as he handed the beautiful wooden chestnut box that had held the swords.

"Well I couldn't let you have all the fun," Richard had said.

Richard stared at the swords for a moment. If the Duel happened in his lifetime he would take those two blades down off the wall and pack them in the chestnut box so that he could face his destiny with weapons forged by the fires of trust and friendship. Weapons quenched in spilled blood from the distant past.

Richard finished the rest of his tea and rose from the table. Time for a shower then catch Manchester United on the telly then down into the basement with his boys for a few hours of practice. He passed the pantry door and walked through the short hallway. There was a book case in the hallway. Tomes by Chaucer and Ramsey Campbell and Clive Barker and Agatha Christie lined the shelves. The collected works of Shakespeare shared space with John Kennedy O'Toole's classic, "A Confederacy of Dunces".

On the middle shelf one book sat alone. It had an ancient leather bound cover. The spine was riddled with creases from the book being opened and closed thousands of times. On the front of the book affixed over the leather binding was a large metal cover. A sort of extreme dust jacket. On this metal cover there was an etching. It depicted three large hooded figures looking down from a great height over two figures locked in combat. The figures held weapons in their hands and appeared to be in a battle to the death. Richard touched the metal cover. Its surface was cool to the touch.

It was *The Book of Seven Swords*.

Not *the* book of course. That was locked in the library in the Grand Hall protected by the Archivists. This was just a copy. A painstakingly maintained, well cared for copy. The book was part historical document, part spiritual guide and part practical manual on the Way of the Sword. Between its ancient covers there was almost two thousand years of wisdom and knowledge, observation and testimony .It was what guided the Men of the First Order and the Men of the First Chaos through the centuries. It was an archipelago in the middle of an ocean of time. Something for the Men of the Brotherhood to grasp on to while they waited for the rising tide of the coming Duel. The Book was a direct conduit to their ancestors. All the men who had fought and died for the Covenant had their story recorded in the Book of Seven Swords and spoke to their descendants from its weathered pages.

Richard began to loosen his tie when he heard a knock at the door. Richard stopped in his tracks. The knock in and of itself was innocuous enough. It could have been some traveling salesman. A lost relic from a simpler time who didn't realize his kind were virtually extinct. It could have been a lost and weary traveler looking for someone, anyone who could tell him to how in the hell you got out of Poppingthistle. It could have been one of his neighbors stopping by to say hello or even perhaps to borrow some tea. Richard didn't believe it was any of those mundane possibilities. His gut was twisted into a heavy knot. His skin broke out in a body-wide tingle. It was not a neighbor. It was not a salesman. It was not a traveler. He didn't know how he knew this but he just knew. Richard rushed to the fireplace, covering the space between him and his sword with an economy of movement that belied his size. He pulled one of the swords from its moorings. The solid heft of the hilt and the wicked edge of the blade comforted him. His father Simon Darn had always told him that the feel of a sword in your hand was all the protection a Darn man would ever need. Richard walked to the door with the sword in his left hand down by his side. He walked with a nearly sideways gait. Breathing deeply he walked to his back door. He slid back through his kitchen and grabbed the brass door knob. The back door to his home was narrow, just nine light solid wooden slabs. To open it you had to grasp the handle and give it a rather aggressive pull. Richard peeped through the willowy white curtain over the nine light window of the door.

There on the stoop was a black box. It looked to be about the size of an urn. Richard glanced to the left and the right. There was no one on the stoop or in his backyard. Richard twisted the doorknob and flung the door open with little trouble. A small warm breeze blew into his kitchen. Richard heard some of the usual sounds of a small English neighborhood. Kids laughing and playing. Far away voices of adults, indistinct in the afternoon air. The box sat on his step mute as a mime. Richard squatted down and placed the sword on the floor by his foot. It was within easy reach if he needed it. He picked the box up and shook it. Nothing jingled or jangled inside. Richard stood and put the box under one arm and picked up the sword with the other one. He closed the door and sat down at the kitchen table.

Thoughts seemed to have been emancipated from his mind. He could not focus on any one idea. On a subconscious level he knew what was sitting on his kitchen table. On a conscious level he could not seem to articulate what he was seeing or what he was feeling. It was the Invitation. It was the first step to fulfilling the Covenant. A validation of all of his sacrifice and training. Of his sons sacrifice and training. Of all the sacrifice of all the Darn men and women for over a thousand years. Here was his ticket to the dance. This was possibly the first step to his death but also a validation of his life. Richard felt a lump rise in his throat.

"Time to stand, boys. Time to let our blades strike true," he whispered.

Lost in his epiphany he never heard the sound of light footsteps on the roof of his quaint little home. He never looked out his bedroom window to see the camouflaged figures scaling the homes of his sons. He didn't notice these figures entering windows unnoticed or impeded in anyway. He had no idea that in little over an hour everything he loved and cherished would be irrevocably changed forever.

Robert Darn waited for his son to move his pawn on the chess board his grandfather had carved for him. Langdon bit his bottom lip as he contemplated his options. Langdon resembled his mother more than he did Robert. A thick head of black hair cut into a faux hawk and wide blue eyes that seemed to be constantly on the verge of spilling tears. He was tall for his age but quieter than most twelve-year-old boys. Robert waited with a bit of a smile on his lips. Langdon was a better chess player than Robert .He understood the nuances and tactics in a way Robert never would but he lacked decisiveness. He hesitated and second guessed himself so much he invariably made silly mistakes. In five years he had never defeated Robert. And despite Rebecca's repeated requests Robert had never let Langdon win.

"The world is a hard cruel place. No one is ever going to hand him anything. No one is ever going to let him win in the real world. No one will let him win in a duel." Robert had told Rebecca the last time she had broached the subject. Rebecca was a woman of the Brotherhood. She was a distant cousin of the prefect of the House of Winter Night, Victor Crizwell. Her father and mother had died years ago and she was an only child. Her father had been born with Cerebral Palsy. He had never taken up the sword but he had made sure Rebecca Koloff Darn knew the history of her family. She understood the importance of the Covenant even if her immediate family were not represented in the coming Duel. His brother Seth was the only Darn man married to slaepan. Yet Corrine was a woman with a unique ability to accept what others would have dismissed. It didn't hurt that Seth had saved her life with his swordsmanship outside of a pub the night they met. She was a fine companion for his little brother and one hell of a cook. And she obviously liked a good rogering. Four kids in sixteen years meant someone was fulfilling their marital duties. Robert wondered if his brother knew how lucky he was to have a wife who loved to shag. A wife who didn't have to be cajoled and begged for a hand job, never mind some good ole fashioned head.

"Pawn takes bishop," Langdon said. Robert shook his head slightly and looked at the board. He had left his bishop exposed and Langdon was removing him from the table.

"Hello now. Good move son. Hmm let's see what the old man can do with only one bishop. Of course I still have two knights, two rooks, a queen and a plethora of pawns. You see son when you play chess you have to be willing to sacrifice every piece on the board as long as the King survives. It's all about the King," Robert said before moving his black rook to challenge the white knight. Langdon had a brilliant mind for chess but he played like he was in love with every piece on the board. His son had not yet learned one of life's harshest lessons. Everyone is expendable once the battle begins. No one is safe, whether it was chess or love or war. No one is safe once the battle commences.

Rebecca laughed from the kitchen as she watched her two favorite men engage in their nightly battle of wits. Robert hated to lose .At anything. He even approached lovemaking like it was a competition. Sometimes it seemed like he wanted to make her orgasm just to validate his manhood. She loved him that was not the issue but sometimes he fucked her like a man chopping down a tree with a dull ax. His jaw set at an odd angle, a grimace across his face and a grim determination in his eyes, he would pound away. It was like her orgasm was incidental to his subjugation of her vagina. When they were young she enjoyed his aggressiveness. It excited her and made her feel wanted. But as she got older she realized she wanted some tenderness. She desired a bit of playfulness in the boudoir. Every night didn't have to be a battle to take the Isle of Clitoris by force. She sighed. Robert was great father and great provider. He was a man of great passions. He was passionate about The Brotherhood, passionate about his honor. He was passionate about his needs. She shouldn't care that he wasn't the tenderest of lovers. She just couldn't seem to shake the idea that this lack of sensitivity was somehow indicative of a lack of respect for her.

Robert heard Rebecca laugh and craned his neck to peer at her standing in the kitchen. Her long black hair was tied into a thick braid trailing down her back. It stopped just above her firm round backside. When Robert had met Rebecca she had been a promising ballet dancer. Even after having Langdon her body had lost little of its tone and definition. She had willingly given up ballet to move to England and be his wife. She worked in the front office of the furniture store and picked Langdon up from school or attended his rugby games. She was a good wife and a good mother.So why did he go to the Du Mor's brothel in London?

Robert knew that was an internal rhetorical question. He knew exactly why he went to the brothel run by a family of the Brotherhood. He was able to procure the hot, rough, dangerous sex he desired from his wife. As to the more philosophical why he knew the answer to that as well. He liked it. He liked the danger of being in the den of the enemy. It added a very tangible excitement to his interludes in the House of Love and Agony. Robert believed in the Brotherhood. He believed in the Covenant. His faith was unshakable. But there was a devil inside him. A twisted perverted little imp that found the idea of screwing around in the very mouth of the beast exhilarating.

Through his scholarly studies with the Book of Seven Swords he learned all about the history of the House of Love and Agony at an early age. He learned that they were basically high class pimps. The last revision to the Book by the Archivists noted that the Du Mors operated brothels all over Europe including one in London. The last time the book had been updated was in 1913 after the last Duel. Much like Ford or IBM the Du Mor brothels were a business with a long tradition and some considerable staying power. As a young man Robert had searched out these experts in the erotic arts. The advantage of being in a secret society was that many of the members didn't recognize each other. The Book of Seven Sword was not illustrated with pictures of all the members of their dark fraternity. Unless individuals crossed paths during the normal course of their lives no one from the Houses of Chaos knew or interacted with those from the Houses of Order. Robert had found the stories of the dark House of Love and Agony intoxicating. His father and grandfather had spoken of that house in hushed tones that were equal parts desire and disgust. Robert had wanted to find out for himself if that house was really as decadent as it was in the stories.

So as a teen Robert had found his way to the lair of lasciviousness. He didn't go every week and he didn't spend all his money there. He would bide his time and save his wages from the furniture business. Then when he had saved the appropriate amount he would sneak away from the scent of sawdust and tung oil and embrace the smell of lilac perfume and cinnamon massage oils. The devil inside him was awoken within those fur lined walls of that inconspicuous pit of passion. The devil liked it rough. The devil liked to defile and debase the harlots of the House. He liked it a lot. Until he met Rebecca he thought that the devil was something he left behind when he walked out of the House of Love and Agony. He did not. The devil clung to him with an implacable grip. It was the devil's face his wife saw sometimes when they were clinging to each other in that wild place in the middle of their bed in the middle of the night. The thrill of possibly being in the presence of those who might wish him harm, the deliciously twisted feel of taking a woman whom you had bought and paid for, a woman who had to do whatever you told her to do was like a drug to Robert. He told himself he would kick the habit but he wasn't really trying.

"White knight E5 to black rook G4," Langdon said. Robert looked at the board. Langdon wasn't close to winning yet but he was taking more and more of Robert's defenders. Robert laughed but it seemed conspicuously devoid of mirth.

"Well look who is trying to step up to the big time. Hmm..." Robert said. Studying the board he saw that in his rush to take his father's rook Langdon had left his Queen exposed to Robert's knight.

"It's all about the King," Robert mused as he moved his knight to take Langdon's Queen.

A soft grunting sound came from the kitchen. It sounded like Rebecca had a chest cold and was coughing up some phlegm. Robert sat back silently laughed to himself as he took in the look of shock on Langdon's face. The old man still had some tricks to teach him. Robert stopped laughing when noticed the look on Langdon's face went from mild shock to a pale bewilderment. Robert heard soft, almost imperceptible footfalls coming toward him from the kitchen.

Years of training his senses and his reflexes had prepared him to act quickly and decisively when it was necessary. His conscious mind receded to the background and his training took over. He stared at Langdon's big blue eyes and noticed a strange reflection there. A figure was coming up behind Robert. It was a distorted figure in his son's eye but he didn't waste time trying to figure out what or who it was. He grabbed the chess board and flung it over his shoulder keeping his eye on his son's eye and the reflection there. The chess board was carved out heavy mahogany and trimmed in chrome. It had hinges on the side so one could open the board and store the pieces inside. Robert threw it hard in a sharp arc over his left shoulder. He didn't wait to hear it make contact. He grabbed Langdon and pulled him out of the chair, then flipped the table over behind them as they headed for the basement.

Robert heard a sound like the buzzing of a small propeller multiplied by a thousand erupt behind him. His training asserted itself and grabbed the upturned table by the leg and held it up like a shield.

Metal throwing stars buried themselves in the table top like they had been fired from a nail gun. Robert tossed the table toward the assailants coming through his kitchen window and stepping over the prone form of his wife. They were dressed in some kind of strange camouflage that seemed to consist of all the foliage and terrain that surround his little neighborhood.

.Swords. He had to get to his swords. The closet near the front door had one. A light weight modified long sword. It was hanging on the inside of the closet door. He pushed Langdon toward the back of the house toward the pantry.

"GO, GO!!! TO THE TRAINING ROOM!" Robert yelled at his son. Langdon looked confused for a moment until Robert pushed him with all his strength. The boy went flying, caught his balance, then ran to the basement door. Robert ran into the living room and did a hand spring over the couch, landed on his hands in a push-up position then sprang up and ran for the closet door. All around him he could hear glass breaking and furniture being overturned. The assailants were tearing through his house. They were closing in on him like wolves on a lone sheep. Robert grabbed a wooden stool by the door and threw it over his shoulder in the same way he threw the chessboard. He grabbed various knick-knacks off a shelf near the door and began hurling them at his assailants with deadly accuracy. A ceramic bulldog struck one assailant between the eyes. A pair of crystal swans took out two other assailants. The remaining five attackers ducked and dodged the collectibles with dizzying acrobatics. One dropped to the floor in a split while another leaped into the air and grabbed one of the exposed beams with his short tanto blade before dropping to the floor in front of his prostrated comrade. Robert ripped the shelf from the wall and hurled it at his attackers.

"I never liked that shelf. I told Rebecca when she brought it home all the shelves were crooked. But she fixed it. She wouldn't let me touch it. She did it all by herself," he thought.

A bright red plume of rage bloomed in his heart. A super-nova of anger exploded in his soul. He had reached the closet door. One of his assailants was right behind him. The attacker pulled out his wakizashi sword and raised it above his head. He brought it down quickly and full of deadly intentions.

Robert spun around with the long sword in his hand.

He blocked the strike from the ninja in front of him with both hands. Without thinking, acting on instinct he kicked with his left leg at the man's wrist. The force of his kick knocked the sword from his enemy's hand. It stuck in the wall quivering like a tuning fork. Robert sliced his long sword to the right, then the left, then the right again in a flash of steel. Brotherhood steel. The sharpest steel on earth. Blood splashed onto the walls of his quaint little home...the home he had shared with Rebecca. There was blood to the left of him, blood to the right of him.

The ninja fell to the floor in three sections. His leg and thighs slid away from his torso which in turn slid away from his head and arms. A bitter coppery scent filled the house as the contents of the ninja's thoracic region spilled across the floor. The four remaining ninjas converged on Robert. One picked up a fallen comrades sword and attacked.

The long sword in Robert hand had been made by his father. It was a modified Zweihander broadsword with a sharp point and large parrying lugs just above the hilt. The cross guard was a straight cylindrical barrel above a long grip with a weighted pommel at the end. It was a sword designed to be a two-handed weapon but through rigorous and dedicated training Robert could wield it with one hand. The sword did not gleam. It did not sparkle .Robert had mostly given up training with it in favor of lighter shorter swords. He didn't polish it regularly or even dust it. He just left it in the closet just in case. His father had warned him that one day as the Duel grew closer their enemies may come looking for them and they would do well to be ready. Robert believed in the Duel, in the Covenant. But as time passed the idea of the Men of the First Chaos showing up at his door lost its potency. It slipped to the back of his mental Rolodex along with his mortality and talking to Langdon about sex. It was still in his mind, just not at the forefront. He never really thought the day would come when he would be fighting for his life in his own home. He was fully prepared to die fighting in the Duel for the good of mankind. He didn't think his wife would be a casualty of the war the men of the Brotherhood had pledged to fight. She didn't deserve to be lying on the floor of her own home leaking her life's essence all over the linoleum floor.

The ninja swung his two blades at Robert .One blade went high the other blade went low. Robert blocked the lower strike then let the sword roll up and around his wrist on the handle. The five-foot blade sliced through the air with a faint whisper. He caught the sword and blocked the high strike as well. Robert spun to his right just as one of the other attackers drove the point of his sword at his back. He dodged the blade of the katana and gripped the long sword in both hands. His forearm muscles strained against the white fabric of his white shirt. He completed his revolution while at the same time bringing the sword down across the outstretched arm of the ninja who had tried to stab him in the back. The blade sliced through the man's arm like a meat cleaver. The arm and the sword fell to the ground. More blood spurted onto the foyer floor. The now one-armed ninja grasped at his bleeding stump and stumbled backwards toward the door. He didn't make it.

Robert followed him and drove the point of the longsword through his rib cage almost to the hilt. Still holding on to the sword with both hands he used all the strength and power he had earned over the years and picked the man up off the ground with his sword. Grunting Robert whirled around and tossed his body at his approaching comrades. Two of the ninjas nimbly dodged the flying corpse of their brother. One caught the corpse in an awkward embrace and slipped on the bloodied floor. He fell backwards with his brother on top of him. He struggled to remove his bulk and rejoin the fight.

The two remaining ninjas pressed forward again. Robert was being pushed into the front foyer area.

"Need more room," he thought to himself. Robert struck at his enemies. The sound of metal crashing against metal filled the room. He then leaped into the air over their heads. He held the long sword out by his side as he executed a front flip. He landed on the dead ninja and his brother who had not yet extricated himself. The force of Robert landing on the ninja and his dead brother sent all three of them sliding along the hard wood floors on a slick layer of blood. Robert surfed on the two ninjas until the bodies of the two men slid up under a heavy wooden coffee table in the living room. Robert hopped off the two men .The living ninja found himself trapped by the arms of the coffee table and his dead brother's body.

Robert kept his balance as the ninjas turned and attacked again. He waited with his sword raised near his head like a baseball player about to hit a grand slam.

The attacker on his left reached him first. He pulled out a chain with a long blade attached to one end and handle on the other end. He launched the blade and chain at Robert. Robert watched the blade as it flew toward his head. Time slowed down. The world slowed down...he could see the sharp edge of the blade and the miniscule nicks from poor sharpening. Robert could see beads of sweat bubbling up out of the eye holes of his attackers mask. It looked like a Guy Fawkes mask had mated with a ghillie suit.

Robert waited for the second attacker to reach the dance. Then he moved.He took his left hand off the hilt of his sword and caught the blade where it was attached to the chain. In one fluid motion he took the blade chain in his left hand and turned his body slightly to the right. As the second attacker raised his swords to strike, Robert drove the point of the blade chain into his throat over his left shoulder while at the same time driving the point of the longsword into the chest of the first attacker who was still holding the handle of the chain blade. It was a version of the kusarigama with a detachable blade. Robert didn't know that and he didn't care. All he cared about was hearing the death rattle of his enemies as he stood there between them. The sight of his attacker's blood dripping down the length of his sword did not fill him with relief. The rage inside him bloomed even brighter. It was not satiated .Not even close.

Robert let the blade at the end of the chain go and pulled his sword out of his enemy's chest. Both men fell to the floor. Robert took his sword and slammed it point first into his hardwood floor. He walked over to the body of the ninja he had stabbed with the kusarigama and searched his body. He found a short tanto blade, several more shurikens and a long pointed metal pin.

"Blimey you blokes have a lot of pockets! You fellas are like kangaroos! Ninjas. I'll be damned! You blokes have had movies and television shows made about you but they don't do you justice. I mean you fellas are some cold-hearted pikers. You kill an innocent woman standing in a kitchen making dinner for her family. Ooh ice water in your veins lad. You okay under there? Don't worry I'm going to be with you in just a minute lad." he said as he searched the body. He picked up the tanto dagger and walked over to the coffee table. He squatted down and saw the last ninja struggling under the body of another ninja. Additionally his arms were pinned to his side by the legs of the coffee table. Robert reached out and pulled off his mask. The face that stared back at him was young but hard. Tiny black eyes stared back at Robert with a naked malfeasance that boiled the air between them.

"Are you blokes after my da and me brother too? Of course you are. I think they will find that task a bit more difficult than they anticipated. So I will make this quick. I only got two questions for you, laddie. Who sent you and how did you find us? I'm pretty sure I know the answer to the first question but I'm at a loss about the second one. The Men of the First Chaos sent ya didn't they? So that means the Duel is happening. I wager we will be receiving an invite very soon if we haven't already." Richard leaned in close to the man behind the mask. He took the point of the dagger and pushed it against the thin membrane of the man's iris. He did not pierce the eyeball. He just pressed against the tissue of the iris with the point of the blade. The man under the table did not flinch.

"Laddie, who sent you? And how did you find me? Did you get my info from that whorehouse? Tell me now and I'll kill you quick. Just like you killed my wife. She's laying on the floor over there. Does she have a lot of ya little throwing stars in her back? Is that how you killed her? Throwing those little stars in her back? IS IT YOU FUCKING BASTARD?!" Robert screamed. This man would not talk. It was immaterial if he spoke English or not, this man would not speak. So why were they playing this game?

Robert slid the dagger into the man's eye...slowly. The eyeball popped with a wet squishing sound. Robert drove the dagger in deeper. The man squirmed. A tear fell from his other eye. Robert's left cheek began to twitch as he pushed the dagger into the man's brain. The man stopped thrashing. Robert stood up and put his hands to his face. Sobbing he walked over to his sword and pulled it out of the floor. Robert stepped over the fallen bodies and walked into the kitchen.

Rebecca was lying on her side. Her legs were askew and her dress was pulled up a bit exposing her thighs. Robert went over to her body. There were six long cylindrical bolts sticking out of her chest in an erratic pattern. Robert knelt to the floor and dropped his sword. Gently he grabbed her upper body and pulled her into his arms. Blood soaked his white shirt as he held his wife tightly. He rocked slowly side to side.

"All my fault my love. Tis all my fault," he whispered.

Robert heard footsteps rapidly coming up the steps to his front door. He lovingly lay his wife's body back down on the floor and grabbed his sword and hopped up off the floor. The front door flew open.

"Robbie! Are you in here!?" Seth screamed. Robbie walked out of the kitchen and met his brother.

Seth looked just like their dad. A big boxy head and close set eyes which gave him a permanent scowl. Seth was covered in blood. His white button up shirt was cut to ribbons and his pants were not in much better shape. It didn't appear that he was bleeding so the blood was probably not his. He was holding a long saber in his left hand. It was saturated with blood, the stench of it making Robert sick to his stomach. Seth walked up to Robert and draped his right arm over his neck.

"Are you okay brother? Those grimy bastards came at me while we was in the midst of a Doctor marathon. The boys are okay but Corrine is going completely bonkers mate." Seth said.

"Where's Da? "Robert asked. Seth patted Robert's neck again.

"That piker is with the boys and Corrine in my garage. Those bastards thought that they had found an easy meal in the old man but he showed 'em he wasn't nobody's fish and chips. Tough bastard does not have a mark on him!" Seth said.

"Is Langdon with the other boys?" Robert asked stiffly. Seth put his forehead to his brother's.

"Yes brother he is with my boys. Da says we have to get out of here. Get on the first flight across the pond. Make it to the Grand Hall. We'll be safe there. Well until the Duel starts. So let's get Becca and get the fuck out of here," Seth said quietly. Robert pulled away from his brother and sat down on the arm of his couch. Seth looked at Robert as a sense of dread filled his heart.

"Robert. Where is Becca?" he asked. Robert nodded toward the kitchen. Seth shuffled around the prone and dissected figures on the floor and peered into the kitchen. He saw Rebecca. He rushed back to his brother. He dropped to one knee in front of Robert.

"Oh Christ Robbie I'm so sorry .So fucking sorry lad. Let's go talk to Da. We need to take care of her Robbie. We gotta.....aw Christ Robbie I'm sorry!" Seth said. He stood and grabbed his brother in a bear hug. Robert didn't move.

"Come on brother let's go talk to Da," Seth said. It was the only thing he could say at this point. Rebecca was dead. He couldn't imagine how Robbie was feeling. His own wife and children were frightened and crying but alive. Rebecca who had made the best rum cake for his birthday last year was lying on the floor dead. Seth knew what was at stake with the Covenant and the Duel but he couldn't think of that right now. All he could do was hug his brother hopes that Da would know what words to say to make this not so fucking awful.

There was a sound at the door. Both Seth and Robert stood up and raised their swords in smooth practiced movements.

"BOYS!!" Richard Darn yelled as he came through the door.

"Da we are here," Seth said as he lowered his saber. Richard came into Robert's living room still carrying his two swords. There was a small splatter of blood on his face and some drops on his vest. Other than that he looked like he was ready to go back to the office. Richard looked at his boys and saw the shadow over their faces. He dropped his swords and walked up to Robert. He took his head in both his hands and stared in his eyes.

"Langdon told me he saw his Ma fall down when the men came through the window. Robbie I'm so sorry me boy. We will call Sanders and Son to come get her. After we read the Invitation. Then we will go to the States and take those Men of the First Chaos to task my son." Richard said in his deep rumbling voice.

"I'm not waiting til the Duel. You call Sanders and you take Langdon to the airport. I'll meet you there in a little while," Robert said. Richard dropped his hands to his sides.

"Robbie what do you mean you're not waiting?" Richard asked.

"Da, does it look like they are waiting?" Robert said. Richard crossed his arms.

"Son, I know you loved Rebecca. I know that you are feeling the worst pain a husband can feel. If that was you mum I would feel the same way. I would want to go and take my revenge on anyone connected with the Men of the First Chaos. Then I would remember I am a Man of the First Order, a member of the Brotherhood of the Blade. Then I would remember our Oath. Not for vengeance Robert. That's our Oath. Our pledge to the Covenant. Robert we are not like them. We are not killers .We are warriors in a battle that determines the fate of the world. Son, this isn't just about you and Rebecca or me and your mum or Seth and Corrine. It's about all of mankind. Forget for a moment what happens if we lose. Think what would happen if we broke the Covenant. If we descended down to their level and fought them face to face in the hills and the cities it could break our pack with the Judges. Once that was done it wouldn't matter whether we were Men of Chaos or Order. The world as we know it would cease to exist. Is that what you want son?" Richard asked quietly. He stared at Robert.

"It is about me Da. You don't understand," Robert said flatly.

"Robbie what are you saying to me? "Richard said. Robert looked off to his left. He looked at a picture on the wall of him, Rebecca and Langdon in Spain last year. He looked back at his father.

"I know where one set of these buggers hang their hats. I know because......I've been there before. I've been going there for years. That's how they found us Da. If I wasn't such sex-addled bastard they would never have found us. All my life I have trained for the Duel. I have come to grips with the idea that I might die under the sword. But once I met Rebecca and had Langdon I consoled myself with the idea if I did fight in the Duel and I did die she and Langdon would have each other. Now that won't happen. My wife is dead because I couldn't keep my cock outta the snatches of Du Mor whores." Robert said flatly. Richard grabbed his son again. He kissed him on the forehead.

"Robbie. We are warriors not saints. You didn't cause this, the Men of the First Chaos did. With their money and their influence and their connections. They make the world dance like a marionette. Robbie we can cut those strings with our swords at the Duel. If you go to their brothel on Canal Street you are no longer a warrior. You are just a madman with a sword," Richard said. Robert gently pulled his father's arms from around his neck. He smiled.

"Da that's just what I am," he said. He stood and put his longsword down on the ground.

"Go on I'll meet you in a little while. I won't keep the Judges waiting," Robert said. He started for the basement door.

"Robert! The Men of the First Chaos are not these ninjas. They are the most skilled swordsman on Earth other than us. Robert, what I am saying is you could...Robert I don't want to lose you in a whorehouse. I don't want to lose either of you. I don't want any of us to die but dammit Robert if we do die let it be for the Covenant!" Richard said at the top of his lungs. Robert looked back over his shoulder and winked at his father.

"Save my Invitation Da. I would hate to be barred from the dance," Robert said. He opened the basement door and descended the steps.

Seth and Richard stood there and stared at the open door for a few minutes.

"Da we should go after him!" Seth said. His voice was bordering on the edge of hysteria. Richard stooped down and picked up his swords.

"We can't Seth. We have to read the Invitation. We have to prepare. Robbie's made his choice," Richard said. A cold feeling seeped through his body. Somehow he had failed his boy. Robert could repeat the words in the Book of Seven Swords verbatim, but he didn't know what they meant. He did not understand that honor was not just standing true but sometimes standing down. In spite of how much it may pain ones heart. There were three parts to true honor; courage, dedication and sacrifice. Robert did not lack the first two. But Richard knew his son. He knew his son felt he had given more than his share of sacrifice. Richard wished he could have articulated to him that true sacrifice was not accepting Rebecca's death but carrying on with his duty despite it. Richard hung his head .But only for a moment.

"Come now Seth let's check on the boys and Corrine. We need to call the police and the funeral home. Then we need to get to some place quiet and open the Invitation. And pray to Mother Earth and Father Sky and all the gods that may be that your brother finds the courage to be the man I raised him to be. Pray that he comes back to us," Richard said. He turned and walked out of Roberts's house. Seth followed him. He looked back once. A tear seemed to be poised to fall from his eye. He threw his head back and it fell back into place.

Robert walked along the long familiar underground chamber that ran beneath all of the houses his family occupied in Poppingthistle. A row of fluorescent lights ran along the roof. To the left and the right long wooden racks ran the length of the room. Each rack held a different type of sword; katanas, sabers, foils, epees, broadswords and scimitars. Robert ran his hand along the racks as he walked. He knew which pair of swords he wanted. There were two sabers at the end of the rack just before the ring his father had built with old barrels. Two finely wrought sabers with polished black handles and bright brass hilts. Lightweight but unbelievably strong they were his favorite swords. They were made for his father by the sword maker Garn Whiteborne many, many years ago. Robert reached the two sabers. They were lying side by side on the outstretched wooden arms of the rack.

Robert picked them up and gripped them tightly. They felt right.

They felt just.

Robert grabbed a leather pool cue case and put the two sabers inside. It was how he and his brother and his father sometimes left the house. Much like the longsword in the closet they wore the swords just in case. There was a thick black wool sweater hanging on a hook in the basement. It was probably left over from one of their endless practice sessions. Robert pulled off his bloody buttoned shirt and put on the sweater. He put his arm through the strap on the case and walked back the way he had come. He passed the set of stairs that led to his home and went further until he found the stairs that led up to his garage. Before he ascended the steps he looked back down the long connected basement and saw the old tree trunk sitting beneath sickly yellow lights at the far end of the room. It comforted him, the family motto on that well-worn chunk of wood. Taken from the Olde Grove itself not one hundred years after the first Duel. Or so the story went. Robert knew that what he was about to do would separate him from the Brotherhood forever. He was not like his father or his brother. He obviously was not a man of honor so why pretend to be one? His wife was dead because of his actions, not because of his membership in the Brotherhood. His pain, while enormous, would pale in comparison to the pain he was about to rain down on the House of Love and Agony. Robert bowed his head.

"I beseech thee Judges of Man Stewards of all that ever was. Allow my father and my brother to stand. Allow their blades to strike true. Deliver my enemies into my sight. That is all I ask. Let me see my enemies. I will do the rest,". Robert said. He climbed the steps and jumped into his car. Crying, he backed his car out of his garage and tore out of Poppingthistle. Wheels spinning he left a cloud of smoke in his wake.

Langdon ran to the window of his Granddad's kitchen and saw his father's blue BMW tear out of their neighborhood. The boy didn't cry or speak. He just watched the car until it drove out of the range of his sight.

"Langdon, Come now son. We have to get going too. Your Dad's gonna be alright," Richard said. He wasn't sure if he was lying to the boy or to himself. Or both.

HAPTER FIFTEEN

Carcone stood in front of his son with two long pieces of thick rope in his hands. Each rope ended in a small tennis ball sized chrome plated spheres. Each sphere was lined in sharp inch long spikes. The sphere looked for all the world like sea urchins dipped in metal. Carcine was standing just ten feet away from his father. He was shirt and shimmering with sweat. His longish hair fell in a wet clump, around his head. He was barefoot as well. On his hands were two steel and Kevlar gloves with long cuffs that extended up to his elbows.

Carcone began to spin the lengths of rope. Faster and faster he spun them letting them build up a huge amount of centrifugal force. Carcine watched the balls as they flew around and around on the end of the ropes. His eyes focused on the spikes. Soon they seemed to be moving in slow motion. He concentrated even more. Eventually he could see the individual spikes as they caught the light from the overhead lights. They were in the training room for the House of Blood and Steel. This was the dungeon of their duty.

Without warning Carcone launched one of the metal spheres at Carcine's head. The rope moved through the air like a whip. Carcine saw it approaching from his left. He raised his left hand and blocked the sphere with his metal and fabric covered hand. The sphere clanged and bounced away from his face. Carcone launched the other sphere at Carcine. Carcine blocked that one as well. Carcone advanced on his son. He hurled the spheres faster and faster. Carcine blocked them one after another. Backing up but still concentrating he blocked and ducked and shimmied away from the spheres.

The door to the training room opened with a creak. Carcine looked toward the door. It was an involuntary move. One of the spheres cracked him in the side of the head. He tried to snatch his head away and to the right. He did not get the full brunt of the spikes but he felt a warm sticky substance begin to trickle down the side of his face.

"Fuck!" Carcine yelled. Carcone twirled his arms and wrapped the rope around his forearms until he caught the spheres in his own gloved hands.

"Never lose your concentration. Not for one minute. Be assured your opponent will not let a creaking door impede him from slicing off your head," Carcone said. He looked at Carcine. His son was angry and embarrassed. Good. He would not soon forget this lesson.

"So I suppose that black box sitting on the coffee table is the Invitation. Congratulations Carcone. You were right. There really is a Duel. You really will put our son in harm's way," Agrippina said as she stepped through the door. She stood at the top of the stairs and looked down upon her husband and her son. Carcone couldn't help but feel that was an apropos position for her. She always seemed to be looking down on him .Despite his disdain for his wife he could not deny the striking figure she cut when she entered a room.

Agrippina stood almost six feet tall. She was a half an inch taller than Carcone. Her snow white hair was cut into a severe page boy style. Her light silvery blue eyes stared out at him from a heart shaped face with a sharp aquiline nose in the center. Her long lean arms were crossed over her pert and firm breasts. Her torso was wrapped in a skin tight gray cashmere sweater blouse with a light blue and white Hermes scarf. A long black skirt caressed her sharp angular hips and her defined calves. Grey thigh high leather boots strained against her muscular legs. Many times over the course of their marriage Agrippina had been asked to entertain the idea of modeling but she refused. Carcone knew she liked the idea of others coveting her beauty but she liked the idea of control more. Carcone could never see her being directed to tilt her head a certain way or pout on cue. It went against her nature. Those who viewed their marriage from the outside, like Vivian, thought that Agrippina was weak and waifish. Carcone knew the truth.

There was something missing in Agrippina. What other saw as weak was really apathy. She literally did not care about or for anyone or anything. What some saw as vacuousness was actually a cool unemotional cunning. Her beauty was exponentially opposite to her personality. She was a beautifully wrapped present with a scorpion inside.

"Agrippina, so good of you to make the trip. Of course I was right. Did you think I was playing cricket down here for all these years? And our son will come to no harm if he keeps his eye on the ball," he said as he held the spiked sphere in her direction. Agrippina raised her head and sighed. She retreated from the stairs like a phantom in an haute couture sheet.

"Never let anything break your concentration, Carcine. It is a sign of weakness. Weakness gives off a scent like blood. It will draw sharks. Do you understand?" Carcone asked.

"Yes of course," Carcine said.

"Come, we will be reading the Invitation very shortly. I wanted to wait until your mother arrived. I want her to see this in person," Carcone said.

"See what?" Carcine asked.

"The truth, Carcone said cryptically.

Agrippina walked out of the wine cellar and into the kitchen of the chateau. She glided past the staff preparing the meal she would share with her husband and her son. She slipped past the manservant Chavalle and up the grand staircase to her bedroom. Carcone slept in the bedroom next to his den. On occasion they would agree to have intercourse but they never spent the night together. Agrippina did not like the feel of another person against her skin for the entire night. Carcone was hairy and he sweated like a horse. Shakir was exquisite with skin like amber butter but she didn't like for her to lay against her for an extended period of time either. She liked to touch and be touched within clearly defined parameters. Shakir understood that in a way Carcone never would.

Agrippina lay down on the bed and slipped out of her shoes. She felt a warm tingly feeling in her belly. The Duel was coming. Pretlow would be there. Finally after all these years she would have a chance at satisfaction...Agrippina believed in the Duel, in the Covenant, in the Judges, everything. Carcone thought she eschewed all of the history of the Brotherhood because that is what she wanted him to believe. She played the role of agnostic to avert any suspicions until it was too late. She would take her retribution on Pretlow through her son Carcine. Carcone was a good swordsman but he wasn't the equal to Pretlow Creedence. She had seen Pretlow's skill up close and personal. Even as a young boy he had been a maestro with a blade. She was sure his skill had just increased in the intervening years since those halcyon days in Italy in Garn Whiteborne's studio. For her plan to work she needed a swordsman with skill without as much hubris as Carcone. A swordsman with a touch of petulance and not above some chicanery. In short she needed Carcine. Carcone had too much pride to accept the tool of her revenge. He would deem it beneath him. Carcine had no such compunction. She had raised him to be that way. While Carcone tried to fashion some code of honor out of the duties of the Brotherhood while still being as ruthless and cold as his Hellenic ancestor Agrippina had taken a different tack. She ascribed to no code except Winning. At all cost. Oh yes she believed in the Duel and the Covenant but they were just means to an end for her. Her true religion was Revenge. To this theology she was a devout disciple.

Pretlow had committed the most egregious offense a man can commit. He had awakened love in her heart and then not had the courage to return that love. Everything that happened after that was his fault. Some would say it was unfair, insane even, to blame Pretlow for what happened to her in Italy. To those people Agrippina would say that they had never known the pleasure of meeting their soul mate then experiencing the agony of having him turn his back on you. To those people she would have said that they did not know what it felt like to be willing to sacrifice everything for someone to only realize they would not do the same for you. Those people did not know the true meaning of pain, of despair. Those people were just like Pretlow. He didn't understand what she had been willing to give up for him. He didn't understand the pain and agony she had endured while trying to build a world for the two of them. But soon he and his family would become very well acquainted with pain. She would see to that personally.

Agrippina slid her hand down the waist band of her skirt. Her delicate fingers tiptoed to her center. She touched herself in the quiet stillness of her bedroom. Carcone, Carcine, Shakir, Vivian all these

THE BROTHEROOD OF THE BLADE

faces faded away until the only face she could see was Pretlow's. She touched herself more aggressively. Yes she imagined his face as her plan unfolded. She would be there. She would insist upon it and Carcone would acquiesce. She had studied the Book of Seven Swords. Once the Invitation was accepted the Prefects and the members of their respective houses that were fighting would go to the appointed place. Family could attend. She had read accounts of wives being at the Duel. It was up to the discretion of the Prefect. She had to be there. She had to see his face.

Her body began to convulse. She cried out in ecstasy. "Pretlow see what you have done to me. I will see all that you love in ruins!" she thought as she climaxed.

CHAPTER SIXTEEN

Raul Esperanza parked his truck in front of his villa. The evening sun was setting and his day in the olive groves was at an end. He climbed out of the creaky old panel truck and dusted off his pants before he walked in his home. He and his son Alan worked in the olive groves for the San Solce olive oil company. Raul had been with the company since he was eighteen. Now at fifty he was the foreman for the entire propagation and processing division in Andalucía Spain. Alan had started in the groves last year after finishing school. Raul did not want him working in the groves next year. He wanted his only son to go to Madrid. He dreamed that Alan would enter university and pursue a field of study not work in a field. Providing they did not receive the Invitation next year.

Raul walked toward the porch and whistling a tune under his breath. He was a tall and lean man with leathery skin like an old catcher's mitt. His black hair was tied into a pony tail that reached his shoulder blades. There were only flecks of gray here and there in his thick hair. His long arms ended in huge gnarled hands with thick callused fingers. Many years of working in the groves had toughened his hands. Some days it seemed those huge trees went on forever in endless rows for days. As the years passed and he rose in the San Solce olive oil company he never forgot those hard days in the field. Days when it felt like the sun was five feet from his face and the air was so dry it was hard to breathe.

There were days when all he could think about was coming home and practicing with his saber. Raul laughed to himself. You know a job was tough when you looked forward to sweating in an attic with a saber in each hand.

Raul stopped in his tracks. There was a shiny black box sitting on the bottom step of the porch. Raul looked around his property with wide eyes. His villa was at the end of a long dusty lane out in the Spanish hills. He could see someone approaching before they got within a hundred feet of his home. He saw no one.   The box appeared to be made out of polished ebony or obsidian. It was a gorgeous piece of craftsmanship. Raul slowly backed up to his truck and opened the door. He glanced around again as he reached behind the bench seat and pulled out his dueling saber. Four feet long with a coppery basket guard and a handle wrapped in brown leather. The saber was sharpened every day by Raul himself. He could throw a piece of paper in the air and let it float down to the blade it would be sliced in two. Raul resumed his journey to the porch.

A symphony erupted from his pocket.

It was the ringtone he had given his cousin Sonna. His uncle Lorenzo was long in his grave but as long as Sonna was alive his image would still walk the earth. Raul fished his phone out of his pocket. "Yes?" he asked.

"Raul, are you okay?" Sonna asked. She sounded out of breath.

"Yes, is there a reason I shouldn't be?" he asked.

"Richard wants to talk to you." she said. Raul could hear a man's voice in the distance .Then Richard was on the line.

"Raul, Richard. Have you received your Invitation yet?" he asked in his thick cockney accent.

"Well my friend I just got home and I see a large black box on my step... I am assuming that is the Invitation." he said.

"Raul we are under attack. Assassins came after us today. They killed Robert's wife. I can only assume they are agents of the Men of the First Chaos trying to thin our ranks before we even get to the god blessed Duel. Be careful my friend. In a few hours we are boarding a flight for the States. I drained the savings account and we are heading to the Grand Hall, neutral ground that even those bastards won't sully. I hope," Richard said. Raul craned his neck again and looked around his home. He didn't see any assassins but that didn't mean they were not there this very minute.

"Richard, keep my cousin safe. Alan and I will see you at the Hall soon" He cut the phone off and put it back in his pocket.

Alan was in town with some friends playing some futbol after work. Alan's mother had died several years ago. It had been a quick but painful death from kidney failure. Neither he nor Alan was a viable donor. He had watched Esmerelda de le Chain waste away in front of him and Alan. He never felt so helpless. All his skill and abilities as a swordsman meant nothing that day in her dreary hospital room. His strong hands could not hold her as she went on her way to whatever lands lay beyond the wall of eternal sleep. In the years since he had not taken another woman to his bed. Not out of some pious desire to remain pure or a devotion to the memory of his deceased wife. He just didn't have the energy to make the effort. He really didn't feel like playing the game of jumping bones. He had plenty of offers on a regular basis but he just couldn't seem to find the on button to his libido. He poured his energy into the Way of the Sword. The House of Sun and Stone was a small fraternity but a devoted one. He and his

THE BROTHEROOD OF THE BLADE

son Alan and his cousin Sonna were all that was left of that fabled House. But what they lacked in numbers they made up in zeal.

Sun and Stone. The name had come from the first of their ancestors who had fought in the Duel. Meridius the Stone Mason had been plucked from Roman perdition to fight for the fate of all mankind.

When questioned by one of his enemies about his pedigree he had reportedly said:

"I come from the hills. I dig stone out of the ground with my own two hands. I build structures that will stand as long as the Sun shines on those hills."

Sun and Stone, two constants that endure for centuries. Raul hoped that he was not the last prefect of his house. Alan was a young man who might have lots of children. Raul did not want the House of Sun and Stone to die with him.

Raul ran up to the porch grabbed the box and turned around to jump in his truck.

Two men clad in black, loose fitting robes rolled from under his truck. Their faces were covered by tight fitting masks.

"They must have been holding on to the under carriage near the exhaust pipe," Raul thought to himself.

"Well I see the dead men I was expecting have arrived," Raul said. One man pulled out a short wakizashi and attacked. The other hung back near the truck and pulled out a collapsible bow. It was a gun metal gray metallic contraption that he unfolded with a practiced efficiency. He then pulled a bolt from a hidden pocket on his hip. The bowstring became taut once the bow itself was fully extended. The ninja then drew a bead on Raul as he fought against his brother.

302

The man in black stabbed his blade toward Raul's chest, his stomach, his legs. Raul blocked each blow with his saber while still holding on to the box. He tossed the box toward the man in black. As the man swatted the box away with his sword Raul advanced. His movements were as sharp as his blade. He feinted toward the right then brought the saber back across his body to the left. The man in black barely got his sword up in time to block the blow. Raul tossed his saber from his left hand to his right hand and spun around in a tight circle. As he did this he dropped to one knee. He sliced the saber through his opponent's left leg as he completed his circle. Popping to his feet before the man could fall he used a back hand motion to slash through the man in black's neck. His head leaped from his body as his leg fell away from his thigh. The ninja fell to the ground and his sword clattered on the hard dusty soil.

Raul watched the body fall for a moment before turning to face the second assassin.

The ninja let his arrow fly as Raul turned.

Raul caught the arrow only millimeters from his face. He then shook it back and forth slowly in a "no no no" gesture as if he was admonishing a child and tossed to the ground. The ninja pulled another arrow out of his hidden quiver and fired again. Raul sliced the arrow in half with his saber and languidly began walking toward the ninja. The ninja fired again. Raul sliced the arrow in half once more. The ninja fired again and again Raul sliced the arrow down the middle. The ninja reached into his quiver again. It was empty. Raul put the tip of his saber against the man's throat.

"No. Enough of that my friend. No more arrows. No more swords. No more trying to kill me. Time to die," he said softly. The man did not move. He spoke. Raul did not understand what he was saying. The man spoke again broken Spanish.

"Time for your son to die too." he said. Raul smirked.

"My son is better than me," he said. He pulled the tip of the saber away from the man's throat. The ninja moved quickly and reached inside his shirt. But he could not move as quickly as Raul. The tall man brought the saber around in a deadly arc. The shimmering blade cut through the ninja's   vertebrae and muscle with ease. His head rolled off his shoulders and fell to the hard earth. The man's body slid down the door of the truck spouting blood from his neck like a fountain in Hell. Raul stepped back out the way of the arterial spray. It splattered across the dry soil like warm rain.

Raul walked back over to the other body on the ground and picked up the black box. It was not scuffed or damaged. In fact the dirt did not stick to it. It rolled off the slick surface and danced away on the wind. Raul tossed it in the truck. He turned the key and the truck roared to life. He headed off to find his son. He had not been speaking with hyperbole when he said Alan was better than himself. Raul thought his son might be the finest swordsman he had ever seen. Alan looked like a younger, more muscular version of himself. The boy was insanely athletically gifted even by Brotherhood standards. He could dunk a basketball while performing a standing back-flip. Raul had watched him carry a 200 pound crate of olive oil on his shoulder with one hand. His sword skills were equally amazing. But what made Raul most proud of his son was his absolute belief in the Covenant and what it meant for the world. Alan Esperanza believed. No questions, no doubts no fear.

Raul backed up and turned on to the road. He didn't call the police and he didn't call his boss to let him know he would not be in tomorrow. Or the next day. Or perhaps ever again. The dead bodies in his yard and his employment were of little concern to him now. Now the time of the Covenant was at hand. He had to pick up Alan and go somewhere quiet and open the Invitation.

Now was the time for their blades to strike true.

CHAPTER SEVENTEEN

Hatred.

It filled the halls of Catlow's heart. It suffused every part of his being. It was bitter sour thing in his belly that etched a scowl on his face from the inside out. He drove through the street like he was riding a lightning bolt. The wind clawed at his face and nearly took his breath.

Harmony was dead.

The words seemed to be floating in space in front of his eyes... sharp Olde English letters that shimmered. It wasn't that he couldn't believe it. It was that he couldn't stop believing. It was too big, too awful to be true but he couldn't erase the image from his mind. Harmony lying in his arms, her blood spurting out of her neck like water from a whales' blow hole...He had showered but he knew her blood was still on his hands. If she had never met him she would still be alive. He was responsible. But he did not bear the blame alone.

The Men of the First Chaos...they bore the weight of this crime. Those seemingly mythical bogey men from his childhood were real. Real and just as crazy as his father. They believed in the Brotherhood so much they had sent assassins after his family. They were infected with the same psychosis as Pretlow. His father. Harmony's death was on his hands as well. In fact all of the members of the Brotherhood shared the blame for Harmony's death. It was because of their fanatical beliefs that Harmony was lying on the floor next to Frank, cold and lifeless. He would never hear her voice. He would never feel her touch again. He hated the Brotherhood, he hated the Covenant. Most of the all he hated the Men of the First Chaos He would find them and he would kill them all. No Duel, no fantastical world ending covenant, just swords and screams and blood.

He would go home and wait for his father to come home. Once his mother and Calla were safe he would jump on his bike and begin his quest. It was a simple mission: separate the heads of the Men of the First Order from their bodies.

Pretlow did not panic after Saed had abruptly ended their call. Saed was a good friend and a great swordsman. He had little doubt about his ability to handle the assassins at his door. He wasn't so sure about his son. Pretlow had the makings of a great swordsman; strength, agility, speed, power, and intelligence. In recent years however, he had seemed to lose the most important attribute a swordsman could have in his arsenal. Dedication. Pretlow didn't know why Catlow had stopped believing or when but he knew now was not the time for any men of the Brotherhood to give in to doubt. The wolves were at their gates.

"Perhaps I did push him too hard. Perhaps I didn't do an adequate job of really explaining what we are and what we do. I don't know," Pretlow thought to himself. Catlow was a good boy. He was funny and kind and sweet to his little sister. He was strong and healthy and....that's all Pretlow really knew. He didn't know his favorite color. He didn't know what cartoons he had liked as young boy or whether he was a dog or cat person. He didn't know if his son was still a virgin. The list of things he didn't know about Catlow could fill a phone book. Pretlow had trained him but had he taken the time to really understand him? Seeing the guitar in the living room had shocked him. He had not known Catlow even knew how to play the guitar. He vaguely remembered Saed teaching him something on that African instrument he carried with him. The memory was indistinct in his mind. Pretlow shook his head. He was great sword smith, a good husband but was it possible he was a bad father?

He was an hour away from Richmond. Pretlow pushed those thoughts away and focused on the road ahead. It was his way.

Catlow pulled up to his house and parked his bike. He walked to the front door. He touched his brow with a trembling hand. He was still wearing Harmony's bandanna. His heart cracked once more and fresh pain filled his soul. Catlow saw a shiny black box sitting on the front step of his house. He picked it up and shook it. It made no sound. Catlow tucked the box under his arm and turned the door knob. The door was not locked. Catlow's chest grew tight. His mother always locked the door. It was a holdover from growing up in Baltimore. Catlow eased the door open and stepped inside his house. He was barely all the way in the house when a sharp pain bit into his left leg. Catlow jumped into the air and executed a front somersault. In mid-air he turned his body so that when he landed he would be facing his door. He grabbed the closest thing handy. It was with horror he realized he had grabbed his guitar. He was holding the instrument by the neck. He raised it above his head to strike at his attacker until he realized his attacker was a little eight-year-old girl. An eight-year-old holding an ice pick. Catlow felt a thin trickle of blood begin to drip down his leg.

"Calla, what the hell?" He lowered the guitar. Calla stood up and put her hands on her hips, still holding the ice pick.

"Mama said that bad men were going to try an' hurt us. You won't here. Daddy won't here. Somebody has to do something," she said condescendingly. Catlow shook his head and tossed his guitar on the couch..

"Come here Stinky," he said. Calla ran to her brother and he dropped to one knee. They embraced in a way that only siblings can. Calla breathed deep and took in his scent. She felt the warmth of his cheek and the sound of his heart and she wasn't afraid anymore. Catlow was home. Whatever was going to happen, Catlow was home.

Catlow held his little sister tight .Her small little body was as tense a piano wire. Caught in a maelstrom of pain and anger and blood and death she was a beacon of light that brightened his heart the tiniest bit. He released his grip and stood.

"Calla, give me Dad's ice pick." Calla hesitated then handed him the stiletto. Their father loved ice in his drink but did not like ice cubes. The shape of the cubes disturbed him. Catlow thought it was so odd that a man dedicated to order did not like the relentless rigidity of ice cubes. His father was an anachronism and an enigma. He was a man who held himself to the highest moral code like an errant knight, a man who had never divulged anything about his own childhood or his life before he met his wife. Oh Pretlow would tell Catlow tales of the Brotherhood and their storied history. Or mythology depending on your point of view. Pretlow never talked about his own father or his mother or where he grew up or any of his friends. It seemed as if Pretlow had been born as an intimidating robotic warrior of a lost age.

"Where's Mom?" Catlow asked.

"She went downstairs to the shop. She been crying. She think I don't see it but I do," Calla said.

"Okay. I'm gonna go talk to Mom. You stay here. And lock the front door please," Catlow said.

"Well it's part of my trap for the man in the backyard," Calla said. Catlow froze in his tracks.

"What man?"

"The man that was standing in the backyard this morning. He's gone now. But I'm ready for him. That's why I need the ice pick," Calla said. Again she spoke as if she was explaining how to open a book to an idiot. Catlow grabbed her arm.

"Come on. You just sit at the top of the step while I get Mom then we are getting the fuck out of here," he said as he pulled her along.

"OOOOOH you said the f-word. Daddy is goanna kill you!"she howled. Catlow ignored her and plopped her down on the top step of the basement stairs.

"Stay. If you hear ANYTHING you come running down here. You hear me Calla? I mean what I say," Catlow said. Calla started to say something but the look on Catlow's face shut her mouth. He looked like Daddy when he was done being sorta playful. It wasn't scary but she knew he was serious.

Catlow walked down the steps and into his father's shop. So many hours of his life had been spent in this basement and others like it across the East Coast. To the left of the stairs was his father's work bench. To the right was the training space. A wide twenty by forty rectangle that was the proving ground for the men of the House of the Green Hills and the House of Sand and Fire and the House of the Olde Grove. He and Shian and Seth and Robert had gone from playing with wooden sticks to dull sabers to real swords over the course of these many years. He and Shian had become close over those years. Seth and Robert were older and as years passed they got married and had children. They no longer visited. Catlow and Shian were only a few hours apart and were blood relatives. It was only natural they would become close friends. He envied Shian. His father trained him but also let him have a life. He didn't move every couple of years. Shian had gotten to go to the same school with the same people for years. He had been allowed to attend college and go on dates. He was not a slave to the blade like Catlow.

Shian had experienced a much more normal life. Or as normal as a member of the Brotherhood could expect. That was why Catlow found it incomprehensible that Shian believed in the Covenant so vehemently.

Once a couple of summers ago after a particularly intense sparring session they had been sitting on the floor of this very room. Catlow had been sipping from a bottle of water and Shian had been sharpening his scimitar. Catlow took a large sip and then asked his friend a question.

"So do you really believe in all this?" Catlow had asked. Shian had not looked up from his sword. He continued sharpening it but responded to Catlow's question with a question.

"Do I believe in what?" Catlow sighed.

"Do you believe in this? In the Covenant. Do you believe that immortal Judges gather the good and the bad to do battle every one hundred years to determine the fate and path of the world? That if we lose the world will be plunged into another hundred years of death and destruction yadda yadda yaddda..?." Catlow had asked. Shian stopped sharpening his scimitar and looked at his friend. Shian was a shade darker than Catlow with long curly hair that framed his sharp face. He had started growing a wispy beard that gave him a vague sinister appearance.

"What I believe isn't important. What I know is one day Men of the First Order will show up at our door intent on taking our live and the lives of all the people we care about. What I know is that my dad and your dad are good men who wouldn't put us through all this for nothing. What I know is I plan on being ready when they show up," Shian had said.

"You didn't answer the question." Catlow said. Shian sighed.

"Yes. I believe. I believe in it all. I am not afraid to die, Cat. I'm afraid to lose. Because if we lose then everyone loses," Shian had said before returning to his scimitar.

Catlow looked to the right again and what he saw took him aback. His mother was on the proving ground .With a sword. Darnicia was wearing a pair of black yoga pants and a white sports bra. Her thick braids were tied back from her forehead with a blue ribbon. She was wielding a thin epee like sword that his father had made for Catlow when he was a younger.

Darnicia was training.

Catlow watched as he slashed and parried and attacked. She ducked and spun and stabbed. Her speed was amazing and her foot work was impeccable. Suddenly she executed a back flip and Catlow cried out in shock. She turned in a flash and held the rapier aloft in a defensive pose.

"Catlow!" she exclaimed. Darnicia dropped the sword and ran to her son. Catlow embraced his mother and felt another minute spark of light fight against the darkness in his heart. She released him and rubbed her hand against his cheek.

"My baby boy. You do not know how happy I am to see you. I was so afraid for you my son," she said

Catlow shrugged her hand away from his face.

"Harmony is dead. Because of me. Because of the Brotherhood." Darnicia took his face in her hands. She had to stand on her tiptoes to do so.

"No, no my son .It is not your fault or the fault of the Brotherhood. It is the Men of the First Chaos. They fear they will lose the Duel and..." she started to say but Catlow cut her off abruptly.

"Oh God Mom don't talk to be about that bullshit right now!" he yelled. Darnicia stepped back from her son. She crossed her arms. Catlow felt his face get hot. Despite all he had been through today the way he had just spoken to his mother shamed him.

"I'm sorry Mom. I didn't mean to curse but I just can't hear about the Duel and the Covenant right now. It's bad enough Dad believes all this stuff but now some other crazy people believe in it too! And they hired killers to take us out and now Harmony is dead. I watched her die. She bled to death in my arms," Catlow said, crying. Darnicia did not move. She looked up at the ceiling for a moment before she spoke.

"You think this is all a big game Catlow? You think that your father and I and your uncle and all the men and women of the First Order have just wasted our time for over a thousand years? You think it's all rather silly, don't you? I guess that's our fault. Your father and I. He for pushing you too hard and me for not speaking up as I watched him push you. But believe me when I tell you it is not a game. It is not a fantasy. It is as real as this house or you motorcycle or even your love for Harmony. It encompasses all of that and more. You have never seen the Grand Hall. Or the real Book of Seven Swords. You read the accounts in the copy gathering dust on your shelf but you have never seen the sword of Aron the Wounded Eye. You have never touched the skull of Tonkon the founder of the House of Sand and Fire and felt the heat that emanates from it even now a thousand years later. He was touched by the Judges with their immortal fire. He lived for 200 years .He was the only man to fight in two Duels. But here is where I failed you Catlow. You shouldn't have to touch or feel anything. Your faith is weak and that is our fault. Faith is not just believing in the unseen. It is believing in what you see in your heart. When a person takes a leap of faith they don't know if they will fly or if they will feel a firm path under their feet or if they will hit the ground but arise unscathed born anew in another world. But they know SOMETHING will happen. We failed you Catlow .I failed you. And because of that we may fail all of mankind. Our ancestors did not ask for this duty. But they did not run from it either. That type of honor is in your blood Catlow. I hope it finds its way into your heart." Darnicia said. Catlow saw she was crying as well. He turned away from her and started to walk up the stairs. He spoke with his back to his mother. He didn't feel like facing her.

"I think we should sit in the living room. If something does happen we need room to move or run. Until Dad gets back. Your foot work is good. But you drop your sword to the left every time you are going to attack," he said. Darnicia uncrossed her arms.

"Thank you. I haven't held a sword in years. But I felt I needed to get the rust off if ....it was just going to be me and Calla. I'll bring up your sword. And mine," she said. Catlow nodded his head.

"What's in this black box?" Calla yelled from the top of the stairs. Catlow and Darnicia looked up and saw her holding the shiny black square.

"The Invitation!" Darnicia said with a whisper. Catlow looked over his shoulder at his mother then quickly back up at Calla.

"Calla put it on the coffee table. Me and mom are coming up and we are all gonna wait for Dad," he said. He turned and faced his mother.

"Why do you think it's the Invitation?" he asked. Darnicia put her hands to her face and then spoke.

"You really haven't read the Book in a long time have you? After the first Duel in 185 A.D the Invitation was always sent in a black box made of unknown materials. It appeared on the doorstep of the Prefect of each house and only the Prefect can open it. It has begun," she said breathlessly.

"Good. Then I can get all the Men of the First Chaos in one place and kill them all," Catlow said.

"Catlow remember the Oath," his mother said. Catlow turned his back and walked up the stairs.

"Fuck the Oath," he said under his breath.

Fear. It was a not a feeling that Yakita Takinori knew very well. He was used to inspiring that feeling in others. On assignments, he had seen the face of countless men when he appeared out of the shadows. Clad in his black mask and robes he would watch as their eyes widened. Some begged for their life. Some ran. Some would fight back but all were afraid.

Not the men of the Brotherhood.

If the goddamn chief of his unit was to be believed these men were not only not afraid but they were doing the unthinkable. They were killing ninjas. Not just one or two but dozens. Yakita had never considered the possibility of dying on one of his missions. The Clan of the Swift Death taught its members discipline and dedication. They were instructed from an early age to show no mercy and no fear. Yakita had never had a problem adhering to either of those tenets.

Following those tenets was proving more difficult today. He was hiding in the crawlspace of the attic of the house of Pretlow Creedence. He had his bluetooth in his ear. He was wearing a thin, black silk mask and matching silk shirt and pants. He was armed with a short tanto blade and a longer wakizashi sword. He also had fifty shurikens and fifty bolt-type shurikens. He was the backup plan. He was stationed at the house in the off chance that Pretlow Creedence escaped his three brothers. Escape. Not if he slaughtered them in the middle of a field. After they had not checked in a second unit had converged on the Ren-fair. The information they were able to gather was terrifying. All three brothers were dead, defeated in quick succession by a man who was for all intents and purposes a blacksmith. Yakita could not process it. Three of his brothers versus one man and they didn't even leave a mark on him according to witnesses. It was unbelievable.

The heat in the crawlspace was incredible. He was soaked with sweat .The silk fabric clung to his body like a second skin. He was uncomfortable but he would not move until he was given the order to do so. Young clan members were often left in hotboxes for weeks at a time with only a cup of water a day and no food. Those who passed out or cried out were taken out. Yakita didn't mind the heat.

He was more concerned about the man who was only forty minutes away from this house. Yakita may have been more concerned about Catlow if he had known Catlow had killed the head of his Clan. He did not have that information because his unit chief did not have that information yet. If he had and he had passed it on to Yakita the young man may have just eased out of the crawlspace and left his old life behind. But he didn't know so he didn't move.He waited on orders and silently meditated to calm his troubled soul.

"They are just men. They are just men. They are just men. They die like all men die," he repeated to himself again and again. He thought if he said it five thousand times he might just begin to believe it.

Catlow sat on the couch with Calla sitting in the floor and his mother in the kitchen. A three foot long Hellenic style short sword was across his lap. He was holding his guitar, strumming it lightly. He was playing a song he had heard on the radio. He was playing from memory. It was Green Day's Boulevard of Broken Dreams. He had his eyes closed. He was feeling the taut strings with his fingertips of his left hand while his right hand moved along the fretboard. He didn't really know the chords of the song or what key it was in; he just played what he heard in his head. What if he was wrong? What if there really were Judges and the Duel was real? He opened his eyes and stared at the black box on the table. What if they really were the guardians of mankind? His mind felt like a balloon filled with water. It was malleable and tight all at the same time. He couldn't think straight. Ninjas, apocalyptic duels, mysterious immortal Judges, it was all too much to comprehend but he couldn't stop thinking about it. If the Duel was real it didn't lessen his desire to gut the Men of the First Chaos. It didn't bring Harmony back to life so ultimately it didn't matter. He closed his eyes again.

A car pulled into their driveway. The lights flashed on the far wall of the living room through the front window. Calla jumped off the floor.

"DADDY!" she yelled. Catlow tossed the guitar aside and picked up the short sword.

"Wait, Calla. Stay behind me," he said. He stood in front of the door with his sword down by his side.

The sound of keys being inserted in the lock filled his ears. Catlow still didn't relax. The assassins could have stolen his father's keys if they had killed him. He was being cautious. Deep down inside he didn't think those assassins had fared well if they had battled Pretlow Creedence. Pretlow was not the most affectionate father or the best listener or the most understanding man in the world. What he excelled at was wielding a sword. He did that better than almost anyone in the world. Catlow watched the door knob turn inch by inch. He felt his stomach tighten. Calla was behind him peeping between his legs. Darnicia had come out of the kitchen holding her foil.

The door swung open. There was no one standing there. Catlow took small steps toward the doorway.

Pretlow came flying through the door. He had hopped up to the transom and then swung himself into the doorway. He hit the floor in a roll and then stood with Aequitas in his hand. Catlow had raised his sword and pointed in the direction of the figure that had come flying into his house. He and his father stood there for a moment lost in their training, both wrapped in the cloak of concentration.

Pretlow dropped his sword and ran to his son. He grabbed Catlow in a bear hug and lifted him off the ground. Calla grabbed Pretlow's leg and Darnicia dropped her sword and wrapped her arms around her son. They stood like that for some time. Catlow could count on one hand the times his father had hugged him. Pretlow kept whispering. "My boy. My boy," in his ear. Catlow had not returned his father's embrace. He was still holding the short sword in his right hand. His left hand was empty. The anger inside him bloomed bright for a moment. Like a thunderstorm it raged inside him then just as suddenly as it appeared it vanished and he finally let go of his sword and returned his father's embrace.

"Family is another word for those who can hurt you and heal you in equal measure," Catlow thought to himself.

"My Father, my father," he whispered back.

CHAPTER EIGHTEEN

Chaos.

That was what the lobby of the East London House of Love and Agony embodied at this moment. There was blood on the floor and the walls and the ceiling. Body parts littered the foyer and the hallway past the check-in desk. The lovely reproductions of Renaissance era paintings looked like they had been sliced and slit with a buzz saw. Guards, working girls and patrons could be seen among the dead. A head here, an arm, the brothel had been transformed into a slaughterhouse. Vivian stepped carefully through the pools of blood on the lush carpeted floor. She was wearing a black leather skin-tight one -piece suit. A silver zipper snaked up the front of her outfit. A large scrunchie held her long red hair back from her face. Black boots with three inch stiletto heels finished off her attire. In her left hand was a four foot long epee like weapon. The blade was a thin, elongated pyramid no wider than pool cue. It was sharp on all four edges. The hilt had a large circular guard above the handle. The handle was wrapped in leather then sealed with a grip enhancing substance. Vivian walked down the hall alone. She had told her slaves to stay at the brownstone she owned in London. Her sons were on their way to the Du Mor mansion outside of Paris. She was here alone. Just as the madman had commanded. She eased down the long hall that led to the large master ballroom. The ballroom was where the guest met the various girls amid the sounds of a live band and entertainment of a definitively adult and ribald nature. The guests were plied with fine wines and spirits. They were given whatever recreational drug bit their fancy. Fine cigars and Viagra could be obtained for an outrageous price. Once the guest found a woman they liked they would then adjourn to any number of rooms that made up the rest of the House. The House prided itself on not only providing a gateway to every erotic fantasy of their guest but inundating them with epicurean delights. The House of Love and Agony was not just a whorehouse. It was the place where desire met reality. It was where seduction was practiced with impeccable virtuosity. It was a cathedral to the amatory arts.

Vivian cautiously opened the huge wooden double door of the ballroom. The large ornate brass handle was sticky with blood. The door creaked open and she could see that the carnage continued.

Two more security guards lay in pieces on the Turkish rug that lay in front of the bandstand. To the left was a collection of large round table covered with red tablecloths and black skirting. There were dozens of leather lounge couches and love seats sprinkled around the room. The walls were lined with silky black mink drapes. A two hundred light chandelier dominated the ceiling. There were statues of Venus and Aphrodite positioned around the ballroom. Fresh flowers sat in crystal vases on short Corinthian columns.. The two dissected security guards were the only dead bodies in this part of the house. However there was one of her working girls sitting on the floor Indian style. The girl had long blond hair and big bright baby blue eyes. All she was wearing was some expensive mascara which had begun to run. She was weeping softly. Vivian guessed she was crying because of the man sitting in a chair behind her with a sword to her throat. The man was handsome, if a little square-headed. He had piercing eyes and strong masculine jaw. Fists the size of small hams held two swords. One was at the girl's throat the other was hanging at his side. The blades were painted a deep shade of scarlet. There were splashes of blood on the man's face but Vivian didn't believe it belonged to him.

"Do you know what my wife Rebecca liked to do more than anything else in the whole world?" the man asked.

"I do not know your wife." Vivian said softly.

"Oh dearie you have to use the past tense when talking about my wife. She's dead ya see. I'll tell you what she liked to do more than anything else. She loved to dance. She just loved to move to a piece of music. When I met her she was dancing ballet in a small company from the Ukraine that was performing in London. A friend of our family's had gotten my mum the tickets. Rebecca was gorgeous. She moved like a dream if a dream had a smile that could warm a snowman's heart. Her family is a member of our little secret club ya know. So I let her cousin know I was interested and the rest as they say is history. It really is history now 'cause this afternoon some Asian blokes stuck her full of throwing stars and she bled to death on our kitchen floor. In front of me and my son," Robert said choking down a sob. Vivian eyed him coldly.

"I won't insult your intelligence and tell you I am sorry about your wife because I am not. She is nothing to me but the root of an inconvenience to my business. I can, however, assure you that neither I nor the members of my House had anything to do with the attack on your family today. While I can appreciate the panache and reasoning behind such an action, this," she said as she swiveled her head around the ball room and glanced at the bodies strewn about "is counter-productive. I would not have taken such a wasteful action," she said. She tapped the end of sword on the floor casually.

"My you're a cheeky tart! Well I tell you what Miss Emma Peel I have been coming to this den of depravity since I was sixteen years old. I came for the thrill of being near people who may want to kill me one day. My wife paid for my hedonism and self-destructive and loathsome behavior with her life. I will carry that weight for the rest of my life. But somebody here told those black suited wankers where to find us. You must have gone through my wallet or bugged the room I used or something. So I'm here to make this here House of Love and Agony feel my pain. I'm not waiting till the Duel. I can't chance my vengeance on a turn of a black pebble. I may not get a chance to fight the Prefect of this House if I play according to the rules of the Duel. Ha ha Ha that rhymes! I can't ....I can't let Rebecca's death go unpunished. So run along dearie, and get the Prefect of the House on the phone. I told them girls I wanted the Prefect not another whore. No offense I'm sure you are a good whore."

"And what of the guards and the young women in the foyer? Who shall be punished for their deaths? For the revenue I have lost and the expenses I will incur having this building cleaned? Blood is not unknown in this House but this is ridiculous." Vivian said coolly. Robert chewed his bottom lip.

"I'm sorry 'bout the girls, I truly am. I went a bit bonkers there for a moment. I guess seeing my wife filleted in front of me sent me over the edge. The guards, well that was their job ya know. They are supposed to protect the girls from crazy people. And in the last four hours I have become the craziest bugger you will ever meet. Now go along...what's your name dearie?" Robert asked. Vivian raised her sword.

"I am Vivian Du Mor. Prefect of the House of Love and Agony at your service. Robert laughed.

"Well I'll be damned. And what my dear little lass do you think you are going to do with that sword?" he asked. Vivian slashed her sword to the left then to the right.

"I expect I will kill you with it. If we hurry you can catch your dead wife before she crosses over into Hell." Vivian said as she waved her sword side to side.

A black cloud of rage rolled across Robert's face. He pushed the young blond woman away and stood. At his full height he was 6'4. Vivian was 5'8. Robert cleaned the blade of each sword on his pants leg.

"I'm going to cut you open and see what your insides look like," he said quietly. Vivian felt her blood rushing through her veins. All her years of brutal physical training, of study and practice, of pushing her body to its absolute limits had been in preparation for this moment. To face another member of the Brotherhood in combat. She realized this was what she wanted more than anything. All those years ago she had told Carcone she wanted him to teach her sons because her style was not beneficial to them Now was the chance to see if maybe she had been wrong. Perhaps her style, cobbled together from the journals and tomes of past members of the Brotherhood plus her own self-taught techniques could triumph. She was a mistress with no master. As it always would be. Countless hours of studying the Book of Seven Swords, days spent running the path behind her chateau with hundred pound weights in a back pack, night after night of pull-ups until she threw up, sparring with her servants, watching the old prefects at the Bilderberg as they demonstrated their particular styles. It had all come to this. She would either win or she would lose. She would either live or she would die. She thought she could live with dying as long as she acquitted herself admirably. She could not live or die with the idea that all her dedication had been in vain.

Robert screamed and ran at her. Vivian screamed as well and ran toward him. Their howls sounded better suited to some primeval forest than a beautifully decorated ballroom. They met in the middle of the room. Robert took the saber in his left hand and slashed it toward Vivian's head. His hand moved in a blur, speed and power moving in perfect synchronicity.

Vivian blocked his strike with her modified rapier. She dropped to one knee as he swung the saber in his right hand and ducked under the blow. Vivian slashed at Robert's legs but the large man leaped into the air and flipped over her head and landed on one of the large circular tables. Vivian hopped up onto the table and stabbed at Robert's mid-section. Robert brought the saber in his left hand down and parried her rapier while stabbing at her throat with the saber in his right hand. Vivian leaned back until her ponytail brushed her calves. Robert kicked her left ankle with his right leg. It was a hard vicious blow. Vivian felt an electric shock of pain race up her right leg. Pushing with her left leg she back-flipped off the table and landed unsteadily on the floor. Robert jumped off the table with all his might. Vivian watched in shock as he literally flew over her head and landed ten feet away. His momentum caused him to slide just a few more feet when he landed in a crouch. He stood and twirled his sabers in each hand before advancing on her again. Vivian waited for him to approach this time.

Robert swung his sabers one after another at Vivian's head. His arms moved like pistons on in an engine. Vivian blocked each blow her frantic parries matching Robert's strikes. Vivian ducked under sabers and delivered a crouched spinning back kick to Robert's thigh. Her black stiletto ran across his firm quadriceps and opened deep red gash like a clown's smile. Robert jumped back and looked down at his leg.

Vivian pursed her lips and made a kissing motion. Robert howled. It sounded like a werewolf assuming his final form. He ran at Vivian but she leaped back up on the table. Robert followed hurling his saber strikes at her like lightning bolts. Vivian blocked and parried his blows as she hopped backwards and blind from table to table as Robert followed. She didn't need to see the tables. She knew where each one was in relation to the floor plan. She had designed it herself. Soon they reached the edge of the ballroom. She was running out of tables. She leaped to the last table, the one closet to the fur-lined far wall. Instead of just landing on the table and standing to fight she stepped back a bit more. As Robert prepared to follow her once more she hopped off the table and brought her rapier down on it with both hands. The table was sliced in half. Robert tried to adjust his landing by doing a split but the halves of the table slid away from his large feet. He fell to the floor. The back of his head struck the table behind him. As Vivian began to advance for the coup de grace Robert executed a kip up and in doing so planted both his feet in her chest. The force threw her against her fur-lined wall. Robert was on his feet and running toward her as she hit the wall then slid down its length.

Vivian felt like her chest had caved in on her internal organs. By the Gods he was fast. As she slid down the wall she saw him coming toward her. She grabbed the fur drape that hung from strong iron rings attached to the ceiling. She tightened her abdominals as she reached the end of the drape which hung a few inches above the floor. Suddenly Vivian began to turn to her right while her free hand held onto the drape. She began to turn furiously. She rolled herself up up up into the air with the drape wrapping around her like a cocoon. Robert increased his speed. The bitch had marvelous swordsmanship. She was self-taught. He could see that from her fluid improvisation. If he didn't intend to kill her he would have been impressed. As she rolled up the wall Robert followed her. He ran up the sheer face of the wall. He planted each foot as fast and hard as he could. He had to reach her before gravity pulled him back to the ground. Years of practice had given him the ability to dodge her for a moment or too but Mistress Gravity would not be denied. He planned on grabbing the edge of the drape and letting his weight pull it and him back to the floor. To do so he dropped the saber in his right hand. If he had been a member of the local Anglican Church, he might have heard the old homily "If you want to make God laugh make a plan." But he wasn't Anglican. He was Brotherhood.

Just before he reached the edge of the drape Vivian started turning the other way. The drape began to unfurl. As it did it covered Robert's head. He was plunged into darkness. Cursing he let gravity do its work and fell to the floor where he landed in a crouch. Vivian also reached the floor. She saw his abandoned saber. Quick as a cat she grabbed the sword and hurled it sideways at the strong iron rings in the ceiling. The saber spun like the blades of a helicopter and sliced through the rings with a wicked snap. The fur-lined drape fluttered to the ground just as Robert began slashing his way out of its inky embrace. Once his torso appeared through the ribbons of the drape she struck.

Grunting she stabbed forward with her rapier. She aimed her strike for Robert's head. Right at his throat. She saw the epee sliding through the air in slow motion. She saw his carotid artery pulsate as she pushed her sword forward.

Robert brought his remaining saber up swiftly and with great force. The force was more than Vivian had been expecting. The blow pushed her sword away from her body.

A lightning bolt of pain shot up her arm. For a moment her entire world was filled with agony. Quicker than a cat, Robert punched the inside of her wrist. She watched helplessly as her hand opened and her sword fell to the floor. She stood for a nanosecond staring at her fine manicured nails, her soft creamy white skin and her empty hand. Her stomach felt like it was being pulled to the depths of Tartas. She watched as Robert raised his saber and began to bring it down with deadly intentions. His face was a grim mask of hate and ecstasy.

Thought was useless now. Vivian's body reacted with instinct.

Vivian fell forward and landed on her hands. As she did so she brought her feet up and over as if she was performing a handstand. Robert's momentum drove him toward her feet. Toward her razor sharp stilettos. For a moment she resembled an upside down "L".

The last thing Robert Darn saw were those razor sharp stilettos rushing toward his eyes. The heels entered his eye sockets with the force of a punch. They slid through his eyeballs, past his optical nerves and almost into his brain. Robert screamed, this time in agony. He stumbled backwards and blind. Vivian landed back on her feet and rushed to find her epee. She saw it lying on the floor a few feet away. She grabbed it and ran toward Robert.

Robert could hear her footsteps coming toward him from his right. He swung wildly with his saber.

Vivian ducked under Robert's desperate flailing.

Gritting her teeth she drove her rapier into his throat with both hands. She grunted and bared her perfectly capped teeth as she pushed the sword up and into his neck. Robert dropped his sword and wrapped both his hands around the epee. Blood began to ooze from his neck and his hands. Vivian pulled the blade backwards and Robert's hands fell to his sides. As the blade exited his throat Vivian heard a wet gurgle. Blood ran like tears from his ruined eyes. Blood was pouring from his throat. Blood dripped from his lacerated hands. Robert Darn wobbled on his feet for a moment. He fell backwards like a great oak from the Olde Grove and hit the floor.

The ballroom was filled with silence. Her chest was on fire. She wondered if she had a fracture in her sternum. She walked over to Robert's body and looked down at his bloodied visage. Every cell in her body was humming like the strings of a cello playing a concerto.

Vivian turned and walked out the ballroom and back through the lobby. As she walked she pulled the ribbon from her hair and let her red locks fall to her waist. Her hips swung with a new swagger. Gavin was waiting for her in the lobby. He was holding a smooth brown wooden box. The box was the same length as her sword. She placed the epee in the open box and Gavin snapped the lid shut.

"Gavin, please have our friends who work with Harry Orange and his associates come and clean up this mess. Then call the London police to report an attack here at the House. And Gavin, please make sure I get his swords," Vivian said. Gavin smiled and nodded his head.

"So glad to see everything went your way Madam," Gavin said. Vivian ran her fingers through her hair and glanced at Gavin.

"Did you ever doubt it would? Now I wish to have my desires satisfied. Call ahead and have Seville, Marcel and Noel prepare themselves," she said softly. Gavin raised an eyebrow.

"All three of them, Madam?"

"Yes Gavin all three. Make sure my whip and my candles are available. Then prepare our jet for takeoff in three hours. After I attend to my needs we will be returning to the mansion and opening the Invitation." She walked toward the door and the limo waiting outside.

"And once you open the Invitation, what then Madam?" Vivian stopped.

"Then we go to the Grand Hall and fight for our lives Gavin. We fight for our lives."

CHAPTER NINETEEN

Catlow sat on the bottom step of his father's shop as Pretlow gathered his best swords and his blacksmith tools. Pretlow worked quickly and efficiently. Catlow watched as his father moved around the shop with speed and purpose. No wasted movements. It was just his way. Catlow understood that but it did nothing to quell his rage or satisfy his curiosity about why Pretlow had asked him to join him in the shop. Alone. Catlow thought that after their tearful embrace that they had reached some unspoken truce. He guessed he was wrong and Pretlow was going to berate him for something. Catlow sat on the step waited. He no longer feared his father's rage. His own rage frightened him more. He could feel himself slipping away, becoming a creature he didn't recognize. His hatred of the Men of the First Chaos had changed him. He would go with his family to the Grand Hall. He would go through the motions of the ritual and all the silly traditional genuflecting. Then he would take a sword in each hand and kill every Man or woman of Chaos he saw. Nothing his father said to him now could change his mind. His mind was not in control. His heart was running the show now. His shattered heart.

Pretlow gathered a replacement basket guard for Aequitas and packed some other swords in a smooth velvet lined wooden box. He placed his blacksmithing tools in a large iron tool box. Once he had packed his tools both deadly and artistic he turned and faced Catlow. Pretlow leaned back against his work bench and crossed his arms. His son looked much older than his seventeen years. He had aged a decade in the twenty four hours since Pretlow had slapped him and watched him rush out of their house. Pretlow sighed.

"Catlow. Your mother told me about your friend, Harmony. I am truly sorry for you my son. I ....I overreacted to what you said in the kitchen. I see now that I did not do a very good job of preparing you for the weight we have to bear. I mean I prepared your body but not your mind. Not your heart.

The responsibilities we have are not for everyone. We are different Catlow. We are not just the slaepan. We are painfully aware of our duty. What we do is hard. I don't want you to think that I don't understand that. Sometimes I wish for the peace of the ignorant. It makes life so much easier. They don't have to worry constantly. They can sleep well. Their world is very simple. The ignorant are like ants. Ants don't know they are small. So they don't fear the giants that periodically come through their kingdoms and lay waste to their homes or smash them out of existence.

But we are not ants, Catlow. The Brotherhood is not something we do or participate in. It is who we are. It is a duty passed down for almost two thousand years. I take that duty very seriously. So seriously it may seem that I don't care about anything else. But never ever doubt my love for you, your mother and Calla. You are my family. You are my whole world," Pretlow said. Catlow was a bit stunned. Pretlow was not given to emotional soliloquies. He had never heard his father express any doubt about his duty or his commitment to the Brotherhood. But his rage was not quieted. Not one inch.

"You don't understand," Catlow said. His head was hanging down and his long arms were dangling off of his knees. Pretlow stepped forward and put his hand on Catlow's shoulder. Catlow flinched and looked up at Pretlow.

"What don't I understand? How it feels to be in love? To lose someone that you felt your heart could not function without? To see someone you love is hurt and even though you knew it wasn't your fault you felt you should have been able to save them? "Pretlow said. Catlow stared at Pretlow.

"Did something happen to Mom and you couldn't...you couldn't stop it?" Catlow asked. Pretlow put his hands on his hips.

"No not your mother. Someone else. Someone who was very dear to me. Someone I knew a very very long time ago." Pretlow motioned for Catlow to slide over on the bottom step. He sat down next to his son, the very image of himself, and patted his leg.

"I want to share something with you. Something that happened to me long ago. I want you to see that I do understand. This is something I've only talked about with Richard Darn. I've never told your mother or your Uncle Saed. It is something that shames me but I want to share it with you so that you can see that I am not just a member of the Brotherhood or Prefect of the House of Green Hills. I am also a man. A man that was once a boy and that boy made some awful mistakes. I learned from those mistakes. But the price of my education was high. It was 1989 and I was spending the summer in Florence Italy...

****

Pretlow got exited the plane in the Tuscany International Airport with his carry-on bag and a belly full of trepidation. The bag carried all his worldly possessions. His father's Book of the Seven Swords, his father's dueling sword, and his few pants and shirts. He was wearing his only pair of shoes and his only jacket. The temperature was a balmy 70 degrees and the sun was sitting high in the clouds like a huge white onion. Pretlow looked around the lobby of the airport. The Archivists had told him that Garn Whiteborne would have one of his apprentices pick him up from the airport to take him to the studio so that he could begin his own apprenticeship to the master sword maker. Pretlow had not wanted to leave the Grand Hall. The libraries and studies and rooms of that ancient citadel were comforting to him. The Menagerie made him feel connected to his father and his ancestors. The vast collection of venerable swords spoke to him in whispered confidences and hushed agreements. Seeing those honorable artifacts always re-affirmed his commitment to his duty and his mission. Touching the longsword of Maul the Druid or staring at the long dagger of Aron the Wounded Eye was like speaking to those warriors of yore. They told him it was all worth it. They told him their duty was real. Whenever he thought of his father or his mother mouldering in their graves he would wander down to the Menagerie and walk among the glass cases and his path would become clear once more. His father and his mother had believed in the Covenant. They had believed in the Brotherhood. That was never the issue. The fact that his father couldn't live without his liquor and his mother could not live without his father was the real issue. But standing in the Menagerie their faults and flaws become inconsequential in the face of the relics from Duels of the past. Their human frailties disappeared in the shadow of their awesome charge. It was in those moments that they ceased to be alcoholic father and suicidal mother and became instead Prefect and First Lady of the House of Green Hills. It was in that moment he could love them again.

Pretlow shook his head and mentally returned from his reverie. He scanned the airport lobby and tried to pick out an apprentice sword maker among the bustling throng of people. He was leaning against short bank of plastic chairs when someone tapped him on the shoulder. He spun around with his right hand near the flap of his weathered green gunny sack. He was reaching for his father's sword.

"Whoa there, Tiger! You don't wanna go slicing up your only ride in Italy!" the man in front of him said with a laugh. He was a trim mid-sized man. He was not as tall as Pretlow but he wasn't short. He was dark-skinned but with thin lips and a narrow nose. His hair was twisted into an impregnable knot of twist and locks that looked as if they hadn't seen water since the seventies. The 1870's. A bright orange leather jacket was wrapped around his narrow shoulders. Wide legged blue jeans ended just above his brown hiking boots. A black t-shirt hugged his frame and black chunk of obsidian hung from his neck on a woven hemp necklace. Pretlow was shocked by the man's eyes. Most dark-skinned people did not have blue eyes. Especially bright baby blues like the man standing in front of him. The man held out his hand

"Garn Whiteborne, artist, designer and sword maker extraordinaire. You must be Pretlow. The old biddies at the Grand Hall told me you were a tall drink of water." Pretlow took the man's hand and was surprised by the strength of his grip.

"Yes I am Pretlow Creedence." Garn laughed again.

"I...Am Pretlow Creedence. You sound like a Jedi. How old are you? Seventeen? Oh my we are going to have to loosen you up a bit. Come on let's get to the studio and I'll try to see about getting that stick out of your ass," Garn said as he headed out of the terminal. The man was walking incredibly fast.

"Sir I was under the impression that I would be learning how to make swords with a member of the Brotherhood not a..." Garn stopped.

"Not a what? A clown? Pretlow, one thing I have learned in my long long life is that life is a tragic comedy and the almighty is the biggest joker of all. Why not laugh along with him instead of living behind a veil of tears? Don't let my Versace coat fool you. I am the best sword maker in the world and if you are half the young man the Arks say you are you will learn more than just sword making this summer."

"I am sorry sir I meant no disrespect." Garn laughed again.

"Man have you ever smiled? Like ever? So damn serious. Come let's get back to Florence. You can meet the rest of the gang." Garn headed toward a bright orange Fiat. Pretlow tossed his bag in the backseat and climbed in the passenger seat.

"You get scared easily?" Garn said. Pretlow turned to look at him.

"I am not afraid of anything." he said. Garn smiled.

"Good so you won't complain about my driving. I just love automobiles. I can't even tell you how much I love these little horseless carriages," Garn said. He turned the key and hit the gas. He left the airport parking lot with a cloud of smoke trailing behind his spinning tires.

Forty-five minutes later they arrived at a huge villa on the outskirts of Florence. Garn hopped out the car and stretched his arms. Pretlow removed his fingers from the dashboard and tried to forget the little car going up on two-wheels as they came through some of the more narrow roads along the hillside.

"Come Pret let's get you settled in. Your actual training won't begin until tomorrow. "Garn said. He and Pretlow walked into the villa. It was a large two story Spanish style villa with a large wrap-around front porch with a roof supported by marble columns. The front door opened onto an expansive foyer that was lined with black marble tiles with white veins. The foyer gave way to an enormous parlor filled with plush chairs, bean bags and love seats. The walls were lined with all manner of art from multiple time periods and styles. Pollocks were hung next to Picassos which shared space with Andrew Wyeth landscapes and Norman Rockwell portraits. The floor in the parlor was a dark Brazilian cherry wood that glistened with a thick polyurethane finish. A beautifully colored parrot sat in huge black bird cage in the corner of the room. The parlor led into the kitchen and dining area. A wide central island dominated the room. It was covered in rough travertine tiles. Pretlow followed Garn through the kitchen to a short hallway that ended in a gorgeous black wooden door with corbels and a small speakeasy window in the center. Garn grabbed the door knob and stopped. He held his hand up to Pretlow.

"Wait. I want to open this door with a flourish," he said grinning.

"Welcome to Whiteborne Studios!" he said as he flung the door open dramatically.

Pretlow walked through the door into another world. Behind the door was a gigantic combination warehouse and studio. Large skylight let in the afternoon sun and illuminated all the nooks and crannies of the studio. Man-sized twirling mobiles hung from clear plastic twine in the ceiling. Da Vinci's hang glider twirled in the air next to an early 19th century bicycle. A Chinese dragon trailed from one end of the studio to the other like some great-grandson of Smaug.

Scattered throughout the studio were several elephantine work tables. Projects of all shapes and sizes were being fabricated by several individuals with looks of deep concentration on their faces. Pretlow scanned the room and took in each and every table. To his left a young man wearing dark goggles was welding some type of suit of armor. To his right a young woman was molding a mask of some type out of clay. Straight ahead an older gentleman was painting a mannequin with bright green red and black colors. The dummy had a gag around its mouth. Far to the right a figure wearing a full welding mask was cutting through a large sheet of metal with an acetylene torch. Far to the left a young woman with her back to him was sketching on a white canvas. The sketch appeared to be of some type of holster or bandolier.

"Mr. Whiteborne," Pretlow began but Garn held up his hand.

"Garn. Not Master Garn or Sensei or Mr. Whiteborne. Just Garn. Titles truly don't matter here. Only discipline and dedication matter in this house," he said softly.

"Garn I thought you made swords," Pretlow said. Garn laughed. It was a full and somehow fleshy laugh. It came up from his gut and exploded out of his mouth.

"Oh Pret you tickle my humerus bone. We do make swords here. But just making swords doesn't pay the bills. So we make suits of armor for S&M dominants in New Jersey. We create works of art for political movements in South Africa so that they may make some kind of statement. Whatever that means. We create wall murals for wealthy folks who wish the Victorian Age had never ended and spend their weekends dressed in clothes that Charles Dickens loved to wear. But make no mistake. We make the finest swords you will ever see. I have acquired skills over a long and interesting life that allows me to forge blades with no equal. Not every Garn Whiteborne sword is a Brotherhood sword but every Brotherhood sword is a Garn Whiteborne sword. Now let me introduce you to the crew," Garn said. He went to the middle of the studio and clapped his hands. The sound was louder than Pretlow had expected. It made his ear drums sting.

"Folks we have a new member of the team starting with us tomorrow. So let me get you guys acquainted. This tall and slightly attractive fella is Pretlow Creedence. Pretlow, the fella with the goggles is Cliff. The young woman making a slave mask is Aria. The older gent is my good friend and assistant August. The scary guy over there that looks like Vader is Richard and the aloof young lady sketching a sword holster of her own design is Agrippina. Come over here and make him feel welcome folks," Garn said in a loud booming voice that filled the cavernous studio. Everyone immediately stopped what they were doing and came over to shake Pretlow's hand. Everyone except Agrippina. She only turned around on her stool and peered at him. Pretlow felt a strange nervousness when her gaze settled on him. She was an incredibly attractive young girl. Long auburn hair that was parted down the middle fell to her waist. Her face was sharp but softened by keen blue eyes. She was wearing a light muslin shirt and fade blue jeans. Her feet were encased in moccasins. She stared at him for a moment before she dropped her gaze.

"Alright let's get back to work! Pretlow let me show you your room."

The next few weeks flew by for Pretlow. He began to learn blacksmithing and metallurgy, metal shaping and fabrication. He tried to keep his temper in check but he was rapidly losing patience with Garn and his stubborn refusal to teach Pretlow how to make swords. On the Saturday of his fourth week at the studio Pretlow as sitting outside the studio on the patio eating his lunch and looking out at the Tuscan country side. His excellent vision allowed him to see vineyards

341

and farms miles away from the villa. He ate his bruschetta quietly and efficiently while he pondered his options. Perhaps he should write to the Archivists. Let them know what was going on at their master sword maker's little studio.

Or maybe he should just wait and see what happens in the next couple of weeks. As he sat there he heard the French door open with a creak. He turned quickly and saw Richard Darn coming out onto the patio. Richard was a tall boy like himself but wider and thicker through the middle. He had sandy brown hair that was pulled back from his head in a ponytail. He had a twinkle in his eye and always seemed to be laughing inside to a private joke. He started to run toward Pretlow then turned his run into the lead-up to a cartwheel which in turn became front somersaults. Richard flipped four times before he landed on his butt next to Pretlow. Pretlow was impressed. The older boy had good form.

"Why you sitting out here all by your lonesome, mate? You're not afraid of Aggie are ya?" Richard said, his eyes crinkling at the corners. Pretlow turned his head to look at the countryside again.

"No I am not afraid of Agrippina. I just don't like the way she stares at me," he said as he finished his bruschetta.

"Well she used to stare at me the same way. I think she thought we would look like monsters, Richard said smiling. Pretlow turned to look at him.

"Why would we look like monsters?" he asked. Richard rolled his eyes.

"Well we are members of the Men of the First Order and her family is a part of the Men of the First Chaos. I think she thinks we are going to cut her head off in the night." he said. Pretlow felt his stomach twist into a million tight little knots. He stood and let his plate fall onto the hard red patio stones. He started to stride to the door.

"Where ya going mate? What's wrong fella? I thought you knew that!" Richard called after him but Pretlow barely heard him. He stomped through the villa and up the marble staircase to Garn's private office.

He turned left at the top of the stairs and headed for the double doors at the end of the hall. They were tall, intricately designed doors with a vast carved tapestry of the scenes from some ancient ceremony. Pretlow recognized Machu Pichu and the Mayan Pyramids. Small wood cut silhouettes dotted the door and a sun in splendor was dominant in the left hand corner of the doors.

Pretlow did not knock or announce himself.

He grabbed the cast iron knobs and pulled the door open with all his strength. Garn was sitting with his feet on his desk. His eyes were closed and Pretlow heard Vivaldi playing on a boom box sitting in the corner under a stone bookcase. Garn was wearing purple and black checked pants, no shoes and a white linen shirt open at the throat. He was caressing the black stone that lay against his chest. His toes were adorned with an assortment of rings with various symbols carved into their surface.

"Garn. I am the living Prefect of the House of Green Hills. I am a member of the Brotherhood of the Blade and I have sworn my allegiance to the Men of the First Order. I will NOT break bread with a member of the Men of the First Chaos. I DEMAND you arrange for me to leave this place today!" Pretlow said. His voice boomed through the office. His head was throbbing and he felt the beast that was his temper testing the bars of its cage.

Garn did not open his eyes.

"You hear the strings in that piece? They sound like the way angels speak. Clarity beyond our understanding but it speaks to our hearts. You demand nothing of me Pretlow. I work with the Brotherhood at my own discretion. I am not of the Brotherhood. I make swords for the Men of Order and the Men of Chaos. My mission, my reason for existing is the art the blade. I have lived for a long, long, long time, Pretlow. Sex, money, violence; none of these vices hold much interest for me anymore. Ah but the art. The craftsmanship, the aesthetic pleasure of a finely wrought sword keeps my long days and longer nights from overtaking me. It soothes me, comforts me to see what I can do with just my hands. Your Archivists didn't send you here to just learn how to craft swords. They sent you here to find a center inside yourself. They sent you here to learn to channel that ferocious temper. Would your dead parents be proud of you if they could see you now?" Garn asked.

Pretlow felt the bars snap. He saw a cheap sword in a scabbard leaning against a lounge chair to his left. He grabbed the sword and threw the scabbard aside. He turned to face Garn. But the man was not in his seat. The old wooden office chair was spinning around in a lazy circle. Suddenly Pretlow felt a stinging in his left thigh. Garn was standing to his left and had just struck him with the scabbard. Pretlow was not a boy given to flight of fancy or daydreaming. He did not ponder how Garn could have gotten out of the chair, moved around him, picked up the scabbard and struck him with it all within five seconds. The beast was free. It would not be satiated until he had run the Garn through.

Pretlow turned as fast as he could, which was very very fast. He slashed at Garn's face but the older man blocked the blow with the scabbard. Pretlow stabbed forward with the sword. His eyes were focused on Garn's throat. Garn took the scabbard and caught the point of the sword. He slid it along the length of the blade until the weapon had been sheathed. Pretlow was so amazed at his speed he hardly felt it when Garn twisted the now sheathed sword out of his hand.

Garn struck at the soft spot behind Pretlow's knee. The tall boy fell to his other knee. Quick as a hiccup Garn moved around him placed the scabbard against his throat and then entwined his own arms around it until he had Pretlow in a modified full nelson. They tumbled to the floor.

"I know you are angry and scared. Your father died and your mother died and you bear an awesome responsibility. I know you do. Trust me I know what you are feeling. But if you don't get control of this hatted and anger it will eat you alive from the inside out and you won't make it to the Duel. You are angry at your father for driving drunk and dying. You are angry at your mother for taking her own life. You feel ashamed of that anger so you channel that anger into hate for the Men of Chaos. You think you honor your father with your hatred and in turn it eases your shame. I understand how you would make that assumption but you are wrong. I knew your father. If he was here he would tell you that your hatred narrows your vision. It corrupts you. This Duel is not about you, Pretlow and it's not about Agrippina or Richard. It's about everyone. The whole world. You are trying to use your hatred to focus your mind. You need to learn how to just focus. Let go of your anger for your parents. Let go of your hatred. Cool the fire of your passion so it doesn't obscure your true mission. You are the generation that will fulfill the Covenant. You must be brave and skilled and vigilant but most of all you must be men of honor. Men of honor don't run. Men of honor are not prejudiced. They judge people on their own merits not on what house they come from. You have honor in you Pret. It's my job to shape it. Just like the steel. Now say the oath," he said. Pretlow could barely breathe. The scabbard was biting into his neck. He strained and twisted but Garn had him in an anaconda's embrace.

"Pretlow, while I am not at all homophobic this looks really gay. Say the oath. Promise me you will be a man of honor." Pretlow gritted his teeth. He closed his eyes.

"We are the men of the Brotherhood…" he began…

Weeks later Pretlow was in the workshop finishing up an iron harness for a client of Garn's. Pretlow had learned not to ask about the clients and why they needed certain things but he was pretty sure this harness was for a person to wear around their neck and head. Pretlow shook his head and continued to polish the brass metalwork.

"Goddammit!" he heard someone exclaim. He turned and saw Agrippina standing in front of a metal work of her own. Richard and Garn were standing next to her. She was running her hands through her hair and her face was tight and pinched. Pretlow wandered over to her workstation. He had tried to take to heart what Garn had said. Being bested was not something he enjoyed. However he could now see that it had been necessary. Humility and honor walked along life's road hand in hand. In the Grand Hall when the Archivists would put down their book and scrolls and spar with him he beat them easily. After his mother passed away he sought out the old masters that would visit the Grand Hall and seek counsel on techniques and conditioning. Being subdued by Garn had taught him that he still had a lot to learn. Abut fighting and about himself.

"What is the matter?" he asked Richard. Agrippina wouldn't look at him.

"Well Aggie here is designing a rig to be worn by a certain fella who shall remain nameless but apparently he needs to carry daggers in such a way that they are concealed yet easily accessible. " Richard said.

"And Agrippina is having some difficulty finalizing her design," Garn said gently.

"The daggers are supposed to be hidden up his sleeve. But he want's daggers that are eight inches long. From his shoulder to his bicep is only 4 inches. His forearm is six inches. If I rig them to his forearm the tip will stick out of his sleeves." Agrippina said. Pretlow could hear the exasperation in her voice.

"No one wants to see this man's tip." Richard said with a wink. Garn shot him a withering look.

"Can I...can I look at the rig?" Pretlow asked cautiously. Agrippina looked at him out of the corner of her eye. Then she nodded curtly. Pretlow stepped forward.

The rig was a series of metal channels no wider than a dagger's blade. The channels were lined with some kind of elongated spring system. The dagger was nestled on top of the spring and held in a small black shuttle. At the top of the rig was a square actuator and attached to that were two tubes. One ran the length of the rig down to what Pretlow assumed were some type of gauntlets. The other was attached to a small cylindrical canister of compressed air. It appeared the entire contraption was designed to be worn like a coat beneath a coat. Or a coat's sleeves beneath a coat. Pretlow stared at the rig for a long time. Finally he turned to Agrippina and looked in her eyes.

"Split the blade from the hilt. Fabricate a blade with a locking mechanism. Re-calibrate the delivery system to that the hilt is worn up by the bicep and the blade on the forearm. When the gauntlets are activated have a two stage actuator. Hilt releases and locks onto the blade. Blade releases and flies into the wearer's hands. He will just need really fast reflexes," Pretlow said. Agrippina's cold blue eyes ignited like a furnace.

"Yes, I see what you are saying. I'm not that good at fabrication. I really like to design. Could you help me with the blades?" she said. Her tone was not halting or shy. It was saturated with a frankness that belied her years. Her request took Pretlow by surprise.

"Um I guess I mean I have to finish that harness," Pretlow said. Garn laughed.

"Nonsense. Richard can finish polishing the harness. You and Agrippina get to work on this rig," Garn said as he turned and walked out of the shop. Richard grinned at Pretlow.

"Better give me your polishing rag mate," he said. Pretlow handed him the rag in his hand. As Richard passed him he whispered.

"Seems like you might be getting something polished y'self mate," he said in low conspiratorial tone.

Pretlow ignored him. He turned to Agrippina.

"Shall we begin?" he asked. She smiled and nodded her head.

The next week saw Pretlow and Agrippina working very closely together. Pretlow showed her how to bend and shape metal and

Agrippina showed him how to put the images in his head down on paper and drafting boards. During a lunch break she joined Pretlow on the bench in the middle of the patio.

"So you are not at all what I thought you were going to be,." Agrippina said as she stole one of Pretlow's orange slices. Pretlow chuckled.

"And how did you imagine I would be?" Pretlow said. Agrippina smoothed a loose lock of hair behind her ear.

"I don't know. Richard is a silly. I never really think of him as a Man of the First Order. He is just funny ass Richard. When Garn told me another Man of Order was coming I expected someone.....cruel and austere. But you're not. You're just quiet," she said taking another orange slice.

"Well you are not what I imagined a member of the Men of the First Chaos would be either," he said as he bit into a huge slice of orange. Agrippina reached for the last orange slice. Pretlow grabbed her wrist. His grip was firm yet gentle.

"And what did you think I would be like?" Agrippina asked staring into his eyes.

"Evil." Agrippina laughed.

"Who says I'm not?" she asked. Pretlow released her wrist.

"I guess you could be. I don't know. I have little experience with women," Pretlow confessed. Agrippina smiled.

"Did you just make a joke?" she asked.

"Was it funny?" Pretlow asked. He was smiling. "Yes it was," she said as she snatched the last piece of the orange.

"So your father never sat down and had the talk with you about girls and how we are just the best thing to ever happen to men and you should always make us happy?" Agrippina asked as she swallowed the orange. Pretlow hung his head.

"My father is dead."

"Oh I'm sorry. I didn't know."

"How could you? I don't like to talk about it. My mom's dead too if you were wondering," he added. Agrippina put her hand on his knee.

"So you are all alone?" she asked.

"No I live with the Archivists at the Grand Hall. I work in the Menagerie..."

"Do you have any other family?"

"Yes but they don't want to be bothered with me or the Brotherhood, he said. He had never said that out loud. His uncle wanted no part of the family legacy. His mother had no siblings. He was utterly and undeniably alone.

"I wish I was alone. My family has my whole life planned out for me. They want me to marry another member of the Men of the First Chaos. My father has basically sold me off like a prized mare." she said. Pretlow turned and faced her. He pushed another wayward lock out of her face.

"And what do you want?" he asked. Agrippina smiled.

"I'd love to design swords for a living. I love coming up with ideas. I'm just not that good at making them."

"Obviously," Pretlow said. Agrippina punched his arm.

"Seriously. I would love to stay here and work with Garn forever." she said wistfully.

"He is a unique personality," Pretlow said. Agrippina threw her head back and stretched like a cat.

"Well he isn't any stranger than some of the people I've seen come through the doors of our House," Agrippina said. Pretlow shrugged his shoulders.

"He is just really different. I've never encountered someone like him."

"Well he makes me feel like he really cares about me. Like what I want is important," Agrippina said.

"It is important," Pretlow said. Agrippina smiled again.

"I'm serious. You should be able to do what you like."

"Well it's for the good of the Covenant." Agrippina said. Her voice was dripping with sarcasm.

"What good is the Covenant if you are miserable? If you can't give your whole heart to it? I believe in the Covenant. It's all I have. But you have real talent. I've seen your drawings. Your designs are incredible," he said.

"You are just trying to get into my pants," Agrippina said with a smile. Pretlow felt his face get hot.

"No. I am just saying that you have a right to live your own life. "

"What, you don't want to get into my pants?" she asked. Pretlow felt his face getting hotter.

"I...uh...I mean I don't know about that. I mean I don't want to just get into your pants. I mean I don't want to get into your pants unless you want me to. No that's not what I mean..." Pretlow stammered. Agrippina stood. She laughed. It was a deep throaty sound that made Pretlow tingle all over his body.

"You are so cute when you are totally embarrassed. Come see me after lunch we have to try the rig out today. Sorry about your parents. I really am," she said as she rose. Pretlow stared out at the country side.

"Yeah me too."

Later they were in the shop. Agrippina had put the rig on Pretlow. He had his arms outstretched as she made adjustments.

"Don't move..." she said quietly as she pulled and tugged the components of the rig into place Garn and Richard were standing near the worktable as Agrippina darted around Pretlow checking and re-checking the air lines and the aluminum channels. Richard was grinning like a Cheshire cat. Pretlow stared at him with a baleful expression.

"You smell good," Agrippina said under her breath. Pretlow felt his whole body tingle. It wasn't what she said but how she said it that stoked the fire of his passion. Her timbre, her inflection, her tone were in unison speaking to a part of him that he had never really explored in all his seventeen years. Her light blue eyes caught his light green ones every now and again as her hands moved over his body. She cinched up the rig around his biceps and tightened the gauntlets around his wrist.

"That's tight," he whispered.

"It has to be. Don't worry. Be a good boy and I'll let you go," she said. Humming, she finally took a step back and looked over her work.

"Well, I must say it looks like it will work, Agrippina. But as the boygirl in Thailand said, looks can be deceiving. Let's see how," Garn said. He was standing with his chin resting on his fist.

"Comfy, Pretlow? I mean it's no good if it's uncomfortable," Agrippina asked.

"I'm fine. Let's try it," he said curtly. Agrippina nodded.

"Okay. Just press the pressure releases when you are ready." Pretlow looked at her. She stared back at him.

"I hope it works," her eyes seemed to say.

"It will," Pretlow tried to say back with his eyes. He pressed the two small round toggle switches in his palms that were attached to the gauntlets. A large hiss filled the room. That was followed by two distinct metallic clicking sounds. The handles flew down the aluminum channels and slammed into the blades and locked into place. The now-intact daggers were launched out of the channels. Pretlow grabbed both of them as they exited the channels just above his wrist. All this happened in less than three seconds. Pretlow stood there holding the two blades he had fabricated for Agrippina.

"There is a warrior," Richard thought to himself. Agrippina jumped into his arms and hugged him in a tight embrace.

"Thank you," she said in his ear.

"Well we can call the client and tell him his product is ready for whatever he wants it to do with it," Garn said. "Good work you two." And with that he turned and walked out of the shop.

"Damn fine work," Richard said as Agrippina began to release

Pretlow from the rig.

"It is a nice piece of work but when are we going to learn how to make swords? And not just swords but Brotherhood swords? That's why I came here," Pretlow said.

"I don't know but it has been nice getting to know you. Both of you," Agrippina said as she stood behind Pretlow detaching the air lines.

"Well I'm going into to town with Cliff. Gotta go pick up some scones. I'm feening for those things. You coming, Pret?" Richard asked.

"No. I am going to practice," Pretlow said. He felt Agrippina's hands stiffen on his back.

"Well suit yourself. You want me to bring you anything?" Richard asked.

"No." Pretlow said.

"How bout you Aggie?" Richard asked.

"No thank you Richard," she said as she finished unbuckling her invention from Pretlow's body. She placed the rig on the worktable and walked out of the workshop.

"Talk to you later Richard," Pretlow said as he followed her.

Agrippina had walked into the kitchen and got a bottle of wine out of the refrigerator.

"Are you old enough to drink?" Pretlow asked her. She pulled the cork out of the bottle and poured herself a glass. She took a long sip and closed her eyes.

"In France we drink wine with every meal." she said.

"You don't sound French," Pretlow said.

Agrippina took another sip. "My parents had me learn English as first language. I speak both fluently. In addition to five other languages. It's a holdover from our old family tradition. When courtesans had to be multilingual," she said as she swirled the wine around in her glass.

"Courtesans?" Pretlow asked.

"I'm a Du Mor, Pretlow. From the House of Love and Agony. Or otherwise known as the House of Pimps and Whores. Courtesans and concubines. Trollops and working girls. We have cornered the market on vice," she said with a laugh.

"I...didn't know," Pretlow said.

"When you said you were going to go practice it reminded me of why you were here. Why me and Richard are here. To learn how to make swords that we will use to kill each other. I guess I had kinda put it out of my mind," she said.

"I would never hurt you Agrippina," Pretlow said. He moved around the large island and gently took the wine glass from her hand and placed it on the table. She turned her face away and put her hands on his chest. She could feel the muscle there solid like granite.

"I watch you in the garden sometimes. Practicing without your shirt on. I watch you with your sword," she said softly.

"I know." His voice was husky and low. His mind and heart were racing at galactic speeds. She was a member of the House of Love and Agony. One of the Houses of the Men of the First Chaos. Literally men who were his sworn enemies. She was also beautiful and intelligent and smelled of cherries and cinnamon. Her light ice blue eyes were soft and rimmed with the threat of tears.

"I know you wouldn't want to, Pretlow. Hurt me I mean. But that's a promise you can't keep," she said. She leaned forward and pushed her face into his chest. Pretlow pushed her away gently and looked down into the smooth mountain lakes that were her eyes.

"I keep my promises," he said. Agrippina took his face in her hands. Pretlow felt their softness against his cheek. It was the first time any woman other than his mother had touched him. He moved his face closer to Agrippina's. Their lips were millimeters apart.

"Um, ya want me to bring some rubbers back from town?" Richard said with a laugh. Pretlow stepped back from Agrippina and bumped into the stone covered island. He turned and walked out of the kitchen.

"Richard sometimes you are a real dick." Agrippina said as she left the kitchen.

"Blimey no one around here can take a joke anymore," Richard mumbled as he walked out of the kitchen.

"Wake up Pretlow," a voice said. Pretlow instantly sat up right in his bed. His hand reached under his pillow for his father's sword.

"You won't need that. After tonight you will be able to make your own sword," Garn said. He was standing at the end of Pretlow's bed. He was wearing a black shirt and a white heavy canvas apron.

"Come to the workshop," he said. Then he left the room so fast Pretlow almost thought it was a dream. Pretlow jumped out of bed and threw on his clothes and hurried downstairs to the workshop.

Agrippina was there as was Richard. They were standing next to a cast iron kiln. The skylight was open for ventilation. A bright orange fire raged under the kiln and deep reddish molten steel was swirling within the cauldron of the kiln. Garn was standing next to the kiln. The pale Tuscan moon cast eerie shadows throughout the workshop. He was wearing two large Kevlar gloves.

"I need your full attention. What I will show you tonight I have shown a precious few. I have been a friend of the Brotherhood for many many years. I do not take sides. I make art that can be used as weapons and weapons that are works of art. I do this in recompense for a debt I owe and can never repay. You are the generation that will fight the next Duel. That will fulfill the Covenant. No not take this duty lightly or without deep and serious reflection. The Covenant is not about just you and how you feel but about every man, woman and child on this planet. It is the reprieve the Judges gave our species. Do not waste it. You know that Brotherhood steel is different from any other steel on earth. It's is stronger, more flexible, more durable than regular Bessemer steel. I am going to show you why.

"I have lived a very very long time. That long life has shown me certain things. Some I wish I could forget, some I am blessed to remember. One of the things I have seen is the blood of an angel spill upon the ground. A real angel, not an angel in the sense that the multitude of different denominations and religions would have you believe. But a terrible and awesome emissary of the Judges. Now how that Angel's blood came to be spilled is not a tale I will tell here but from that blood was made a mineral that when added to the highest quality steel makes it incredibly flexible yet incredibly strong and sharp. In short it turns a regular piece of steel into a Brotherhood Blade." Garn stepped back into the shadows out of the moonlight. When he re-emerged he was holding a large glass container. It had a metal lid similar to a mason jar but infinitely more ornate. The glass was almost black. The lid was locked in place with two brass latches on each side. Garn sat the jar on the nearest workstation and grabbed his welder's gloves.

"Angel's blood. It is the soil that was under the emissary's feet when it was felled by an ancient warrior of the Men of the First Chaos. The blood mixed with the soil and created something new. Something that the alchemists of the twelfth century learned could be used to make a cavalcade of things, including unbreakable steel. But it is highly corrosive to human skin. It is highly flammable. It is very dangerous. If you are true to your craft and to your duty you will learn how to handle it. For now watch and take instruction," Garn said. He undid the clamps on the jar and poured a bit of the contents in his hand. A fine blue substance was in the palm of his hand. It seemed to glow with an ambient light.

"Stand back." His voice was low. The three of them took several steps backwards. Garn threw the blue powder into the kiln. A bright blue flame erupted out of the kiln. Pretlow watched the flame dance and cavort for a few moments before it extinguished in a flash of even bluer light.

"Now I will teach you how to create works of art that bring death," Garn said.

Pretlow would reflect later that the rest of that night passed in a blur of steel, sparks, fire and pain. By the time the sun rose his arms were exhausted from swinging a shaping hammer. His fingers had blisters and his face had a few small burns from sparks flying off of the steel as he willed it into a blade.

By the time Garn released them he was so tired he couldn't think straight. The world he knew was fuzzy around the edges and seemed ready to fray. Pretlow wandered up the stairs to his room and fell across the bed. He was so tired he didn't even reach for his sword when he heard the door creak as it was opened.

"Go away..." he mumbled. A soft delicate hand touched his neck. He turned over on his back and grabbed the hand that had touched him. Agrippina stared at him. Her face looked as exhausted as Pretlow felt.

"Can I lay with you?" she asked simply. Pretlow released her hand and raised himself up on his elbows.

"Why?" Pretlow asked. Agrippina smiled.

"Pretlow, when a girl asks to lay with you don't ask why. Either say yes or no. So is it yes or no?" she asked. Pretlow did not speak but instead moved over to one side of the bed to allow Agrippina to lie down beside him. She turned on her side and laid her head on his sweaty chest. She ran her fingers over his defined pectoral and abdominal muscles. She coiled her right leg around his left one. Her lips found his neck.

"I'm ... I'm all sweaty," he said. His voice was faintly hoarse.

"I don't care," she said as she licked his jaw.

"I ... don't know what to do Agrippina," he said softly.

"I do," she said as her hand reached for his belt.

The next few weeks passed in storm maelstrom of passion for Pretlow and Agrippina. Passion for the swords they were creating and passion for each other. Mornings spent hammering the Brotherhood steel into blades with deadly intentions and night spent finding hidden places around the villa to touch and kiss and explore their bodies. And their hearts.

Pretlow finished his sword before Agrippina finished hers. It was a short scimitar with an ivory handle. As he held it in his hand he thought he could hear his father whisper in his ear. He closed his eyes and thought he could hear Astor Credence's raspy whiskey soaked voice.

"It is your destiny to win the Duel of Generations."

Garn had inspected the sword to determine if Pretlow really was done. He held it up to the light then gripped it with one hand away from his body. He looked at the bone handle and the brass pommel. He looked at the blade and checked to make sure it was plumb and true.

"Very good, Pretlow. You may keep this sword. The next one you build will be for a client," he said as he handed it back to Pretlow. Garn leaned forward and whispered in his ear.

"Shaping steel is like focusing your anger. You mill it and form it and give it a precision and a purpose. Remember that."

Pretlow had gone outside on the patio to practice with the new sword. He let it hang loosely by his side for a moment before going through his movements. He took a deep breath and let the cloak of concentration wrap around his mind. It was a technique Garn had taught them.

"Think of your mind as a knight in an old fairy tale. Your skill and your training is your armor. Then imagine a magical cloak. It is the cloak of concentration. It wraps around your mind and gives you a laser focus. It narrows your vision until all you can see is your enemy and all his movements and possible movements. It slows time around you so that you can react with instinct *and* intellect. It will take time but once you master this technique you will begin to see the world as true warrior of the blade and not just a pretender on a stage."

Pretlow began to let the cloak of concentration wrap around his mind. It unfurled and encapsulated his brain and his heart. He closed his eyes and took deep breaths. He could hear his blood pumping through his veins. Finally he opened his eyes.

He looked out onto the countryside. His already excellent vision seemed a hundred times clearer. He could see humming birds flying around the patio. He could see their wings flapping in slow motion. He could see bees lazily floating among the black eyed susans and gladiola and camellias.

Pretlow began his movements.

He slashed the scimitar to the left then the right. Without pausing he dropped to his knees and tossed the sword to his opposite hand then popped up from his kneeling position to spin around in a complete circle. He tucked his head and did a front flip punchout. In mid-flip he grasped the scimitar with both hands so that as he completed the flip the blade was swinging down with all of his centrifugal force behind it. He tossed the scimitar in the air, spun on one fit and executed a spinning heel kick and caught the scimitar before it hit the ground. He paused for a moment. He heard clapping behind him and turned.

Agrippina was standing at the door of the courtyard. Her dark hair was pulled straight back in a pony tail. She was wearing a light green off the shoulder blouse and skin tight leggings. She was wearing her moccasins even though they didn't really match. She smiled at him.

"You really know how to handle your sword don't you?" she said. Pretlow felt his face get hot. Her frankness still embarrassed him. She was the first woman he had ever kissed, ever touched, ever made love to and yet he felt very inferior to her in matters of the heart. She was sophisticated and witty and very passionate and sensual. When he was around her he felt awkward and uncoordinated. She made a mockery of his skill and training. She exposed him for the boy he was without even trying. Yet despite all that he loved her in way that was new and exciting. And frightening.

"I'm just practicing." he said sullenly. Agrippina walked over to him and ran her hands over his chest.

"Aw baby I was just teasing. You are so cute when you are embarrassed." She hugged him. He hugged her back.

"What's going to happen at the end of the summer?" she mumbled into his chest. Pretlow stroked her hair with his free hand.

"I try not to think about that," he said. Agrippina raised her head.

"I can't stop thinking about it. Pretlow I have never felt as happy in my entire life as when I'm your arms. I don't think about Carcone or my family's whorehouses or my father looking disappointed with everything I've ever done. I meant what I said. I want to stay here forever." Pretlow looked down at her and kissed her forehead.

"We can't stay here," he said. It wasn't as if the idea hadn't crossed his mind. Just stay with Agrippina here in Florence. Forget the Brotherhood, forget the Duel. Just live a life, spending every day creating with metal and every night creating with flesh.

But the voice of his father expelled such thoughts.

"Who says we have to stay here? We could go somewhere else. We could go anywhere. We are skilled craftsmen Pretlow. We could earn a living. We could get an apartment or house. We could build a life together," she said. Pretlow stepped back from her embrace.

"Aggie we are from different worlds. You come from a family that is rich. It doesn't matter how they got that way they are wealthy in ways I can't even imagine. I have nothing but my sword and my skill and my oath to the Brotherhood. You deserve to be with a man who can take care of you."

"I can take care of myself. I don't' need you, Pretlow. I want you. I thought you wanted me too," she said sadly. She turned and started walking to the courtyard door. Pretlow reached out and grabbed her arm and pulled her to him.

"I do want you Aggie. But we have to be realistic. We belong to different Houses. Different ideas. Chaos and Order. If we did just run off we would need money. I don't have any and your family would cut you off. And I have a duty to fulfill. Just like the men in your family have a duty to fulfill. The Duel is bigger than us, it's bigger than anything. It's about the whole world not just us. I have enjoyed this summer. You are my light I have been in the dark for a very long time but you showed me that there is still beauty in the world. I do love you. But we can't just run away together," he said. The words felt like razors in his mouth. It hurt to speak the truth. The truth may set you free but it takes a bit of skin with it when the shackles are unlocked. Agrippina pulled away from him and crossed her arms.

"If I had 100,000 dollars would you stay with me?" she asked. Pretlow rolled his head on his shoulders.

"Aggie you don't have that much money."

"Answer the question. What if I did? Would you be with me? Because I would be with you without thinking about it. I don't care what my family would think or do. I love you Pretlow Creedence. I love your lips and your eyes. I love your laugh and your kisses. I love the way you won't eat ice cubes even though everyone else thinks it's weird. I love your skill with the sword. I love the way you make me feel when we make love. You are my whole life. I don't want to be a Du Mor anymore and I don't want you to be a Creedence. I don't want to belong to Men of the First Chaos and I don't want you to belong to the Men of the First Order. I want us to belong to each other!"

"Aggie if you had that kind of money we could do anything we wanted to do. But you don't. We both have responsibilities to our families and the Brotherhood. If this was another world, if we had that kind of money yes I would be with you for as long as I had breath in my body," he said. Agrippina stepped forward and kissed him. Her tongue slipped inside his mouth and tickled his teeth.

"That's all I wanted to know," she said. She smiled and kissed him again. She stepped back and turned. He watched her ponytail flip as she walked toward the courtyard door. A sour feeling permeated his body. He knew he had said the right things for the right reasons so why did he feel like a steaming pile of excrement? He began his movements again. When all else fails grab hold of the steel. That was one of his father's favorite sayings. For the first time in a long time he wished Astor was still alive and sober so he could talk to him. But he was dead and in his grave and Pretlow was the Prefect of the House of Green Hills so he would have to soldier on alone. His movements became more frantic, more intense. Pain was a muse for his skill and he was overly acquainted with her.

The day moved forward and it wasn't until dinner time that Pretlow noticed he hadn't seen Agrippina since their talk in the courtyard. He sat down with his plate of broiled chicken and green peppers and a glass of apple juice next to Richard. Richard was wolfing down his food with reckless abandon.

"Rich have you seen Agrippina?" Pretlow asked.

"Yeah French girl, dark hair, killer arse," Richard said. Pretlow did not laugh.

"I'm serious. I talked to her earlier and have not seen her since," Pretlow said. There was a feeling in his gut that something was wrong. It was a feeling he would learn to trust as he matured. Richard stopped gobbling his food for a moment.

"Did you two have a lovers spat?" Richard asked, grinning. A piece of chicken breast was caught in his teeth.

"Huh? What are you talking about? I'm just concerned because I have not seen her in four hours," Pretlow said sipping his juice.

"Oh because everyone knows you two have been shagging like a pair of jack rabbits," Richard said.

"What? We are not shagging or whatever. We are just friends." Pretlow said. His face was burning.

"It's okay mate. I'd do her if she even gave me the time of day. But she only has eyes for her cream colored prince," Richard said with a laugh. Pretlow stood up from the table.

"You know Richard I like you but you are not nearly as funny as you think you are." he said as he stomped out of the kitchen area. Garn watched him over the top of his mug of beer. His blue eyes were gleaming.

Pretlow went to his room and slammed the door behind him. How did Richard know? How did anyone know? Granted he had nearly no experience with this sort of thing but he thought they had been careful. What if the Archivists found out? Or....then he stopped thinking and just sat on the bed. There was really no one who would care what he was doing or with whom. He was the last scion of his House. Perhaps Agrippina was right. Maybe they should just run off together. Pretlow fell back onto his bed. As his head hit the pillow he felt something hard under it. Pretlow flipped onto his belly and reached his hand under the pillow. There was a small wooden box about the size of a blackboard eraser. He sat up and touched the smooth walnut surface. It was hinged like a jewelry box. He opened it and looked inside. There was a folded piece of a paper and small metal bracelet. The bracelet looked like a small piece of chain mail. Pretlow unfolded the piece of paper.

It was a letter from Agrippina. Reading it made Pretlow's blood run cold.

Dear Pretlow,

I hope you like the bracelet. I made it myself just for you. Thanks to your kindness and patience I am actually half-decent a metal forming (smile). Pret I asked you a question today and I was overjoyed at your answer. Because there is nothing I want more in this world than to spend the rest of my life with you. But you are right. We will need some money to get started. Did I tell you I would do anything to be with you? (smile) I have done something that I know will make you mad at first but if you love me the way you say you do you will understand. I talked to Cliff today and he told me that people pay a lot of money for

Garn's swords. Like hundreds of thousands of dollars. Especially some of his older ones. He wants to help us Pret! For a small fee of course (ha ha). So he and I have taken one of Garn's swords to Civitavecchia near Rome to meet with some gentlemen from a certain organization that shall remain nameless. I think 50,000 dollars will be enough for us to start don't you my love? I will write when I have the money. If you meant what you said you will wear that bracelet and meet me in Civitavecchia. If not then I guess I was wrong about you and about us but I will still go on. I won't be returning to Garn's either way. And I can't go home. I won't. I hope I see you with that bracelet soon.

All my love,

Aggie

Pretlow folded the letter and walked down to the courtyard. Richard was there working off his meal by practicing his own movements with a large broadsword. Richard was a practitioner of a very different style than Pretlow's. It was less acrobatic and more brutal. Richard had said his father did not believe in finesse. He believed in fatalities. Pretlow watched as Richard made short, harsh, but incredibly quick movements with his sword.

"Richard." Pretlow said. Richard turned and pointed his sword toward Pretlow. He quickly lowered his weapon.

"Sorry mate didn't see ya there. Damn you look like you've seen a ghost." Pretlow handed him the letter.

"We both may be seeing a ghost very soon," he said quietly. Richard scanned the letter and then looked up at Pretlow.

"Oh God. If the gentlemen she is talking about are who I think they are she is in the bollocks mate."

Richard said as he handed the letter back to Pretlow. Pretlow folded it and put it in his pocket.

"My thoughts exactly. I think she is talking about the Mafia. Or some group attached to them. And if they know who Garn is they won't want him coming after them. They are going to kill her and Cliff," Pretlow said.

"We have to tell Garn," Richard said. Pretlow shook his head.

"No. We have to go to Civitavecchia and find them before they try and sell the sword."

Richard laughed.

"Even if we know where they were, which we don't, Civitavecchia is at least an hour away so they have a three hour head start. She and Cliff are probably already..." Pretlow shot him a stern look.

"Don't say that. Just don't say that Richard." Pretlow's face was clouded with anger and worry.

"Don't say what Richard?" Garn said. He was standing behind Richard. He had not been there two seconds ago. Pretlow would swear on a stack of bibles he had not been standing there a moment earlier.

"What is it you don't want Richard to say Pretlow?" Garn asked. His blue eyes seemed to shine. He was wearing a purple blazer and a black t-shirt with plaid purple and black pants and no shoes. He looked clownish but his voice sounded anything but. He was staring at Pretlow intently like a snake might stare at a bird it was about to devour. Pretlow was not a coward. He could be called many things. Sensitive, dour, humorless but not a coward. He stared back at Garn. He held the letter out to him without dropping his gaze.

Garn read the letter then handed it back to Pretlow. His face was dark as a storm cloud.

"You would think after three thousand years I would stop being shocked at man's capacity for treachery. It's not about the money. I have more of that than I could spend in twelve lifetimes. It is the trust. That is priceless and not easily given. It seems once again I made a miscalculation. Oh well what can ya do? I'll be in my office drinking some Sambuca," he said as he walked past Richard and Pretlow. Pretlow grabbed Garn by the arm. Garn slowly turned his head and looked down at his hand.

"You're gonna be wanting to let go of me Pret," Garn said. His voice was as cold as the embrace of a corpse. Pretlow did not remove his hand.

"We need to go after them. They are in danger," Pretlow said. Garn pulled his arm away from his grip.

"A danger of their own making. I feel no compunction about letting them sleep in the bed they have made. If it becomes their deathbed so be it."

"When I first came here you spoke to me of honor. Yet now you forget yours. A man of honor protects the weak. He helps those who are in danger. He helps his friends." Pretlow said.

"Pret there is a difference between a man of honor and a hero. A man of honor lives a life that adheres to a personal code. He fulfills his duty. Every hero eventually becomes a villain. Heroes fall Pretlow. They are put on pedestals that are eventually knocked out from under them. Don't be a hero Pretlow. Be a man of honor. Trust me it is less painful in the end," Garn said wistfully.

"I don't want to be a hero. I just want to make sure she is safe. Can you help us?" Pretlow asked.

"Whoa what's this us stuff kemosabie?" Richard said holding his hands palms out in mock surrender.

"I can't go alone. I will need your help," Pretlow said simply.

"Have you forgotten that she belongs to the Men of the First Chaos? A group who will most likely try to kill us one day? I say she made her bed now let her lay in it," Richard said. He tried to sound tough. He tried to sound blasé but in truth he was terrified. He knew he was a skilled swordsman. But he had never tested those skills in real combat. Against men who would probably have guns and the resolve to use them.

"Richard it doesn't matter if she is of the First Chaos or the First Order. We have a duty to help her if we can. And I can't do it alone. Look I didn't really have any friends or family when I came here. But then I met you and Agrippina and I finally realized what it means to care about something other than my sword or the Brotherhood. I can't just let her.....die. And if you are the person I think you are you can't either." Pretlow said. Richard looked up at the sky for a moment.

"Bollocks let's do it," he said. Pretlow clapped him on the shoulder. Garn sat down on the bench in the courtyard with his back to the two young men. He took his necklace off and it held it by the clasp. The dark obsidian stone turned ever so slightly in the soft breeze.

"Well I guess you did learn something since you've been here Pretlow. I am sure the Archivists will be so proud. I forget sometimes that for normal people death is really a big deal. My anger about Cliff's and Agrippina's betrayal blinded me to that for a moment but now the glare of rage is gone and I can see clearly now. Richard is right. You don't know where she is at this moment. But I can find her," he said. He grasped the black stone in his hand.

"This is called the Deathless Stone. Or the Philosophers' stone. Or the Immortals' Lapis. I guess it doesn't really matter what you call it. It's what it can do that is important now. Boys, every person ever born is going to die. While that thought may disturb you it's actually a very peaceful transition. I've done it a few hundred times. Everyone's death is specific to them. An ending written in the time before time and as inexorable as the rising of the sun. This little doohickey in my hot little hands is a stone from the beginning of time. From the time before time. It's like a cosmic sponge. It absorbs the energy that would have been released upon ones death. Thus persons who touch this stone never die. It's like taking the food out of a refrigerator before it rots. The fridge never stinks or needs cleaning. It just hums along forever until the power is disconnected. Boys I am that fridge. This stone came into my possession over 3,000 years ago when I was just a poor young man playing on the lush and fertile fields of the Egyptian delta. Because I touched this stone you can stab me, shoot me, hang me from the gallows and I will just keep humming along. I know it sounds incredible but if you stay with the Brotherhood the list of incredible things you will see will be longer than a phone book. I've learned a lot about this little gem over the years. If Agrippina is dead I won't be able to find her. But if she is alive and I can lock on to her energy I will be able to get you boys pretty close to her location. I still think you are foolish for wanting to be a hero Pretlow. I also think you are right. Men of honor help those who are helpless. So fuck it here goes," Garn said as he gripped the stone tightly. He pressed the hand holding the stone to his forehead.

At first nothing happened and Richard glanced at Pretlow with a raised eyebrow.

Then then the stone began to glow. A glowing purple illumination so deep it was almost black began to spill from between Garn's fingers. It was pulsating like a strobe light. Garn began to sway back and forth on the little bench. He hummed a low soft tune.

He began to rise off the bench. Not standing. Rising. His whole body rose slowly off the bench. Two feet, then three feet then finally floating above the bench lazily with the stone still pressed to his head. Pretlow felt Richard grab his arm and squeeze it tight. Garn floated just above the bench for a few minutes more then crashed back down onto the bench. He let out a moan and pulled the stone away from his head. Richard and Pretlow rushed to his side.

"No, no, I am fine just give me a moment," Garn said as he put the stone back around his neck. His face was coated with a thin sheen of sweat. He is eyes were red and his breathing was deep and ragged.

"She is still alive. Somewhere near the docks of Civitavecchia. I.....I couldn't see Cliff's energy. That's not a good sign boys," Garn said.

"We need to get there now. Can you drive us Garn?" Pretlow asked.

"Crimeny that bloke was just floating in mid-air!" Richard mumbled to himself.

"No alas after touching the stone I am no good for at least an hour. My equilibrium is off and I have vertigo. Happens when you touch the eternal. You guys can take the car. I assume Cliff drove his truck," Garn said.

"I can't drive," Pretlow said. He hung his head. Richard snapped out of his trance.

"Don't worry I can. Where are the keys Garn?" Richard asked. Garn rose and wobbled a bit. He did not look very steady. He reached in the pocket of his pants and produced a ring with keys on it. He tossed it wildly at Richard. The ring sailed past Richard's head. Richard turned on his heel and caught the keys without looking.

"Car is out front. Take me upstairs to my office," Garn said as he wobbled a bit more.

"Garn we have to go," Pretlow said urgently.

"Not before you get some swords. Real swords that are meant to spill blood. Come on help me you big bastards." Garn said. Richard grabbed one arm and Pretlow grabbed the other one. They walked him through the French doors and headed for the stairs. Aria came down the staircase holding a book and a glass of water. Her face twisted into a mask of confusion.

"What is going on?" she asked in her high Australian accent. Richard and Pretlow walked right by her as Richard replied.

"Cliff and Aggie stole one of Garn's swords to sell to the Mafia. Cliff's dead Aggie is probably on her way to joining him and me and Pretlow are going to rescue her. If we don't make it back you can have my Dr. Who poster."

They entered Garn's office and he half stumbled half fell into his chair. He pointed at Richard.

"On the key chain is a fob. It doesn't open the car. Press it." Richard pulled the keys out of his pocket and pressed the gray button on the black fob. Pretlow heard the whirring of gears and chains coming from behind Garn's chair. The wall began to separate down the middle. 'The wall was actually a remote controlled pocket door. It opened to reveal a small room that was lined with polished wooden racks. Swords sat in the racks like wine bottles in a cellar. Garn swiveled his chair around to face the room. Pretlow noticed on slot on the rack was empty.

"Ah…ah shit they took the Charlemagne longsword. I like that one. Gilded blade with six diamonds in the hilt. Pure Brotherhood steel and a green emerald embedded in the pommel. Charlemagne never even got to see the damn thing. Cliff knows that it's the most expensive one in the whole damn rack," Garn said woefully. Pretlow stepped into the room. It smelled of old oil and leather. Steel and wood and blood. The scent of blood was hiding among the other smells but Pretlow could sense it even more than he could smell it. He walked over to the right side of the little room. A weak light bulb with a pull chain hanging from it fought valiantly against the darkness. There were two sabers side by side in the rack. Their blades were dark and burnished almost black. The hand guards were functional not overly dramatic. But the blades looked wickedly sharp. The light glinted off the edge. Pretlow grabbed one of the sabers and pulled it out of the rack.

"It speaks to you. To a true swordsman. Those sabers belonged to a good friend of mine. Let's just call him the Fox. After he passed away I reclaimed them. Those are swords well suited to a quest like yours

Pretlow," Garn said as he sprawled over his chair. Richard walked into the room and grabbed two long swords. Richard gripped the dark ebony handles with the chrome pommels and cross guards. He pulled them out of the rack with a quick flick of his wrist.

"Fine choice Richard. They were owned by a fellow named ….well let's just say he was once a noble knight but lost his way because of a beautiful woman. He was a member of two influential groups. One is chronicled in story books. One is chronicled in the Book of Seven Swords. Garn struggled to his feet and leaned against his desk. His eyes were red and his skin was still slick with sweat but he seemed to be a little less the worse for wear. The stone laying against his chest pulsed with a bluish neon light like a heartbeat.

"If you want to save her you better hurry boys. She is alive but bad things are being done to her as we speak. Vile things," Garn said as he swayed ever so slightly. Pretlow nodded his head.

"I'll meet you downstairs," he said to Richard. Richard waited till Pretlow left the room then turned to Garn.

"Garn, how old are you?" he asked. As he asked the question he rubbed his thumb along the chrome pommels of the longswords. Garn laughed. It was a deep rich sound that filled the room.

"If I told you, you wouldn't believe me. But I can remember when the plains of Giza were green and not filled with pyramids," Garn said as he stared into Richard's eyes. The younger man dropped his eyes. Garn pulled open a drawer in his desk. He reached inside and pulled out two white featureless masks with leather straps. He tossed them to Richard.

"If you boys are going to do what I think you are going to do it might be wise to hide your identities. Godspeed warriors," Garn said as he plopped down in the chair. Richard looked at the masks then hurried down the stairs.

Richard stood next to the Fiat waiting. Finally Pretlow came through the front door to the car. He was wearing a black trench coat and a hooded sweat shirt. Richard had on a tan London Fog trench coat and a black watch cap. They put their swords and scabbards in the back seat and then got in the car.

"So how will we know what warehouse she is in?" Richard asked. Pretlow pulled his hood over his head.

"We will start with the warehouse that has the least light, that looks the most dilapidated. The one the furthest from the cruise ship docks. If I was going to do some illegal stuff I'd want to be someplace like that," Pretlow said. Richard started the car.

"And if we do find it ? "Richard asked

Pretlow turned to face Richard. His tawny face was grim.

"Right. Gotcha." Richard said as he put the car in gear.

They did not speak at all as they made the hour-long drive to Civitavecchia. They both kept their own counsel as the Italian countryside gave way to the more urban landscape north of Rome. Eventually they passed a sign that said "Welcome to Civitavecchia" in Italian. Richard guided the car into the large port city and followed street signs to the docks. He parked the little Fiat in the lot of a little bistro about 200 yards away from the docks. Pretlow hopped out of the car. Enormous white cruise ships loomed in front of him back lit by the setting sun. Further past the cruise ships lay the industrial docks of Civitavecchia. He could see container ships and large cargo ships. The far end of the docks was dotted with several warehouses. Richard got out of the car as well. Pretlow reached in the backseat and carefully grabbed his swords and attached them to the thick belt he was wearing. Richard did the same.

"Let's just start walking that way,." Pretlow said as he nodded to the far end of the docks.

"She couldn't have gotten kidnapped by some blokes in a five star hotel could she…" Richard complained.

"There is a service road just past those cruise ships to the right. We can take that road and check the building as we go," Pretlow said. Richard nodded curtly.

"Well let's have at it," he said as they began to walk side by side.

The Dapper sat at a large metal desk eating a cannoli and some lasagna. His given name was Arturo Gamiano but everyone called him the Dapper because he was always so well groomed. His hair was always neatly combed. His beard was always trimmed and clipped to the same precise length. His black blazer and black shirt were pressed and creased expertly. A person could see their reflection in his leather shoes. His fingernails were buffed and manicured. No matter what violence he visited upon an individual or several individuals his carefully maintained appearance was never besmirched.

A few feet from the where the Dapper was eating a man's body lay across the cold concrete floor. There was a single bullet hole between his eyes. The Dapper daintily dabbed at his mouth with a paper napkin. The Dapper had been buying swords from Cliff for about a year. Cliff would bring him the original sword and replace it with a forgery so as to not alert his employer. The Dapper would sell the sword for triple what he paid for it to some unscrupulous collector, tell his bosses he sold it for only twice what he paid for it, give his boss his cut and pocket the rest.

Cliff was a master blacksmith. Unfortunately he wasn't a master at picking the winner of futbol games. Every sword he sold the Dapper just served to give him more money to lose on the next soccer game. It was like a condemned man buying rope from his hangman. Then last night Cliff called him with an offer he couldn't resist. Cliff had a figured it all out. A priceless sword that could not be copied. A patsy to take the blame for the sword's theft and a young girl that could be sold to the highest bidder at a flesh auction. The patsy and the young girl were the same person. The Dapper had listened to Cliff's proposal with great interest. He calculated the risk versus the reward and decided to humor Cliff enough to get him and the girl down here to the warehouse his Family owned. A sword here and there was fine but Cliff was talking about stealing the sword of Charlemagne. That would be noticed by his employer. The girl as a patsy was a nice idea but who was to say that Cliff wouldn't have a crisis of conscience and tell his employer who he had sold the sword to and who had kidnapped the young girl? No Cliff had to die. The girl would be sold to one of those oily Arabs sheiks. The sword would be sold to a very wealthy and very discreet collector. The Dapper's bosses would never know about this sale. The Dapper was going to kill the four men that had accompanied him to the dock tonight. He would tell his bosses that they had been attacked by some of Cliff's associates. In the ensuing chaos the sword was lost but the girl would be a suitable compensation. Once the sale of the sword was done the Dapper would disappear to some small nameless island in the South Pacific to spend the rest of his days sipping coconut juice and eating pineapples.

A scream echoed through the darkened two-story warehouse. The Dapper took another mouthful of lasagna.

Since they were not long for this world the Dapper didn't see any harm in letting his men break the girl in by breaking her down. They were in the middle of the loading dock taking turns. The Dapper did not participate in such deviancy. He felt it was unseemly. The Dapper dabbed at his mouth again and then checked his watch. It was almost six. The sun had almost set. Once it was full dark he would execute the four men and then take the girl to his bosses after hiding the sword. All in all a very neat and orderly plan. He put another forkful of lasagna into his mouth. The girl screamed again. My but those men were insatiable.

"I don't guess you thought about just calling the coppers did you?" Richard asked as they climbed down off of a dumpster after peering in the window of another dark warehouse. Pretlow shrugged his shoulders.

"If Garn's vision was correct and they are meeting with Mafia types I just assume they have the local police in their pocket. I've read accounts of these types of men," he said. Richard laughed.

"Well I've known men of that type and I guess you are right about the coppers," he said. There was only one more warehouse. It sat at the very end of the service road with its backside to the sea.

"Well, last one mate. If they aren't in this one I guess Garn's magic rock was wrong," Richard said.

Pretlow was about to respond when a scream pierced the air.

Pretlow and Richard looked at each other for a moment. The scream had come from the last warehouse.

Pretlow took off running full speed toward the warehouse. Richard was right behind him. The building had two large roll doors on the first floor and two huge windows on the second floor. A rusty dumpster sat to the right of the roll doors and some empty crates were littered around the dumpster. Richard tossed Pretlow one of the masks Garn had given him as they ran stride for stride. Pretlow put it on without breaking his gallop as did Richard. They were running incredibly fast and their long coats were unfurling behind them like war banners. Pretlow jumped onto the dumpster then jumped to the top of the roll door. He landed on the metal canopy that housed the door when it was in the up position. Then he pushed off of the canopy until he reached the ledge of the second story window. Richard jumped off one of the crates to the other door then off that door until he too was hanging on the ledge of the second story window. The two young swordsmen nodded at each other and then pulled themselves up over the edge until they were completing a handstand but just for a moment. They let their body weight fall against the window. The glass shattered like fresh ice over a mountain stream. Both young men plunged into the cavernous structure turning in mid-air until they landed feet first onto the concrete floor. Countless hours of poly-metric and ergonomic exercises prepared their bones and ligaments to exceed the limits of what was commonly thought to be humanly possible. Glass fell all around them like razor sharp rain. They both landed in a half-crouch. Pretlow raised his head and took in his surroundings. A few large crates to the left and the right. A cordoned off section toward the back of the building that was most likely some kind of office. There was a loading dock to the right with another roll type door that when opened would expose a pier that ships could dock alongside as they were loaded.

There was a group of men crowded around another man at the loading dock. The three men were all laughing and exhorting the fourth man in Italian. At first Pretlow thought the fourth man was having a seizure or was in some other type of medical distress.

Then he saw a pair of moccasins on the ground near the man. Another scream pierced the night. A scream so mournful and full of rage and hopelessness that Pretlow's heart broke into a million pieces and those pieces broke into a billion pieces; an exponentially increasing fracture of the heart that made him want to retch. Instead he pulled his trench coat back and pulled his sabers out and advanced upon the group of men. The men who would soon be ghosts.

Richard saw what Pretlow saw and his spirit was filled with such pain he thought he might just go insane. He pulled his trench coat back and pulled out his longswords. Richard blinked back tears of rage and advanced with his friend toward the jackals that were holding Agrippina down on that filthy floor.

The four men were caught off guard for a moment. With their white mask and long coats and swords Richard and Pretlow looked like angelic warriors as they fell from ceiling. But the men quickly regained their composure. They were hard men who had spilled much blood in their short violent lives. They knew the simplest way to deal with any enemy was to shoot it. A lot. They pulled their semi-automatic weapons from their waistbands. The man who had been having his turn on the girl stood up pulled up his pants and took his gun out of his shoulder holster. They stood side by side and fired at the masked interlopers.

Pretlow watched the men fire their weapons at him and Richard. He slowed his breath. He waited for the cloak of concentration to wrap around him. When it did he felt his rage meld with his skill in a way he had never known. He saw the bullets flying at him like the bright little bits of a meteor arcing through the air. He brought his sabers up and deflected the first bullet. Then the second and the third and the fourth and then he was swatting aside every bullet as he moved forward. He passed the sabers back and forth in front of him in an intricate dance of gestures.

Richard had never felt so alive in his entire life. The melding of his extraordinary skill and these exceptional swords was like grabbing a lightning bolt by the tail and cracking it like a whip. The men shooting at him had appeared very confident when they had pulled their weapons. As he deflected each and every one of their bullets they no longer looked confident. They were beginning to look afraid.

Richard didn't want them to be afraid. He wanted them to be terrified.

The Dapper didn't understand what exactly was happening but he thought he had a pretty good idea. He saw the men flying through the window and he could see them actually deflecting bullets with swords. Perhaps Cliff's employer had gotten wind of his scheme and had sent some of his minions to reclaim the sword. Well he would not let that happen. He had the sword right next to him. And as his four associates fired upon these mysterious assailants he saw the girl crawl to her feet and take off running toward the back door, which only opened onto another short dock. The Dapper did a quick little calculation in his head. These men were blocking each bullet. Each gun had sixteen bullets in the clip and one in the chamber. That was 68 bullets. That gave him about two minutes to get out of the warehouse. He couldn't go out the front door obviously. He would have to follow the girl out the back door. He quietly rose from his desk and grabbed the wooden box that held the Sword of Charlemagne and tucked it under his arm. He walked swiftly out the back door as the guns continued exploding behind him. He had a feeling the mystery men were going to eliminate his associates for him. The irony of the situation was not lost on the Dapper. He smiled just the tiniest bit.

Pretlow seemed to be outside himself watching his body move against his enemies. He crossed his sabers in front of himself until his right hand was touching his left bicep and his left hand was touching his right bicep. The two men standing in front of him were out of bullets but they were still pulling the trigger. They seemed to be in shock. Pretlow uncrossed his arms. As he did the sharp edge of the sabers sliced through the necks of the two men standing in front of him. Their heads fell to the concrete floor with a meaty slap. Blood flowed from their severed carotid arteries as their bodies collapsed. A splash of crimson landed on Pretlow's mask like tribal marking.

Richard dropped to his knees in front of the two men that had been firing at him. He sliced the longsword in his left hand to the right, right through the gunmen's legs. The sword sliced through their knees at the joints. Richard rose from his knees and decapitated the gunmen with the longsword in his right hand as they fell to the floor. The scent of blood filled the warehouse. It was hot coppery scent that Richard never forgot.

"AGRIPPINA!" Pretlow screamed. Richard pointed with his sword toward a metal door just to the right of the cordoned off office area. Pretlow ran toward the door.

Grunting he sliced through the door diagonally with his saber. The door fell from the frame and Pretlow walked through the opening followed by Richard. They stepped out onto a short little pier with a small power boat moored to it. Standing between them and the boat was a well-groomed man holding a gun to Agrippina's head. He had a smooth wooden box on the pier by his feet.

Agrippina's face was red and swollen. Both of her eyes were black and bruised. There were thumb prints on her neck. She was naked from the waist down and there was blood on her thighs. The well-dressed man said something in a language Pretlow didn't recognize. He said it again louder.

"He wants you to throw down your swords," Agrippina said. Her voice was flat and listless. Pretlow thought she sounded like a wholly different person.

"Not bloody likely" Richard growled. Pretlow stepped forward and dropped his sabers on the pier. The sound of waves lapping against the pier washed over him as he let his sabers fall from his hands.

"Do it Richard," he said. Richard hesitated.

"Trust me my friend. I have a plan," Pretlow said. Richard stepped forward and tossed his swords onto the pier. The well-dressed man said something else.

"He wants you to raise your hands." Agrippina's monotone voice was like nails on a blackboard to Pretlow. He raised his hands as did Richard.

Pretlow extended his left arm with his palm out as if he was directing traffic. He pressed his second and third finger against the palm of the gauntlet he was wearing. Richard heard a familiar whirring and high pitched whistle. The well-dressed man looked puzzled for a moment.

A dagger flew out of Pretlow's sleeve and sailed through the night.

"Clever." The Dapper thought before eight inches of steel buried itself in his left eye and punctured his frontal lobe. He fell backwards on the pier with his gun still in his hand. Agrippina fell to her knees. Pretlow rushed to her and put his hands under her arm pits. He picked her up effortlessly. Once she was on her feet she pushed against his chest. He tried to wrap his arms around her. She punched and kicked him. She fought his embrace.

"Get off of me! Get the Fuck OFF!" she screamed. Pretlow removed his mask. So did Richard.

"Aggie it's me!" he said. She continued to punch and kick and scream.

"Fuck you! Get off of me! I know it's you Pretlow Creedence. I would not have been down here if not for you Pretlow Creedence. This would not have happened to me if not for you Pretlow Fucking Creedence!" she said as she reached between her legs and slapped him with her bloodied hand. She left a red smear on his face.

"Aggie, please!" Pretlow said. She began to claw and scratch at his face. Richard didn't know what to do or say so he picked up the swords he and Pretlow had surrendered and wrapped them in his trench coat.

"Please Aggie girl we came to help you,." Richard said.

"Agrippina please stop!" Pretlow howled.

"Oh I asked them to stop Pretlow. I begged them to stop and they just laughed. They laughed and laughed. It is so goddamn funny! I see that now! A woman of chaos and a man of order being in love it's a fine fucking joke!"she screamed. She began sobbing. Richard wiped his face and spoke to Pretlow in low voice.

"She has been through something awful laddie. But we can't stay here on this pier yelling at each other. There are six dead bodies here and we killed five of them. We have to get back to the car with great haste."

Agrippina please come back to the studio with us," Pretlow said softly. This elicited a great gale of laughter.

"Oh you really think I'm going to step foot in Garn's studio after I stole his most valuable sword? You are really stupider than I have realized. No I will walk to the nearest police station and tell them who I am. A Du Mor family jet will be here within the hour to pick me up. And they will hire cleaners to erase any trace of me from this place. They have cleaners for everything. Even me. They will clean even me," she said.

Agrippina walked past Richard and Pretlow back through the ruined door and through the warehouse. Pretlow picked up the box with the Sword of Charlemagne in it and followed her back into the warehouse. He watched her pale form move through the darkened building. She idly kicked one of the severed heads of her attackers out of her way as she walked. Richard followed Pretlow.

"Agrippina," Pretlow said. He didn't yell but his voice seemed to belong to a man many years older. She stopped.

"Tell me Pretlow. Did you wear the bracelet?" she asked with her back to him. Pretlow hung his head.

"Aggie...." he said. She turned and looked at him. Richard was there too but he knew she was only seeing Pretlow.

"Don't ever call me that again. That was the name of the girl you pretended to love. The girl who would do anything for you. That girl died right over there. You see that place where the blood and the piss and the shit have pooled? Yes she's dead. I am Agrippina Du Mor." She turned and walked over the broken glass to the large roll door. She seemed oblivious to the pain. She pulled the door at the door but it didn't budge.

Pretlow removed his trench coat. Richard could see he was wearing the rig he and Agrippina had constructed. He walked to the overhead door and put the coat around Agrippina's shoulders. This time she did not fight or curse. He stepped back and looked at Richard. Richard thought he had never seen such a lost and anguished face in his life.

"Agrippina you should at least let us drive you to the nearest police station. We will leave you there but you can't just walk into the night like this. It isn't safe. Richard said. Agrippina laughed.

"What could happen to me now that is worse than what just happened to me Richard?" she asked.

Thirty minutes later they had pulled up to the Civitavecchia police station. A few uniformed policemen were walking down the white marble steps of the station house. Richard parked the Fiat across the street from the station house. He got out of the driver's seat to let her climb out of the backseat. She started striding across the street. Pretlow jumped out of the passenger seat and ran around the front of the car. He had taken off the rig and was just wearing his black hoodie.

"I tried to save you Aggie,." he said his deep voice carrying over the sounds of the light traffic careening down the street. Agrippina stopped and turned to face him. She walked up to him and placed her hand gently on his cheek.

"All you did was to show me that the men of the First Order are weak. They lack the courage of their convictions. If you really had loved me you would've have just left with me. I wouldn't have had to go to that savage place and try and sell a priceless sword." She stood on her tip toes and kissed his cheek. She whispered in his ear:

"One day I will make you pay for this stain I have received. One day you will learn to love. Love the way you professed you loved me. And I will see all you love in ruins. I swear it by the blood of my ancestors and the honor of my House. You will know love and you will know agony. I promise you."

Then she was gone. Pretlow stood there for a moment more.

"Come on laddie. We gotta go," Richard said. Pretlow climbed back in the Fiat.

"I just wanted to save her Richard," Pretlow said. Richard put the car in gear.

"I know ya did mate. We tried. We tried." he said as they pulled away from the curb.

Pretlow ran his nimble fingers over the links of Agrippina's bracelet as they drove back to Florence.

Catlow sat next to his father on the bottom step of their basement speechless. Pretlow flexed his large hands and tapped them on his thighs.

"You see Catlow. I am human. I have known loss. Loss of someone who made my spirit soar every time I saw her face or when she entered a room. So believe when I tell you I understand the pain you are feeling. I know Harmony is no longer with us but something in Agrippina died that night at the docks. I saw it wither and putrefy in her eyes. We never spoke again. She was right of course. I should have never let what happened between us happen. But I was young and alone and weak. And she was so very beautiful," Pretlow said.

"Do you ever regret not running away with her?" Catlow asked. Pretlow sighed.

"Not when I look at you and your sister and your mother. But I would be a liar if I said I never thought about the road less traveled. But that road was never really open for me. I am a member of the Brotherhood. As was my father and his father. We are warriors. We fight, we stand for those who cannot," Pretlow said.

"So you understand why I must kill all the Men of the First Chaos. I have to stand for Harmony," Catlow said through clenched teeth.

"I understand you want to. But you won't kill them all. Only the ones in the Duel. I won't tell you to deny yourself vengeance. You know the words of the Oath. But channel that vengeance. Combine it with all that I have taught you. Shape it and mold it into a weapon that helps you fulfill the Covenant. Because if you don't you won't avenge Harmony, you won't survive the Duel and you won't honor our ancestors. Don t think me cruel when I tell you do not lose your focus on why we are participating in this Duel. If you lose your focus with these Men of Chaos I will lose a son. And I don't want that. I need you as sharp as the sword in your hand Catlow. When we get to the Grand Hall we must honor the terms of the Covenant. It is neutral ground. Do you understand me?" Pretlow asked. Catlow nodded his head as if he agreed with his father's sage words.

"I am not going to this Duel for the honor of the Creedence name or the fucking fate of humanity. I am going to see the heads of the Houses of Chaos at my feet," he thought to himself.

Pretlow stood.

"Come my son. It is time." Catlow looked up at his father.

"Time for what?" he asked. His voice was low.

"Time to read the Invitation. Time for you to see behind the curtain." Pretlow turned and walked up the steps. Catlow stood and followed his father. It was hard to imagine Pretlow Creedence ever being young and nervous. But somehow the image comforted him. Despite the events of the last few days he felt closer to his father than he had in years. He didn't believe some immortal sword maker had used a magic rock to tell his father where his girlfriend was being held. He did believe that his father loved that girlfriend though. He could see the pain on his face as he told his story. It was the same pain Catlow wore on his own face now. He wanted the Men of the First Chaos to see that pain right before he slit their fucking throats.

In the attic Yakita repeated his mantra.

CHAPTER TWENTY

Abdul El-Aki carried the light black box into his sitting room. It was an actual room where all he did was smoke from his hookah, drink Russian vodka and....sit. There were huge silken pillows scattered on the floor.. A large bay window overlooked the east courtyard of the House of the Black Rivers' seat of power. He eased his large frame down on one of the plush pillows and sat with the black box in his lap. Davi sat down next to him in one fluid moment. Alton plopped to the floor. He was his mother's son. He was short with soft features and a weak chin. His thick black hair hung in lank strings in front of his face. He was carrying a crystal goblet rimmed in gold. It was full of whiskey. His fingers were weighted down with gold and silver rings. Alton had entered the room barefoot. His toes were adorned with silver rings as well. Abdul El-Aki was 54 but he was still built like a solid length of maple. His long black hair was tinged with gray and the skin around his chin was beginning to sag. But his eyes were still a predator's eyes. Wolf eyes. Abdul sighed. He honestly didn't know if he was Davi's father. Whenever he looked at Alton, drunk and fat and weak he wanted it to be true. He had considered taking a DNA test but Nazir went apoplectic. She would not be the second woman to bear him a son. There was only one El-Aki heir in her mind and there could be no others. He could have had the test completed without her knowledge but he loved Nazir. Deep down inside he loved Alton. But his disappointment sometimes outweighed his love. He knew that was a shameful thing but it was the truth and Abdul did not spend much time bemoaning the truth. He pushed his hair behind his ears.

"Long ago after the first Duel the Judges in their wisdom and benevolence and their dichotomous love and disdain for us gave each member of each House a choice. Agree to fight in the Duel of Generations, accept the Invitation or leave the Brotherhood," Abdul said in his deep voice. Alton giggled. Abdul shot him a look that could have spoiled a glass of milk. Davi was wearing his sunglasses and looking straight ahead.

Thousands of miles away Barton Crisp was telling his charges the same story.

"But to leave the Brotherhood is to leave all the protection our victory would bestow," he said as he and Danny and Thad sat in his study with the door locked and shades drawn.

Logan Akinyele was sitting in his house going over the story in his mind. His father had taught it to him years and years ago.

"And so the Invitation is sent. It calls the warriors of all Houses to their duty. It calls the Men of the First Order and the Men of the First Chaos to the Covenant made lo these many years ago," he thought to himself. His hands were covered in dirt. He had buried his father in the macadamia grove. He had burned the bodies of the ninjas.

Arato, Miko, Lauren and Arato's father Lin sat in the kitchen of the house they all shared as Arato repeated the story of the Invitation.

"It is the first step in the long journey on the road to Perdition or Paradise. "Arato said.

Silas Boon grasped the hands of his sons as he recited the story to them in the sun room of their mansion.

"What way that road turns depends on the actions we take and the battles we fight…and the strength of our resolve," he said staring into their eyes.

"And the strength of our swords," Richard Darn said as he and Seth and Langdon sat in their shared basement.

"It is not an Invitation to be taken lightly or without great consideration. For to accept this Invitation..." Taang Sang said to his sons as they sat across from him.

"...is to pledge your life to this Covenant, this Brotherhood. Once the oath is given there is no turning back, Carcone said to Carcine as Agrippina sipped a glass of wine.

"So as Prefect of this house I will ask this question now and for the last time. Are you prepared to accept this Invitation?," Vivian asked as she held the hands of her two sons.

"Are you prepared to fulfill this Covenant and keep the oath? Are you prepared to give your very life? Because if you are not then we have already lost," Saed said as he and Shian sat in the parking lot of the Baltimore Washington International Airport.

"If you are not then do not accept this Invitation. To break this Covenant is to court damnation." Raul said to Alan as they sat on the hood of his truck near the bright white beach of Caldetes near Barcelona.

"I tell you that not to frighten you but to impress upon you the seriousness of what we are about to undertake. The fate of the world, of our families and our friends' families as well as our children and our children's children hang on the edge of our blades. By accepting this Invitation you accept the duty and the responsibilities that go along with being a member of this Brotherhood. The day after the Duel is done will be a new world for those that are left. What world that is depends on us and our will. So I ask. Do you accept?" Pretlow said to

Catlow as they sat in the living room of their house. It had begun to rain outside. The droplets beat against the window pane with a slow and steady rhythm. Catlow looked out the front window into the darkness. He thought of Harmony. Of his frightened little sister. He thought of his mother swinging a sword. He thought of all the years of distance between himself and his father. He thought of the Men of the First Chaos warm and safe in their mansions. He turned his head and looked his father in the eye.

"Yes," Catlow said. Pretlow nodded and put the black box on the coffee table in front of them. Darnicia was upstairs with Calla packing their bags. Pretlow rubbed his hands together for a moment. It sounded like two pieces of sandpaper rubbing together. Catlow looked at his father.

"Dad?" he asked. It was a single word but it conveyed a troubling question that Catlow did not feel comfortable asking.

"Are you afraid to open the box Dad?"

"All my life I have worked and trained and sacrificed for this moment. My father and mother are dead because of this Brotherhood. My father drank too much to dull the things he had seen as a member of this Brotherhood. He died in a car accident. He was drunk. My mother could not live without him. So she took her own life. Many people that I know and love could be dead. My son was attacked. Your girlfriend was killed in front of you. Up until a day ago the last few years of my life have been some of the best I can remember. To see you and your sister settle down here. To see you both grow and yes have you test my authority has been frustrating, gratifying and peaceful. I just wanted to remember how our life here made me feel for a few seconds," Pretlow said as he stared at the box.

"How did you feel Dad?" Catlow asked. Pretlow put his arm around Catlow.

"Happy, my son." He smiled at Catlow. Catlow found himself smiling back before he even knew he was doing it. Pretlow turned his attention back to the box.

He placed his hand on the lid.

"I am Pretlow Astor Creedence. I am the unquestioned Prefect of the House of the Green Hills. I accept this Invitation as do all the kinsmen of this House. We are the men of the Brotherhood. We pledge our lives to the Duel of Generations. We pledge our lives to the fulfillment of the Covenant until the end of all time. We pledge to take up the sword the first instrument of order and the first weapon of chaos.

Not for love.

Not for hate.

Not for vengeance

Not for pleasure

Not for pain

But for the lives of all the people of the world.

Cry Discordia!

Cry Decretum!

Let our blades strike true!

Let our blades strike true!" Pretlow said. His voice rose with each word until at the end he was yelling at the top of his lungs. Catlow looked at his father as if seeing him for the first time in many, many years. He was the Prefect of the House of Green Hills. He was a member of the Brotherhood. He was not a man to be trifled with or cajoled or intimidated or taken lightly. For a moment Catlow believed again. In everything.

Pretlow took his hand away from the black box. Nothing happened. At first.

Suddenly the box began to vibrate. Catlow could hear a loud hum coming from it as it sat on the table. The lid slowly opened on its own. Catlow felt his eyes go wide as he watched. Pretlow reached a trembling hand into the box. He pulled out a clear circular plate of glass. It had a strange set of symbols acid etched around its perimeter. Other than the symbols the plate was clear.

"Where is the Invitation?" Catlow asked in a hushed voice.

"Hand me my sword." Pretlow said. Catlow got up and retrieved his father's sword. It had been leaning against the wall. Pretlow sat the plate on the coffee table and took his sword from Catlow.

He stood and rolled the sleeve of his blue flannel shirt up to his elbow. He bit his lip. Grimacing he slid the blade of his sword across the inside of his forearm horizontally. A thin red line formed on his arm. Pretlow held his forearm over the glass plate. Three or four red drops fell from his arm onto the plate. Pretlow sat down on the couch. He grabbed the plate and held it up to his face. The blood began to run across the surface of the plate, but not in accordance with the laws of gravity. The blood ran up and then down across the plate. Sideways and diagonally. The white etched symbols began to glow with a crisp yellow light. Catlow stood next to his father. His heart was thudding in his chest. He instinctively put his hand on his father's shoulder as they both watched the blood dance across the plate and the symbols pulsate with a steady yellow light.

Finally the blood stopped prancing across the plate. The symbols grew even brighter. Catlow shielded his eyes and Pretlow looked away for a moment. When the light finally extinguished itself Catlow opened his eyes. There were words written on the plate. The blood had been fused to the surface of the plate and spelled out the words:

YOU HAVE ACCEPTED THIS INVITATION VOLUNTARILY AND OF YOUR OWN FREE WILL. THIS HAS BOUND YOU TO THE DUEL OF GENERATIONS AND THE COVENANT BETWEEN MAN AND THE JUDGES. MAKE YOUR WAY TO THE GRAND HALL IN THREE DAYS TIME.

MAY YOUR BLADES STRIKE TRUE.

"Still think it's a fairy tale?" Pretlow asked.

Visit www.hcspublishing.com for the release date of book two: "The Brotherhood of the Blade: The Covenant".

ABOUT THE AUTHOR

S.A. Cosby is a writer and poet originally from Mathews County. A fan of fantasy and sci-fi since an early age S.A. started writing in high school and continued during his studies at Christopher Newport University where he majored in English. His short story "The Rat and the Cobra" was published by Thug-Lit.com in their tenth online issue. He is currently finishing up his second novel "The Brotherhood of the Blade - The Covenant".

He lives in Gloucester with his pug .... Pugsley.

Made in the USA
Monee, IL
11 March 2021